SAVING DR. WARREN

God Bless America!

Jeff M.

SAVING DR. WARREN...

A TRUE PATRIOT

JEFFERY J. MCKENNA

Saving Dr. Warren...A True Patriot

Cover design by
Felix Erman Yudi (Pixal Clan – 99 Designs.com)

Image – Portrait of Joseph Warren, by
John Singleton Copley, 1765.
(Museum of Fine Arts, Boston)

Interior design by
Sue Balcer

Editors
Ellen Brock, Wendy Jo Thornton
and Lisa Messinger

Paperback ISBN: 978-0-9999012-0-5
Ebook ISBN: 978-0-9999012-1-2

I dedicate this book to
God, Family and Country

My Three Great Loyalties

CONTENTS

ACKNOWLEDGMENTS

First, after twenty years of repeatedly researching, writing and editing the novel, I thank my best friend and wonderful wife, Mimi. I could not have done it without her love and support.

I also thank my daughter Meghan for reading and editing the book. As a middle school History teacher, she is the ultimate resource for understanding and relating to the target audience. She has been an indispensable inspiration to help me finish the book in 2020. Her reading of the manuscript to her students in the fall of 2019, and their suggestions and encouragement, made this book a reality.

I thank many others that have helped the novel. Brent Brindley, Steve Wood, Christine Schijf, Kyle Reid, Andy Huxford, Peggy Jardine, Anton Kuhlmann, Austin Mild, Alex Tholen, Stockton Wittwer Samantha Proffit and Fariba Mahmud all had an influence in shaping the final version.

Finally, I acknowledge many students at Canyon View Jr. High School. My opportunity to speak to them at their school and experience anew the challenges and enthusiasm of middle school, confirmed to me that twenty years to create something that they might enjoy, was worth all the years of effort.

"Mrs. Truman's 2020 History Class"

Abby Davidson
Abi Goodey
Aden Black
Ahria Skipps
Alexa Ramirez
Alondra Gomez Mejia
Alondra Landeros
Andee B
Andrea Frutos
Astrid Cielo Gil
Austin Flynn
Brandon Johnson
Braxton Hartle
Brenna Demharter
Brett Karr
Brooklyn Bradley
Bryan Yaya
Carlos Mendez
Carolina Velazquez
Galeno
Charlotte R. Cochran
Chase Riggs
Chase Wolsey
Chelsea Gaines
Christian Prugue
Clara Contreras

Coleman K Maya
Connor Headman
Courtney Maxwell
Cumorah Olayan
Dylan Brandner
Eliza Barkdull
Elsa Esplin
Emily Anne Greer
Emily Ernstrom
EmmaLee Duersch
Eva Green
Garrett Brown
Gordon Ellingson
Grace Swan
Gustavo Torres
Hannah Schofield
Hayden Lleuedyn
Indie Bulkley
Jace Tunnell
Jack Nixon
James Craddock
Jameson Gardner
Jamie Cody Adams
Jan C. Chico
Janet Ruiz
Jayden Palmer
Johann Costa
Jon Gilchrist
Joseph Crawford
Joseph Eggett
Josh Atkinson
Justin Hull
Kaden Pope
Karla San Juan
Katie Carlson
Kayawna Welch
Kaylee Rae Longhurst
Kaylee Zarate
Kole Porter
Kowin Sperry
Koya Burg
Krista Keele
Kyson Taylor
Landry Christensen
Lauren Carlos
Leah Hammer
Leslie Carvajal
Lia siufanua
Lilly Ann Elias
Lily Wald
Logan Walker
Luke Cherrington
Madeline Garside
Mahlia Aznar
MaKenna Barraclough
Marcus Smith
Marilee Hodson
Mary Clark
Mason Harmon
Matthew Kummer
Max Clint
Maya Inouye
McCall Thaxton
Mckay Nelson
Michael Burr
Mya Valdez
Nicholas McKinley
Nicholas Santa Cruz
Noah Davenport
Olivia Bristol
Paola Arkell
Pedro Jared Mateo Febres
Porter Olsen
Robert Chase
Roman Richards
Ruth Guerrero
Ryan Noorda
Ryder Pack
Sadie Jarvis
Sadie Walker
Samuel J. Backman
Sarah Millett
Sofia Macedo Flores
Sophi Deucher
Sophie Clark
Spencer Bateman
Stephanie Duarte
Steven Matthew Bernal Hernandez
Stone West
Stratton Lewis
Sydney Baca
Talon Parkinson
Talon Sisoutham
Taylor Ramage
Travian Haslam
Ty C. Jacobs
Tycen Whitaker
Vincent Jablonski
Wilson Haddock

ACKNOWLEDGMENTS FOR PHOTOS AND IMAGES

Part One

New York City, September 11, 2001 - Unattributed 9/11 Photographs, Library of Congress/Public domain.

World War II Soldier Helping Fallen Comrade - USMC photo.

Part Two

Boston Massacre, March 5, 1770 - Boston Massacre, Image Engraved Printed and Sold by Paul Revere, Boston/Public domain.

Boston Tea Party, December 16, 1773 - "The Destruction of Tea at Boston Harbor," 1846 Lithograph, Nathaniel Currier, Public domain.

Part Three

Jason Russell House - From the Collection of Jeff McKenna.

Map of Lexington and Concord - © Meghan D. Truman.

Scene from Battle of Bunker Hill - Death of General Warren at the Battle of Bunker Hill, oil on canvas, John Trumbull, Museum of Fine Arts, Boston, Massachusetts.

Part Four

Abigail Adams - Portrait of Abigail Adams, pastel on paper, Benjamin Blythe, Massachusetts Historical Society.

John and Abigail Adams House, Quincy, Massachusetts - From the Collection of Jeff McKenna.

Part Five

Bunker Hill Monument - Bunker Hill Day, Charlestown, Massachusetts, Library of Congress Prints and Photographs Division/Public domain.

Freedom Trail Map - © Meghan D. Truman.
Statue of Dr. Joseph Warren at Bunker Hill - From the Collection of Jeff McKenna.

Patriots' Page

Mercy Scollay –*Portrait of a Lady in a Blue Dress*, oil on canvas, John Singleton Copley, Chicago: Terra Foundation for American Art. (Although the young woman in the portrait was never identified, many believe it is a portrait of Mercy Scollay. See drjosephwarren.com; "Miss Mercy Scollay is John Singleton Copley's 'Lady in a Blue Dress.'" Samuel A. Forman).
Lee Warren – Courtesy of ourlocalveterans.com, St. George News.
Robert Eugene Bush – U.S. Navy photo.
James L. Day – USMC/Sixth Marine Division photo.
Todd Beamer – Family Photo/Associated Press.
Brent Taylor – Utah National Guard photo.

Time Traveling Talismans

They Existed before the first pyramid rose from the desert.

They will exist on the day the last drop of oil is pulled from Earth.

They appear.

They vanish.

No one controls them.

Certain societies guard them.

They are Time-Traveling Talismans.

They are called "T3s" within the societies that care for them.

You will see.
You will learn.
You may believe.

— Boston Historic Genealogical Society

Part one

SEPTEMBER 11th ESSAY

New York City, September 11, 2001

World War II Marine Helping Fallen Comrade

Prologue

The Haunting – September 11, 2001

He was old, but his dog was older.

He covered a cough and then another. "Come on Pal." The Labrador mix started to come. He always came. With pained and halting steps, Pal came.

While he waited for his companion to limp to his side, he coughed again and looked at the left field line. He wiped his face and put his gnarled hand on the chalk dispenser. His faded grey eyes noted the zags. Not as straight as he used to make them. After fifty-one years of lining baseball fields, he knew how to spot imperfections in outfield lines. Yet, despite how badly he wanted to make them straight his body just couldn't do it anymore.

Pal finally reached him. The old man stretched down and scratched his bone-thin, friend. Pal's stiff and brittle tail wagged, while his big, brown eyes tried to hide the pain his worn-out body caused. The man turned his eyes towards home. He hated seeing the end of another "best friend," really, an only friend. Since he had first brought the chubby pup home, Pal had followed his master everywhere for more than fourteen years.

Together they walked home as the sun dipped below the horizon. The two of them lived in a one room, oversized equipment shed. The old man had lived there for half a century. "Here you go Pal." He lowered a bowl of their evening stew. He watched as his closest friend nudged it away. Pal rested his head on his paws. His pained eyes turned up to his master. Another day of not eating. It wouldn't be long.

Shaking his head, the old man thought of *Tex, Bud, Sal, Ann.* He couldn't do this again. He coughed. He coughed again and again. He wondered if he could just stop eating.

He changed and then lay in bed. Sleep never came easy.

He looked at Pal curled up by his feet, then his eyes turned to their one small table. With the moonlight creeping in, he saw his two worn photos propped up next to that old leather satchel.

In the first photo, he was sixteen. His brother Walter was fourteen. Their black and white grins stretched ear to ear and his long right arm hung over his brother's shoulders.

From the second photo, his brother alone stared at him. This picture was taken in 1945, right after Walter turned eighteen. He was perfectly dressed in a World War II Navy corpsman's uniform. He looked as sharp as any soldier ever had. It was the type of photo that should be in a family scrapbook somewhere, passed down from father to son. But Walter never became a father. There were no sons. No one else living can remember that smile, those eyes. No one else in the world remembers Walter. No one but him.

Knowing it might be hours before he could fall asleep, he turned on the dusty TV. It took a moment for the grainy image to appear, and when it did the old man still couldn't figure out what he was looking at.

A billowing grey cloud seemed to engulf the screen. As the camera panned out, he realized it was a building. A huge, towering building with fire pouring out from its sides.

The news reporter entered the screen, and as she talked, the video continued to play in the background. The old man sat there mesmerized by the footage from earlier that day. He watched the north tower crumble. He caught phrases of what the reporter was saying.

"Attack on America..."

"The Pentagon…"

"Survivors…"

"At war."

Feelings rushed over him that he hadn't felt since listening to the radio with his family on December 7th, 1941. America was under attack!

A reporter started interviewing a man at Ground Zero, and the old groundskeeper turned up the volume. "He's trapped down there! I'll be here all night to dig him out. I'll be here all week if I have to. I'll do whatever it takes, he's my *brother*!"

Hearing that last word, the old man switched off the news as fast as his trembling hands would let him. He sat there with his head in his arms, his body shaking. It wasn't until Pal licked his cheek that he realized he was crying.

Half the night later, he lay there tossing and turning in his sleep.

"Walter! Walter! Get back!" The sounds of the mortar's explosion and cries of the wounded covered his pleas. He tried to grab at his brother's arm, but missed by less than an inch.

Cries of "Medic!" and "Doc!" surrounded the crater that was as big as a giant meteor. The Japanese mortar had done its job. Torn Marines lay all around.

The haunting continued. He couldn't stop his brother. Bullets. Bombs. Death. It was everywhere...

He screamed again, "WALTER!"

This scream escaped the dream and rattled the dirty window.

Startled, Pal looked up.

The groundskeeper sat straight up in bed. Sweat beaded across his forehead as he tried to breathe.

Nightmares like this had haunted the old man for over fifty years. Yet, unlike so many times before, tonight his shaking hand didn't reach for the photo of his brother. Instead, he picked up the worn, leather satchel.

For over fifty years, he'd protected and guarded the satchel. For over fifty years, he'd lived with the knowledge that the items inside it – letters from the 1800s, a stack of faded and torn pages, and a strange, old musket ball - should've gone to his brother. Yet, the old man had been the one tasked with passing the satchel down the Warren family line.

These dreams reminded him.

He failed on Okinawa.

He failed since Okinawa.

He failed for fifty years to find the right owner - the next owner - of the leather bag.

People called him a hero.

All he could see when he looked in the mirror was a failure.

Chapter 1

"Patriots' Day" on the Adams Family Farm

April 19, 2002
221 Days – After September 11th

"WARNING! Beware of Unaccompanied Bags or Belongings"

The man read each word.

Through dark sunglasses, in a perfectly pressed black suit, the tall, middle-aged man with obsidian colored eyes, read again the warning.

Patchy clouds drifted in front of the April sun as the rays fell upon the 9-11 precautions. The man turned from the sign.

He'd noticed a few of these warnings dotting the national park. He knew these signs had been installed since the attacks last September.

He glanced around this particular sign posted on the edge of the flower garden. It stood next to a cement path that widened and wandered through well-trimmed lawns. His eyes followed the trail that led him and the other visitors from the park's Welcome Center to a house built over 250 years ago.

He stepped from the sign without admiring the spring flowers bursting in yellows and purples. He'd already noted that more than one park ranger had stared at him, surely questioning his intentions and wondering if he might be a security threat. So far, they'd said nothing.

He now followed a group of twenty or so tourists as they walked the pathway to the house. Some members of the group admired the historical residence at the end of the trail. Others listened to the guide explain the history of the national park. He already knew the facts. He knew the history. He knew the building. He didn't come today for sightseeing or history lessons. He came for one purpose.

His eyes stayed focused on the boy. Walking with his head above the rest, he watched the teenager's every step. His Society — a group older than the historical home he approached, and more prestigious — had assigned him to track the boy. For five months, he'd spent his days and nights watching and sending reports. Since November, he'd followed the boy's every action. So now, he watched the young man walk up the three stairs of the porch to the old home. The man from the Society had studied, he'd been trained, and he knew exactly why the boy had come to this house on this day. He would wait. He would watch. Today, he would finally make contact....

"WARNING! Beware of Unaccompanied Bags or Belongings"

The boy read each word.

Ignoring the people around him except for his mom and his friend, Steve O'Dell followed the path while reading the second sign he'd seen warning about strange bags and announcing the defensive side of The War on Terror. President Bush had talked to everyone on TV and said the country would protect itself from another terrorist attack. Steve had never seen these kinds of signs before last September. Now, they popped up wherever there were a lot of people, or at any important national place.

With faded jeans and brown hair tousling in the April breeze, Steve an 8th grader at Needham Middle School, slowed as he walked behind the park ranger. Surrounded by a small group of visitors, he looked toward one of America's oldest and most cherished farmhouses. He knew this house. He'd seen it two centuries earlier in its prime. Back then, it was a real farmhouse, not some museum or something in the middle of traffic. Over two centuries, the old house had been engulfed by the city of Quincy as its buildings and busy streets had changed. The city, with rows of homes, now slithered around and squeezed the old Adams Farm like a boa constrictor.

Steve remembered the countryside that had surrounded the house. He remembered the fields and fruit trees. Now, Steve looked at the city beyond the two-story home. No one else on the tour could truly appreciate what the Adams' sprawling farm had once been like. Over two centuries before, he and his younger friend Johnny had explored every inch of the rolling fields. Now, buildings and concrete covered everything around the old house.

Steve looked out towards the ocean and a smile crept over his face. He saw the hill where he and Johnny had been together on his last day in Braintree. Their talk on that hill had changed everything. Two hundred years later, it still affected Steve.

Then he glanced up at the chimneys poking from the roof. He remembered open hearths and warm fires filling the Adams' home in the days of the Revolution.

Steve stopped. He'd arrived in front of the weathered granite steps forming the stairs to the front porch. He took a deep breath and prepared to climb the same granite stairs he'd climbed centuries earlier.

His mom walked ahead with his best friend, Grace Levy, by her side. Grace had missed soccer practice to join Steve, something rarely done on her premier level team. Grace wore her blue plaid skirt and her crimson soccer hoodie, her golden ponytail bouncing between her shoulders as she walked up the front steps to the entrance.

Facing the entrance, Steve took another deep breath. He wondered. He paused again and pulled a Revolutionary War musket ball from his pocket. He turned it around in his hand, then gave it a squeeze. Silently, he expressed his deepest hope, a thought so strong, he almost heard it out loud, Could the Adams' Farm on the anniversary of the start of the American Revolution do it? Would this visit, on this day, electrify the ball and produce one more trip in time?

For two seconds he held his breath, closed his eyes, and stretched his right leg through the 250-year-old doorway. The antique wood squeaked under his first step, and then again at his second. Smells of the old walls, floors and furniture flooded his senses. He felt the 1770s wrapping around him, but when he opened his eyes . . . nothing. No bright light, no talismanic portal, nothing but the Adams' home, still in April, 2002. The musket ball sat cold in his hand. Dang! Why wouldn't it heat up? Why wouldn't it turn on?

Grace turned to Steve. She gave him a questioning look and he saw her hope. Behind her, the park ranger, wearing an old-fashioned tri-corn hat as part of his Revolutionary uniform, continued the tour. He stretched his long, branchy arms towards the front of the parlor. Steve thought he looked like a tall, skinny scarecrow with long arms and a pointed nose. The ranger pushed the group together until they bumped up against one another. He rambled on about this and that piece of furniture in the parlor. Steve overheard the strange-looking ranger say something about the unfinished portrait above the mantel. Ignoring the ranger and the mantel above the fireplace, Steve finally answered Grace by shaking his head no, causing the dimple in her cheek and the glow in her eyes to fade.

So frustrating! Not even a visit to the Adams Farm on this really important day, April 19th, Patriots' Day, could activate the musket ball. He thought for sure that the First Day of the Revolutionary War would cause it to begin working again. Grace stepped over and squeezed Steve's hand. This was not something she would've done before the September 11th Essay Contest, before the musket ball, or before his adventures with Dr. Joseph Warren.

Steve nodded to Grace, but his attention refocused on the antique parlor. He remembered it so well. Over 200 years ago he'd walked on this same floor. He'd knelt in the middle of the room with the Adams family in prayer, and played chess by the fireplace with his friend Johnny. Now, he looked over to that same fireplace. Nothing had changed, but then he glanced above the hearth.

He saw for the first time the old painting[1] that the tour guide had been talking about. The smile and warm eyes in the portrait pierced through his chest. He felt a current zap up and around his spine like he'd laid his tongue on the end of a fresh 9-volt battery. He stared at the painting of the Revolutionary War hero. In a low whisper, the words popped out, "That's Dr. Warren."

---

1 *Dr. Joseph Warren Portrait* – The dramatized image of Joseph Warren on the book cover is from an original 1765 portrait of Dr. Warren by John Singleton Copley. He painted the image on the front cover and partially completed a second painting of Dr. Warren that was very similar to the first. The artist gave the partially completed version of the portrait to John and Abigail Adams because Dr. Warren had been a very close friend to the Adams family. Abigail hung the portrait above the fireplace in their home. It has stayed in that place of honor for over 200 years.

The lanky ranger kept speaking, "Abigail Adams hung this painting of Dr. Joseph Warren above the hearth in 1788, and never permitted anyone to move it." He added, "For over 200 years, the family, and now the National Park Service, have honored her wishes."

Steve remembered the doctor's smile, his voice, his constant fire in those battles at the beginning of the Revolution. He rolled the ball with his fingers. The Massacre, the Tea Party, the speeches, the battles – he recalled them all. But one thought bounced between everything, *Will I ever see him again?*

The scarecrow-looking guide continued describing the house. He moved his long arms, redirecting the group from the parlor. His group moved on just as a new group came in. Steve waited to bring up the rear.

He squeezed the musket ball again – still nothing.

The ranger pointed his three-cornered hat towards the hall and shepherded the group in that direction. Grace looked back towards Steve, and then she and his mom followed the other tourists. Steve maneuvered behind the ranger, sneaking back to the edge of the parlor. He turned to the portrait of his friend for a minute while he was alone . . . at least, he thought he was alone.

The man in the black suit stood to the side of the hall, hidden from Steve's view. He'd removed his designer sunglasses and raised his eyebrows. He pressed forward, straining and tilting his body toward Steve's extended hand. Steve opened his hand and looked at the round piece of lead. In a mumble that the representative of the ancient organization had to strain to hear, the boy said, "Can't I have one more adventure, just one more?"

The Society's assigned agent straightened and stepped toward Steve.

Finally, it was time to make contact.

Every journey has a beginning.

The first steps of this journey may be unclear. You may be confused. Why a dying groundskeeper? Why the Adams' Farmhouse? And, why does a fourteen-year-old boy have a Revolutionary War musket ball? Don't worry. Each page will make more sense.

I'll be your guide through these pages.

I'll introduce myself this way. Imagine a canvas with a pale blue sky as the background and an artist searching for a color. With a dab and then a stroke, the colors from her brush flow onto the canvas. Her brush has created a blend of red, white, and navy blue that seem to ripple in the pale sky. They appear as three separate colors, but somehow as one. I'm that brush of color. Memorial Day, Presidents' Day, Flag Day and all those other days you wake up and wonder why extra flags are flying? Those are my days. Each of these days consists of the hues of red, white and blue.

Now, to understand the connection between the groundskeeper, the farmhouse, the ancient musket ball, and the man in a black suit, we must go back in time. Not to the Revolution and the days of Joseph Warren but to the moment when Steve's story becomes my story. We will go back six months to the essay contest. The essay that changed everything, by introducing Steve to ME.

Chapter 2

"Patriot Day[2] 2001"

October 10, 2001
29 Days – After September 11th

Grey clouds, tons of smoke, and huge patches of orange flames all poured out from the upper floors. Steve O'Dell had seen it before, and he figured everyone in the classroom had too – more than a dozen times. By October 2001, who hadn't seen the New York skyline that September morning?

It had been a month since September 11. Like every other American, images of that day were seared into Steve's memory. He could tell you exactly where he had been, who he was with and what he was doing when he first saw the burning towers decimated by a terrorist attack. He'd been in school, in math class. After the second plane crashed into the South Tower, there was a knock on the classroom door. The aide from the office whispered something to his teacher, Mrs. Timothy. She turned on the television and everyone watched.

Andy Huxford, a popular football player, sat two rows from Steve. He sat frozen as the class watched the towering buildings burn that September morning. Then Mrs. Timothy gasped. Everyone just watched in shock as the first skyscraper of 110 floors crumbled. It just disappeared. A huge billow of smoke replaced the building. It was then that Mrs. Timothy turned off the news.

---

2 *Patriot Day versus Patriots' Day* – Since September 11, 2001, there have been two special dates with very similar names. September 11 is called "Patriot Day" and the date is designed to remember those who were injured or died during the terrorist attacks in 2001. April 19 is called "Patriots' Day," and certain states honor this date in memory of the first day of fighting in the first battles of the Revolutionary War in 1775.

Andy shot up out of his chair. He kept shaking his head as he took a couple of staggered steps. He kept muttering over and over, "My brother works there." Mrs. Timothy left with him to get help from the office, as the whole class sat silently, still in shock from what they'd just seen.

Now, a month later, Steve wondered why everyone in his school was watching the attacks again. After the video of the falling towers was over, Mr. Rodriquez turned the lights back on. He paused as he looked at the class. In a low tone, he said, "Okay class, here is your new assignment. Each of you gets to write an essay. The topic is, '*What is 'Patriotism' after September 11, 2001?*'" Steve watched faces twist and heard some groans rumble in the room. In his more usual, enthusiastic voice he added, "Hey now, this isn't a normal assignment. The reason we watched these attacks again is that now you get to write this essay as part of a contest for Needham Middle and Needham High."

Everyone in the school knew Mr. Rodriquez, or knew of him, and everyone called him "M-Rod" for short. Steve's favorite teacher shined – a star in the classroom, every bit as much as the famous baseball player, A-Rod, when turning double plays in sold out stadiums. M-Rod taught Honors English at Needham Middle in Needham, Massachusetts. Because they wanted M-Rod as a teacher, Steve and many other seventh graders in Needham Middle School stayed up late on Thursday nights the previous year, studying extra for spelling tests and vocabulary exams so they could be selected for 8th grade honors.

In his usual voice, M-Rod said, "So, guys, the grand prize is $500 for the best essay." Steve lifted his eyebrows. "AWESOME!" and "SWEET!" replaced groans. "Lee Warren is sponsoring the contest. He's Needham's very own Pearl Harbor survivor and retired businessman." M-Rod didn't need to tell them about Lee Warren. Unless you were a new kid in Needham, you knew the *Flagman*. Lee never missed a parade, veteran's celebration or soldier's funeral. Armed with a pocket full of flag pins or flags attached to wooden sticks, he'd visited every elementary school in Needham on more than one occasion. No Needham kid escaped without one of the Flagman's flags.

The bell rang and M-Rod raised his voice. "Lee Warren started this contest after 9-11 to help our schools and community heal. So, think about what makes our country great!" Steve figured M-Rod, more than any of his other teachers, knew about what made the United States great. Every kid in M-Rod's class had heard his stories. He'd keep things interesting, talking about how he'd been raised in south Boston by Puerto Rican parents and married a "*hot*" Mexican wife (M-Rod's words, but the photo of her on his desk had every boy looking twice) while attending graduate school in California. M-Rod spoke perfect Spanish but chose to teach Honors English. He grew up poor and got scholarships for both business and law, but chose instead to be a teacher.

M-Rod had a lot of unique experiences that he wasn't afraid to share with his students. Oftentimes, his stories were funny and had the whole class laughing. But the story Steve remembered most was when their class was reading a book about the Great Depression. M-Rod told the story of when his dad had lost his job, and how he and his family had gone without food for two days. M-Rod wasn't ashamed of his past. He was proud that he came from hard-working immigrants. M-Rod had an energy for life that helped him to be successful, and it was that energy and love for teaching that made him a favorite at Needham Middle School. Raising his voice a bit, M-Rod said, "The essay is due by Wednesday, October 17th." As everyone bumped towards the door talking about the prize money, M-Rod's last words squeezed through; "Good luck!"

Nudged and plowed, Steve's mind raced. Five hundred bucks! He could buy some really cool stuff! He stepped into the busy hallway and a favorite voice edged out visions of five one hundred-dollar bills spread out on his bed.

"Steve?" He turned. Then he saw it, Grace Levy's smile. It blossomed as her right cheek winked that amazing dimple. She said, "Hey, I was wondering if you want to work together – like, you know, on our essay? Maybe we could help each other with some ideas." Tilting her head, she said, "Besides, I need help being patriotic, you know, so I can write the winning essay." Grace's smile, framed by her pretty face with olive-colored skin and rich, milk chocolate eyes (they weren't hazel, they weren't brown – they were pure "milk chocolate"), was enough to short-circuit the brains of middle school boys and melt their hearts like a Hershey's kiss on the Fourth of July. But Steve, a plain eighth grader, who managed with a few misplaced freckles, ordinary, wavy brown hair, and no flair on field or court, saw just Grace, at least he liked to think that.

Quickly he said, "Sure. How about today?" He figured the sooner they started, the sooner he could claim the prize money. He just needed to clear up one thing first.

"But, Grace, you don't need to stress about feeling 'patriotic.' This isn't a contest about loving your country or something."

Grace nodded as they walked. "Yeah, but I'm just thinking if you're more patriotic you can, you know, maybe, write a better essay?"

Steve and Grace made their way up the hall and around three giggling girls standing in front of the stairs. The leader of the group, the one caked in make-up and earrings lining the length of her ears, stepped in front of Steve and bumped him. "FROG! Watch where you're walking!" The other two girls laughed. Steve ignored them and was glad Grace just shook her head.

He wanted to finish his point before Grace went the other way to her class. Steve turned to her, "Trust me. This contest has nothing to do with patriotism or loving your country or how much blood you can donate for 9-11 victims or anything like that. It's about writing. That's it."

Steve stopped and waited. Finally, those milk chocolate eyes caught his. He cemented his point, "Grace, being patriotic has nothing to do with this contest."

Chapter 3

Writing the Essay

Later that day, Steve walked home with Grace. They plodded past autumn trees with leaves in shades of orange and dark reds that reflected the crisp New England sunlight. Between the canopy of leaves, Steve saw a fluttering of red, white and blue. Every house in the neighborhood that owned a flag had been flying it every day since 9-11, and many who didn't own a flag before September 11th bought one.

When they got to Steve's house, he went to the kitchen and laid out paper and pens near the bay window. The light poured across the room and the rays warmed the oval oak table. With the O'Dell's dining room on the other side of a swinging door, Steve's hide-a-way in front of the bay window served as the perfect place for hanging out when writing or doing school stuff.

Grace put her bag on the table and Steve walked over to the pantry. Looking through the etched glass window within the door, he cracked the door and asked, "Grace, you want some potato chips?"

"Yeah, sure," she said, pulling papers and pens from her bag.

Steve sat down and handed her a small bag of chips, then opened his bag and put it on the table. "Okay, Grace, I've been thinking about this. The people judging these essays will like symbols. You know, M-Rod is always making us figure out what the stuff in a book means. I'm going to make the two Trade Towers symbols and I can include some other patriotic stuff." Grace listened and nodded.

Steve kept talking, "You know, it's like if you compare the twin towers to Lexington and Concord from the Revolution, then the judges will be like, 'Wow, this kid knows some history.' And then if we add some famous quote, like 'Give me Liberty or Give me Death' or something like that, it'd be even better." Steve started making notes, but looked up at Grace. "Remember, the key is we've got to figure out what the judges want to read." He popped a handful of chips into his mouth as he began to scribble down his ideas.

Grace tapped the end of her pen up and down, but didn't say anything. Steve was too busy writing to notice her tilt her head and squint her eyes. After a minute she said, "I'm thinking patriotism means – other things. I think it's like doing something for others, you know for the people in your country. Someone isn't patriotic just because they say they are. They need to be doing something. Like the people that gave blood at our school or like when soldiers go away to fight for our freedom. You said something about Lexington and Concord. Well, I'm thinking that it's like the same feelings of patriotism; like leaving your farm and fighting back then are similar to what people do now. Kind of like regular people giving stuff up, even dying, to help others; like on September 11th, when the police and firefighters ran into the buildings to try to save people or when the passengers on the one plane made it crash in the field in Pennsylvania so it didn't bomb the White House. It's that kind of patriotism that is the same after September 11th."

Steve stared at her, "Awesome! I love it. But how would you write it for the judges? You have to be thinking about who's going to read these essays. I've been studying about writing and what the experts say is, 'think about your audience.'" Steve wrote 'Pearl Harbor' on his paper, then said, "See, Lee Warren, he's sponsoring this contest, right? And he was at Pearl Harbor. I'm going to include something about Pearl Harbor because that's what he's going to like reading." He popped another chip into his mouth.

For a moment Grace looked at Steve in silence. Then she asked, "Is that everything – what the judges will like?"

Steve smiled, "Always think about what your audience wants to read, and for this essay it's about the judges. That's how you win. That's how you get the $500 – but I totally love your ideas."

Grace stopped tapping her pen and stared across the table, "So you think Lee Warren is sponsoring this essay just so you can figure out what he or the other judges want to read?"

"Yup." Steve didn't even look up. He kept smiling as he wrote the thoughts tumbling around him. The ideas kept coming and he didn't want to lose them.

Grace pushed away from the table and started picking up her stuff. "You're done?" Steve asked with surprise. "You don't want to write?"

She shrugged. "I need to go home and get ready for soccer practice."

Steve looked at the clock. "Now?" Grace just nodded. He said, "I like what you said, about how patriotism is the same now as when our country started, in the Revolution and stuff." Grace looked up at him, the twinkle in her eye showing.

Then Steve said, "What did you say patriotism meant again? Was it something about doing something or . . . what was it you thought the judges would like?"

But his question had blown out any spark in those milk chocolate eyes. She looked to the door, "Being patriotic means doing something, like doing something for others, not just thinking about you or what you can get. It's about helping others or protecting those in your country who need help."

Steve smiled. "Sweet. The judges are going to love that kind of stuff!"

Chapter 4

Lee Warren

"*. . . one nation under God, with liberty and justice for all.*" Steve sat down with the rest of his first period class and waited for the morning announcements. Ever since the 9-11 attack, his school had started saying the Pledge of Allegiance. Before that, he hadn't said it since elementary school. Now, over a month later, it was just another part of their morning routine.

"Welcome students, we have some important news today." The otherwise pleasant voice of the principal scratched through the school's halls and classrooms, distorted by the sound system. "First, you have one week to get your Halloween costumes ready. You can wear a costume next Wednesday for Halloween, but costumes must be appropriate, and no masks will be allowed." Steve smiled along with his classmates. What was Halloween without costumes?

"Now, some really exciting news!" Mrs. Pollard's voice scaled up a few notches. "Lee Warren, our own World War II and Pearl Harbor Veteran and sponsor of the essay contest, called this morning and told me that the winner of the Patriotic Essay contest is from our school! Yep, one of our middle school students beat all the high school entries." Steve lifted his head. Normally he could sleep through his principal's announcements but not now – not when there was five hundred bucks on the line. Mrs. Pollard continued, "At lunch today, Lee Warren will be here to present the prize money and personally congratulate the winning author."

Steve thought, *lunch.* Now if only he didn't have four more hours to wait.

Finally! The bell rang and he and a hundred other kids slammed through the lunchroom doors.

Principal Pollard stood up front at the edge of the cafeteria tables with Lee Warren and a bunch of other grown-ups that Steve didn't recognize. Mrs. Pollard always smiled a lot. Her brown hair, cut below her shoulders, flowed behind her as she talked and greeted those up front. Lee Warren stood by Principal Pollard. Mr. Warren looked like a short version of Santa Claus, with a round stomach, white hair and a jolly twinkle in his eyes. Next to Lee, Steve saw a tall guy with wavy, sandy-colored hair and a big camera hanging from a thick strap around his neck. There were two other guys and a woman, too, who Steve thought looked important; probably other judges.

"This is so cool!" The voice came with the prettiest smile in Needham.

Turning to Grace, Steve nodded and said, "Yeah, lots of people."

Grace said, "What do you think?" Then she added, "So cool that it's someone from the middle school!"

Steve nodded, biting his lip. "I messed up."

Grace furrowed her brow, "What are you talking about?"

Now, nibbling the inside of his lip, Steve shook his head, "I messed up; I could've done so much better. I ended my essay talking about a tree. The judges would've rather read about the church."

Grace looked like she just drank sour milk, "You're still just thinking about what the judges would rather read?"

Steve nodded. "I wish I'd known about the real old church. It's this St. Paul's Chapel[3], right next to where the two towers were. I saw it on the news. Like, all the other buildings next to the towers were totally wrecked but this church that George Washington worshipped in somehow got protected. Dang! I blew it." Grace frowned. Steve sighed, "The judges would've loved it. The church is like where all the rescue workers went, and all the family members stayed when they

---

3 St. Paul's Chapel, also known as "The Little Chapel that Stood," is a real chapel built in 1766. George Washington did attend church there. It is less than 100 yards from where the Twin Towers collapsed. Everything around the chapel, including much larger buildings were destroyed. However, the little chapel was untouched, not even a pane of glass was broken. It became a refuge and beacon of hope for rescue workers and families searching for survivors.

were hunting for survivors. Comparing patriotism to this St. Paul's church would've been a perfect way to end my essay. I'm so mad!"

Grace wouldn't even look at him; she just shook her head.

Steve watched the large cafeteria room buzz with kids wandering through and around the rectangular tables, all of them wondering who would be five hundred bucks richer. Grace sat next to Steve at one of the long white tables that always smelled like bleach. Mrs. Pollard called into the portable microphone, "Students. Students. It's time to start." Steve fidgeted in his seat.

Mrs. Pollard said, "Well, I'm so excited that Lee Warren sponsored this essay. I've been talking to him about it and he told me that he just wanted to do something to help after the 9-11 attacks." She smiled at Lee. "He told me, 'When I saw it all happen and heard that it was terrorists and the Taliban that did it, I wanted to sign back up with the Navy and go over to Afghanistan and fight 'em myself. But, when you're 80 years old, the Navy doesn't want you.'" Mrs. Pollard turned to Lee, "So Lee decided he'd focus on the good of our country and sponsored the contest for our Needham young men and women to help them remember patriotism. Now, what's so cool is that one of our students was the most patriotic!"

Steve saw Grace smile, but he thought, *What the heck – most Patriotic? An essay contest is about the best writer.* He didn't have time to think about what that meant before Mrs. Pollard rushed forward, announcing the winner. "Yes, Steve O'Dell is Needham's most patriotic student! His essay topped 'em all!" Mrs. Pollard started clapping and everyone else did too. The principal looked out over the cafeteria tables trying to spot her most patriotic student. Lighting up when she saw him, she called out, "Steve, come on up!"

Smiling and clapping with everyone else, Grace nudged Steve, "Go on up, most patriotic." Grace's smile was totally genuine, but he felt a sting in each word. Then, he forgot about everything else and thought about the five hundred bucks! He shot right up. He hated being singled out in a crowd. He knew his face was beet red, but for $500, he'd go up front.

With the students and the other grown-ups clapping, he headed to the cafeteria stage. As Steve reached the front of the room, Mrs. Pollard handed the microphone to Lee and stepped over to Steve. With a big smile, she said, "Congratulations!"

Steve hated feeling like he was on display, so he directed his gaze from the principal to Lee Warren's left hand, where Lee held the check. He just wanted to get the prize money and sit down. Lee began to talk, and the old Navy man's voice rang deep and salty from years on the ocean, "Well, young man, congratulations!"

He wasn't tall – he was actually about the same height as Steve. Lee put a wrinkled but firm hand on Steve's shoulder. His eyes twinkled as he added, "You did a fine job, son. Yes, sir. That was a mighty fine essay and certainly you are a true patriot. Yes siree, you are." Lee raised the envelope. "Please accept this $500 prize for the most patriotic essay." He handed the envelope to Steve, and the reporter snapped off a dozen quick photos. When the reporter finally finished, Lee said to Steve, "Mayor Barney would also like to give you something." Lee turned to the man in the blue suit and Steve groaned inside. He had his $500. He was done. He didn't want any more attention, but he looked over at the mayor.

The mayor buttoned the top button of his jacket and approached Steve carrying a framed certificate. Steve tried to read the certificate. He could only make out the top word "patriotic." His stomach tightened. The mayor turned his round face from Steve to all the other kids. Everyone seemed ready to be done and start eating lunch, especially Steve. Once the money was awarded, who wanted to keep listening?

The mayor said, "Guys, I won't take long. I know you want to eat, but I've got something important for Steve." Turning from the crowd to Steve, he said, "As the Mayor of Needham, I told Lee we want to give you this. The Town of Needham thanks you for helping our community to remember." Steve thought the last word seemed strange. Mayor Barney went on, "After the attack on 9-11, we need to remember what a great country we have. Students, I hope you will always remember the veterans. Please remember their sacrifice for you.

I've known Lee Warren for over 20 years. He's the greatest patriot I know, because he never lets me or anyone in Needham forget the veterans who fought for our country. He's told me more than once about the slogan '*Remember Pearl Harbor.*' He told me that every American during the war – that's World War II for you guys that may struggle with your history – *remembered* the Japanese attack.

"So, what I'm saying is, Lee's essay contest was to help you Needham middle students, and all of us, remember what a great country we have. Remember those firefighters and police officers who ran into the burning buildings to save Americans. Remember all those that lost their lives when the buildings crashed."

Steve just stood there. The mayor went on and on. A warm feeling flowed up Steve's neck to his ears, like the sick warm feeling that flowed down your leg when you were a little kid and you wet the bed. This talk about patriotism and patriots and remembering embarrassed him more than if he were standing in front of everyone in his underwear. Finally, the mayor said, "Alright, now, I'll give Steve this certificate from the City of Needham. Steve, please accept this award from the city honoring you as the winner of Lee's essay contest and the Most Patriotic Teenager in Needham, Massachusetts." Steve couldn't believe this. He wrote an essay. He won $500. He just wanted to take the money. The mayor could keep the plaque, the certificate, stop the talks. He just wanted to sit down with his envelope. He wrote an essay. He liked writing. That's it. He didn't want to be some great American!

Reaching over to take the plaque, Steve didn't even try to smile. He wanted to leave, but Mayor Barney held his arm. Then the Mayor said to all the students, "Unless Mrs. Pollard has something else," the mayor looked to the principal and she shook her head, "you can go enjoy lunch." By his grip, Steve knew this meant everyone but him.

As the other kids scrambled to the cafeteria windows to be first in line, the mayor smiled at Steve. "Thanks for your essay, Steve. It really helped me remember that patriotism is more than just saying 'I'm an American' or repeating the Pledge of Allegiance."

Steve saw Grace coming towards them, and he tried to get away before she heard all this patriotic stuff. "Yeah, okay, well, thanks. I kinda got to . . . " Just as Grace reached Steve's side, Lee Warren, with his eighty-year-old legs, waddled back over to Steve. Tilting to his left side a bit, like a lopsided toy ship in a bathtub, the old Navy man reached out and grabbed Steve's arm. "Son, I'm proud of you. It's not many your age who have a love for their country like you. Yes, sir, you're a special young man." Lee looked directly at Steve under his bushy white eyebrows. "You know, yep, you bet, you understand the price paid by others so you can live in the greatest nation on God's great earth. I want to thank you." Lee tilted his head and nodded a bit. "Your reference to Pearl Harbor . . ." Lee paused. He continued through a tightening throat, "excuse me." He paused again, "Thank you." He moved his hand to Steve's upper arm and gently shook his shoulder. "Thank you for remembering Pearl."

Steve saw Grace staring at Lee. Steve looked in Lee's direction but not in his eyes. He thought how he had manipulated the essay at the kitchen table. He nodded to the old sailor. When he was ten, Steve had taken a bag of *M&Ms* from a store without paying. He ate the candy, but each piece tasted worse than the one before and he threw away the last ones. He never did it again. The guilt of eating stolen chocolate outweighed the cost. Holding the envelope and check for $500, and listening to Lee, he felt like he'd just eaten stolen chocolate.

Steve didn't look up, he just walked away.

Grace walked with him.

Neither said anything.

Chapter 5

An Invitation

The next day Steve's full essay and a photo of him with Lee Warren appeared in the Needham Times. All the lines Steve had included just to impress the judges were blasted across the entire front page. Too many people saw it. Too many people thanked him for it. Teachers he knew and even those he didn't stopped him in the hall, patted him on the back and thanked the *patriotic teenager.* He hated it!

One hundred miles away, the article and essay had upturned a small, simple, very sad home.

On an old kitchen table, the article lay, spread out. Behind it were two photos and a leather satchel. Next to the Needham article, was a small wooden marker with the name *Pal.*

Covering his mouth from a rib-breaking cough, the old man leaned over for air. The groundskeeper looked again at the article. For two days he'd done little else besides watch over his dying friend and read again and again, the article – especially the essay. He straightened, picked up the wooden marker and wiped another tear from his cheek.

He walked gripping the grave marker in his right hand, while the Needham article weighed on his conscience. Could there really be someone he could give the old satchel to?

At the end of the maintenance road, at the back of the outfield walls, he'd created a special spot. For over thirty-five years, no one but him came back there.

He stopped and looked at the four other markers - Tex, Bud, Sal, Ann. He knelt at the edge of the line of names. His knee sank as he pushed Pal's marker deep into the freshly shoveled ground. Taking a minute to look at the five markers, a wave of coughing hit him. It knocked him to his hands and knees. The coughing kept rolling over him from every direction. His motivation to keep fighting was no longer for Pal. Now his lungs fought back for the boy, the satchel, and most importantly, for the memory of his brother.

When the coughing finally passed, he heard the rumble of a car pulling up.

Standing, he looked past the outfield wall and saw a grey-haired man in a green army uniform standing by his front door. He recognized him.

He slowly started towards his home just as the old soldier was getting ready to get back in his car to leave. As the retired Colonel opened his car door, he spotted the groundskeeper.

With a tone of relief, he said, "Harold, there you are. I was worried."

Harold just nodded.

The Colonel took off his hat as he tried to straighten his own, worn down body. "Harold." The Colonel paused, "Is it really true? Are you backing out of our Veterans Day celebration?"

With Steve's and his parents' full names in the article and his entire essay in the newspaper, more than a few businesses and strangers in town sent him letters congratulating him. Embarrassed, Steve had started making sure he got the mail before his mom. If his mom saw the letters, she always wanted to read them and talk about the essay, which only made him feel more like he'd stolen chocolate. Just when things began getting better, it came.

On the first Friday in November, Steve came home from school in time to see the mailman close their mailbox and drive away. Steve headed to the box, grabbed the cold metal, and opened the lid, taking out the five or six letters. Sorting as he walked, he saw two names in the corner of an envelope, American Legion and Veterans of Foreign Wars. The letter came from Portsmouth, New Hampshire, addressed to, "Mr. Steve O'Dell and the O'Dell Family." Strange. Steve had never seen one of these "loved your patriotic essay" letters come addressed to him and his family and never from New Hampshire.

He tossed his backpack and the other letters across the kitchen table, one letter sliding off onto the ground. Steve slumped in the wood chair nearest the pantry door and opened the Portsmouth letter. He read,

Dear Steve and O'Dell Family,

A Joint Committee of Veterans Affairs from Portsmouth, New Hampshire wishes to invite you to a special ceremony honoring one of our nation's heroes, Marine Sergeant Harold Keith Warren, a World War II Congressional Medal of Honor Recipient and Purple Heart Veteran. Because Veterans Day falls on a Sunday, we will be celebrating Monday, November 12. The ceremony will be held at the Portsmouth, New Hampshire Veterans Center and will commence at 10 a.m.

The American Legion and Veterans of Foreign Wars have been requested by Sergeant Warren, himself, to extend this special invitation to Mr. Steve O'Dell and his family. Mr. Warren asked that Steve arrive at 9 a.m. He would like to speak to him and give him something he says is very special.

If you have questions, please call.

Sincerely,
Colonel D. Doughman
Commander American Legion Post 168
238 Deer St. Portsmouth, NH
(306) 703-9567

Steve finished the letter and read it again. It looked like it had been written on an ancient typewriter. Who was this Sergeant Warren guy or Colonel Doughman, anyway? And why would they want to talk to him? And give him something? What could be so "special?" Steve read it again. When he got to the end and saw the phone number, he debated. Should he show this to his mom, call the number or just throw it away? He wasn't in the mood for some group wanting to honor the Great American Teenage Patriot, but he did wonder what a Marine sergeant would want to give to him.

He walked to the swinging door at the end of the kitchen, pushed it open, and hollered, "Mom!" He waited a bit, and then again, "Mom!" Nothing. Steve picked up the kitchen phone and stared at the number on the letter. Then he punched in the number.

A woman's voice answered, "Hello, American Legion Post 168."

Steve stalled and almost hung up but then said, "Can I talk to Colonel Doughman?" He tried to sound official. It must've worked because the lady said, "Wait one minute and I'll get him."

This helped Steve's confidence. A moment later he heard a deep but shaky voice say, "This is Colonel Doughman, may I help you?"

Now, what the heck to say? Steve froze and the older voice said, "Hello?" Steve took a breath, and then gulped out, "Yeah, I guess . . . I'm Steve O'Dell," he paused, "and I just got a letter. Some letter to me and my family."

Steve had no idea what to say next, but Colonel Doughman jumped right in. "Oh, good. I'm glad the letter made it. Sorry to send something without much information. I'm not much of a writer. You're probably wondering what this is all about."

Steve said, "Yeah, I'm kind of wondering why I got this letter." Looking out the window, he saw his mom pull up into the driveway, get out and begin tugging white grocery bags from the back seat. She popped through the kitchen door carrying three or four bags.

Colonel Doughman's voice poured through the phone, "Here in Portsmouth, we just recently learned that your great uncle, Harold Keith Warren, got awarded the Medal of Honor during World War

II and a Purple Heart, as well. We've known about him for years. He took care of our baseball fields, but we had no idea he'd been a war hero. Anyway, here in Portsmouth, he only went by Harold Keith. So, until some new YMCA man from New York found out that Harold, our field keeper for almost 50 years, was really Harold Keith Warren, a Medal of Honor recipient, we had no idea. So, when we found this out, we organized a special Veterans Day celebration to honor him." The old voice continued, "We've been plannin' this for a while. Then I just learned the other day, that Harold won't do it unless you come." I guess you and your family don't know him, but Harold is your mom's uncle. He was your grandma's brother."

The old man paused. Steve thought, *What the heck?* This letter from some old typewriter coming from some old veteran's group in New Hampshire seemed really strange, but now this conversation was too weird. How did this old guy know about some long-lost great uncle? Steve wished he'd never made the call!

His mom could see him fidgeting. She spotted the torn envelope and letter on the table. She picked up the mystery letter. Mom's eyes zipped across the lines, once, then twice. Steve stared back with a blank face. The voice on the other end of the line asked, "Are you there, son?"

Panicking, Steve decided to tag-team the call and handed the phone to his mom, saying, "It's this Colonel Doughman guy from the letter." Steve pointed and his mom's eyes got really big as she stared at the phone and heard the remote voice through the receiver.

Pausing, she put the phone on speaker. Then she said, "Hello, this is Mrs. O'Dell. Are you calling about this veteran's celebration?"

Edging closer to Mom, Steve could hear the old man's voice readjust a bit, "Oh, you must be Steve's mom. I'm sorry to be saying all this in such a jumbled mess. I didn't call though. Steve called me. I was just telling your son that your uncle, Harold Keith Warren, requested that Steve come to a program we are having to honor him."

Mrs. O'Dell cut the man off, "But I don't have an uncle named Harold. What's this about?" To the old colonel's credit, he didn't back down or get flustered. "Yeah. Harold said you wouldn't know him. He explained that he is your mom's brother. I guess he and your mom, Esther, had a terrible falling out after the war, after World War II, that is."

Mom's face fell, her voice soft, "How did you know my mom's name?"

"I'm sorry. I know this is strange. I was explaining this to your son but I'm glad I can talk to you." Leaning closer, Steve heard the man say, "Your Uncle Harold has lived in Portsmouth since after the war. He came up here from Massachusetts and played baseball for an old minor league professional team here in town. But when the league folded, the team did too, and Harold had no job. He stayed in Portsmouth and became the town's field keeper. He lives at the baseball fields in a small equipment house – a real private life." Colonel Doughman paused, "Until now." He paused again, "No one knew until a few months ago that Harold's name wasn't Harold Keith, but that it was really Harold Keith Warren." Mom's face shifted again. Steve knew his Grandma's name before she got married had been Warren.

Colonel Doughman said, "Harold Keith Warren served our country as a Marine sergeant during World War II. He fought at Okinawa and received the Medal of Honor. We didn't even know he'd served in the War."

Mrs. O'Dell looked at the letter. Then she said, "Mr. Doughman, is that right?"

"Yes, ma'am."

"Well, Mr. Doughman, you're right, this is really strange and I'm sorry, but I just don't know what to think." She looked at Steve as she spoke. "How does this involve my son?" The question made Steve fidget.

In a low voice that Steve could barely make out, Colonel Doughman said, "For some reason, Harold insists that Steve come to the Veterans Day ceremony. He's got something for him. He doesn't ask much, and he isn't happy about this event even being planned. He originally only agreed when others convinced him that the ceremony could help our country after the 9-11 tragedy. But, now, after he's already agreed and we've planned everything, he just told me this week that he won't come unless your son, Steve O'Dell, came too."

Steve's mom interrupted, "Steve, or Steve and his family?"

"Well, both, but he wants to see Steve." The colonel went on, "Harold has been pretty sick the past few months. He said he has something he wants to talk to Steve about, and I guess he feels like it's something that needs to be done soon. He'd like Steve and all the family to come early and meet him before the ceremony. If you can come at 9, he can explain this more. He said he's got something to give to Steve and he said he's going to do it before he dies. I'm sorry this is so strange, but I really don't know much more than that."

Steve's mom shook her head, "Well, I need to talk to my husband. We'll see. Is that okay?"

"Yeah. Just let me know, because I honestly don't know what I'll do if you don't come. We've got a lot of people planning to come for Veterans Day this year, since 9-11, you know, and people finding out we have a Medal of Honor Veteran with us. Without Harold coming we would be in a real mess." Even Steve could hear the colonel's desperation.

"Okay. Thanks, Mr. Doughman. I'll call you back after I talk to my husband." She looked at Steve and Steve wondered, What will Dad say?

Chapter 6

An Unwelcome Trip

It was a holiday. To be more specific, it was Veterans Day. Not that Veterans Day meant much to Steve O'Dell. It merely meant one less day at Needham Middle School. Still, it was Veterans Day, November 2001.

Mom and Dad had involved Steve in making the decision. The night after the call, Steve told his dad he didn't care if they went. Sure, he wanted to know what his long-lost great uncle might give him, but going to some veterans' thing in Portsmouth on a day off from school didn't sound like much fun. He was fine to stay or go. Dad called Colonel Doughman and Steve and Mom listened in on the conversation.

After a couple minutes, Dad said, "Lee Warren did what?" Steve tilted his head. More talking went back and forth, and Dad hung up and said, "I guess a bunch of planning for their Veterans Day program is wasted if Steve doesn't go. This Colonel Doughman says Harold isn't coming without Steve."

Mom looked to Dad. "Why Steve? And why did you ask about Lee Warren?"

"I guess Lee sent your uncle a copy of the newspaper article with Steve's essay." Dad turned to Steve, "Now your Uncle Harold says he won't participate unless Steve's there. He said something about it having to do with these things that your uncle wants to give to Steve. I don't get it, and this Colonel Doughman doesn't either. He just says without Steve there's no ceremony." Steve sat there in the kitchen, hating his stupid essay even more. How could some dumb essay cause so many problems?

Then, Dad made the decision for the family. Looking towards his wife and son, he said, "Let's go. We'll all go and meet this family war hero." Putting a cheerful spin on the strange calls and occurrences, he added, "It'll be a good way for the family to celebrate Veterans Day after 9-11!"

Four days later, though, things weren't so cheerful.

"You're coming and that's final!" The words ricocheted off the front window and into the back seat. Dad and Steve's older brother, Rob, had been arguing since the family left their home in Needham, a town that was a suburb of Boston.

As the battle raged between Dad and his brother Rob, Steve watched the New England landscape roll by. Steve and his brother had two choices; they could hopelessly argue about going to a Veterans Day ceremony 100 miles away or accept their fate. Steve chose the latter, Rob the former.

"Dad, it's stupid! You know it's not fair. I had plans, and spending my day driving two hours to some dumb veterans' thing that you want to go to is wrong. I'm wasting my holiday!" Nothing original – for the last thirty minutes Rob had rewound and played the same complaint.

Rob's long legs were bent, his knees propped against the back of Mom's seat. He was over six feet tall and muscular from countless hours of training and years of playing every sport. He had chiseled cheekbones and wavy blond hair that always seemed a bit ruffled, in a cool way. Regardless of whether he was dribbling a basketball down court or sitting in the back seat of a Ford Explorer, Rob had his world under control. Squeezing his hands, Rob rubbed them on his jeans. At only sixteen, he looked ready for a college campus.

Steve on the other hand, could barely pass for his fourteen years. His brown hair always looked messed up, but never in a cool way, and his muscles were missing in action, easily hidden under his shirt. He looked like nothing but a typical kid with a few misplaced freckles and hazel eyes.

"By the time we finally get home the whole day'll be wasted." Rob kept fighting. Rob always fought. He never gave up. He was the starting quarterback on his football team, and they had only lost one game, and that was when Rob had played with the flu. "It's not fair. Why do you and Mom get to decide what we do on our vacation?

None of my friends are going to some veterans' thing. Why do we have to? It's lame."

Dad's knuckles whitened at the wheel. "That's it. I don't want to hear another word." Dad cracked each of his words one by one to emphasize his point and control his anger. "The purpose of Veterans Day is for families to spend time together attending ceremonies just like the one you're going to. Do you understand?" Dad looked in vain for an acknowledgment. "This is a family event."

Steve looked across the back seat just in time to see Rob rolling his eyes. Rob said, "I've got basketball practice today. Instead, I'm going to this veterans' crap!"

Dad gritted his teeth and his eyes bulged as he glanced at the rearview mirror. Steve wondered if his brother really thought this was an argument he could win. Forty miles north of Boston, Dad wasn't going to turn around and drive back to Needham.

Mom tried to save the sinking trip. "Rob, give this a chance. After 9-11, many Americans are trying to do something special today. As a family, we can do something too."

But Rob pounced, "Yeah, if it's supposed to be a family trip, why didn't you make Lizzie come on this stupid trip?"

Steve thought about his older sister Lizzie, whose full name was Elizabeth Georgette. At seventeen, she was the oldest of the three O'Dell children. Steve knew the answer to Rob's question and in this case, it wasn't because his IQ was four categories higher than his brother's – whether he liked it or not. In this case, everyone knew the answer. Like a balloon being poked deeper and deeper with a broken stick, Dad had reached his limit. Mom, however, reminded Rob that Lizzie had to work and couldn't get time off.

As the New England fields whizzed past the side window, Steve's thoughts veered a thousand miles away from the car conversation. He mulled over something he thought about a lot. How could he be smarter than Rob? Steve wasn't just a smarter eighth grader than Rob had been when he was in eighth grade. Steve was smarter in general. He knew it and he figured Rob knew it too.

As the Ford Explorer rounded a turn, Steve's thoughts rounded back to the situation at hand. He wanted to team up with Rob, in a way that Steve could never do on a court or field. Though he didn't think he could win Rob's case, Steve said. "Mom, Rob's right, it isn't fair. He really didn't have to come today. I changed my plans, but he didn't have to."

Rather than wait for Mom or Dad, Rob rebounded and pounced. "Really? What were your plans? Were you headed to the library with Grace? Going to read some poetry? Oh, yeah, I forgot. The library would be closed. I guess it would be the bookstore. Do they still give you guys lemonade? Or, are you drinking herbal tea now, while you talk about books or, like, try to write one?"

Steve stared past the front window. It took a second or two for the sting to set in. The previous summer, Steve had mowed lawns every day. Pushing a lawn mower with hot, sweaty hands, he got painful blisters the first days and weeks. After his hands suffered enough, the body's natural defenses kicked in. Hard, protective calluses formed. Not the same with Rob's cuts and digs; they always stung.

"Rob!" Mom used a sharp tone, one that came out often when defending her younger son from her older.

"Mom, it's true! Really, it's just weird, him hanging out and writing stories and crap with a girl." Rob glanced at Steve and then back out the window. The green sign informed them that they were approaching the New Hampshire state line.

Steve thought, he's right. He would've spent the day with Grace. Whether at the bookstore or the library, they would've talked about books. Steve knew that his best friend, a girl, and his favorite pastimes, reading and writing, were not cool or normal for eighth grade boys. He also knew that Rob's friends questioned Rob, more than once, about his younger brother.

Steve totally got it. Rob and his friends figured that regular eighth grade guys, at least real guys, played sports. Steve liked watching sports, he cheered for the Red Sox and hoped this new quarterback, Tom Brady, would keep winning games for the Patriots, but Steve could never be the athlete Rob was. Rob and his buddies worshiped anything that could be kicked, thrown, dribbled or swished. Steve, on the other hand, liked to read and write – especially to write. The only person Steve knew who liked to read and write as much as him wore more skirts than pants. Rob had his teammates with balls, bats, hoops and adolescent athletic glory. Steve hid with Grace, sharing essays and books and hoping for middle school anonymity. For Steve, the less said about this matter, the better.

The Ford Explorer continued towards New Hampshire. Rob had lost the battle. He persisted only out of instinct, "Mom, I just don't get why we have to go all the way to Portsmouth for a Veterans Day celebration?"

Steve saw Rob looking out the window, eyes darting and attention far from Mom's front seat. As they made their way off the main highway and into Portsmouth, Mom explained, "Rob, we're going to be honoring a member of our family, a decorated war hero. . ."

Rob interrupted. "Mom – really? I know what we're doing. We're going to see some relative, some guy we didn't even know existed, get honored by people we don't know and have never met. And, this long-lost relative is being honored because he got some Purple Heart medal for getting shot, and some other stupid medal."

Dad looked straight into the rearview mirror and aimed his finger at Rob. "That other medal happens to be the Congressional Medal of Honor, young man. And I've had it with your attitude. Do you understand?"

Dad's stare remained laser focused at Rob, but Rob smirked and shook his head as he looked out the side window arms folded. Steve thought, Wow! Rob is either too dense to discern the fire in Dad's eyes or he really is brave.

Either way, Rob kept looking out the side window, "Well, I just don't get it. What's the big deal about getting yourself shot? Do you really deserve some congressional medal?"

Steve could tell that Mom hoped they could make it without a total catastrophe. She spoke before Dad exploded. "You don't get the Congressional Medal of Honor for 'getting yourself shot.' The Medal of Honor is only awarded to the bravest of soldiers. It's a very special medal, Robert. So is the Purple Heart. It's given to soldiers who are wounded while serving our country. It was started by George Washington when he was a general."

Mom's explanation bounced right off Rob. Instead, he latched on to a new point, "Well, tell me, does it really make sense to encourage soldiers to go out and get shot? Do we want our guys saying, 'Hey, look at me, I get a medal because I got myself blown up?' Don't you think we should give medals to the guys smart enough not to get shot?"

Luckily for Rob, trying to find the Veterans' Memorial Building in a strange town required all of Dad's attention. Steve watched Mom shake her head and heard her say something about how the Purple Heart represented a soldier's sacrifice and that Rob should change his attitude. Steve watched Rob pick at a hangnail, shaking his head.

Steve himself wondered, should they honor a soldier who had gotten himself shot?

Really, though, it didn't matter. Before too long, Steve saw the Portsmouth Veterans' Memorial Building and realized that whether Rob or Steve thought someone should be honored made no difference. Steve and his brother were in Portsmouth, New Hampshire, and were about to be part of the town's 2001 Veterans Day ceremony, whether they wanted to be there or not.

Chapter 7

Portsmouth's Memorial Building

Portsmouth's Veterans' Memorial reached three stories. The building directory on the inside foyer showed that the first floor was dedicated to the American Legion and the Veterans of Foreign Wars, while the other two floors were offices for Portsmouth businesses.

The first floor opened up and Steve stumbled into a military museum. Uniforms and war equipment protected by glass cases covered the walls. Steve spotted the guns with bayonets first, and then saw the long, serrated knives. A machine gun, flame thrower and even a grenade stood out in the center display. Steve stopped, looking at the grenade, and wondered if it could still explode.

The walls were dotted with photographs of young soldiers, uniforms, and letters from the 1940s written to home in the soldiers' own handwriting. A few of the photos had medals next to them, with more than one Purple Heart hanging from a ribbon.

There was a feeling in the room that made him stop. He only occasionally attended church services, but the first-floor lobby reminded Steve of his family's church and Grace's synagogue. Not that you'd ever find flame-throwers or grenades lining the walls of a church, but the small museum just felt like church. The faces of the soldiers made a guy not want to say or think anything he didn't want someone to hear. In church, you guarded your thoughts for God; here you did it for the men in the photos.

Steve wanted to keep looking around, but his mother's grip on his elbow and gentle tug toward an older man in uniform cut short his tour. Mom herded both Rob and Steve toward the man who Steve figured must be Colonel Doughman.

Mom put a hand on Steve's shoulder and said, "This is Steve." Colonel Doughman smiled, reaching out his hand and leaving it there long enough that Steve decided he'd better shake it. He hated these moments. He never knew how to act. He finished shaking the colonel's hand, and for some reason the colonel's shiny black shoes were more interesting than the officer's aging brown eyes.

With a warm smile, Colonel Doughman said, "Well, it's nice to meet you, Steve. I can't thank you enough for coming. Your great uncle is excited to meet you, too." Spoken with authority, the colonel's tone still seemed nice.

"Yeah." That's it. What else could Steve say?

A few seconds of silence emphasized Steve's awkwardness and made his cheeks turn red. Colonel Doughman finally said, "Well, follow me, Steve, and I'll introduce you to Harold."

The colonel walked, steadying himself with each step to keep his balance. Steve and his family slowly followed. They entered the assembly room, which was filled with twenty to thirty round tables, each covered with a red, white, or blue tablecloth. In the middle of every table was a vase holding flowers and an American flag.

A dozen or more old people in uniform sat in the hall. At a table about halfway to the podium, three men looked over to Steve's group as they entered. Steve saw the clock above the stage and noted that it was 9:25. He remembered the letter requesting they arrive at 9.

When they approached the table, the three men stood to greet them. Two wore military uniforms. The third man, who was much younger, wore a regular blue suit and tie. The younger man pushed his suit sleeve back and glanced at his watch. He lit up a simulated smile. The smile produced tons of shiny white teeth, but his eyes didn't light up. Steve looked to the shorter, older man in the white Navy uniform, and recognized him right away – Lee Warren!

Lee, holding the backs of nearby chairs for balance, was the first to greet them. "Well, hello, son!" Lee shook Steve's hand. "By golly, it's good to see you, young man, and your family too." Lee looked beyond Steve to his Mom, Dad and Rob, and gripped each of their hands in turn. "Boy, it's good to see you all. Ol' Harold kept telling

Mr. MacLachlan here," he gestured to the younger man in the business suit, "that if you didn't come, he was walking home."

The other man popped up, "Nice to meet you. I'm Mr. MacLachlan from the local YMCA. I'm the man who discovered your uncle, our own community war hero." Now the man's smile had teeth shining from ear to ear like a used car salesman. Squeezing Steve's hand, MacLachlan said, "You must be Steve. I recognize you from the newspaper article that Lee sent to Harold." This man's voice had a hollow, tin sound. "Yep, that's the article that almost ruined all our plans." Steve saw Mr. MacLachlan glare toward Lee. Lee seemed not to notice. Or perhaps he simply didn't care.

Lee reached his hand out to help the final man at the table approach the family. The last man's grey eyes were sunk deep and when he lifted his hand to cover a cough, his skin looked like thin, tan paper over bones. He held an old leather-handled bag in his left hand and used his right to mute another small cough. Then he nodded in the direction of Steve and his family. He wore a dark blue uniform with red trim, and a white hat with a gold eagle, globe and anchor emblem above the words, United States Marine Corps. Two medals were attached to his navy blue jacket, a heart-shaped one hanging by a purple ribbon, and an anchor holding a bronze star that hung by a light blue ribbon. The old Marine said nothing.

Finally, Dad stepped up. "Mr. Warren? Or, I guess –," Dad looked at the uniform, "Sergeant Warren? I'm not sure, but it's a pleasure to meet you. I'm Tim O'Dell, this is my wife Kathryn and these are my boys, Steve and Rob." Dad shook the old sergeant's hand. The Marine's eyes scanned the family and stopped at Steve. A slight smile cracked his lips, but he held his silence.

Lee said, "Harold, this is Esther's grandson, Steve O'Dell." Lee turned to Steve's mom, "Harold and I are second cousins. Growing up we weren't just cousins but friends." Steve could see out the corner of his eye, Harold still looking at him, while Lee kept talking. "You didn't know this but I knew your mom Esther growing up. Yes, sir. We were all of us friends." Lee nodded and looked back over to Harold.

Harold Warren didn't say anything. He just kept staring at Steve, while Steve let his eyes roam around the room, uncomfortable with the old man's focus on him, and the icy silence. Steve didn't know what to say.

After a long pause, Lee hobbled up next to Steve, put his arm around him and said, "Yes, sir, this is the young man who won the contest. When he won, I didn't even think about him being Esther's grandson. No sir! I forgot that Esther's Kathryn here," Lee looked to Mom, "wasn't a Warren anymore but had married Mr. O'Dell. Yes, sir." Steve watched Harold listening to Lee and nodding his head, but the old man stood silent, still staring at Steve.

After what seemed like a century of silence, Harold Warren finally spoke. He had a voice like sandpaper. "I should've reached out to you a lot earlier. I'm just real glad you came today. I'm real glad I can tell it now." Harold coughed, turned his head. The former Marine sergeant lifted his old leather satchel, holding it with both hands, and looked to Colonel Doughman. "Should we talk here?"

The colonel shook his head and pointed to a door behind the stage and podium. "No. This room over here is better. More private." With an arm extended in the direction of the door, he helped direct the group. The MacLachlan guy stopped smiling, looked at his watch, and shook his head as they all walked to the room.

A sharp, tall man with a stylish overcoat watched the group gather in the assembly hall. He stepped forward to get a better view. As the group walked toward the side room, the man, who was wearing designer glasses, stared at Steve and the old sergeant. He'd traveled from downtown Boston – the old Boston, where the buildings smelled of a concrete that was cured before the Civil War. Although he hadn't received an invitation, the man knew about the event. He knew about Harold. He knew about Harold's younger brother, Walter, that had died in the war. He understood Harold's need to tell Walter's story to Steve. He knew about Steve and the essay contest. For this man, there were only two questions that needed to be answered that day. First, did Harold Warren bring The Society's talisman? Second, when does Steve get it?

Chapter 8

The Corpsman on Okinawa 1945

Sergeant Harold Warren walked behind the group, staring at his grand-nephew. The young man was actually there. The Marine sergeant gripped the leather satchel closer to his chest and fought back the cough. The cough, the last few weeks his life had been nothing but fighting back the cough. The cough was winning, and he knew it would gain the final victory soon; he couldn't keep fighting it. He knew it, no doctor need tell him more. But, he had today, and he had Steve here. After waiting fifty years, he'd finally give the satchel to the right owner.

Harold lowered himself into a chair and watched as Steve, his family, Colonel Doughman and Lee sat down and turned their chairs to face him. Mr. MacLachlan refused to sit, and instead stood behind the group with his arms folded. Harold shook his head. He had no desire to make MacLachlan happy by participating in his perfectly planned ceremony, at least not until he'd finished saying what he needed to say.

With everyone arranged in place, Harold looked on. He'd waited for this moment for fifty years but he didn't know how to start. Then his old gray eyes fixed on Steve. He tried to clear his throat to talk but instead a terrible wave of coughing erupted. Holding his hand up, Harold battled the enemy surges around his lungs and managed to stop the attack.

He may not know how to start, but Harold knew every twist of the story he was about to tell. He could remember every detail like it happened last week. He'd thought about each event over a thousand times. While guiding a rake gently across the pitcher's mound or pushing the chalk dispenser like an arrow slowly behind third base line, he'd relive Japanese sunsets and snipers, as well as island mornings and marauders. For him, the war never ended. It replayed over and over inside him. He'd become a quiet man. But, before the sands of time had accumulated, there had been many days where he'd led men with a voice that boomed over Japanese bullets.

For fifty years, he thought the Warren family chain of those possessing the artifacts in the satchel had been broken. Now he had Steve in front of him. He adjusted the leather bag on his lap.

From the corners of a remote island in the Pacific, and from a time before computers and cell phones, the Warren brothers – Sergeant Harold Warren, and his younger brother, Walter, – had made lasting footprints in black, Okinawa mud. Harold had tried to forget his memories of Okinawa for so long that the thought of retelling these stories made his stomach ache. But he had to do it. He was the only person living who could remember Walter's sacrifice. If he failed, if he didn't share these things, Walter would never be remembered.

The former Marine sergeant looked at his nephew. He didn't know what Steve would do with Walter's story. But the moment Harold read Steve's essay, he knew Steve was too patriotic to just let Walter's sacrifice fade away. With a deep breath for strength, Harold began to tell his brother Walter's story.[4]

The whistle pierced his ears before the explosion knocked him to his back. Bullets zipped, muted for a few seconds by the roar of the explosion. Black mud from the island spewed upward and fell like vomit on the young Navy Corpsman. The giant explosions covered up the sounds of Japanese bullets, but the metal bullets still sliced and tore advancing Marines.

"Medic!" When the mortars' echoes ended, the regiment's medic, Corpsman Walter Warren heard the shouts from every direction. "Doc! . . . Doc!" The shouts were booming through the scrambling

4 *Walter's Story* – The story shared by Harold about his brother, Walter, is based on a true story. At age 18, Navy Corpsman, Robert Eugene Bush was the youngest member of the Navy to receive the Medal of Honor in World War II. He received it for acts of great valor and heroism on Okinawa in 1945. His story can be found on the internet. He was a True Patriot.

Marine lines, from the front to the back. Overwhelmed by the cries of injured men, the eighteen-year-old corpsman closed his eyes. Tears would do nothing.

A Navy corpsmen had one job on the battlefield, provide emergency medical service to fallen Marines. With legs and arms that barely filled his uniform, and a helmet two sizes too big, he was supposed to be a savior to fallen comrades.

Before he darted across the battlefield to help the injured men, he took in the scene. The once tropical refuge now looked like a torn, bloody scab of burned trees and scorched mud. Bullets continued to splatter the ground and men screamed. The last island before Japan, Okinawa remained the Japanese Empire's last hope.

When the ground stopped trembling, he pushed himself up onto all fours and crawled towards the closest bleeding Marine. The bullets rained down and splattered mud all around him. He pushed through and settled in the red mud beside the bleeding soldier. The young man looked barely older than Walter. He lay shaking, almost vibrating, his eyes widened in shock, blood flowing from his split left side and mixing into the black mud surrounding him. He gasped for air. Seeing the medic slide next to him, the torn Marine squeezed out two words, "Thanks Doc."

For the next two hours, Walter dodged Japanese bullets. He scrambled from one injured Marine to another. There were always more. Those who could talk never missed thanking their "Doc."

Then the words boomed, "Santos is down!"

Walter turned. He recognized the voice. "I need a medic! The Captain's down!" Lincoln, a friend to Walter the minute he stepped onto the island, continued to shout as he scanned the field. Cupping both hands to his mouth and shouting above the roar of battle, he yelled again, "Walter, Santos needs you!"

Walter spotted Lincoln and the injured captain on a ridge thirty yards away. He scrambled up the hill. Bullets from a group of Japanese snipers riddled the ground behind him, splashing mud on his ankles. Lincoln fired back at the snipers, hoping to provide some cover. When Walter finally reached the top, Lincoln put his rifle to his side and grabbed him by the shoulders. "Man! I can't believe you made it. I'm glad your brother didn't see that."

Wasting no time, Walter crawled towards the dying captain while Lincoln continued firing at the enemy. Lincoln was a big-boned Marine who smiled more than most and had a small gap between his two front teeth. He'd been best friends with their sergeant since the battle of Peleliu, long before Walter joined the Company. Lincoln's Daddy, who was from Texas, loved the sixteenth president and loved the Lord. Lincoln had been taught from an early age to stand tall when the flag passed and to bow your head often in giving thanks.

After quickly examining the captain, Walter began inserting a four-inch needle connected to a tube into the captain's arm. His supplies were almost gone; he knew this would be the last plasma he administered for the day. Looking at the unconscious captain, whose eyes were closed and face ash white, Walter hoped it wouldn't be wasted. Moving fast, he taped the needle to the captain's arm and lifted the life-giving plasma bottle.

"Aggh . . ." The death cry cut through the shooting and Walter saw a Marine no more than three feet away split over backwards. There would be no checking his wounds. The first Japanese bullet bent the Marine to the side, while a second from a different direction, surely meant for Walter, twisted and ripped the Marine in two. Walter narrowed his eyes and knelt lower. During Walter's four weeks on Okinawa he'd seen many a soldier torn through by an enemy's bullet. He knew this scene would become just another part of his replaying nightmares.

The two Japanese soldiers who had combined their shots to end the life of the Marine covering Walter now advanced towards the medic. Still holding the plasma above the captain, Walter reached for the captain's holstered pistol. There were other Marines around, but none were close enough to protect him. They were all engaged in attacking Japanese forces. Although the purpose of the Navy corpsmen was to save lives, not take them, you could not place a man on the front lines of battles and not educate him on how to defend himself. The Navy provided brief training on firearms for corpsmen and Walter had excelled. The young corpsman aimed and fired straight ahead.

The closest Japanese soldier folded in half, with Walter's first round buried in his stomach. His second shot blasted the chest of a Japanese soldier old enough to be his father.

Upon seeing his comrades fall, a third Japanese soldier dropped down to his knees to fire from the island's brush. His shots zipped past Walter, one so close the vibration of the bullet stung Walter's right ear. With two shots from Walter's pistol, the third Japanese soldier fell.

Lincoln ran towards his corpsman. In his hurry to help Walter and Captain Santos, Lincoln didn't see two Japanese soldiers stepping from behind a rock and taking aim. Walter fired first. He shot the last round in his captain's gun, ending the life of another Japanese soldier. Walter tossed the spent pistol and grabbed the loaded M1 Carbine of the fallen Marine next to him. Swiveling around and leaning the rifle on his left arm, while still holding the plasma, Walter fired two more rounds. The first missed, but the second removed a large portion of the second Japanese soldier's face and skull.

Ducking and dodging while holding his helmet with one hand and his rifle with the other, Lincoln slid in next to his company's medic. He nodded in the direction of the fallen attackers. "Thanks, Doc." Lincoln looked at the other three crumbled Japanese soldiers, his eyes doing the math, as he studied his sergeant's younger brother. They had little time to catch their breath as they both saw a final Japanese attack emerging.

Still holding the plasma, Walter again repositioned himself, balancing the rifle over his left arm. Lincoln leveled his carbine in the same direction. The four Japanese soldiers made a run at Walter and Lincoln, but the first two were leveled with two shots by the Americans while the other two positioned themselves to fire. Shots were exchanged and other Marines came to the aid of Walter and Lincoln, as the medic continued to aid the captain.

With the firepower from Americans increasing, the enemy retreated off the ridge. As the last Japanese soldier disappeared into the island trees, he managed a shot almost too true. Walter dropped his rifle and grimaced as his hand flew to his right eye; he'd been hit just at the corner of his eyebrow. Blood flooded into his eye. Now he could only make out muted images. He pressed his hand against his own wound, while raising the bottle with the last of the plasma for the captain.

Walter tossed the now-empty plasma bottle to the side, and ignoring the blood oozing between his fingers, he began applying bandages to the open gash above the captain's right hip. As he rolled him to his side in order to apply the bandages, the captain woke enough to look at Walter's blood-covered face and managed two words, "Thanks, Doc."

"Well, thank you, Harold!" Mr. MacLachlan's words sounded like they'd bounced through an empty tin can. "What a great story." Motioning to his wristwatch, MacLachlan said, "But, I think it's time. We need to get going. The program is supposed to start in less than nine minutes."

Harold looked at MacLachlan. The Marine sergeant shook his head, coughed, and said, "Nope. We'll finish." Harold looked around. The old sergeant's gray eyes stopped at Steve and froze on the young man. Steve squirmed. "I'm not going into that room," he nodded to the door, "until I've told all my story. I've waited to share it for longer than you've been alive."

MacLachlan tried again, "Harold," MacLachlan's voice turned from tin to brass, "I'll be telling all about how you got your medals on Okinawa."

Harold cut him off. "You think I brought him," nodding towards Steve, "to tell him about my medals? Sir, I think you ought to sit down and listen because I'm not walk'n through that door until I'm done, and I've got a whole lot more tellin' to do." Harold stared at MacLachlan. MacLachlan looked to Colonel Doughman for help. The colonel walked over and got a nearby chair and brought it to the group. He nodded to Mr. MacLachlan. "Come sit down, son. I promise that everyone out there" the colonel motioned to the door, "will wait."

Sucking in his cheeks, MacLachlan closed his eyes and marched to the chair next to the O'Dell family. Whether he liked it or not, he would listen to Harold unfold the story of his younger brother.

Harold turned to Steve. Finally, after decades, the right person was here, right here in front of him. He would not fail, not like on Okinawa. He'd preserve Walter's memory by passing his story on to Steve. Then, he'd preserve the aged legacy contained in the old leather satchel by passing it, too, to Steve. The rest was in God's hands.

Chapter 9

The Sergeant on Okinawa 1945

Four Days Later

The sun was rising. He could hear it.

Sergeant Harold Warren recognized the sound. Every dawn for weeks, he'd heard the buzzing. The huge, island blowflies came alive at the graying of morning. For now, only their low buzz stirred the tropic mist. Soon, the creatures, as big as rotten, molding cherries with wispy, hair-like legs and metallic-colored bodies, would be hovering over the remains of war. The island's messengers of morning, the rotten metallic creatures flourished among dead Japanese soldiers and even unburied U.S. Marines. Leathernecks[5], left with the dead. Blood-scabbed and muddy. The sergeant shook his head. Only war's darkest reaches could cloak the light of *Semper Fi.*

The sergeant knew his creed. Every Marine sleeping in the black ooze around the sergeant knew it. *"Semper Fi*[6]*"* – two words seared on a Marine's soul like a branding iron on the right flank of a Texas steer. It didn't matter if they were in boot camp or on islands with strange names and stranger bugs, Marines live by this code. *Semper Fi* translates to "always faithful." To Marines, this meant loyal to "your brothers," even dead brothers.

The beaten sergeant shook his head, staring through the gray light at the fallen, decaying soldiers. He knew Marines retrieved the bodies of their fallen brothers. It's just that Okinawa in 1945 proved a terrible exception.

---

5 *Leatherneck* is a slang term for a member of the United States Marine Corps. It originated during the time of pirates, when Marines wore a thick leather collar to protect their necks against the swords of pirates.

6 *Semper Fi* is the motto of the United States Marine Corps. The full Latin term is Semper Fidelis, which translated means "always faithful."

The buzzing grew louder. It was an awful way to start the day, but after weeks of killing, the island hosted flies better than men. Back home in New England, birds - not gigantic flies - announced the coming of morning. Morning rays lit up the tops of trees, *not* unburied mounds of men. Less than three years earlier, the sergeant had welcomed morning because it meant the start of a new day. Now, he welcomed morning because he'd lived through another night.

Days on Okinawa haunted the strongest men, but nights heaved up even greater monsters. During the day, the sergeant had a chance. He could see the burned-out ridges or blasted-out rock knolls. He could spot the favorite hiding places of Japanese snipers, and protect his men.

But, once the sun sank, a darkness rose up that haunted those left alive. Japanese marauders emerged in the corners of the sergeant's mind like black, night fog. Quickly he pinched his eyes shut. One of a thousand dark memories marched through his mental barricades. Behind clenched eyes, visions of dying Marines and cries of buddies crashed through his barriers. It had been a long night.

Sergeant Warren gathered his thoughts. Every morning the same smell, moist earth mixed with decaying flesh. Every morning the same scenery; scarred land, shredded trees, burned dirt. Today, the rocky ridges stuck out, stark and crisp against the sky. The peaks that had once seemed far away now loomed over them. He stared at the silhouettes called the Shuri Heights. After three weeks of bloody attacks, his company had won enough ground to strike. For three weeks, they'd inched toward the ridges.

"Winger, look, we're on *Hell's Door Mat*!" A warm, familiar voice brought the sergeant around. For two years, the sergeant had shared foxholes and mess kits with that voice. He laughed with it in better days and heard it above the cries of dying Marines during the worst of days. He recognized his best friend Lincoln's voice, "Linc" to his buddies.

Harold thought about the name "*Winger.*" He liked to hear it, especially from this thick-haired, ever-smiling leatherneck. Most of the other Marines now referred to him as Sergeant Warren or just Sergeant (never "Sarge" – maybe in the Army, but not in the Marines). However, a decreasing few still called him "Winger." This buddy with a wide smile, wider because of the small gap between his front teeth, and big shoulders to match that big smile, stood out among the remaining few.

Winger. How long has it been? He remembered his first sergeant's words, "Boy, I ain't never seen someone throw a grenade like that. Write your Momma and sign the letter 'Winger' cuz that's your new name." From that moment on, the name "Winger" had stuck. After the battle of Peleliu, the Marine Corps made him a sergeant. New men called him Sergeant. The buddies who survived Peleliu still called him Winger. The sergeant that coined the name never heard it said after the battle of Peleliu, because he went home with a flag draped over a coffin.

"How many do you think are left from Peleliu?" Winger asked.

Shooing a fly away, the big-boned Marine with his white teeth and black hair smiled. The hair pressed down from his helmet, forming a halo around his head. Lincoln thought for a second, then looked across the unevenly dug foxholes. "After the last four days, Winger, I'll bet there ain't more than 15 or 20 of us." He turned to the ridges, "And now, with us here staring down that big hill, I ain't so sure any of us are ever gonna kiss our girl again." Linc's words echoed what they all felt, as they secured ground near the Heights.

Lincoln tried to sound optimistic, "But I'm guessin' we're close enough to charge that chunk of rock and get'r done." Both knew that to "charge that chunk of rock" meant exposure to enemy fire from every ridge. Despite this, Linc's enthusiasm in such a dismal situation refreshed Winger's soul.

Linc always managed to give Winger a needed boost. Back home, Winger had football teammates and neighborhood pals. He'd known those guys since he was a kid, but none of them matched Linc. Nights spent together in a foxhole covered in black mud and watching a buddy struggling for their last breath welded their souls like brothers.

"Hey, Winger, you alright?"

Winger barely heard his friend.

Brother . . . a dry heave started deep within his stomach, tearing and clawing at everything inside. Now, Winger realized that just thinking the word "brother" resulted in anxiety, and triggered a twisting in his stomach like a hoard of snakes he couldn't control.

For days his stomach had tightened around his insides whenever he thought of his kid brother. The closer they got to the Shuri Heights fortress and the terrible battle ahead, the stronger the reaction. He took three, four, five deep breaths. He could do this. He looked at Linc and then over to the young soldier with barely any stubble on his face who shared his foxhole.

Following his friend's gaze, Linc said in an almost reverent tone, "Winger, I ain't never seen someone work like him." Still staring at the sleeping soldier, he continued, "You know every 'Doc' we've had since Peleliu has been the best. I'd have risked my tail-end for any of 'em. You know it. But, heck, Wing, I ain't never seen any of 'em do the things your brother does." Winger cringed at that word again.

"I know it hurts you all over, havin' em here, and I know you're thinkin' it's your fault and all. But, Wing, ya gotta know our company couldn't ask for a better Doc than your little brother. Did you hear what he did for Santos?"

Winger pushed a fist into his stomach, as he looked past Linc. He stared over black earth and scorched stems that used to be trees, and rubbed his face. He didn't want to hear the story again. He'd heard . . . Walter had killed Japs, dodged bullets, kept the plasma flowing to save the captain. No one, including Lincoln, understood the torture of trying to protect a younger brother on Okinawa.

Instead of listening to Linc talk about Walter saving Santos, Harold's thoughts drifted back to when he learned about Walter coming to Okinawa. It'd only been a couple months ago, but it seemed like a different lifetime. When Harold first found out that his brother had requested to join their company, panic gripped him. He felt terrible for writing to his family. He had written only one letter. After Peleliu, he wrote to tell his family how the Marine Corps promoted him, how they made him sergeant.

Winger hated writing. His younger brother, now cramped in the black ooze of an Okinawa foxhole, could write like Ted Williams could swing a bat. Winger, in comparison, felt comfortable with a ball in hand, not a pen or pencil. He fumbled with words and sentences like a point guard dribbling a football. But once, when their captain on Peleliu made him a sergeant, he did it. He wrote that one letter.

Then, he got his younger brother's reply. "Harold, thanks so much for writing. After reading your letter, I enlisted in the Navy. I want to serve as a corpsman and have requested to serve with your company in the Pacific Islands." The words hit Winger like bricks.

What was Walter thinking? He read the letter a third time, cringing at the last lines, "Harold, I want to be with you. I want to be in battle with you and use whatever skills I possess to preserve the lives of those under your command."

Navy corpsmen were deliberately targeted by the Japanese. Everyone knew this. Everyone but the young eighteen-year-olds signing up to be Marine medics. Everyone but Walter. Unlike the Germans, who tried to honor the red cross of a medic, the Japanese actually targeted them. Even before Peleliu, the Marines had long removed all medical insignia on the corpsmen. However, the minute the Japanese saw one run to the aid of a fallen Marine, they knew they'd found a "special target."

The death of any Marine pierced a soldier's soul, but the death of a corpsman produced a special venom. Watching a Navy corpsman aiding a fallen Marine brought silent prayers. "God protect him." When such prayers fell short and bodies were riddled with bullets, you could turn and look across the heavens, but you'd find no answer.

Away from his buddies, alone in the dark, Harold's body shook with sobs the night he learned Walter enlisted to be a corpsman with him, all because of the letter he wrote.

Now, months later, he and his brother slept together in a foxhole. The younger brother, Walter, the one he'd looked after in the schoolyard, now slept covered in Okinawa sludge with a bandage that oozed blood and puss over his right eye.

As brothers growing up, they were so different. Winger led his football and baseball teams. Walter read and studied. He followed in Harold's shadow, content to follow, just to be near his older brother. But, despite their differences they respected and loved each other.

Now they were both in the Pacific, and they were more similar than Winger had ever imagined. The younger brother who never counted for much on a ballfield or in a neighborhood fist-fight, proved his worth when another man's life teetered on the steepest brink.

Chapter 10

Shuri Heights Unleashed – 1945

Winger reached over to wake his brother, shooing a fly from the gash above Walter's right eye. The large fly lifted off but returned twice before it flew from the juicy wound. Winger rocked Walter by the shoulder.

"Walter, hey . . . wake up." Rocking harder, he raised his voice, "Little bro, it's time to wake up. You need to get ready." He paused and then said the words he'd been thinking about all night. "We make the assault today." Winger hated to wake him. Rarely did their corpsman sleep a full night.

Blinking into the morning sun, Walter spoke to his brother and Linc. "Is there a reason I got to sleep the whole night?" Turning to his older brother, his voice had a bite, "You didn't wake me. Did you cover the watch all night?"

Harold said, "Today we make the assault . . . letting our medic sleep made sense." Harold's voice sounded apologetic, but he figured all those listening knew the truth. He wanted his brother rested even at his own expense.

Lincoln, upon hearing Winger confirm what many had wondered the last few days, asked, "Today, Wing? We attack the ridge today?"

Harold nodded "Do you mind telling the guys?"

Standing, Linc asked, "When did you find out?"

"Top brass decided yesterday afternoon, or at least that's when Lieutenant Reid told me." I couldn't say anything 'til morning. Well, now, it's morning." Harold gestured at the sun cracking the horizon. "We need to get 'em ready."

Linc nodded. Saluting, he said, "We'll get all the men ready." Unprepared, Harold returned the salute – it wasn't like his buddy to be so formal. He watched Linc begin spreading the news from foxhole to foxhole.

Turning back to his younger brother, Winger could see his anger. The medic resented the special treatment. "How is it that the medic needs a full night's rest but not the sergeant?" Walter's tone still had an edge to it.

Not wanting an argument, Winger explained, "I'm the sergeant. I went to the meeting about storming the hill. I had to know about the attack. I'd be awake no matter what. Do you think I could sleep?" He didn't wait for an answer. "You could sleep, not me. That's why. You needed it." Although his explanation made sense, Harold knew Walter resented the situation. He hated preferential treatment, but Winger knew that Walter couldn't stay mad at him for doing something nice.

Walter forced a meager, "Thanks."

The sun crept up the sky like any other day on the island. Winger's company, like all the other companies surrounding the hill, prepared for the assault. No one talked much. A dark feeling wrapped Winger's men like a larva-infested blanket. The seasoned veterans had experienced this kind of "dark" feeling before battle, before waves of death. New recruits had not.

Winger and all his men feared death, but the veterans knew that unseasoned Marines confronted a greater haunting. Veterans had fought through it. The new soldiers' souls wrenched with the question, "In the black of battle, will I crack? Will I be a coward to friends?" You could see soldiers' bladders confirm that this was their first assault. The wet stained pants exposed them for the coward they so feared they would be.

Manmade thunder banged through Sergeant Warren's eardrums like a sledgehammer direct to the head. He heard the artillery cannons behind his company unleash their roaring shells and felt the Japanese response, with the enemy's mortars landing around their positions close enough to rattle the tightest jaws.

Thousands of Marines prepared to storm Shuri Heights. He looked at the other companies, and then at the ground between them and the hill they must take. Where a grassy valley once sprawled, an open sore gouged the land.

No trees, no plants, just mud laced with black, decaying bodies lay before him and his men. Death slimed the mud, filling the air with a thick, damp stench. In some spots, mud reached deeper than a soldier's knees, swarming with maggots. More than once, Winger had encountered squirming, white larvae infesting the muck around a decaying soldier's body. Winger and his men prepared to plunge themselves into the eye of battle, what combat soldiers in prior wars and other battles had labeled, "The meat-grinder."

Winger watched with his men as the companies assigned to the frontal assault began the first wave. The boys stood no chance. Winger watched the Japanese annihilate the charging Marines like they were insects crashing into the front windshield of a speeding truck.

The second wave followed. The wreckage from the first company provided little benefit to the second wave. Small groups of Marines pushed farther, using as cover the discarded tanks and carriers from the previous assault.

True to his orders, the sergeant led his men forward.

Members of his company on both sides were cut down as they advanced. His men's torn bodies joined hundreds of Marines face down in the Okinawa mud. He could do nothing except urge his men forward.

Moving ahead, he saw Linc. His buddy, who had dodged death and Japanese bullets with him for over two years, rolled snake eyes. Snake eyes, the lowest roll of two dice, was also the unluckiest. The Japanese bullet hit, too true. From the corner of his eye and to his left, his best friend wrenched backward. Lincoln's chest absorbed the bullet. Linc's arms spread wide and his head arched back. Winger watched his buddy fall.

Linc's soft brown eyes were still looking heavenward when Winger slid in next to him and buried himself over Lincoln's torn rib cage. Linc's eyes never closed, but he was gone before his head splattered into the black mud.

In the middle of the chaos, the sergeant knelt beside his buddy. There was nothing he could do, but he couldn't seem to leave him. Calling for a medic was useless, and even if something could be done, a medic would never hear him above the terrible chaos. The voice, the smile, all gone. Harold held a piece of himself in Linc's lifeless body, a piece lost forever.

He got to his feet and spotted Walter, who was crouched sixty yards away next to a fallen Marine. Harold pushed forward, continuing up the hill, following commands. But before Walter left Harold's view, machine gun fire cut a direct line across Walter and the injured Marine. His brother's body jolted, thrashed, and fell to the ground.

"NO!" Harold shouted. The scream rattled Harold's entire body, but it was just another sound lost in the chaos of battle.

Too much pain. Harold crashed full speed toward Walter, covering the remaining 40 yards in mere seconds, collapsing next to his brother's body.

Walter lay on his side, trying to administer aid to his own wounds with trembling hands. Seeing Walter's hands dripping red, fumbling, unable to grip and hold the plasma bag, Harold reached over to help. Walter tried to tell his older brother what to do, but Harold heard nothing but a strained gurgle.

The plasma bottle fell from Walter's hand. Harold knelt there, helplessly watching his brother's chest expand with air one last time.

Within minutes, he had witnessed the death of his best friend and his younger brother. Winger buried his face in his brother's neck and waited for a bullet to cure his unquenchable hurt.

With face and arms shielding Walter's body, Winger would've remained there forever, but a retreating soldier tripped over him, ending the moment. Winger did not recognize the retreating Marine, but the abrupt collision awakened him to his situation and surroundings.

Winger used the back of his hand to clear his eyes. He looked at his brother's muddy, blood-stained body and a fury erupted. His entire being surged with one purpose – eliminate the entire Japanese army and die.

His company and the other right flank companies had received orders to pull back. Ignoring the command, Winger surged forward. He moved up the hill, hiding, running and killing. He advanced for over an hour after the order to pull back. When night came, he continued. He would not stop. It would be the last thing he ever did.

The door burst open. A very short, very wide lady in a very yellow blouse let out a long sigh. "Well, there you are! What are you guys doing? The program should've started eight minutes ago!"

Harold had focused so hard on the story that the sudden interruption shattered his concentrated effort and sent him into a rattling cough attack. He had exerted all his strength. He had nothing left. He'd fought the shadowy cough which was inching through the last, uncontaminated parts of his lungs. There seemed to be no breath left. His lungs held no air. He looked at Steve. He looked at the satchel. He had failed. He had not explained the contents and failed to give the satchel to Steve.

God knew he had tried. He turned his thoughts to Him. He hadn't talked to God since 1945 on a blood-stained battlefield. If God wanted these items to get to Steve, He would need to help. After a half century of "forgetting God," Harold turned to his last resort. He barely moved his lips between the deadly coughs, "Please help."

He didn't know where he'd find the strength to stand.

MacLachlan jumped up, nodding his head, and moved toward the door.

Nobody else in the room moved. All eyes were on Harold. Colonel Doughman's eyes glistened, and Lee quietly looked at Harold, nodding his head in small forward motions, while gingerly nibbling the inside of his lower lip. Steve's mom stared at her uncle, while his dad put his arm around her and pulled her in close. Rob too, now looked at the old Marine sergeant differently. Steve wondered if Rob's attitude about soldiers being awarded the Purple Heart had changed.

Harold turned his eyes to look at the grand-nephew he had summoned from Needham. With eyes fixed on the relative, the sergeant went to lift the leather satchel toward Steve. He opened his mouth but said nothing. Instead, he coughed two lung-rattling, chest-deep eruptions. He doubled over and his whole body shook.

Both Lee and Colonel Doughman helped Harold into the banquet room. Steve watched them walk in but paid little attention to the leather satchel that Harold still guarded.

Steve had no idea the importance of that old leather case.

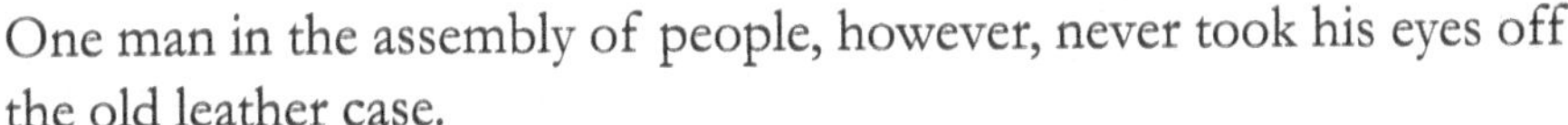

One man in the assembly of people, however, never took his eyes off the old leather case.

Chapter 11

The Honored Guest

The tall, finely dressed middle-aged man in the back of the room focused on Harold, and more specifically on the leather satchel. The gentleman in the black suit stood to get a better look as Harold sat down with the help of Colonel Doughman. Through his tinted glasses, his dark, piercing eyes noted the care Harold gave to the worn leather case.

The agent was one of the most experienced in the Society. He guessed by the way Harold Warren carried the leather bag that it contained the talisman and that Steve had not yet received it. As he watched Harold collapse into his chair while placing the bag on his lap and wrapping two arms firmly around it, he knew he'd guessed right.

Steve and his family found the table reserved for them near the front. The large assembly hall was bursting with people; many stood in the back. Steve figured every old person in Portsmouth must have come to see Harold.

Colonel Doughman stepped up to address the audience. "Welcome." Everyone turned their attention to the colonel. "I want to thank you for coming and being part of Portsmouth's Veteran's Day banquet. I apologize for getting started a bit late."

The colonel announced the commencement of the ceremony, and a retired chaplain offered a prayer. The chaplain's voice carried through the room, "Will everyone please stand with me. Father, we thank Thee for the chance to gather this day . . ." Steve closed his eyes and bowed his head. Steve attended church with his family on Christmas and Easter, but his family didn't pray at home. He'd wanted to learn to pray but he'd been too embarrassed to ask his parents, so last year he had asked Grace. He remembered Grace saying something about how praying was like talking to a friend. He liked the idea. He'd just never tried it.

The prayer ended, but Steve was still wrapped in his thoughts. When his mind finally returned to the present, he realized that not only had the prayer ended, but a veteran had finished leading the audience in the Pledge of Allegiance. Steve had recited the pledge with the rest of the audience. The years of reciting the pledge in elementary school, and now since September 11th, enabled Steve to recite the pledge without any meaning, no thought, no feeling, and certainly not remembering what it meant.

The veteran leading the pledge sat down, and Colonel Doughman returned to the podium. Clearing his throat, he addressed the audience. "At this time, I would like to acknowledge what an honor it is to have a decorated war hero like Harold Keith Warren in our midst. Many of us only know Mr. Warren as Harold Keith, the keeper of the ball fields here in Portsmouth.

"It was an honor to discover that our own Harold Keith is actually Harold Keith Warren of the United States Marine Corps, a recipient of the highest honor that can be given to a United States soldier." The many men and women in uniform began clapping. Colonel Doughman continued, "Yes, both the American Legion and the Veterans of Foreign Wars are proud to sponsor this event for Mr. Warren. Although we've benefited from Mr. Warren's generosity for years, when he made large anonymous financial gifts, neither the Legion nor the VFW could ever have guessed that the gifts were coming from Harold or could've known what a hero we had in our midst until Mr. MacLachlan from the local YMCA discovered Harold's true identity and accomplishments.

"At this time, I will turn the microphone over to Mr. MacLachlan, as he requested the chance to introduce our special guest." Turning to the YMCA man, Colonel Doughman strained a smile, "Mr. MacLachlan."

The lights bounced off Mr. MacLachlan's tailored suit and white teeth. The polished man stepped to the microphone. "Wow! Can you believe we're all here today because I followed a hunch?" Grinning and nodding, MacLachlan turned to Harold and flashed his overextended grin. He looked at the audience and secured his reading glasses.

"I want to read the account of our reluctant hero. But, to understand the significance of what Harold Warren did, we really should know more about the Medal of Honor. Of all the medals issued by the United States Government, there is one which has a somber glory all its own. Since 1941, this medal has been awarded more often to soldiers who died in combat than to living men. Only three out of every ten actually live to personally receive the award. For the other seven, the highest medal is placed on their coffin."

MacLachlan paused and looked up. Despite the man's unpleasant nature, Steve was riveted. "This Medal can only be awarded by the President of the United States. President Theodore Roosevelt said that he would rather have the blue ribbon of the Medal of Honor around his neck than be President of the United States.

"Now, let me tell you what our very own Sergeant Warren did to earn the Congressional Medal of Honor so many years ago."

Adjusting his reading glasses, he read, "For bravery at the risk of his life above and beyond the call of duty, as a sergeant serving with Company K, 3d Battalion, 5th Marine Regiment, 1st Marine Division, in sustained combat operations against Japanese forces on Okinawa, Ryukyu Islands in May 1945. On the first day, Sergeant Warren rallied his men and the remnants of another unit and led them to a critical position forward on the front lines of Sugar Loaf Hill on the Shuri Heights. Soon thereafter, they came under an intense mortar and artillery barrage that was quickly followed by a ferocious ground attack by some forty Japanese soldiers. Despite the loss of over one-half of his men, Sergeant Warren remained at the forefront, shouting encouragement, hurling hand grenades, and directing deadly fire . . ."

Steve listened to MacLachlan but watched Harold. He seemed hypnotized. His eyes had lost focus and his stare faded into the words of his story. The Marine sergeant listened, but Steve could see that his uncle's thoughts were far from November 2001. It looked like his great uncle was being swallowed up in his memories of the mud and blood of Okinawa in 1945.[7]

7 *Sergeant Harold Keith Warren's Story* – Harold's story is based on a true story. The story shared by Mr. MacLachlan and re-lived by Harold, is Corporal James L. Day's story. He was a young Marine that received the Medal of Honor for acts of valor and heroism on Okinawa in 1945. You are encouraged to look up Marine Corporal James L. Day and read about him. After World War II, he served in the Korean War and Vietnam War. He was a True Patriot

Chapter 12

To Die on the Shuri Heights of Okinawa 1945

Harold sat and listened. Memories materialized in his mind, one after another. As MacLachlan bounced on, telling his story, Harold actually relived the story. The battle of Shuri Heights became more than just words on paper. The room around Harold disappeared. The crowd of grey-haired men in clean uniforms disappeared, replaced by young, frightened soldiers stained in blood and mud. November 2001 had become May 1945.

While most soldiers followed the repeated commands to retreat, Winger marched forward. He would not retreat, not one inch, not one step, not until every Japanese soldier suffered the same fate as Linc and Walter.

Time passed. The battle spread. Though he'd said nothing to members of his company, the sergeant now noticed that six of his men had followed him up the ridge. They needed no words or command. They just stayed with their leader, their friend.

When he'd decided he would die on his impossible mission to kill every Japanese soldier, he didn't realize his decision would affect the lives of six of his fellow Marines. These men had missed their opportunity to retreat and regroup. A hive of enemy soldiers now encased them.

Loud words came from his left, "Winger, what's the plan?"

Harold turned towards the man who had shouted. Standing nearby, with his head swiveling in every direction, stood Private Sal Damiano. Harold knew Damiano well. A Marine a little shorter than most with curly black hair. Sal was an Italian from North Boston whose parents had come to the United States when Sal was just a baby. Damiano loved his adopted land. No Marine said anything negative about the U.S. around Damiano.

A few weeks earlier, Harold had watched a new Marine get caught up in downgrading the country he fought for and Damiano told him he'd heard enough. Damiano said he preferred the new soldier stop talking about Roosevelt being a corrupt Democrat. Sizing up the shorter Marine, the new man just chuckled, threw his head back and laughed.

The new soldier found the smaller Marine true to his word. Damiano said nothing more. He just walked up to the bigger man. When the six-foot Marine stood up, he smiled, looked to his side and laughed as he started to talk about this easy fight. Damiano didn't talk. Instead, the Italian Marine kneed the bigger fellow full-strength in the crotch, and placed a right uppercut to below his jaw as he doubled over from the knee to the groin. Then Damiano kicked him hard enough in the ribs while on the ground to lift him half a foot. After that, the new Marine spoke with more respect about his country and its president.

Sal Damiano yelled again above the crack and snap of the bullets, "Winger! Got Japs everywhere!" While he waited for his sergeant's orders, he leveled his rifle and fired a few well-directed shots towards the enemy. Sal's coolness and resolve, even while the enemy swarmed, came as much from his inner character as the seasoning he'd received in earlier battles. He'd watched the fingers of death stretch in every direction; he'd watched the same fingers snatch buddies on one side and then the other.

"Damiano, you and the others dig in behind this bluff." Harold motioned for the soldiers to tighten in behind the small ridge. Using their KA-BAR[8] knives to dig, they managed to produce six foxholes, while continually firing rounds at a circling enemy. Winger looked at the meager foxholes designed to shelter them from hundreds of

8 *KA-BAR Knife* – This is a Marine's fighting/utility knife. The knife is a foot long with a seven inch blade. The polished steel is engraved with four, proud letters "USMC" – United States Marine Corps. These knives were the prized possession of every fighting Marine. Marines depended on their knives for everyday tasks such as pounding tent stakes, driving nails, opening food cans, digging foxholes and of course, defending their lives.

Japanese soldiers. Winger had been willing to die to avenge his brother and his friend, but he hadn't counted on the deaths of Sal and five other Marines because of his decision.

He and Sal gathered grenades from the six living Marines, as well as from the dead bodies around them, dodging bullets in the process. They collected almost thirty grenades.

Harold could throw a grenade better than any Marine on the island. His ability to throw small bombs the length of a football field generated stories that had spread from one company to the next. But Harold's accuracy and timing proved more deadly than any distance. Whether throwing a grenade eighty yards or just over the nearest bush, he placed the explosive exactly where he wanted, and despite the differing distances, he knew how long he should hold the bomb after pulling the pin. His timing and his throw resulted in Marine Corps legends. With every throw, the bomb landed and less than a second later it exploded. The enemy, if they even knew a bomb had landed, had no time to react.

Harold had an athletic gift for hurling grenades but also an enormous amount of practice. Ever since his first sergeant saw him heave a grenade and dubbed him "Winger," he'd become the designated thrower for the company.

Seeing two Japanese soldiers working together, shooting and covering as they approached the foxholes, Winger waited. Thirty yards from their encampment, the soldiers darted behind a darkened and charred boulder. The sergeant waited. He saw the enemy's rifle poke out. Winger pulled the pin. The first enemy soldier darted forward and the second popped out to cover his companion, but never saw what exploded. Winger's toss had landed in front of the first soldier just as the second tried to help with cover. Both absorbed the explosion of a perfectly-timed and placed grenade. Both were dead.

Throughout the day, Winger hurled grenade after grenade while his comrades used their rifles. They made it into the night.

The Japanese soldiers now had the cover of darkness; sleep was not an option. Winger knew that the Japanese had isolated their location and that they fully expected to eliminate them before morning.

Throughout the night, Winger and his men withstood three enemy assaults.

When morning came, two of their comrades were dead and one was wounded. Those left alive needed more grenades and ammunition if they were to have any chance. Winger left the bunker on his own to find weapons for his men.

As he maneuvered to the right of the hill, gathering grenades from fallen soldiers, the sergeant heard a voice. "Corpsman." A little farther to his right and twenty or thirty feet up the hill he saw the Marines; there were four behind a group of bushes. He had to crawl upwards to get to them.

When he got closer, he could see that all four were badly injured. One by one, he helped the first three stumble and walk to the relative safety of the foxholes. However, the most seriously injured soldier appeared to be so near death that any jarring might kill him. Harold looked at the torn-up soldier. His only options were to leave him to die alone or carry him to the foxholes. Crouching low to avoid being seen, Harold slung the injured Marine over his shoulders and brought him to the makeshift bunker. Somewhere between the two locations, the Marine passed on to join Linc and Walter, but still, Harold had honored his creed. *Semper Fi.*

The additional three Marines had with them enough firepower to get Harold and this small group through another day.

Night again proved the most difficult. All the Marines that Harold had carried to safety died that night and three of the original six passed on as well. When the morning of the third day arrived, only Harold and Sal remained. As they struggled to hold off the enemy, both received injuries, Sal more seriously than Harold. In total, nine men died under Harold's watch.

The dawn of the third day brought relief. The Marines' counterattack had finally caught up to Harold.

The Major heading the attack looked to Harold and Sal and asked, "Fellas, how'd you manage to maintain your ground in this space?" Looking at the few dead Marines compared to the dozens and dozens of Japanese casualties, the Major asked in amazement,

"You've held this position since Tuesday?" Harold talked to no one; he just nodded his head. He would let someone else do the math. He'd forgo the Japanese body count.

The reinforcements confronted a stench that made their stomachs turn and their eyes water. Strong men grabbed for something to cover their noses. Two days and dozens of dead bodies under a blistering sun produced a wretched smell.

Two of the new Marines helped Sal onto a stretcher; he would lose his leg but he would live. He asked for his sergeant. When Harold came, Sal grabbed him by the arm. "Winger, you're a national hero!" Harold didn't look into his eyes. Sal said it again but this time each word came through a choked-up throat. Harold looked up and saw the moisture in Sal's eyes. Harold's innards tightened. He didn't feel comfortable. A seasoned Marine like Sal didn't choke up.

But Sal wasn't done. "I've never seen anything like that. Not ever. The way you fought for the Corps, for your country! You're a HERO!" Now, Sal spoke slowly, "What you did, it ain't gonna be forgotten." Sal then let go of his arm. He turned to the others around them and shouted, "This man killed a hundred Japs! He's Superman! The Japs can't kill him!" Harold turned. He couldn't listen. Slowly he walked away.

Harold looked at all the dead. He'd wanted to avenge Walter and Linc. He'd wanted to kill the entire Japanese army. He'd fully expected to die. His killing of so many humans brought no relief. His sadness suffocated him.

Harold walked away from the bodies and looked down the hill where Walter lay covered. He found himself dropping down the slope, until he kneeled next to his little brother. For a second, he imagined Walter just sleeping under the tarp. He reached for the draped cloth and took the top in his hands. He began to pull it back. Did he want to see his brother like this? He closed his eyes.

He looked away to see if Linc was still there, but his friend's body had already been removed. He thought of his men. All dead. Marines he'd known his whole time in the Corps.

So much death surrounded him. He couldn't understand why he'd lived. He knew he should be lying covered like all those he'd led. The sergeant looked back up and watched Sal disappearing on the stretcher. Through the blackness of grief and guilt, he remembered a distant time with no mud and blood. He remembered clean chalkboards and small desks.

He and his fifth-grade class had struggled to memorize *The Gettysburg Address.* He could see Mrs. Hartley in front of their class with a kind smile and encouraging eyes, explaining the meaning of each phrase, line by line. She'd taught him that someone is giving their life when they give their "last full measure of devotion."

Gazing up, he dropped to his knees. His throat ached. His eyes blurred with tears. His chest stabbed and seemed to pierce him from the inside out. He reached down and squeezed his fists until his knuckles turned white. The black island mud gushed out between his fingers.

Harold whispered Abraham Lincoln's famous words. Turning his face from the stained mud to the cloudy sky, he breathed, "I gave up to you my *last full measure of devotion."* His tears now cut lines in the dirt on his cheeks, "Oh God . . . why didn't you take it?"

Chapter 13

THE ESSAY IN PORTSMOUTH

MacLachlan finished. He looked up, a smile ear to ear, very pleased with his stirring account. The YMCA man turned from the audience to Harold and said, "I now present to you Portsmouth's very own Medal of Honor recipient, known to his men of Company K as . . . *Winger*!"

Hearing that name come from those lips jolted Harold from his memories. The old Marine sergeant stood with a strength he didn't think he had.

As he placed the leather bag up by the microphone, Harold ignored MacLachlan. He looked out over the audience and brought his gaze right to Steve. Steve fidgeted under his great uncle's stare. Harold coughed hard. The cough lasted long enough to make MacLachlan look around for help. Colonel Doughman handed Harold a water bottle, but the old sergeant waved his hand and shook his head. He grabbed both edges of the podium, leaning forward.

Looking across the audience, Harold asked, "Are you looking for a hero? After 9-11, you want to see heroes that helped our country. You came to see some hero that did something great!" He stopped. After a pause, he yelled, "Well, it ain't me! I'm an old, dying man that hasn't fought a battle in more'n 50 years; and when I fought, I left my best friend and my younger brother dead! I couldn't save either of 'em." Harold started coughing again. Then he continued in a raspy voice, "If you want to see a hero, you should've seen my brother, the one that died in Okinawa and all the other men that died with him. They're the heroes!" Harold roared at everyone and his eyes darted out across the audience as if they were a room full of enemy combatants.

The old sergeant looked across the assembly hall at the stunned expressions on the crowd's faces. He dropped his voice, "I should've died with 'em." Harold stopped, barely shaking his head as his thoughts overcame him. He gathered himself and went on in a reverent tone, "I've done nothing for my country in more'n fifty years. If you've come to see a hero, some patriot, you're looking at the wrong guy."

Harold turned his gaze back to Steve and in the same reverent tone said. "I learned a few weeks ago that I have a grand-nephew in Needham." Steve stopped breathing and his face warmed to a red glow. Harold motioned for Steve to come up to the podium.

Steve sat cemented to his chair. He wasn't getting in front of a bunch of old people in uniforms. He looked to the back door and thought about running. His dad caught his eyes and, with a stiff finger, directed him up to the front. Steve shook his head but knowing Dad, he'd chase him down if he tried to break for it.

Harold smiled at Steve and reached into his satchel.

Wondering how this could be happening to him, Steve looked towards his mom, but she was no help. She just nodded toward her uncle.

Once Steve stood, clapping started. Hoping if he went up front, the clapping would at least stop, he started walking. He got to the microphone and his stomach wretched. Harold had pulled from his satchel and spread on the podium the front-page article from the Needham Times with Steve and Lee Warren's photo.

Harold looked to the crowd, whispering into the microphone, "This young man did more with a pen last month than I did with a rifle fifty years ago, to help us remember what we need to be doing as Americans after 9-11. I have here," Harold lifted the newspaper from the podium, "an article published in Needham about an essay this young man wrote. His essay got first place! Unlike me, this member of the Warren family can write. He writes like the younger brother that I couldn't save 56 years and 171 days ago."

As if in a nightmare, Steve heard Harold say, "Now Steve O'Dell, my niece's son, will read his winning essay about patriotism after September 11th." Harold nodded to Steve and stepped back from the podium.

Steve stood alone at the microphone. He looked at the audience, who'd started clapping again, and tried to focus on the newspaper. The words in the article swam around the page. He couldn't read the essay. He could barely stand. His stomach somersaulted, and he grabbed the sides of the podium to brace himself. He'd prefer swallowing a razor blade over this. He looked to his mom. He looked to Harold. They both waited.

Steve took a breath. The clapping faded. He looked out at the audience and back at the paper. Loosening his grip on the podium, he read the words, "What is Patriotism after September 11, 2001?" He paused, sucked in as much air as possible and closed his eyes. He felt a hand on his shoulder. Winger, who struggled to stand himself, was standing by Steve. They would do this together.

Steve began . . .

What is Patriotism after September 11, 2001?

April 19, 1775, patriots planted a seed.

For over two hundred years, the world has watched that seed grow into Our National Tree.

On September 11, 2001, two towers crumbled. The Pentagon burned. But Our Tree still stands.

From April 1775 to September 2001, Patriotism has kept Our Tree alive. The morning of September 11th, a new branch grew. Speeches, songs and flags welcomed the branch as Our National Tree changed forever. The new branch came with promises from Americans who want to remember their country, but too often forget.

New York firefighters and police officers can never forget. They heard a call. Like the minutemen and farmers of 1775, they left family and friends forever. The first responders rushed into the burning giants and the two towers became their Lexington and Concord. On the morning of April 19, 1775, on a field in Lexington, Massachusetts, farmers stood up to a King. Their blood nourished a sprouting seed. On September 11th, regular men and women became heroes buried in dust and rubble while rescuing their fellow Americans. This new branch grows because of patriotic soil.

Other heroes that fell that day flew on a plane. If the walls of Flight 93, which crashed in a Pennsylvania cornfield, could talk, what would the wrecked walls say? Would they tell of a passenger quoting Abraham Lincoln, saying they needed to give their last full measure of devotion? Or, maybe someone on Flight 93 remembered the last words of Nathan Hale, the first American spy, who said, "I regret I have but one life to give my country." Now, Todd Beamer's[9] words, "Let's Roll!" are echoed and etched in history. Todd Beamer's blood and the blood of all the people on Flight 93 mixes with the blood of Nathan Hale, Abraham Lincoln, and the tears of thousands of Americans. Their blood and tears darken and strengthen Our Tree's soil.

Sixty years ago, a surprise attack turned our country upside down. From the shores of Pearl Harbor came a hidden blow that shook the National Tree. After December 7, 1941, a flame exploded in Americans from the beaches of California to the shores of Maine. On September 11, 2001, the world watched as evil again slammed into the Tree's weathered trunk. Our Tree's enemies cheered as the Pentagon burned. As in 1941, The Eagle has sharpened and spread its claws – consequences will follow.

The answer to the question, "What is Patriotism after September 11, 2001?" is found beneath the National Tree. Evil can shake leaves, tear the bark, or burn the branches, but America's patriotism and history are the roots and soil that strengthen Our Tree. Terrorists bombed buildings. They killed people. But democracy's first tree, in the world's first free land, still stands. Our Tree's heroes and history make the country's branches strong as they spread and grow. Like a family through the years, Our Tree's leaves change. The leaves

---

9 *Todd Beamer* was 32 years old when he and everyone on his plane died. He had a wife and two sons. His daughter was born four months after his death. He and the other passengers aboard United Airlines Flight 93, on September 11, 2001, decided to take on the hijackers and wrest control of the plane before it crashed into the White House. Todd Beamer's last words heard by anyone still living, were, "Let's Roll!"

fall. Babies arrive. Grandparents die. But the country's family can always gather around The National Tree. Like the soil and roots of an old oak tree on grandfather's farm that keep the tree strong in the storm and in the sun, that's patriotism after September 11, 2001.

Steve took a big breath, and wondered if he'd remembered to breathe while reading. He could feel his heart pounding and his uncle's hand patting him on the back.

A man in a blue uniform like his uncle's stood and started clapping. Then a man and woman wearing green uniforms stood, then others. And then everyone stood, with some knocking over chairs in their excitement to applaud. In an instant, the entire hall exploded with clapping.

Steve cringed as hundreds of real patriots clapped for the "most patriotic" boy in Needham – heck, the most patriotic in the country! He hated it. Steve knew the lie. *Minutemen*, *Nathan Hale*, references to the *Gettysburg Address* on the airplane, they didn't mean anything to him. Sure, he and his family had visited Lexington and Concord; they only lived twenty minutes away. But none of it had ever meant anything to Steve. Steve just wrote what teachers and judges wanted to read.

It seemed like Steve had been at the podium for an hour, when the clapping immediately stopped. Everyone turned their eyes to Steve's left. Steve turned and saw his great uncle on one knee, bent over coughing so hard Steve figured his lungs had to be shredding.

Lee and Colonel Doughman came to Harold's side. Harold tried to stand as Lee said, "We're going to the hospital."

Harold shook his head and tried to push himself up. He picked up his satchel, pointing to Steve. He waited for the coughing to pause just enough to mumble, "Let me do this first."

"No sir," Lee said, "we need to go now. This can wait."

Shaking his head, Harold said, "No. Please. . ." But the coughing again overwhelmed his words.

Colonel Doughman said, "Can you just give it to him here?"

Still bent over, Harold shook his head.

What the heck could be in this satchel? Steve wondered.

Harold lifted a gnarled skeletal finger and pointed to the private room they had been in earlier.

Colonel Doughman nodded. Lee reached a hand towards Harold and helped him back into the private room, asking Steve to join them. The colonel thanked everyone for coming and directed the crowd to the refreshment table. Steve's family caught up with Lee and made their way back to the room.

Harold's voice strained as he nudged closer to Steve. He wheezed out, "I'm sorry." He coughed and spoke again, "Sorry to make you do that." He kept walking with careful steps and just before getting to the room added, "But after watching you, I know you're the one."

They entered the room, and Harold fell into his chair. "My dad died in '48." He paused for a small cough. "For more than fifty years, I've thought this," the old veteran nodded down to the leather bag on his lap, "was supposed to go to Walter."

He turned to Steve and managed a faint smile, "But, even though I stopped believing in Him, God wouldn't let me. God helped me find you." Harold wheezed, and though he tried, he couldn't stop the final attack. The hacking came through lungs that were too thin to put up any resistance.

Lee stepped in, "Harold, we need to go."

Harold held up his hand, but unable to stop the coughing, he finally nodded. He was doubled over with a now gray, ash-colored face, a skin color Steve had never seen before on a living person. He wondered if his great-uncle would die right in front of him. As the old sergeant was hoisted up, he turned toward Steve, smiled briefly and dropped the leather satchel onto his lap. He managed three words through the chest rattling, "I'll explain more . . ."

Although the agent didn't walk toward the private conference room, he didn't take his eyes off the closed door. He was pretty sure that when the door opened, Steve would be carrying the leather satchel.

He waited.

He watched.

He was right.

Chapter 14

Grace Levy

No matter how hard he fought to focus on the white board in his classroom, Steve's eyelids kept inching downward. He needed sleep. Last night his mind had bounced from Medals of Honor, Purple Hearts and saving Marines on Okinawa, to white-haired veterans standing and clapping. But mostly he thought about Harold and the leather bag. He wanted to tell Grace everything.

English class, the only class he shared with his best friend, finally arrived. Steve loved books and loved to write, and M-Rod brought both words and books alive. But today, Steve wanted to get to M-Rod's class not to hear M-Rod, but to talk to Grace. Steve and his parents, and even Rob had all looked over the weird stuff in the leather satchel the night before. Nothing about yesterday or the strange items in the satchel made sense.

Steve waited impatiently in M-Rod's room until Grace arrived. She smiled, and although Steve had seen that smile a million times, he thought, every cover girl in the country would trade for it if they could.

Grace stopped in the doorway, holding her English book up against her chest. "Hey Steve, what's up?" As usual, she dressed more formal than most girls, but never stuffy. The Star of David necklace lay on the neckline of her sweater. She tilted her head. "Something wrong?"

Steve raised his eyebrows, "I can't tell you now. But wait 'til after class. I'll tell you about what happened in Portsmouth."

"What? Did something bad happen?" Grace's smile turned.

"No. Not bad, just weird." He confirmed with a nod that he had a story—a good one. The second bell rang, and they took their seats. M-Rod began class and Steve tried to pay attention. Instead, his thoughts wandered back six years ago to Hillside Elementary.

He remembered that the event happened after Halloween, but sometime before Thanksgiving. He and his classmates were cutting turkey feathers and writing multiplication facts on each one. Their teacher, Mrs. Harris, asked for everyone's attention. Her third graders obeyed.

The teacher stood in front of their class with a new girl clinging to her hand. Looking up from his turkey feathers, Steve saw Grace Levy for the first time. Her golden hair was tied in a snow colored ribbon and her milk chocolate eyes looked timidly at everyone in the room. Grace looked so pretty, but standing next to the teacher in front of a classroom of strange faces took its toll. Her milk chocolate eyes pooled. She ended up sitting at Steve's table, in Brent Brindley's seat. Brent's family had moved to California just as the leaves were changing, leaving a vacant spot to Steve's left. Their friendship began with a few words and a little help at recess. Later that week, when walking home, both realized they lived around the corner from each other. From that time in third grade to now, Steve O'Dell and Grace Levy had been friends. In fact, they were best friends.

They both endured teasing for it. Everyone, boys and girls, teased Steve; he projected a big target. A tough, cool or athletic kid might have escaped the comments, but because Steve liked books, writing, and had little to no skill with a ball or bat, he had no chance to avoid being teased. In the middle school hierarchy, he approached par at best.

Grace, on the other hand, topped the charts. No boys dared tease her. Olive skin, chocolate eyes and hair like honey made most boys lose all ability to even talk in her presence. Then, when she smiled, any thought of cool middle school conversations short-circuited and went up in flames. To add to this, since moving to Needham, Grace was the starting left wing for the most competitive soccer club in town. Her workouts on the field resulted in an athlete's figure. Most of the teasing Steve experienced from the boys stemmed from their bewildered jealousy. Even the high school boys, including his own brother, Rob, were amazed that Grace chose to hang out with Steve.

The girls, however, made up for the boys' shortfall. Sometimes to her face, but more often among themselves, the most popular girls, the "in group," referred to Grace as the Jewish Princess. They dubbed *JP* the code term for Grace.

During football season, a cheerleader eyed Grace and Steve eating lunch together, and said, "Look, there's JP and her frog." Upon saying *frog* she pointed at Steve. "Now, if our Jewish Princess will just kiss the frog, he'll change into a prince." Everyone hanging around the cool table laughed. Whether they thought it funny or not was secondary to middle school protocol requiring them to do what the others did.

Ironically, when the girls strayed from the "in-group," they individually loved to be nice to Grace — never to Steve — but to Grace. Each girl dreamed of walking around the mall or going to lunch with a best friend as pretty and kind as Grace. On more than one occasion, Grace had done things with a girl from the popular crowd, not because Grace called and wanted to, but because the other girl had asked. Grace was nice to the girls who later, when in their pack, turned mean.

Steve knew Grace would be warmly welcomed if she played their game. On the other hand, Steve could try all he wanted but the door to the middle school elite would never open. Unlike his brother Rob, Steve could never ascend to the top of teenage popularity.

The fact that Grace could hang out with this group but chose not to made her different. Steve realized that even though he might dream of life within the "in group," if it meant giving up books and writing and not being friends with Grace, he'd pass. The bell rang. Class ended. Grace smiled as she walked toward him. Now he could talk to her about Portsmouth, Veterans Day 2001, and that really old leather bag.

Chapter 15

Portsmouth Story

Steve and Grace rarely argued. He could count on one hand the disagreements between them. But when Steve explained his experience in Portsmouth, he regretted the conversation.

As they walked to lunch, Steve told her the war stories about Walter and Linc and all the crazy things that Harold did. Then, he told her about how he had to read the essay.

"I read it in front of everyone." Steve groaned. "I wish I hadn't written the stupid thing. I hated having all these old veterans standing and clapping for it."

Up to this point, the conversation had been great. Then Grace said, "Steve, I don't get it. Ever since you got the prize money you've been really weird about the essay – like, so negative. Don't you think you're being a bit sensitive?"

Overlooking the sincerity in her tone, Steve jumped on her statement.

"Okay, if you think I'm sensitive, I guess you can just forget I said anything!" Steve's voice echoed sarcasm. "I just don't like my essay being read by people, or, like, being applauded by weird strangers." The thought of all the veterans clapping sparked more fire, "And I hate people thinking I'm patriotic!"

Grace backed up and said, "You don't need to get mad. I just don't get why you're so negative about it. My parents read your essay in the paper yesterday and loved it."

Grace's comment sparked another unintended consequence. Being reminded that the Needham Times republished his essay as part of its Veterans Day edition caused Steve to become even more irrational. Shaking his head, he growled, "Great! Now I'm sure they think I'm so patriotic. What am I supposed to do? Join the army or something? I'm not patriotic Grace. I just wrote some stupid essay for a contest. People who really love this country, guys who fought in wars and stuff, were standing up and clapping for me like I'm some sort of hero. It's wrong!"

Steve paused to catch his breath. "Grace, I don't hate my country. I'll say the Pledge of Allegiance or whatever. I just hate everyone reading that essay and treating me like something I'm not. I'm not patriotic. I just wrote this essay and it won some contest – that's it! And, like, now it's affecting my whole life!"

Steve was more upset about the situation regarding the essay than he was upset with Grace, but he didn't say anything that would make her feel better. Embarrassed because he'd vented his frustrations on his friend, he turned away. He hated the fact that Grace, like everyone else, wanted him to be proud of his lies. He headed to his fifth period class before the lunch bell rang and left Grace to eat lunch alone.

A few rows away, sitting just on the outside of the popular table, sat Nick Reece. Nick watched Grace as much as he could and just put up with Steve obstructing the view. Leaving a table where he knew nobody would miss him, Nick circled around and formulated a plan. He dived in on Grace.

Plunking himself down in Steve's spot, Nick, who was wearing his football jersey with a number normally worn by second string lineman, said, "Hey, finally. It's good to see you alone."

Grace looked at Nick and managed a meager, "Hi, Nick." Nick lived in the same neighborhood as Grace and Steve, and he'd known them both since elementary school.

Nick propped his elbow on the table and leaned his head on his hand. He wanted Grace's full attention. Then he said, "So, he finally spaced you, huh?"

Grace turned to Nick with eyebrows raised. "*Spaced* me?"

"Yeah, you know, putting some space between you. I heard from some of the guys that he was tired of being teased, some guy said it. Yeah, this guy said, 'Watch Rob's little bro and Grace. They're going to stop being friends.'" Nick sat back, lifted his hands and shrugged. "So I'm guessin' that's what's happenin." He could tell he now had all of Grace's attention.

"Who told you that?" she said.

Nick knew he'd stained his credibility with Grace in the past. In elementary school, he'd always invited Grace to his birthday parties but he never invited Steve, even though he always told her he did. And, in sixth grade, he gave her a ring he bought for a couple bucks and told her it was a real diamond.

Now, even as he acted confident, his lie made him a little concerned. "Someone said it. I don't remember who. Someone on the football team." Nick liked reminding everyone, especially Grace, that he played football.

The lunch bell rang, and Grace popped up. She kind of grinned at Nick and said, "Thanks, Nick."

Nick shot up, eager and ready to head in her direction, but Grace made a double turn one way and then another. Nick watched her go as he stood facing in the first direction, standing alone.

Chapter 16

A Friend Needed

Grace didn't have any other classes with Steve, but she thought about him in each period. Could Nick actually be right? Each hour, in each class she thought more and more about Nick's words—"*He finally spaced you, huh?*"

The last class period bell rang. Grace walked to where she and Steve always met to walk home. She watched half the school go by. Again, she remembered Nick's words. As she watched all the school leave, she reminded herself that she did arrive early. She waited a while longer. She thought about other ways Steve could have left the school. After ten minutes of waiting, she felt sick with worry. Was it true? Did Steve want to end their friendship?

Steve sat in his last class, Honors Science – weird teacher, and mostly boring stuff, not a good combination. They'd been watching a video series the last couple of classes about Einstein's Theory of Special Relativity for middle school kids. He first thought it would be terrible, but he'd actually found these weird science theories pretty interesting. Just not on that day. He kept thinking about Grace. He didn't want to be in a fight with her, but did she really need to say he was so sensitive? He couldn't help the fact that he hated everything about the stupid essay! He shook his head and mumbled, "It wasn't worth the $500."

He sat there with his head on his desk, listening to how Einstein figured out that time and distance are only relative and, in essence, disappear upon reaching the speed of light. Kind of interesting, but Steve perked up when the lights popped on. Two minutes and he could race to see if Grace was waiting for him at their usual spot. What if she was mad and didn't show up? What if she walked home alone? As he picked up his books and started getting ready, he saw it. Johnny Conners' hand shot straight up. This kid could never get through a class without having to say something. Other teachers were on to him, but not so in science. Steve hoped Ms. Okenspire wouldn't see his dopey hand before the bell rang, but no such luck.

"Yes, Johnny."

Steve joined half the class in tilting his head back and rolling his eyes.

"Ms. Okenspire, does this mean you could build a time machine?"

The bell rang, but Okenspire shook her finger at the kids closest to the door. Steve and the rest of the class all groaned. They'd seen it so often; Ms. Okenspire's round, pudgy face lit up, talking to the one kid who was as weird as she was. "Yep, Johnny, that's exactly what it means. The first time I learned about Einstein's Special Theory of Relativity, I thought the same thing. I even checked books out from the library to try to figure out how to build one." Okenspire went on and on about her dream to be the first time traveler. Johnny Conners sat listening and smiling. Finally, a kid in the back said something about missing the bus and hopped up, and Steve and the rest of the class joined him. As they made their escape, Steve heard Mrs. Okenspire raise her voice. "Okay, we'll talk a lot more about Einstein's theory and time travel tomorrow."

Steve shot past the door and bounced between the few remaining people still in the halls, hurrying to his and Grace's meeting place. He hopped down the halls, passing hall monitors almost at a run.

Busting through the front doors, he looked to the nearest pole. There stood Grace, holding her books across her chest. Her eyes brightened as Steve approached, but she said nothing. Straightening as he approached, he struggled for the right thing to say. "Hey . . ." was all he got out.

Grace helped make it easier. "I'm sorry about the essay and stuff." Her smile came slow.

Steve nodded and looked away. "It's okay," he said, then asked, "Do you want to come over and I'll show you the stuff my great uncle gave me?"

Grace's smile warmed, "Yeah, I want to know more about your great uncle's leather bag." As they turned to go home, Steve ignored Nick, who was standing with two other guys, staring in their direction. Steve watched as Grace glanced their way, and then ignored them as well.

As they walked home, Steve told Grace more about the leather bag. "It's so weird. So, my mom's uncle made this real big deal about sharing his brother Walter's war story and giving me this leather bag. When I opened it, there was an envelope of old letters and newspaper clippings about some guy during the American Revolution, a musket ball and, like, some ancient papers written by some really old guy. But nothing about his brother or World War II, or anything else he talked about." As they came into their neighborhood, Steve stepped over a kid's bike on the sidewalk. The clouds lay flat but thick. "I don't get it. I mean, I kinda get why he would want to talk about his brother. But, I'm just not sure why he made such a big deal about the essay and me getting this stuff."

Grace walked around the bike, then said, "This manuscript is written by some 'really old guy?' How do you know that?"

Steve shrugged, turning toward his street. "I guess when you see it, you'll see how scratchy and shaky the writing is. It just looks like an old dude wrote it."

Grace nodded and Steve figured she'd see it for herself in just a bit.

Grace said, "And you got a musket ball, too?"

Steve nodded, "Yeah, that's the coolest part." He added, "It's really old. My dad said maybe from the 1700s. Even Rob liked it." Grace and Steve kept walking. When they turned the final corner, they both noticed an extra car in front of Steve's house. Looking at the white car with red and blue stripes, Grace asked, "Who's at your house?" Steve recognized the white car; he'd watched it take his great uncle to the hospital yesterday.

Still staring at the car, he said, "Lee Warren."

Steve and Grace went inside and found Mr. Warren on the couch and Mrs. O'Dell sitting on the edge of the fireplace. Steve paused when he saw his mother's broken expression. Lee raised himself from the sofa to greet Steve and Grace. He didn't look well. His usual seafaring energy had sunk. Mom didn't stand up or even say hi to Grace. She placed the back of her hand over her mouth.

Steve took his backpack off and set it down. He looked at Mom. "Did something happen?"

The words pressed through Mom's throat, "Something terrible happened." She swallowed. "Harold died this morning."

Steve's stomach flipped.

Lee waited and then with the saddest expression Steve had ever seen on the old sailor, added, "Yes, sir. We went to the hospital. Yep, I went with him and stayed the night. The doctors were working on Harold's lungs just fine. He'd battled lung cancer for years; stopped smoking in the eighties but the lungs just don't ever heal. No, sir." Steve now saw Lee's eyes circling like someone confused as much as sad. "The doctors worked on his lungs, got him oxygen, but late into the night his heart just stopped. Doctor said sometimes the cancer treatment can kill a heart as well as the cancer." Lee stopped. Staring at the empty dining room table, he said to no one in particular, "Yes sir, Harold had a massive heart attack at 4:30 this morning."

Steve looked to the Navy veteran and mumbled, "He said he'd tell me more about the stuff he gave me."

Mom turned to Lee. "Lee, do you know anything about the things Harold gave to Steve? You know, the things in the leather bag?"

Steve's eyes were filled with hope as he looked up, but Lee just shook his head. The old Navy man frowned, "I know Harold wanted to give those things to you, Steve, real bad, yes sir. I know they came to him when his dad died. But I don't know much more – don't even know what the items were."

Steve asked Lee, "Do you want to see what Harold gave me?"

Lee kept staring at Steve. Then he said, "Sure. Yes sir."

Steve hopped up the stairs to his room and brought down the satchel. He spread everything across the dining room table as Mom, Grace, and Lee gathered around. Steve took the yellowed letters and newspaper clippings out of an old oversized envelope and handed the tattered stack of pages tied with a string to Lee. "This stuff," Steve pointed to the letters and articles, "talks about some guy named Joseph Warren. I guess he was some doctor or general back in Boston during the Revolution." Steve picked through the papers and found an article from the early 1900s that talked about Bunker Hill and included a picture of Joseph Warren. "Like this stuff, it's all mostly about him."

Lee thumbed through the letters and newspaper articles from the envelope, and then glanced through the stack of papers, looking closely at pages of the manuscript. The previous night, Steve had looked through the stuff. He'd tried to make sense of the dusty bundles. He couldn't even read most of the sloppy handwriting that filled the thick manuscript.

The first page of the bundle started mid-sentence, or at least that's what it looked like. Figuring out what the sentence said would be like reading some Egyptian scroll. The yellowed sheets were torn and curled up at the edges with faded letters scratched on the paper by a guy who could have done better with a pen in his teeth. Few pages made any sense, but you could see the name "Joseph Warren" a lot. Although the handwriting improved some as Steve thumbed through the stack, faded blotches of ink covered all the pages. Even if this stuff was important to his great uncle, Steve wondered, "How could anyone read it?"

Steve found the musket ball and handed it to Lee. "He gave me this too." His hopes that Lee could explain the items were fading.

Lee examined the gray lead ball about the size of a marble. "Oh, well, now . . . interesting." He bounced it in his hand and held it up close. "Yes sir, looks real old. Maybe, it's a Revolutionary War ball." Lee looked at Steve.

Steve and his dad had figured that out last night. Steve had spent more time examining the ball than anything else. After everyone had gone to sleep, he couldn't put it down.

Steve stared at Lee, "Yeah, me and my dad guessed that too." Steve waited for an answer and then asked, "I'm wondering, you know, does this make any sense to you?" Steve motioned to the musket ball, the tattered letters and old articles, and the ancient bundle of unreadable pages on the table.

Lee nodded a few times, "Yes sir, this Joseph Warren looks like he was pretty important and these here papers and musket ball look like they've passed through a lot of your family. Yep. This is very interesting. Yes, sir." Done looking, Lee put his hand on his belly, waddled over to Steve at the head of the table and moved his hand to Steve's shoulder, "Son, this is quite the legacy, you bet. That essay of yours sure made a big difference to Harold. Yes sir, I wish he could be here to tell you himself and explain all this." Lee passed his arm over the table, "He sure wanted to give that old leather bag, with all this here, to you."

Steve was disappointed. He hoped Lee would have something more to say. He even hoped Lee could make the papers and musket ball make sense.

Lee shuffled to Steve's mom and gave her a hug.

Mrs. O'Dell said, "Thanks, Lee. I appreciate you being such a good friend to Harold and us."

Lee shook Steve's hand again and nodded towards Grace. He said a few more things to Steve's mom at the door, hugged her again, and left. No guidance, no help, and nobody to solve the mystery.

Steve turned to Grace, ready to voice his disappointment.

She, on the other hand, sat with an eager look in her eyes, fidgeting at the table, eying the musket ball and the manuscript, all set to start solving the mystery.

PART TWO
TIME TRAVEL

"Talisman – An amulet or charm whose presence exercises a remarkable or powerful influence on human feelings or actions." This is not a perfect definition. It's not a perfect term to describe the Society's musket ball, but close. There are approximately 37,000,000 minutes in an average lifetime, but how many will you remember a thousand years from now? Harold's gift is a masterpiece of moments, a "Time Traveling Talisman," T3 for short, permanently etching experiences into Steve and those around him

Boston Tea Party, December 16, 1773

Boston Massacre, March 5, 1770

Chapter 17

A Manuscript and Musket Ball

Steve joined Grace at the table; she'd already started poring over the pages. Mom had walked Lee outside, returned and now looked over the mess with red eyes. Still in a bit of a daze, she asked softly, "Steve, will you move all this to the kitchen?"

Steve nodded and began gathering up the papers and letters as he watched Mom straighten up the living room. She took shallow steps, paused often, and patted pillows that needed no patting. Steve wanted to talk to Mom about her uncle. It felt weird that he had died right after they met him, but Steve didn't know what to say. Hands full, he pushed open the door to the kitchen.

Steve placed the tattered bundle, letters and articles and the small box with the musket ball on the kitchen table. As he sat down, Grace snatched the thick stack of papers, with fingers darting and began flipping through the pages. "Seriously, can you believe these pages are like, from the early 1800s?" She stopped shuffling and pointed to the last page. "Did you see this last sentence?"

Steve nodded, he'd noticed the sentence too when studying the papers last night. He knew one thing for certain, the primary author hadn't written that sentence. It was written in old-fashioned fancy penmanship, and was way too neat. He could actually read the elegant lettering, *"March 4, 1825, I now believe. Johnny."* The penmanship was nothing like the actual manuscript.

Grace looked puzzled as she studied the last page. "I wonder what that sentence means, 'I now believe. Johnny'?" Steve watched Grace's eyes bounce back and forth. She thought out loud, "It looks like the statement was written in 1825."

Steve shrugged. "Yeah, you got me. I looked over all this last night and none of it makes sense." He moved closer to Grace, sitting next to her at the table. He said, "It's all talking about this Dr. Warren guy. I guess he was some Boston doctor just before the Revolutionary War in the 1770s."

Grace looked up. "Really? So these pages are older than 1825?"

Steve nodded, a bit unsure. "Yeah, I think so." He thumbed through the pages until he came across a date. "See, this date is 1770. But try to read the handwriting around the date. Except for a few words, like 'Dr. Warren' I can't make out hardly anything." Steve nudged the pages away and sat back, acting disgusted, but he closely eyed Grace as she pored over the papers.

"Steve," Grace had her nose back in the document, "I don't think we should give up on something this old so quickly." Her words danced. "We can figure out this stuff. We'll team up and figure it all out."

Steve handed her the other papers that had come with the document in the large, full-sized envelope. "See these letters?" he asked. "I think these are from bunches of people who were related, or something, to Dr. Warren. I think my great uncle may have been related to him too."

Grace read a few of the letters. Her head sprang up, and she said, "Okay! This makes sense. So your great uncle is a descendent of Dr. Warren. That means Dr. Warren is your ancestor, too." These new discoveries made her bounce with excitement as her ponytail, which was tied with a navy blue bow, rested on her shoulder. Even when talking about something as random as Steve's ancestors, her cheek dimpled and her brown eyes sparkled.

Steve's heart beat a bit faster. He held back his smile and said, "Yeah, I guess."

They both flipped through the letters. Each of them was written by a different person. And every person said the same thing. They all emphasized that whoever received the manuscript and the musket ball must pass it on to another male member of the Warren family. According to the letters, all those who received the manuscript and musket ball should be "from Joseph Warren's posterity," or "a descendent of Dr. Warren." The letters also emphasized that the boy or man getting the manuscript "should be gifted with the pen" or "be enamored with the written word."

Grace and Steve struggled to read the letter that appeared to be the oldest. It was also the longest, and its pages were so yellow and the writing so faded that reading it was almost impossible. The author of the note explained that he had received the manuscript and musket ball from a grandfather who'd received them from his uncle. In the middle of the note, Grace stopped and looked up, "Steve, have you read this part?"

Pointing to the middle, she held the page closer and with effort slowly read out loud:

"Although no one is now alive who can say exactly who gave these legacies to Samuel Warren, it is claimed to have been a person of high station. I have been told that a leader of this great nation, possibly even a President of the United States, commenced this chain of bequests. The actual identity is now lost, as it was never written down and the original benefactor intended to maintain some degree of mystery. We, the recipients and caretakers of these artifacts, are left but to speculate as to who began the original chain of bequests. But, the plea with sufficient urgency was to pass these artifacts to a boy gifted in the art of writing and a descendent of Dr. Joseph Warren."

The letter with this statement was signed by Trenton Timothy Warren, February 3, 1873.

After they finished reading the letter, Grace said, "Look at all these Warren family members. Here is a George Putnam Warren that graduated from West Point. All of these people have been passing on the old manuscript and musket ball for over a hundred years to certain people. Now you're that person! Steve, this is beyond cool."

Steve shrugged as Grace stared at him and said, "You can see why your great uncle wanted to get this to you and keep this chain going. Do you think there's ever been someone as young as you? You're only fourteen."

Steve shrugged again. "I don't know." He felt awkward, like when everybody started clapping after his uncle made him read his essay. He reached over and grabbed the musket ball. "Look how cool this is." He dropped the musket ball into her hand.

"Wow, it's heavy." Grace shifted the small lead ball to her other hand and brought it closer for inspection, her eyebrows knitted. "It's kind of weird holding something that you know . . . " she stopped midsentence, still holding the ball. She glanced at Steve. "Do you think this ball ever killed someone?"

Steve heard the words and instantly felt a darkness and gloom pass through him. "I don't know," creeped through his throat.

Grace turned the ball with her fingers. Still looking, she said, "It's so mysterious." She added, "I mean, it's even mysterious without your great uncle and these old pages. Holding it feels, like I'm holding magic." Then with a bit of her signature smile sneaking through, she said, "You know, the musket ball is kind of like the ring in *The Lord of the Rings*." She glanced at Steve, her smile timid. She seemed embarrassed about making a big deal about an old ball.

Steve looked at all the gifts from his uncle, and nodding, said, "Yeah. Kind of crazy – there's Frodo's ring and Steve's musket ball." He smiled at the joke, but he felt it.

The old, scarred musket ball seemed to ooze trapped magic.

Chapter 18

A Door Through Time

Steve lay in bed, turned to the side, then twisted to his back. He looked up at the ceiling, then back to his side. Why did his great uncle make him go to Portsmouth to read his essay in front of hundreds of veterans? Why did Harold want to give him all this old stuff in some beat-up leather bag? Steve reached over and looked at the old musket ball sitting on his nightstand. He thought about Grace. Who would want to read old pages written in the 1770s by some guy with crippled handwriting?

Still thinking about Grace, Steve picked up the old ball. He tossed it into his open palm and then squeezed it. The ball felt warm, strangely warm. He put it in his other hand. It seemed to grow even warmer. He sat up and looked closer at the ball, but his vision blurred. Blinking his eyes and shaking his head, he tried to clear his vision. It blurred worse. He bounced straight up to his feet, and threw the hot ball onto his bed.

Strange.

His vision cleared. The second he had dropped the ball everything cleared.

He looked at the musket ball sunk into the NFL blanket that covered his bed and wondered, *what the heck?* Alone in his room, he turned and saw eerie shadows coming through the window from the streetlights outside. He hopped over to the window, and wasted no time snapping the curtain tight and ending the creepy shadows. Steve thought about the conversation he had with Grace about the old ball. Was it really possible that this old musket ball had killed someone? He looked back at the dark bullet sunk into his bed between the Green Bay Packers logo and the New England Patriots helmet. He shook his head at his own silliness. He wasn't going to be scared of some antique, oversized marble!

Still, it seemed like the musket ball had somehow made his eyes lose focus. That made no sense. The old bullet had no special power – how could it make his vision go blurry?

He picked up the lead ball again. The warmth he'd felt earlier now exploded through his right hand and up his arm. In a flash, as quick as flipping a light switch, his room changed. Now in the middle of the room stood a wooden door, rounded at the top, with light pulsing from its edges and demanding to burst out from behind it. Could this be real? Steve cautiously stepped towards the door. He inched closer, and with two fingers touched the door handle. As soon as his fingers grazed the thick, wood lever, the door swung wide open.

Light exploded from behind the door. Every inch of his room filled with the blinding rays. The blast wrapped him up, and in a hundredth of a second, the burst engulfed him. The portal of light that had once been the doorway pulled him through.

Steve zipped into a portal of light as bright as the sun.

Outside Steve's house, in a black suburban with dark tinted windows, a tall middle-aged man raised his eyebrows. The agent from the Society put the suburban back into park. He'd been getting ready to drive away for the night, when he saw the flash of light burst through Steve's drawn drapes. He reached for his pad. Confident, but not certain, he wrote in his T3 report log:

"November 17, 2001 – T3 appears to have been activated.

Dr. Warren Portal believed to be opened."

Chapter 19

Dr. Warren

When Steve focused his eyes, he saw a new world. Certainly not his bedroom, certainly not a place he'd ever seen before.

The moon glowed. The pale light floated through chilled dark air and night clouds. Steve's head spun. He saw old buildings squished together in narrow rows. He had gone from a warm bedroom to icy streets, from soft carpet to rounded rough stones under his feet. Was this some crazy dream? Had he fallen asleep and dreamed about the musket ball and the burst of light from behind the door?

A voice cut through the air, "William, thank you for accompanying me."

A man walking to the right of Steve turned and gave him a quick smile. Steve was walking but he looked to his left for *William*. No one walked next to him.

Again, the man talked to Steve, "With my duties regarding the Masons, I didn't have a chance to visit John and Abigail." Through the moon's glow, Steve saw that the man next to him wore a long overcoat with tails and had a white wig like George Washington, and a strange hat with three corners. He looked a lot like the guy on the ten-dollar bill, but with a hat. Steve slowed as his mind stumbled.

The man kept talking, "Your role may need to expand given my increased responsibilities to the Masons."

Steve was only half listening. He gaped at everything around him. It all looked like something out of a movie.

Steve was still trying to process what was going on when another man, with a similar three-cornered hat and white wig passed them, saying, "Good evening, Dr. Warren. It's a cold night to be making house calls." The passing man tipped his hat and bowed in their direction.

The man walking beside Steve tipped his hat in return.

This crazy dream became too much for Steve – the strange people, the old-fashioned city streets – he stopped, his head spinning. He bent over with his hands on his knees, struggling to breathe. One knee fell to the ground.

The man he'd been walking with reached back and took Steve by the arm to steady him. "Son, are you all right?"

Regaining some composure and feeling slightly comforted by the genuine concern in the man's voice, Steve asked, "Who are you?"

The man looked confused for a moment, then answered, "I'm Dr. Warren . . . " He paused for a reaction from Steve, but when none came, he smiled and added, "Yes, Dr. Joseph Warren, the most infamous doctor in Boston for overworking his apprentices."[10] Dr. Warren still smiled but he carefully studied the face of his apprentice. "Now, if you can, we really should continue. If we don't press on, we are sure to freeze solid before reaching the Adams' house." With a slight tilt of his head, the doctor asked, "So please, William, may we continue?"

The doctor steadied Steve with a hand while giving him a concerned, questioning gaze. Even with his mind spinning and only the light of the moon to illuminate the man's face, Steve could see how peaceful Dr. Warren looked. Though questions ricocheted in every direction through Steve's mind, the concerned face of the doctor calmed his fears. Not wanting to disappoint the man with the calming countenance, and not knowing what else to do, Steve straightened and walked beside the man he now knew as Dr. Joseph Warren. But who was this Dr. Warren guy anyway, and how was this possible?

As he walked beside Joseph Warren, Steve realized he must be dreaming. But dreams didn't really make you feel cold and he was freezing. Never before had he been able to feel the ground under his feet in a dream, and yet in this one, each round stone he stepped on pushed hard against the soles of his shoes. Plus he hadn't even been

---

10 *Apprentice* is a person who is learning a trade or profession from a skilled mentor and employer. In Colonial America, instead of the traditional path of higher education, students entered into an apprenticeship. This was an opportunity to learn by working directly with an expert.

sleeping. He didn't know what to do but decided he had no choice. He had to act the part of William, the apprentice of Dr. Warren.

Once Steve fully regained his composure, Dr. Warren continued his earlier conversation, "William, my new responsibilities with the Masons, as Grand Master for North America, will require much time. I'll need to rely more than ever on you. Between my role with the Masons and helping calm the disturbance the King's troops are causing throughout Boston," the doctor gestured to the buildings surrounding them, "I worry my time for patients will be slighted."

Steve had been to Boston a lot. Heck, Needham was nestled just outside Boston. But this looked nothing like the buildings and malls of the Boston he knew. Only in the old part of the city, around the red brick path of the Freedom Trail, could he ever remember Boston looking like this.

The doctor continued, "Tonight is a prime example of too much work and not enough time. Thankfully, John and Abigail will receive us at whatever hour." The doctor turned a corner and stopped. "Well, William, shall we see Mr. and Mrs. Adams?"

Chapter 20

An Eighteenth Century House Call

Dr. Warren knocked on the front door, which was opened by a balding man not much taller than Steve. The man, who looked to be in his thirties, gestured for Dr. Warren and his apprentice to enter.

"Good evening, Dr. Warren," the man said. He had bags under his eyes, but his face lit up when he smiled at the doctor. Steve and Dr. Warren entered. The small man closed the door behind them. "We didn't expect you to come so late. And is this William Eustis, the apprentice I've heard about? A pleasure to make your acquaintance." The man shook Steve's hand and offered to help with his jacket. Steve had noticed the strange clothes on others, but only at that moment did he realize that his own coat and pants looked like they were from Thomas Jefferson's closet. His jacket had tails that stretched below his waist. His pants barely inched past his knees. Holy cow! He was wearing knee britches with white nylons!

"Yes," Dr. Warren nodded, "Mr. Eustis will be attending to duties with me tonight." Steve's thoughts bounced in his mind. *Eustis?* That's a weird last name to come up with in a dream. Where was he getting this stuff from?

The man nodded at Steve. "It's a pleasure to have Mr. Eustis join us." John Adams finished hanging the jackets just as a woman entered the room. This lady must have been Abigail Adams. She wore a white nightgown, and held a candle in her left hand. Although she was slim and petite with a very pleasant face, her belly was round under the nightgown.

Mrs. Adams looked at the doctor, "Dr. Warren, thank you for coming. It is so kind of you to come so late, I just hate how I worry ever since Susanna ..." The pretty wife's voice trailed off. Dr. Warren stepped closer and placed his hand on her arm.

Straightening and shaking her head, she continued, "I just miss little Susanna so much," she stammered. "Your willingness to come and check on the family, and to bring your new apprentice, is appreciated more than you will know." Abigail Adams turned to Steve and extended her hand. "It is a pleasure to meet you, Mr. Eustis." John's wife smiled and her face sparkled in the candlelight. Steve smiled back as he shook her hand. Her words were soft and she had a pretty accent. She wasn't tall, about his height, and she had a cream-colored face and coffee-toned hair. Steve nodded.

"You're very welcome," Dr. Warren said, looking at Steve, who said nothing. Then taking a big breath as if to clear the somber air, he grinned. "Besides, Abigail, other than John's cousin Sam, who can I enjoy talking politics with more than your husband and those in his company?"

The names rolled around in Steve's head. John Adams, Abigail Adams, and a cousin. Sam Adams? Was he in the house of the second president of the United States?

Abigail smiled and asked, "Would you like to see the children? They're in bed, in the next room."

The doctor answered, "We'd be delighted." Following Mr. Adams, who had grabbed a candle from the wall, they turned down a dark hall and into the bedroom where two children slept.

Steve watched Dr. Warren place his hand on each little forehead.

"I've been watching both Nabby and Johnny; they seem stronger the last few days," Abigail said. "Do you sense any sign of the fever?" Steve heard the apprehension seeping through her voice, and he looked at the two little sleeping faces. Steve hoped almost as much as the mom that there was no fever. And then he thought, *but this is just a dream.*

Dr. Warren shook his head, and Abigail closed her eyes and smiled. The doctor removed his hand from the boy's head, and little Johnny awoke. He reached a small hand towards the doctor. Taking him in his arms and holding him, Dr. Warren said, "Well, it looks like my *little helper* is awake." Johnny lit up like the candle his father held.

"Can I help give some medicine?" the boy asked in a sleepy voice, eyes only half open.

The doctor smiled and turned to his apprentice, "William, when you become a doctor, maybe you'll be lucky enough to have a helper like Johnny."

Abigail leaned over and stroked little Johnny's hair, "No one is getting medicine tonight."

Steve saw the doctor's smile quickly disappear. Dr. Warren glanced at the empty bed next to Johnny and his sleeping sister. He closed his eyes as he squeezed the child in closer to him. "Even a doctor with the best helper in Boston couldn't beat that consumption[11] demon, could we, Johnny?" The boy shook his head and snuggled tighter against the doctor's chest.

After a long moment, Dr. Warren looked to the child. "Well, Johnny, would you like my friend William here to tell you a story?" With only a slight hesitation, the boy looked toward Steve and nodded.

The doctor stood. "Well, my young apprentice, this will be a fine opportunity to practice your bedside manner with one of our younger patients." The doctor squeezed Steve on the elbow for encouragement and handed him a candle. Everyone left, and Steve looked at the little boy, who was staring up at him, waiting for a story.

Steve placed the candle on a nightstand and tried to think of a story. He decided on *The Three Little Pigs*. It appeared to be a good choice because when Steve finished, Johnny snuggled up closer to him and asked for another. After finishing two more stories, one about a boy named Aladdin with a magic lamp, and the other about a little mermaid in love with a prince (thank goodness for Disney videos), Steve finally slid out of the room. Little Johnny lay in bed sleeping peacefully. Steve looked at the boy; his small, round face was still lit by the candle.

---

11 *Consumption* – This was a medical term used in colonial times to describe any potentially fatal sickness that caused a condition that "consumed" the body through coughing and wasting away.

As he walked back to the parlor, Steve heard John Adams' voice rising. "Joseph, I know you and Paul mean well, but I don't agree. I'm afraid The Sons of Liberty[12] will take things too far. I abhor mobs and the mentality of mobs. Leadership disintegrates, and you're left with men doing things they regret."

Steve stepped into the room and saw Dr. Warren nodding. "John, you're right. But something must be done. The troops can't stay. The people have had enough. They've been here for seventeen months." Dr. Warren's voice now matched John Adams' intensity, "Almost a year and a half, John! We can't let King George take our freedoms or scare us from our rights as English citizens. The King's troops continually marching through the streets of Boston, John – it's nothing less than England flexing muscles of supremacy over us!"

Dr. Warren's voice kept rising, "Are we not Englishmen, John? Shouldn't we be entitled to the same rights our brothers in Great Britain enjoy? Do they have to house the King's Regulars in London or Liverpool? No! If they are not forced to house soldiers, then why should we have to do this here in America? Are we not equal Englishmen?"

John Adams nodded. Joseph continued in a more even tone. "Are English citizens in Britain granted the privilege of trial by a jury of their peers? Yes. Why then are we here in America not granted such rights? Why are our petitions decided by a judge appointed by the King? Why can't we have a jury here in the colonies, with men from our community deciding guilt or innocence?" Steve watched John Adams nod as he listened to his doctor and his friend continue, "You know better than anyone the arguments James Otis makes. John, why are we expected to bear the burden of taxes when we have no representation in the halls of London that are making the laws? This is taxation with no representation. This situation denies all that our ancestors dreamed of when they settled this land!" Steve watched Dr. Warren push his finger into the table, emphasizing his final point.

12 *Sons of Liberty* – This was a secret organization that originated in Boston and eventually spread to the other colonies. The Sons of Liberty were organized to undermine British rule and to oppose British-imposed taxes in colonial America. The Sons of Liberty were not against using force to oppose the British.

"Our fathers came to this land for freedom, John, freedom! Parliament has no right to take from us the liberty our fathers passed down to us."

Abigail had moved next to Steve. They both listened to John's reply. "Joseph, my friend, I agree. I know that Mr. Otis and my cousin Sam have the good of the colonies and their people at heart. I, too, worry that the Crown is walking on liberties that the colonists must protect. I, too, agree that His Majesty's Regulars here in Boston have overstayed their welcome, as you say, 'trying to bring Boston into submission.' They are trying to punish us for not being obedient subjects of the King."

Interrupting, Dr. Warren added, "And why? Why should we here in Boston be brought 'into submission?' We should be punished for what?"

"I know, my friend," John Adams said. "The King's troops are here because we wished to oppose the Crown's measures for taxing the colonies and because we dared to organize the other colonies to oppose those measures as well."

Steve and Abigail listened to Dr. Warren jump in and finish the thought. "Now we must pay for our misbehavior like some disobedient child – now we must house hundreds of Regulars and have them 'patrol' our streets! And for how long, John? For how long?"

"I understand, Joseph. They've overstayed their welcome. I said that. However, I still worry that these 'Sons of Liberty,' as you call them, the men that you and Paul have patrolling the streets of Boston, will form a mob and take actions that no one wants. Since Christopher Seider's death, all of Boston seems positioned on a powder keg."

"But, John, can you expect anything less? An eleven-year-old boy dies because the traitor Ebenezer Richardson was scared! A man who supported the Crown and the Regulars, even when his rights were being stripped away. And when confronted, he hid. Then, in a cowardly act, he fired a musket overstuffed with buckshot into the street to scare them away! He killed a child, John. I myself pulled eleven pellets from Christopher's small body, John. Eleven."

John Adams didn't reply but just shook his head. Steve had never heard the story of a boy killed by a supporter of the British.

Dr. Warren placed his hand on his friend's shoulder. "If a confrontation with the Regulars results, we will call upon all the colonies." The doctor emphasized his point, "All the colonies, John, as united Americans. We will demand that we be treated like Englishman, and that the Regulars sail back to England. No more marching in our streets, no more living in our homes. No more denying us the rights of freedom that our fathers paid for with their lives when they traveled across the seas and fought and died to live in this land." As he pulled his jacket on, Dr. Warren looked into his friend's eyes and said, "After seventeen months, John, I'm afraid they'll leave no other way."

Steve stood at the end of the hall near Abigail. He handed her the candle, and realized it was time to leave. This history lesson was ending. He knew one thing about this crazy dream, his history teacher could never have taught a lesson like that.

Chapter 21

The Confusion of William Eustis

Steve and Dr. Warren said their goodbyes as Abigail smiled and waved from the door frame. The icy snow crunched under Steve's feet. He kept thinking about Abigail's smile. Her smile reminded him of Grace's. Dr. Warren walked in silence, seemingly caught up in his own thoughts from this night.

As they maneuvered through the streets, Steve wondered how close it was to July 4, 1776. He knew it wasn't July because of the cold weather, but he had no idea what year it was, and everyone dressed like it was time to sign the Declaration of Independence.

Mustering up courage and reminding himself, it's only a dream, he asked Dr. Warren. "Sir, what's today's date?"

Dr. Warren gave his apprentice a concerned look before saying, "Well, for at least a few more hours, it is March 5th. It seems a little late in the day to be asking such a question." The doctor tilted his head. "Are you feeling all right, Mr. Eustis? You've been acting somewhat peculiar tonight."

"No, I'm fine." Then, throwing caution to the wind, Steve said, "It's March 5th of what year?"

Putting a hand on Steve's shoulder, the doctor peered into his eyes as if sizing up whether the boy had gone crazy. "It's March 5, 1770." Then after a slight pause, Dr. Warren asked, "Do you feel all right? Have you fallen ill?"

Steve did feel pretty ill about this bizarre dream, but he shook his head. Joseph Warren said, "William, I need to visit Sam Adams tonight, but I think it best if you return home. You need rest. I've pushed you too hard."

Steve nodded in agreement, then realized that he didn't know the way to the house. He did the only thing he could. He asked, "Where's the house?"

Wrinkling his brow and leaning forward, Doctor Warren questioned him. "Did you sustain a bump to your head? I fear you have some sort of amnesia."

Steve shook his head. With confusion still outlining his face, the doctor gave directions. After a second description of the house on Hanover Street, Steve headed off, hoping he'd figure out how to wake himself from this weird dream once he got to the Hanover house.

Dr. Warren turned in the opposite direction.

Steve had no idea he'd see the doctor again that night, or that when they again met, their fingers would be dripping with blood.

Chapter 22

Boston Massacre

As he followed Dr. Warren's directions, Steve wandered past faded brick buildings with low roofs – no building was more than two or three stories high. He thought he recognized some of the buildings from Boston's red-bricked Freedom Trail. He remembered the day he'd walked the path with his class on a field trip. Now, as he passed a cobbler's shop with a sign shaped like a boot hanging out front, he heard shouting, lots of shouting, echoing from around the corner.

He followed the noise to a street sign – King Street. Just up the street, he saw fifty or sixty people gathered in front of a three-story brick building. Backing away from the mob stood one man with a large musket, dressed in a red coat. Steve's eyes widened, a real Redcoat!

In front of the mob of people, a boy Steve's age pointed at the soldier and yelled. "He's the one! He knocked me – used the end of his musket, he did!"

A man with wide shoulders stood in front of the crowd and shouted, "Let's knock him down! See how he likes it!" A man not too far in front of Steve shouted, "Kill him!" Other men in the crowd shouted in agreement.

The young soldier retreated up the steps of the building, backing up against the door. His head swiveled and bobbed. The growing crowd pushed up to the building's front steps. The mob shoved toward the soldier in the red coat as he cowered like a lone wolf fighting an enemy pack. He whistled and hollered for help, hoping that other Redcoats would hear him.

Caught in the current of the pack, Steve moved with the crowd. He started listening to the conversation of two men at his side. The more burly man with a thick neck and thick arms said, "The King's

Regulars started the problem and we is gonna finish it tonight." Neither of the men were dressed like Dr. Warren. Their clothes looked dirty and coarse, and they smelled like ocean water.

The bigger man, who was missing more than a few teeth, pointed to the boy who had been struck. "Some Lobsterback cracked his musket across the barber's apprentice. Willing to dos to him as that wretched Richardson donz to Christopher Seider. Yes, sir!" Steve remembered the talk of Christopher Seider's death at John Adams' home just a few minutes earlier. He saw that the young boy, the barber's apprentice, had blood stains above a swollen eye.

Bending down and breaking off a piece of ice from a frozen chunk on the ground, the burly man turned to his companion. "Seems as the only waze we're gonna get these Lobsterbacks out of Boston is to force 'em out." He straightened up and flung the large chunk of ice towards the British soldier, just missing his target. He bent down and grabbed another frozen missile. "It maze as well be tonight!"

The smaller man reached down and grabbed a hard-packed chunk of snow. They weren't the only ones attacking the soldier. Ice chunks and snowballs rained down on the Redcoat.

Someone shouted, "Here comes more!"

Turning towards the cry, Steve saw soldiers trotting down the street, holding muskets in front of their chests. These new Redcoats were running in two by two formation, coming to help their trapped comrade. The troops forced their way to the front of the building and onto the stairs. Maneuvering into position, the soldiers shoved and pushed. One soldier, who was trying to shove past Steve, almost knocked him over as the soldier leveled a long needle-pointed bayonet on the end of his musket, fighting his way through.

Steve heard these new Redcoats crying out things like, "Move, you dogs!" and "Let the King's men come through!" and "If you rebels want a fight, let's have it now!" Their shouting fueled an already fired-up mob. Steve saw no one in the crowd of people with a weapon other than a few who held sticks. No one, not one person in the crowd, moved out of the way, or backed down to the Redcoats.

A large man with dark skin stepped out to lead the confrontation. He hit a Redcoat with a stick, "Fire Lobsterback! Come on, fire!"

The bigger man next to Steve shouted, "Hit the filthy Lobsterback again, Crispus!"

The soldier turned his musket sideways and shoved the man named Crispus back into the crowd. The men in the mob whistled through cold fingers and kept taunting the soldiers. Steve heard them swearing, and curses filled the air from both groups as the mob threw more ice chunks and snowballs.

The coarse man with the thick arms handed Steve an ice chunk, and clearly expected him to join in the pelting of the Redcoats. When Steve hesitated, the man with the missing teeth sneered, "Are you a Patriot or a cursed Tory!" Straightening his shoulders as wide as a doorway, he stared down at Steve. A fire brimmed behind the very ugly face, and Steve had no thought of opposing this thug. Steve had never heard of a Tory but apparently the guy with missing teeth considered it the opposite of a Patriot.

Taking the chunk, Steve reached his arm back and pointed his lead foot in the direction of the British troops. His target was the soldier standing on the highest step of the building, second from the end, on the right of the line. Steve let the chunk fly, and for the first time in his life, he actually hit his target.

While the soldier had been dodging objects thrown from in front of him, Steve's ice chunk found its mark from the side. The ice missile sailed from the right, twisting with a sharp slice. The pelted soldier turned in Steve's direction. He saw Steve's face and knew.

While the nine soldiers blocked some ice chunks and got battered by others, Steve heard the word "Fire" get shouted above the chaos of the ice pelting and angry cursing. Steve could not honestly say whether the word had come within the phrase "don't fire," but whether it had or not Steve saw seven of the muskets light up and explode. As Steve heard the first blast, he and the target of his ice chunk were still staring at each other. The soldier leveled his musket and squared it in an instant, targeting Steve's forehead. Steve saw the soldier's one open eye looking down the barrel; the other eye closed to enhance his aim.

Steve stopped breathing. The blasts of the discharging muskets echoed and the cries of those being ripped by musket balls stung the air. He stared at the soldier drilling his aim between Steve's eyes. Was he to be shot by a Redcoat's bullet? Then, the soldier tilted the barrel up and discharged its load into the night sky. In the midst of the screams, the smoke and cold chaos, Steve could see the soldier seething at him. Whether he now regretted it or not, he'd spared Steve.

Head spinning, Steve fell to his knees and then down to his knuckles. He realized he must breathe, taking in gasps of air for the first time since the musket had been leveled at his head. He fought the nausea in his stomach. The two men beside him bent down.

One of the men shouted into Steve's ear loud enough to penetrate the crazy noise, "Are you all right, lad? Did you catch a ball?" Not able to speak, Steve nodded. Misunderstanding, the same man barked, "You were hit? Where son?"

Steve sputtered, "No. I'm alright. He fired up into the air."

The man responded, "Well, if ya ain't hit son, you need to be leaving, boy, and quick. The soldiers have reloaded and more willz be joining 'em." The man's large hand gripped around Steve's bicep, fingers squeezing through to his bone. In a second, the man pulled him up. As he got to his feet, Steve saw more soldiers pouring out of a building just up the street, and the bloody victims from the first round of fire lay in front of the steps of the fancy three-story building. At least five men were spread on the ground and others crawled and stumbled out of the skirmish. The large man with dark skin that the others had called Crispus lay crumbled at the front of the steps. Blood pooled around his head; his chest wasn't moving. The Redcoat with the fanciest uniform jumped between the other soldiers, swearing at his men and ordering them not to fire again.

The commotion continued. Steve stumbled off to the side of the street. Hiding and cowering in the shadows, he could still see the bodies and blood in front of the steps. He shivered and watched the men of Boston gather and the King's troops reassemble. He wondered how much more fighting would occur.

Church bells were ringing throughout Boston. Everyone in the town seemed to be gathering on King Street. New troops of soldiers had joined the original nine, and now they knelt in the street with their muskets, preparing to confront the crowd.

Men who seemed to be dressed more like John Adams and Dr. Warren began to arrive. These men gathered, asking questions. "How did the shooting start?" "Who started the skirmish?" Even though Steve had witnessed everything unfold, when he thought about it, he couldn't say who had started it.

The chaos continued as citizens of Boston and the British troops tried to organize the mess. Seconds turned to minutes. The cold night scratched at Steve's strained nerves, and he began to shiver.

Steve continued to watch people darting and dashing about. Then something caught his attention. In the crowd of people in front of the troops, settling the mob and helping the injured, Steve spotted him. Dr. Warren! Picking himself up and walking from the shadows, Steve approached the only person he knew in the crowd. Dr. Warren moved quickly. He knelt and bent over, helping one of the men who had been shot in the upper arm. Steve watched as the doctor aided the wounded. His mind flashed to the story Harold had told him about his brother, Walter. Running to the bleeding, Dr. Warren and Walter both brought hope to the suffering. "Do you know the names of the dead?" Doctor Warren asked the injured man.

"Aye, I don't know allz the dead, but I do know a slimy Lobsterback shot Crispus Attucks point blank!" The injured man pointed to the darker man who'd been in the front. He now lay face down in a pool of blood. The injured man turned from that scene and looked at Steve instead.

The doctor saw Steve too. "William, good to have help. Come apply this bandage."

Not quite knowing what to do, Steve bent down and placed his hand on the bloodied cloth as Dr. Warren turned to look through his bag. Steve hoped the doctor would think his hands were shaking from the cold.

The doctor asked, "Is Crispus Attucks the former slave who works at the docks?"

The man, wincing from the pain of Steve's pressure on his wound, replied, "Aye. He gotz some of uz to come over when we heard the barber's prentice being hacked by the King's Regulars. Crispus stood right in front of a Lobsterback when the filthy swine fired straightz into the crowd!"

Dr. Warren looked at the man's bloody chest. "William, what are you doing?" The doctor adjusted Steve's hand and shifted the bandage from on top of the wound to a bit under it. "I've shown you this before. If applied from underneath with a more broad touch," the doctor again adjusted Steve's hand, "it stops the bleeding and is less painful." The injured man's eyes closed, and he breathed a sigh. Apparently, he appreciated the lesson. Steve followed the instructions and merely nodded. What else could he do? He certainly didn't remember his prior lessons regarding pressure to a wound. As Steve applied pressure the correct way, the doctor wrapped a wide cord over the bandage.

Dr. Warren said, as much to himself as to the injured man, "Everyone knew this would happen."

Touching his bandaged arm, the dockworker nodded. "Aye. Been almost a year and a half, too long, Doctor, for any town to put up with henchmen pigs!" The man spat out the last words, and added, "I promise, Doctor Warren, tonight is their last night. Us Sons of Liberty won't let the sun set again with these filth in our streets. They's either leave'n on their own or next time both sides is gonna have muskets!"

Steve heard the commitment in the rough patient's voice even as he smelled the man's awful breath.

Dr. Warren made no argument. Nodding his head, he looked over the blood-stained ground. Then, Dr. Warren asked Steve, "William, when did you arrive tonight? How much did you see?"

Still crouching beside the doctor, Steve said, "I think I saw it all." Thinking of the blood pooled around Crispus Attucks, and the barrel aimed at his own head, Steve's hands began to shake more violently. He shoved them in his pockets, hoping to hide them from the doctor. As he did, he felt something he hadn't noticed before. The musket ball. Steve looked at it and placed his hand back in his pocket still holding it.

Steve looked at the doctor. His next words tumbled out, "Am I dreaming?"

The doctor closed his bag as he spoke, "Because Boston dared oppose King George, we've suffered the consequence. For seventeen months we've lived through a bad dream, William. Well, now it ends in a nightmare. March 5, 1770 won't be forgotten."

Turning to examine his young apprentice, Joseph Warren said, "Mr. Eustis, tonight you may have witnessed the first blood shed for American liberty. . . "

The words of Dr. Warren faded. Steve watched the doctor disappear. It felt as if Steve was falling in slow motion down a cavern. As the voice dimmed, so did Steve's surroundings. The cobbled streets, old buildings and Boston's cold, milky night encasing Dr. Warren's face faded away. With a blast of light, the crazy world of March 5, 1770, was gone–the blood and bodies replaced by the clothes on the floor and the sports posters in Steve's bedroom.

Chapter 23

Dream Versus Reality

Steve shot up from the floor. Had he come back to his bedroom from some other place, or had he simply woken up from a dream? The red digits on the nightstand clock read 10:17 pm – the same time he'd first picked up the ball – which made it unlikely he'd been dreaming. He looked around his room for clues to explain what he'd just experienced. As he did, he spied the fallen musket ball on the floor.

Steve picked it up and held it. What a crazy night! He'd felt the warmth of the little boy, Johnny, when he snuggled up to him after the first story, he'd felt the cold air bite his skin, he'd felt the sharp edges of the ice chunk before he winged it at the Redcoat. How?

Steve walked to his bed, placed the musket ball on the nightstand and slipped under the covers, but his eyes stayed open. He tossed and turned, thinking about the adventure.

The next morning, Steve waited as long as he could before picking up the phone. He'd called on Saturdays before, but he always waited until after lunch because Grace's family went to synagogue on Saturday mornings. Today was different though. Today, he couldn't wait that long. Just past eight, he dialed. When Grace answered, the whole story came pouring out. After a bunch of stuff about Dr. Warren and the shootings and the musket ball, Steve ended with, "It all seemed so real."

"What do you mean real?" Grace's voice sounded like she'd just woken up.

Steve explained as best he could over the phone. "I think I need to tell you in person."

"Yeah, I'm sure it was just a dream, but I'll come over," Grace said. "I just can't come until after lunch."

Steve breathed a sigh of relief. "Okay. Great. See you then."

He showered, ate breakfast, sat down to watch TV but ended up trying to read the old manuscript. He shook his head while mumbling, "What a mess," but he kept trying. A bit after one, Grace finally arrived. She came through the side door into the O'Dell kitchen. Steve had arranged the kitchen table with the manuscript and musket ball.

As soon as they sat at the table, Steve told Grace about Dr. Warren, the visit to John and Abigail Adams, and everything from throwing ice chunks at the Redcoats to watching the soldiers shoot people who bled and died. Grace listened, nodded her head and finally said, "What a crazy dream!"

Steve shook his head, "I know it sounds way strange, but it didn't seem like a dream. I mean, I looked and the time on my clock didn't change." Steve eyed Grace. "If it had been a dream, wouldn't I have been asleep longer? And then, when I woke up, wouldn't it be later in the night?"

Grace thought for a moment, then said, "But if everything happened last night, like making a house call with a doctor, walking home, watching the fighting and shootings – if this stuff really happened, it would've taken a really long time, like more than an hour." She paused, "How could it be real if no time passed? It's a cool dream. Dreams are weird. You can be dreaming about a lot of things in just a few minutes." She stared at Steve, "It's not like that if it's real."

Steve looked from Grace to the window. He needed time to think. Her explanation made sense, but something didn't quite add up.

"Grace, I've never dreamt and then remembered so much about it. I can remember Dr. Warren talking to me. He treated me like his apprentice, this William . . . Eustis guy. He said I'd be taking on more responsibilities because he'd be doing more with the Masons. And I can remember the name of the black man who was killed. Everybody called him Crispus Attucks. If it's a dream, why would I remember all this weird stuff?" Steve added, "Why the crazy name, Crispus Attucks, and why would I remember a doctor telling me he had things to do with bricklayers."

Grace made a strange face. "What did you say about 'bricklayers?'"

"I said, 'why would I remember that a doctor was taking on more responsibilities with brick masons?'"

Grace shook her head, "Bricklayers or Masons? I think there's a big difference."

Grace waited for an answer. Steve thought for a moment. Then he said, "Dr. Warren said Masons. He said he was going to have more responsibilities with the Masons." Steve looked at Grace, "Does that make a difference?"

Grace nodded, "A big difference." Grinning, she explained, "The Masons were real popular in colonial times. A bunch of the signers of the Declaration of Independence were Masons. George Washington, Benjamin Franklin, Paul Revere, they were all Masons." Grace could see Steve didn't get it. She kept trying, "I don't understand all of it, but last summer my cousins came from Florida and we went on the Freedom Trail. Our guide was a Mason. After he told us he was a Mason, my dad asked like a million questions – real embarrassing, but the guide just talked a bunch about all the things that the Masons did during the Revolution. That's how I know George Washington and the other guys were Masons. I guess they were some secret group that planned a bunch of things, like the Boston Tea Party. At least that's what this guide said. I'm pretty sure Dr. Warren in your dream meant these Masons – like this secret group. He wasn't talking about bricklayers." She smiled.

Steve turned her point on her, "See Grace! How can I be dreaming about things I don't even know about? Ok, sure, now that you explain it, this stuff about Masons makes sense, but I didn't know anything about it 'til now. See, it's crazy! Then there's this guy, Crispus Attucks. What kind of name is Crispus Attucks? Where did that come from?"

Grace nibbled the inside of her cheek. She didn't have an answer. Steve could tell she was thinking the same thing as he was; "How could he dream about Masons or weird names like Crispus Attucks?" Finally she said, "Have you looked up the name?"

Steve shrugged, "What do you mean?"

"Have you done an internet search?" Steve shook his head.

In less than a minute, they were at the computer desk typing in the name Crispus Attucks.

"Wow!" Steve stared at a full page of hits for this former slave. Everything Steve had seen last night now stood out on the computer monitor. The fight he had witnessed was called the Boston Massacre.

On the screen was a picture of a black man with the name Crispus Attucks beneath it. Steve spoke first, "I didn't even know anything about this Boston Massacre." He pointed to the screen. "This guy named Crispus Attucks, he was a real dockworker and see, it even says he died. Grace, I saw it! Why would I have a real guy named Crispus Attucks in my dream? This is so weird."

Grace nibbled her lip. She whispered, "I don't know." She went back to the table, sat and reached for the pages of the old manuscript. After a minute or two, she turned to Steve. "Okay, this document is about Joseph Warren, right? You had a dream about Dr. Warren. At least for now, let's just call it a dream." Steve nodded. Grace said, "I'm guessing these things that you saw in your dream are somewhere in these old pages."

Steve interrupted, "I can't even read that stuff. The guy that wrote that stuff – he was like writing in Egyptian."

Grace stopped. "How do you know it's a guy that wrote this? It doesn't have to be a he. Women could write in the 1700s too, you know." Grace clipped her words.

Steve had already thought this through, "Sure, it could've been a girl, but girls have better handwriting than boys." He flipped the pages. "I've never seen a girl be this sloppy. It just looks like a boy's work."

Grace's glare softened and she looked back to the manuscript. "Steve, I think the stuff you dreamed about is all part of these pages, that's why you dreamed about them." Grace paused, "This document," She pointed to the old pages, "I mean this is a weird gift, right? You got it from some great uncle just before he died, and a bunch of other people from the Warren family had this old stuff for more than a hundred years. It's all pretty mysterious. I mean, maybe these writings about Joseph Warren have some sort of powers that made you have the dream. Maybe the stuff you dreamed about is in here."

Grace scoured the pages, struggling to read the handwriting that Steve had already given up trying to understand. He figured she could probably make out a word here and there, but he was pretty sure she couldn't follow a story. Not only was the writing poor, but the pages were so worn and torn and the ink faded.

But then, Grace's head popped up. "Look! See?" She pointed to the middle of one of the pages. Steve came over. "See, there's the word 'Masons!'" Although it took effort, Steve saw it. Grace looked closer. "Yep, look, here is 'John and Abigail Adams.' Steve, I really think you read about these things in these old pages and somehow the story came out in your dream."

Steve shrugged. Grace's explanation seemed to make sense. Thinking about how he could've read this stuff, he remembered Abigail Adams. He'd later regret saying it, but without thinking, he added, "You know, like, when I met Abigail Adams, she kind of reminded me of you."

Grace pulled up from the document. Her eyes twinkled. "What? You didn't say that earlier." She smiled, "How'd she remind you of me?"

Steve said, "You know, she was, like real pregnant." As soon as he said it, he realized he should have thought this through better.

Ouch! Grace looked like she'd been invited to Overeaters Anonymous. "So you're saying I'm fat?"

Steve put his left hand to his forehead, "No, she wasn't fat." Slipping, he added, "She was real pretty." Panicking, he continued. "I mean, I don't know. She was like nice, and smart." He was tripping up worse and worse. He knew he needed to exit this conversation before doing real damage, "She just reminded me of you, that's all."

Grace looked at Steve. Slowly, her smile returned, until her lips and dimples were beaming at full force. Even when he felt like a complete idiot, Grace Levy's smile fixed things like hot chocolate on a cold day.

Chapter 24

Again

Time passed. Thanksgiving came and went. Christmas advertisements filled the newspapers, and Steve and Grace talked less and less about the "dream." Steve still picked up the musket ball when he was bored or at night before he went to sleep, but nothing happened. It always felt a bit strange when he held it, but there was no warmth, no light, and no new trips to Old Boston. Memories of throwing the ice chunk and helping the bleeding man with Dr. Warren faded. Telling stories to the little boy named Johnny really did seem like a dream. Grace was right. Everything had been a dream.

Just when Steve had finally convinced himself, Sunday, December 16 arrived. The date had never meant anything to Steve. However, the day before, Grace had told him about some commercial she'd seen advertising a documentary about the Boston Tea Party. Grace said, "Yeah, December 16 is the day the Masons helped with the Tea Party. It's going to be a special on the History Channel." She'd added, "Maybe there'll be something about this Dr. Warren guy."

Steve pretty much had the house to himself. His parents were shopping, his sister, Lizzie, was in the kitchen talking on the phone, and Rob and his best friend Curtis were playing basketball. When Curtis came by to get Rob, he'd said "hi" to Steve, which surprised Steve. Curtis and Rob had hung out together since elementary school. As the best athletes in Needham, Curtis and Rob practiced whatever sport was in season. Curtis tended to overlook Steve and everyone else other than his teammates, pretty girls, or someone who could help him get something he wanted. So, a hello from Curtis before he left with Rob was a welcome surprise.

Steve decided to get comfortable in front of the TV. He held the manuscript and musket ball. He knew the old pages talked about the

Tea Party; he'd seen it before. Now, looking at the ancient manuscript, Steve noted again that Crispus Attucks' name appeared in pages talking about what had happened during the Boston Massacre. Fumbling through the lines, trying hard to figure out what the pages said, he could make out enough to tell that what he remembered from his dream was part of the manuscript. This just seemed to confirm that Grace had been right.

He turned from the old pages to the show which was just starting. Steve squeezed the old bullet and tossed it back and forth in his hands as he watched. The documentary showed the wharfs of Boston. Floating in the harbor were three big, wooden ships. Each had tall white sails and tons of wooden crates stacked high on the decks. The program drifted from the harbor to the warehouses to the homes of Sam Adams and John Hancock.

As the scenes changed, it happened. Steve bolted straight up. The ball in his right palm warmed.

His eyes shot from the tv screen to the ball, now hot in his hand. A door appeared, hovering above the floor of the family room. Steve hesitated before stepping toward it. Then, just as he had in his bedroom a few weeks earlier, he reached for the wood handle. The door cracked open and an explosion of light burst from the crack and filled the den. Light swirled around him like gales of wind over an ocean. When he opened his eyes, the family room was gone. And the year 2001 was gone.

Dr. Warren's world surrounded him again.

Chapter 25

A Call for Resignation

The clouds hung low and grey; so low they snagged on the rooftops of the antique, two-story buildings. Steve could see his breath; he'd crossed back into a winter morning.

A man with thick arms, wide shoulders, olive skin and ample brown hair under a three-cornered hat pounded on a closed door. "Messieurs Hutchinson, Clark, Faneuil and Winslow, your audience was anticipated earlier this morning at the Liberty Tree!" The man who had shouted at the door stood in front of a crowd of other men dressed in long coats, with high white socks, knee length pants, and all wearing the same funny three-cornered hats. Steve looked down. Just like last time, he was dressed like them. He stood in the front, near the leader of the group of twenty or so men. Steve's mind started racing as he tried to figure out what was going on.

The man with thick arms continued to yell through the door, "Your failure to appear causes concern regarding your intentions. I represent a committee that demands a meeting at this time." He paused, waiting for a reply.

After a moment, a window opened and a voice squawked from inside the warehouse, "From whom are you a committee?" The patriot standing in front of the door turned towards the open window, "I'm Paul Revere and I'm from the committee of the people."

Steve's mouth dropped. Remembering his history, he stared at the man five feet away from him. This was the man who had started the Revolutionary War. Steve stared at Paul Revere, and the famous words echoed in his head, *The British are coming! The British are coming!*

Paul Revere continued calling out to the people inside the house. "You and the other tea commissioners[13] know why we're here. You will resign your tea commissions!"

A different man's voice called through the window, "We shall have nothing to do with you, Revere. Your committee's incessant demand for our resignations is unfitting for loyal subjects of the King. We openly refuse to resign."

Paul Revere pursed his lips and pulled a piece of paper from his coat pocket. His voice boomed, "It is hereby resolved that having refused to resign, and follow the honorable actions of your fellow tea commissioners throughout the other twelve colonies, you – the tea commissioners of Boston – are hereby deemed an enemy of the people."

Paul Revere put the paper back in his coat pocket and turned to the crowd. Before he even had a chance to speak, a very large man, even huskier than Revere, shouted, "Out with them! Out with them right now!" Without resistance from Revere, the big man pushed forward, bumping into Steve as he tried to push through, while making room for four or five others. One of the men carried a metal bar that he slid between both doors. With the help of another, the two cracked open the two huge doors. Then they tore the doors off their hinges.

Cheering, the crowd pushed forward. A man standing just behind Steve shouted, "Will you resign now, you egg-eating weasels?" The burly man in front motioned for the others to pass through, but Revere and a couple of others restrained some of the rougher-looking men. The commissioners timidly inched forward. With the door gone, these tea commissioners had no place to hide. Steve stepped aside to make room as they walked out of the torn doorway. Thanks to Paul Revere, they remained untouched as they moved through the crowd, although one of the men next to Steve hocked a wad of spit that landed on a tea commissioner's shoulder. The tea commissioner kept walking as the man near Steve said, "You weasels! Go to

---

13 *Tea Commissioners* were also called Tea Consignees. These were individuals selected by the British government to receive the tea and to then sell it to the shopkeepers. These government appointments were considered an act of favoritism. They would receive the tea at a lower price and would then be able to sell it for more to the colonists, thereby making a good profit.

Hutchinson – the Governor can't protect you forever. We'll meet in the streets someday." Steve saw many men nodding. One man's face broke into a really nasty smile. The commissioners kept walking. Steve figured that keeping this tea commission must be awfully important to them, because if these big guys had been demanding Steve's resignation, he'd have resigned in a second.

Many in the crowd continued to taunt the men. Steve felt a hand grab his shoulder and turned to see Paul Revere. "William, I need you to report to Joseph. Tell Dr. Warren and the other Masons that the commissioners will not resign and will not let the tea return." Revere turned with disgust in the direction of the commissioners, who were now down the road. "Also," Revere's voice became sterner, "tell Joseph that I'll ensure that there are sufficient Sons of Liberty monitoring the harbor to make certain the tea is not unloaded from any of the ships – especially the Dartmouth."

Steve stood in a daze. He wasn't really listening to what Revere was saying – he just couldn't believe the real Paul Revere was talking to him.

"Mr. Eustis! Are you listening to me? You must get this message to Dr. Warren and the Masons. They'll know what steps must now be taken." Revere paused and stared at Steve. His words were curt. "Son, do you understand the directions?"

Steve shook the dazed feeling from his head. "Mr. Revere, where are Dr. Warren and the Masons?"

Revere's eyes got as big as quarters and he shook Steve's shoulder. "The Green Dragon, son – for heaven's sake, what's gotten into you? Now go, hurry!"

Sensing Revere's urgency, Steve scurried away across the cobblestone roads and wood sidewalks. As he walked, he thought about what Paul Revere had said about a green dragon. Everything had seemed so real, and then a green dragon pops into the story. Maybe Grace was right – this was all his imagination. How else could he explain a green dragon being part of this Paul Revere and Dr. Warren adventure?

Steve walked on, not knowing where he was going, questioning every step and struggling to remember Paul Revere's directions.

Wondering about all this, he noticed a flyer pinned to a pole, flapping in the breeze, and decided to read it. After all, what message could his crazy dream concoct for the flyer? The faded page looked as if it had weathered more than one storm. Steve stopped and read:

Friends! Brethren! Countrymen! That worst of Plagues, the detested tea shipped for this port by the East India Company[14] is now arrived in the Harbor; the hour of destruction, or manly opposition to the machinations of Tyranny stares you in the Face . . .

The flyer went on, but Steve stopped reading and pulled the paper closer to him. He stared at the date on the bottom, November 29, 1773, and said out loud, "Machinations of Tyranny?" How could this be a dream when he'd never used or even heard such a phrase? He thought about the warehouse, the shouting, the spitting, the men taking the door off. He'd felt Revere's hand, he'd smelled his breath when he talked to him. It was all so real. How could it be a dream?

But then there was a green dragon. So random. Just like a dream . . .

Dropping the flyer and shaking his head, he kept walking. Not far ahead, Steve saw an old man turn onto the lane. Maybe this old guy could be Steve's test person to see whether this crazy stuff was real. He approached the man. "Excuse me. Can you tell me where I might find a green dragon?"

The gentleman stopped. Cocking his head, the old man said, "Excuse me, but did you ask where you might find a green dragon?"

Steve smiled what he hoped was a friendly smile, "Yes. I'm wondering if you can direct me to such a beast."

The older gentleman's disposition was no longer pleasant. After a moment, the old man said to Steve. "I sense you mock me. Yes, I

---

14 *East India Company* – A British international trading company founded in 1600. This company at times accounted for half of the world's trade. In 1773, the company was in financial difficulty and had a huge surplus of tea in London warehouses. The British Parliament passed the Tea Act requiring the colonists in America to purchase tea exclusively from the East India Company and pay a very small tax on the tea. Because the tax was so small and there was so much extra tea, the colonists would pay less for their tea after the Tea Act. However, the Tea Act imposed taxation without representation and limited the colonists' freedom, by making them buy their tea from the East India Company and through the government appointed Tea Consignees. The colonists opposed their loss of freedom – not high taxes or more expensive tea.

recognize you – Warren's apprentice!" He spit out the last words as if getting rotten meat out of his mouth. Straightening himself and lifting his head with an air of dignity, he raised his voice. "Yes. I'm certain you mock a loyal British subject. The Green Dragon Tavern is where Warren and the other Masons hide, and all the other bloody rebels like Hancock and Adams! Traitors to the King they are!" The old man's face contorted, and he started cursing about the Sons of Liberty. He was so angry that his old-fashioned wooden dentures came loose behind his lips. Steve started to laugh, but this guy was serious.

After pausing to adjust his antique dentures, the enraged man approached Steve, quivering from an overflow of energy. "If you think those loyal to the Crown and the rights of law are so naive that you can openly mock them with such foolish queries, you are mistaken! If I had my way, those loyal to the Crown would burn the Green Dragon Tavern to the ground before the so-called Sons of Liberty or Masons of St. Andrews could hold another meeting!" The man stood so close to Steve that spittle sprayed past the wooden teeth. Suddenly, the old man stopped. He gritted his jaw. And, before Steve knew what was happening, the old man lifted his solid wood walking stick. From high in the air, with a strength Steve didn't think the old man had, he brought the stick crashing down onto Steve's left shoulder.

"Ugh!" Steve grabbed his shoulder and ducked back to avoid a second blow. He side-stepped the angry old guy, and holding his shoulder started running in the direction he'd been heading. Behind him, the man kept cursing about the rebel ruffians and swearing his allegiance to the King.

Steve rubbed his shoulder. His mind raced. Why had the man gotten so mad?

His left shoulder ached, but at least the old guy had confirmed that Paul Revere didn't direct him to some fire-breathing green dragon, but to a real place where Patriots and Masons used to hang out.

Panic turned Steve's stomach. If the Green Dragon was real, that meant the message was real. Paul Revere had given him an important message, and he couldn't remember what he was supposed to tell Dr. Warren. Of course, it was about the tea commissioners not resigning and something about the tea and how it would not be coming off the ship. But what was the ship's name? If this really wasn't a dream – and the ache in his shoulder made Steve pretty certain this crazy stuff was real – then if he failed to deliver the message, he could be messing up history and the Boston Tea Party. He wondered if he could even find this Green Dragon Tavern. As he rubbed his sore shoulder, wishing he had an ibuprofen, Steve passed a street sign that said Union.

Looking down Union Street, he saw a small group of men in front of a two-story brick building. Looking toward the waiting men, Steve saw the red sign hanging in front of the building. In the middle of the red sign, which was shaped like a shield, Steve saw it – a roaring Green Dragon.

Chapter 26

Green Dragon Tavern

"William," a man called. He was in his late forties or early fifties, with gray hair above the ears and a bald spot on top. He walked toward Steve. He looked older than the other men who were waiting in front of the building. Placing his hand on Steve's shoulder, he asked, "Any news from Revere? Did they resign?"

Steve just shook his head. Not wanting to mess things up any worse than he feared he already would, he said, "I need to talk to Dr. Warren."

The older man's reply came with a solemn nod, "I'll take you. He's up meeting with Sam Adams and Mr. Hancock. They'll all want to hear the news." Many of the other men followed them into the tavern and up the stairs to the second floor.

Steve entered a long room at the north end of the tavern. Immediately, he saw the doctor with the kind eyes from his last crazy adventure. Dr. Warren sat at a table with two other men. One was in a gray suit that looked like it had been worn for more years than Steve had been alive, while the other younger man wore a coat that shined with new brass buttons. The man with the drab suit spoke first, "Mr. Eustis." His voice sounded like that of a military school principal. "I presume you have word from the warehouses?"

Steve stood in the doorway with all eyes focused on him. His stomach twisted in knots. He didn't want to mess things up. Dr. Warren gave him a reassuring nod and restated the first man's question, "Did Paul have success in obtaining the resignations of the tea commissioners?"

Looking at the doctor, Steve shook his head. "Paul Revere," the name choked in his throat. "Uhm, yeah, he sent me to inform you and the other Masons that the tea commissioners would not resign." Dr.

Warren closed his eyes and slumped in his chair. The man in the worn suit stood at the table and smirked. He shook his head as if he already knew they wouldn't. Steve watched the third man with the fancy suit lean forward, laying two fingers to the side of his temple and rubbing the side of his forehead as if trying to remove the stress.

Steve strained to remember Paul Revere's other instructions. Messing up on a history quiz in school was one thing – messing up with real people like Paul Revere and Dr. Warren was a whole different problem. "Mr., uh, Revere also said not to worry about the tea being unloaded. He said the Sons of Liberty would watch the harbor." Steve knew that Paul Revere had said the name of a ship, but he couldn't remember the name.

The older man in the gray suit, who seemed to be the leader, said, "William, come join us. Mr. Molineux, have everyone come in. This will affect you all." So, the older patriot who had met Steve in the street was Mr. Molineux. Another name he didn't recognize. He and Steve, along with all the other men gathered in the long room.

Dr. Warren spoke first, looking to the man in the gray suit. "Sam, if they won't resign, we have to take action today." The man Steve assumed was Sam Adams nodded.

The other patriot, in the nice blue suit, whom Steve guessed was probably John Hancock, said, "Every colony in North America is waiting to see if Parliament prevails in forcing the tea upon Boston. The tea can't come off the Dartmouth."

Bingo! Steve remembered Paul Revere's directions. He told the crowd, "Paul Revere said the Sons of Liberty would watch the Dartmouth and make sure no tea was unloaded."

Adams stood. "Thank you, Mr. Eustis." He nodded at Steve. "I'll pay a visit to the owner of the Dartmouth. We'll see if Mr. Rotch can prevail upon the Governor. For two months we've kept this tea from landing. John is correct – all the colonies are watching Boston." Sam Adams looked at the men who had come into the long room. He pulled a scrap of paper from an inner pocket of his waistcoat, "Here's what they are saying." He read from the news clipping, "'Our tea commissioners in Philadelphia have all resigned, and you need not fear: the tea will not be landed here nor at New York. All that we fear is that you will shrink at Boston. May God give you virtue enough to save the liberties of your country!'"

Adams looked at each of the men, "This was published in our Gazette three days ago. It came from Philadelphia. Revere and the Sons of Liberty can guard the Dartmouth and the other ships, but now we must take more action." Placing his hand on the table, Adams emphasized, "I'll talk to Rotch and he'll either persuade Governor Hutchinson before the end of the day to grant the Dartmouth passage back to London with its cargo, or we take care of the tea as we've planned. It either goes back to London or it goes into the sea. It cannot come off into Boston markets. Parliament will not dictate what tea we drink, nor mandate taxes, no matter how small, so long as we have no representatives in Parliament."

Sam Adams turned to Dr. Warren and Mr. Molineux, "Will the Masons and the Sons of Liberty be ready?"

Dr. Warren nodded. "The Mohawks[15] will be waiting the word. William and I will meet with Paul."

Mr. Molineux explained how he'd have men at Edes and Gill and he'd meet Dr. Warren there. Steve knitted his eyebrows. He didn't understand what Dr. Warren meant by Mohawks and he had no idea what Edes and Gill were. The doctor stood and motioned for Steve to leave with him. He smiled and Steve relaxed. One smile, one genuine smile made all the difference in this crazy world. Steve thought . . . I'm going to hang out with Dr. Warren, a real patriot. I might be part of the Boston Tea Party. I guess I could actually be in the pages of my own history book.

The doctor's smile and the ensuing thoughts were enough to make Steve smile back.

15 *Mohawks* – The Mohawk people were a Native American tribe that lived somewhat near Boston. In order to hide their identity, the Sons of Liberty had a plan to dress as Mohawks.

Chapter 27

A Tea Party

Dr. Warren and Steve left the tavern and hurried down Union Street, heading north. The cold air made their breath steam as they hurried up the lane. The doctor turned to Steve, "We'll try his house first and if he's not there, we'll check his shop. We'll need every man Paul's gathered."

Thinking for a minute, Steve asked, "So, who is Paul Revere gathering? Like, who are the Mohawks?"

The doctor kept marching forward but turned toward Steve in confusion. "Well, you – for one – and Paul and the other four or five dozen men that agreed to board the tea ships." Wrinkling his brow, Dr. Warren said, "You do recall volunteering, don't you?"

Steve couldn't believe it. He was about to be part of the Boston Tea Party. He nodded. "Yeah, I mean, yeah, I volunteered. I just forgot about being a Mohawk."

After passing a block or two and a few quick turns, Dr. Warren said, "Well, there are to be plenty of tunics and customs at Edes and Gill. You won't need to return home to gather your own." That name again, *Edes and Gill.* Steve thought it sounded like some kind of fish and he was certainly glad there would be extra Mohawk costumes because he had no idea how to go home to get his.

On the last turn of the street, Steve saw a part of old Boston that he actually recognized. His Massachusetts State History class had walked the Boston Freedom Trail. He remembered the wood house. Its brown gables and scores of windows made it a favorite part of his sixth-grade field trip. This was Paul Revere's house. Dr. Warren knocked on the door.

The door opened and Joseph Warren greeted a woman wearing a cloth cap with a few wisps of brown hair dangling by her ears.

"Good day, Rachel. Is Paul home?" The lady at the door nodded as Paul Revere approached.

"I see William found you." Paul Revere tilted a nod toward Steve.

Standing next to her husband, Rachel asked, "Would you like to come in?" She opened the door a bit wider, and Steve could see at least three children gathered behind her.

Shaking his head, Dr. Warren said, "No, our visit must be short. With permission, we'll just talk outside. It's a sunny day for December." Paul stepped out the door, and Dr. Warren guided the three out of earshot of the home. Dr. Warren turned to Paul, and in a low voice said, "Yes, William found us and shared the news." Staring at his friend, Dr. Warren added, "The Massachusetts's tea commissioners are terribly stubborn."

Looking to Steve, Paul said, "After sending William, I began to notify the Sons. They are gathering at Edes and Gill and at Old South."

Dr. Warren nodded, "They will likely be needed. Sam and John will also be at the Old South. Sam will wait for Rotch, who is making a final plea for Hutchinson to let the tea return to England." Shaking his head, he added, "If Hutchinson doesn't grant leave to the Dartmouth, to return the tea to London, then your Mohawks need to be ready to make salt tea of Griffin's Wharf."

Revere and Warren ended their visit, and Dr. Warren turned to leave. Steve envisioned the famous ride that Paul Revere would make and wondered about the connection to today's events. Curious, he had to ask the question that popped into his mind. "Dr. Warren, how does the Boston Tea Party end up causing the Revolutionary War?"

Stopping in mid-stride, the doctor stared at Steve, "What did you say?"

Steve stopped too. He restated his question. "How does the Boston Tea Party cause a war?"

Warren paused and then repeated, "The Boston Tea Party?" He lifted his eyebrows and nodded his head twice. "Where did you hear such a title? Did you create the name?" He grinned slightly, but then his gaze tightened. "William, what do you mean 'cause a war?' If the tea is destroyed, it's certainly not intended to cause a war. With God's help, this is to be a peaceful demonstration to assert our rights as Englishmen in America, to not be taxed without some say over who makes the decisions. It's not to start a war."

Without thinking, Steve let three words pop out, "But it will."

Dr. Warren straightened quickly, "You can be certain of no such thing, Mr. Eustis."

Steve stood still. How should he answer? He waited for something to come to him.

Still looking at Steve, Dr. Warren said, "If Parliament pursues an unreasonable course regarding our peaceful opposition, then I can see this action escalating into violence. Then I suppose Sam will get the military confrontation he desires."

Steve nodded. But he knew enough history to know what was coming. He knew that destroying the tea tonight would lead up to the revolution.

As they turned the next corner, both had their thoughts interrupted. Mr. Molineux, standing at the intersection, greeted them. "Joseph, Mr. Eustis – we've been waiting." He rushed them into a storefront with a sign that said in large, black letters *The Boston-Gazette,* and then, below that, Proprietors Benjamin Edes and John Gill. Ah-ha, now, he understood the references to Edes and Gill.

Steve and Dr. Warren entered. The room became quiet. The twenty or so men inside the shop stopped talking almost at once and turned to Joseph Warren. Looking around at the gathering, Dr. Warren said, "Thank you, men, for joining the cause of liberty today. So much is to be decided in these next hours. Soon, we will know whether the Governor is going to honor our rights as Englishmen or regard us as slaves of the King. His decision regarding this tea, with its accompanying tax, may set a course that will affect the lives of every man in this room." A surge ran up Steve's spine. He knew a war would follow this night. He figured many of these men would fight and some would die.

Dr. Warren continued. "At this time we await word as to what our fate will be. If we are called upon to destroy the tea, we shall do it. However, we will do our tasks in an orderly and peaceful manner. Under no circumstances shall any of the tea be taken for personal use. It must all be destroyed. It must never be said that our actions were done for any other reason than to protest Parliament's treatment of Englishmen on this continent." All the men nodded their understanding.

Dr. Warren then asked, "Do you have your necessary attire?" Those in the room lifted brown tunics or held up bags of clothes. Warren ended, "Shall we be ready if called up tonight, my Mohawk friends?" Steve heard the men shout "Yay!" or "Here, here!" Then he watched the men start to change their clothes into leather pants and tunics with fringes, and darken their faces like Native Americans.

Approaching Steve, Dr. Warren said, "William, we'll find clothes for you, but for now, I need you to be my eyes and ears at the Old South Meeting House. If the tea is to be destroyed, Sam is going to say these specific words – 'This meeting can do no more to save the country.' If he says these words, you need to run back and tell us. Then we'll know to march to the wharf."

While Steve nodded his understanding, Dr. Warren led Steve out of the printing shop, and pointed in the direction of a steeple a few blocks away. The sun had dipped below the horizon, but the moon glowed bright enough for Steve to see the meeting house in the December sky. As the doctor said, "Go to the church and bring me word," Steve was already heading in that direction.

He walked toward the steeple, his hands shaking. He was going to be the messenger used to start the Boston Tea Party! Would Grace ever believe this?

Once he reached the chapel, he saw dozens of men, and some women too, all waiting to hear the outcome of Rotch's meeting with the governor. Steve squeezed past the crowd outside and into the back of the crowded building. He rubbed his shoulder, remembering the old guy with wood teeth. Then a rumble began rippling through the crowd. Men nudged their neighbors and pointed to a very tired-looking man making his way to the front of the church.

Steve realized the man up front was Sam Adams. The other man must be Mr. Rotch, about to give his message to Adams. Every eye focused on the two of them. It felt as if everyone was holding their breath, including Steve. Had a hairpin fallen out of one of their white wigs, Steve was pretty sure he would have heard it.

After a moment, the other man stepped away and Sam Adams straightened his old, grey suit jacket. All the air had been sucked out of the Old South church. Sam Adams spoke less than a dozen words. Steve heard him say, "Gentlemen, this meeting can do no more to save the country." Bingo! Those were the words that would go down in history as starting the Boston Tea Party.

After struggling to get through the crowd, Steve ran to the print shop. He realized that Samuel Adams' coded message had already made its way to Dr. Warren and the other patriots. Mohawks were leaving Edes and Gill. He reached the door, out of breath, just as the last of the Indians left. Steve was relieved to see that Dr. Warren was still there.

"William, the Mohawks are on their way to the harbor. I plan on joining them. Will you accompany me?"

Steve panted, gulping for air. His heart pounded. He coughed out, "Yes." He wasn't going to pass up the chance to be part of one of the biggest events in American history.

Steve followed Dr. Warren into the printing office. He found a small barrel of black grease, an Indian headdress and blanket, a tunic made of leather that looked like something Pocahontas' brother would wear, and a hatchet. With a sense of urgency, Dr. Warren said, "You get dressed. We only have a moment."

Steve hurried to get changed. He threw off his shirt and tossed his knee-high pants to the ground. He heard a small thud. Looking in the direction of the piled-up britches, he noticed something rolling – the musket ball. Bending, he scooped it up. He stared at it, shook his head and searched for a pocket to hold the ball. While Dr. Warren helped apply dark grease to Steve's face and arms, Steve thought about the lead ball. It was strange that the musket ball was the only thing from his world that appeared in these weird 1770s events.

After a few minutes, Steve looked like the men who had left just minutes before. He and Dr. Warren trotted to the oceanfront. Steve was still thinking about the weird coincidence of having the musket ball with him when the view of the ships and the sea swept all thoughts away.

There, in full view, was the Atlantic Ocean, Boston's harbor and the three amazing ships with their names painted on their sides – *Dartmouth*, *Beaver* and *Eleanor*. Each ship looked tough enough to sail across the Atlantic, and beautiful enough to inspire great welcomes upon arrival. Many of the Mohawks were already aboard the ships, and a very large crowd stood on the dock to watch.

The doctor nodded at Steve and pointed to the Dartmouth. "Go join the other Mohawks." Without hesitation, Steve ran through the crowd to the ship and hopped up onto its landing. In less than a minute, he was standing on the *Dartmouth* watching a hatchet blow come crashing down on a wooden crate. The top of the crate cracked and split open under the blow. Although Steve could not be certain, the Mohawk wielding the hatchet had a body that looked a lot like Paul Revere.

The Mohawk who had broken the crate lifted his head and sounded an Indian war-cry. The other Mohawks joined in, whooping and hollering. Not to be left out, Steve squawked out the best Indian war-whoop he could muster. A shout from hundreds of citizens at the docks echoed the howl. Now, the Mohawks wasted no time in doing their work. The bags of tea that had crossed the Atlantic, and had waited to be unloaded for sale through the tea commissioners to the merchants of Boston were thrown over the side of the ship. Crate after crate was pulled from the hull, cracked open, and dumped into the sea.

Steve made his way to one of the recently smashed crates and grabbed a bag of tea. The bag weighed more than Steve had anticipated and it took all his effort to get it up and to the edge of the ship. Once at the edge, he saw the Mohawks on the *Beaver* tossing their bags into the water. He heaved his own bag out to sea, and it splashed into the Atlantic Ocean below. Steve watched it bob in the cold water and thought, "Now I'm officially part of the Boston Tea Party."

Steve continued to heft the bags across the deck and dump tea into the ocean. After the initial war cries, breaking the crates and dumping the tea happened without hoopla. Steve heard little conversation occurring on the boat, and didn't see any talking among the hundreds of people watching from the docks. The minutes turned to hours, but Steve's excitement and energy stayed strong. Then, deep into the night, Steve heard the words from the Indian who looked like Paul Revere, "These are the last ones."

Steve tried to remember specifics from history class. What next? What would happen now that the tea was all dumped?

With the Boston Tea Party ending, Steve wondered what he would do next. He wanted to remember these events. A bag had torn earlier in the night, its contents spilling on the deck. Steve bent down and grabbed a small pinch of the tea and placed it in the tunic pocket with the musket ball. It would be so cool to show Grace some tea from the real Boston Tea Party!

His fingers closed around the tea and the old ball. Just as he was about to turn, someone locked two arms around him from behind. A large Mohawk with forearms that looked like tree trunks squeezed Steve and spun him around, looking down into his face. Another Mohawk said to the one holding Steve, "What ya got there, Kinnison?"

With a voice that sounded like a grizzly bear, Kinnison announced, "We have a snitch amongst us!" The growl from the oversized patriot caused all the men nearby to turn in Steve's direction. The man picked Steve up under the arms and held him a foot off the boat's deck. Kinnison growled, "I caught him sneaking some of the tea into his own pocket!" Shaking Steve side to side like he was a stuffed toy, he continued, "Despite what the good Doctor and Mr. Adams said about no one taking any of the King's tea for themselves, this scallywag thinks he must be above the rest of us!" The giant Mohawk now smiled at Steve. Steve saw at least four missing teeth, and a layer of yellow and brown build-up that would make a dentist grimace.

Steve wanted to explain, but he stiffened in the patriot's grip. Steve's mind and mouth went numb. The other Mohawk tried to rescue him, "Oh, Dave – he's but a lad. Let him go."

Dave Kinnison ignored the suggestion and announced, "If this one thinks he can pocket a pinch of the King's tea, he and the pinched tea can join the rest of the King's brew!" The monster Mohawk's smile grew, showing off more missing teeth as he marched to the edge of the ship. Without the slightest delay, he threw Steve overboard.

Steve plummeted towards the water. His right hand was still in his pocket, still wrapped around a ball that was heating like hot lead in his palm, while the tea slipped through his fingers. As he plummeted towards the frigid, December ocean, Steve looked into the dark Boston sky and waited for the splash. As crazy as it seemed, his last thought was wondering if the bags of tea already floating in the harbor would help or hurt his landing.

He'd never know.

Chapter 28

Sharing the News

For the past two weeks, he'd agreed with Grace. He'd decided the first trip with Dr. Warren had been a dream. Now, after the Boston Tea Party, he knew it couldn't be a dream.

Grace was still skeptical, though. She'd stayed quiet the entire time Steve had been explaining his second adventure. The first word from her mouth was, "Really?" She tilted her head, "It happened again?" Grace sounded like Steve was telling her he'd caught the tooth fairy. She sat in front of him at the kitchen table, looking like she wished she'd stayed home.

"Yeah, I promise." Steve said. "I was just watching the show you told me about, and then there was a door and a bright light, and then all of a sudden I was with Paul Revere."

"You were with Paul Revere?" Steve nodded. Grace made a face like she'd sipped sour milk.

"It wasn't a dream and I didn't fall asleep!" When Steve had invited Grace over, he'd thought for sure that he could convince her that his newest experience in the 1770s was real, but now he was failing big time. "Grace, I know it's crazy, I know. But I really did talk to Paul Revere, I met Dr. Joseph Warren again. And Sam Adams and John Hancock at the Green Dragon Tavern. I dressed up like a Mohawk Indian and dumped lots of tea in the ocean. Dr. Warren, Paul Revere, everybody – they called me William Eustis again."

Still staring at him, Grace asked, "So you're telling me that you met Paul Revere and Samuel Adams and John Hancock and they all knew you?" Her voice wavered, and she looked sad.

Steve said, "Well, they didn't really know me, like Steve O'Dell; they knew this William Eustis guy. Somehow when I go back in time, I must look like William Eustis to them, but I'm really me. I mean I just look like this William guy." He stopped. This sounded crazy, and he knew it.

Grace shook her head. She turned from Steve to the kitchen window. With a voice coated in sarcasm, she said, "So did you meet George Washington and Thomas Jefferson too?"

Steve looked up at the ceiling above the kitchen table. He didn't know what to do. He didn't expect this. He wanted Grace to believe him so bad, but the more he told her, the more upset she got. Speaking to the ceiling, he said, "It really happened Grace . . . I promise."

He turned back to his friend. Still not looking at Steve, she responded, "You said you put some of the tea in your pocket and that's why some guy threw you off the ship?" Steve nodded. "Well, if you put some of the tea in your pocket, where is it? Why don't you have any of it now?"

Steve rubbed the back of his neck nervously. "The tea didn't come back with me."

Grace kept staring at Steve and he could see her eyes simmering, as if she thought he was deliberately trying to make fun of her. "You told me the musket ball was with you, and that you put the tea in the same pocket. If the musket ball made it back, why didn't the tea?"

Steve had no answer. "Grace, I don't know why there's no tea. It must have like slipped through my fingers when I was coming back, but I'm pretty sure this is the key to all of this." Steve picked up the musket ball. "I think that somehow it takes me back to the past." Grace showed no signs of believing him, but at least she was still listening. Steve kept going. "I was holding it both times I went back to Dr. Warren's time, and I was holding it when I came back to the present."

Grace squinted. "You've held the ball a bunch of other times without having these crazy trips. So how does that work?"

Steve shrugged, "It's like it has to be switched on or something." He shook his head. "I really don't get it."

Reaching over, Grace picked up the musket ball, which gave Steve an idea. "Grace, let's hold the musket ball together! You know, let's see if we can both go back in time." Steve held his breath. Grace opened her hand. She stared down at the ball. After what seemed like an hour to Steve as he waited for her answer, Grace said, "Okay. Let's try it."

Grace smiled for the first time since he'd started explaining his trip to Boston's colonial harbors, wharfs and tea ships. Steve moved closer. "Alright," he said, pointing to the table, "we'll put the ball here." Grace placed the ball in front of them.

Steve reached to touch the ball with two fingers. "Okay, let's touch it together, like this."

Grace paused for just a second and then she did the same.

Chapter 29

The Suffolk Resolves

The second Grace touched the ball, a light exploded. When the light disappeared, the kitchen was gone, Grace was nowhere to be found, and Steve's world had become Dr. Warren's.

"Fellow patriots, Parliament's Intolerable Acts[16] are the vilest of laws! His Majesty and Parliament intend to impose merciless laws upon us so that we and the other colonies will shrink from further objection to unfair treatment. The King believes the other colonies will distance themselves from Massachusetts, as if we are a misbehaving child." Dr. Warren's voice boomed throughout the room.

As the crowd murmured, he continued. "Well, let us be witnesses to the error of King George's plan! The Intolerable Acts have closed our ports, prevented all food and goods from entering our wharfs, ended nearly all employment for the husbands and fathers of our colony, and mandated that soldiers live in our homes and eat what scarce food we have. But have our fellow colonies abandoned us?" Dr. Warren whipped his head around and shouted, "No! Notwithstanding the dire consequences of King George's laws! Our countrymen in New York, Pennsylvania, Maryland, Connecticut, and the other colonies have not dismissed us as the naughty child King George claims we are. No, our brethren throughout the other colonies have answered our prayers on multiple occasions.

"Rather than distance themselves from Massachusetts, the other colonies have united in opposition! Food has been sent to our

---

16 *Intolerable Acts* – These were laws passed in the British Parliament in 1774, after the Boston Tea Party. These laws were designed to punish the Massachusetts colonists for the destruction of the tea. The Americans called them the Intolerable Acts. In England, these laws were referred to as the Coercive Acts. The British Parliament hoped the harsh laws and punishments would make the other colonies become afraid to oppose England's authority. Instead, the result of these laws was that the thirteen colonies united, and in April 1775, they started the Revolutionary War.

aid. Letters of support are received daily. We've become a union of colonies."

Dr. Warren pointed to the window behind where Steve sat, and said, "Right now, delegates from the colonies are gathered in Philadelphia. They're discussing our fate and the fate of this American continent. King George's decrees have not alienated Americans, but have instead brought union to the thirteen colonies!"

Around the room, many nodded. A man in the middle of the room stood. "My good doctor and esteemed patriot, I wish to voice an underlying fear." This man was dressed in a suit that shined like Dr. Warren's, and he wore a well-powdered white wig. "I worry this document that we've christened the Suffolk Resolves[17] goes too far, too fast. Can we expect our brethren from the other colonies, serving as delegates in Philadelphia, to adopt these resolves? Will the other 12 colonies pledge a willingness to prepare for war against the British Empire?"

Steve tilted his head in confusion. War? Steve knew the Tea Party had occurred on December 16, 1773, and the Declaration of Independence was signed on July 4, 1776. What year had he traveled to this time? But, more importantly, where was Grace? In the crowded room, he craned his neck to try and find her. As the men continued talking, he scanned through the throngs of people, looking for her.

The patriot in the powdered wig added, "I worry these resolves will not be passed by our brethren in Philadelphia."

Dr. Warren nodded a few times toward the gentleman and smiled in his direction. "No one can deny my fellow patriot William Cooper's genuine concerns. As the Honorable Mr. Cooper points out, the delegates in Philadelphia are not, um, not currently suffering under the King's Intolerable Acts like we are in Massachusetts. This is true." Dr. Warren paused as he looked around the room. "Also, it is true as Goodman Cooper has expressed, that the delegates of the

17 *Suffolk Resolves* – In September 1774, the Suffolk Resolves were drafted in large part by Dr. Warren. These resolves urged all thirteen colonies to raise militias and be ready for war if England continued to ignore the colonists' rights to live free without England imposing unfair laws for those in America. The First Continental Congress in Philadelphia approved the Suffolk Resolves. The Suffolk Resolves would later be used to help guide Thomas Jefferson when he drafted the Declaration of Independence in 1776.

other colonies may look at the resolves we are here to sign and find them too radical. They may refuse to approve them."

Dr. Warren shrugged. "Yes, it is certain that these resolves contemplate opposition to the King's enforcement of these vile laws with armed and trained militias. However!" The doctor's voice boomed through the room. "I do not believe the delegates of this continent's first Continental Convention will cower from their duty. No, I believe September of 1774 will long be remembered for the stance our Continental Congress takes in opposing tyranny. Surely, the actions in our harbors last December have brought the delegates together. Surely, we will continue to resist the King's ever-flailing scepter that inspires all on this continent to rise and stand forth. Surely, our brethren in Philadelphia will stand up to tyranny!" Dr. Warren continued. Then his voice lowered, like a breeze following thunder, "I believe the delegates from the other colonies will pledge to support our opposition to unjust rule and slavery."

Catching his breath and glancing at every man in turn, including Steve, Joseph Warren emphasized, "The delegates recognize the sacrifice that those in Massachusetts are making to preserve the freedoms that our fathers craved when they first came to this land. This land is America. This land is a land of promise. This was a land of freedom for those who came before us. It must remain that way for those who come after! No, my friends and countrymen, the delegates in Philadelphia will support these resolves." Dr. Warren's voice spiked like a crack of lightning, "And they will support an appeal to arms to oppose the wicked mantle of tyranny!

"The King's soldiers have no regard for Americans. They consider the men of this continent inferior. They believe we are afraid of the red-coated soldiers of the King." Dr. Warren's eyes sizzled. His words seared through Steve's chest. "By heaven, these fellows say we won't fight! I hope I shall die up to my knees in blood." William Cooper, the patriot who had voiced concerns, stood again. "Dr. Warren, no man in this congregation doubts your commitment. And, if there is one signature on these Resolves that could serve to persuade the delegates in Philadelphia, it is your signature."

Mr. Cooper paused. He looked through the window and then turned and stared back at his friend, "Joseph, you have my vote. I agree. I pledge my support to these Resolves. If the Resolves are to be approved, we must sign and deliver them." Mr. Cooper then looked to the back of the room. "We have one of the finest riders in the region with us." Mr. Cooper pointed to a man whose shoulders passed beyond the width of his chair. Steve recognized him immediately. Cooper continued, "Mr. Revere has pledged his willingness to deliver the Resolves to the delegates in Philadelphia."

Paul Revere tipped his three-sided hat towards Mr. Cooper. "It's time," Mr. Cooper announced, "Men of Suffolk County, can our Maker in Heaven, the good doctor here and Mr. Revere count on your affirmation of these Resolves?" All the men next to Steve and those around him burst out with cries of approval. "AYE" and "YAY, YAY," echoed throughout the room and shook the windows.

The doctor's smile broadened when he spotted Steve. He winked in acknowledgment at his apprentice. Steve returned the smile, while those in the room began to clap and stand.

Steve stood to join the others in clapping, but as he popped up, something tumbled off his lap. The musket ball! He hadn't noticed it sitting on his lap. Now it rolled across the floor. The uneven wood planks made the ball bounce and swerve as it rolled. Steve dodged through the crowd, following the ball's path, but just before his fingers could close around the old musket ball, it disappeared.

Steve dropped to his hands and knees on the floor, and spotted a hollowed knot in the wood. The ball sat lodged in the small cavity. He grabbed for the ball and tried to work it out of the hole. It had easily rolled within the cavity of the wood, but he couldn't get it to pop out.

Several men now eyed Steve as he twisted around on the floor, but he didn't care. He had to get the musket ball! As far as he knew, there was no way back without it. Steve clawed at the ball with new vigor. Sweat beads formed below his hairline. Finally, the ball popped free, with a small part of the wood floor.

His fingers wrapped around the ball. As soon as he grabbed it, the men, the chairs, the walls of the room – everything, began to blur. A second later, the room exploded into a flash of light. Everything else vanished.

Chapter 30

Grace's Reaction

Steve jerked back to 2001. He blinked, trying to clear the dazed feeling from his head. "Grace, were you there?"

Steve's words were as sincere as he could make them, but her reply stung like hot ice, "Steve, what are you talking about?"

Raising his eyebrows and hoping, Steve asked, "Did you see Dr. Warren? I mean –" Steve fumbled the words. "Did you see the Suffolk patriots sign the declaration? Did you hear the stuff about the First Continental Congress[18] in Philadelphia?"

Grace handed the ball back to Steve and responded in an icy tone. "Steve, you know I was here. You know," Grace nodded to the chair, "sitting right here, next to you." Grace's brow furrowed and she shook her head. "Are you telling me that you went back in time again?"

Steve shrugged his shoulders and bit the inside of his lip. This was exactly what he wanted to tell Grace. But when he saw her confused expression, he realized how crazy it sounded. "I did go back, Grace." He paused, hoping she would say she believed him. Grace didn't say anything. His best friend just looked away, shaking her head. Sadness now replaced frustration. Steve didn't like either of these emotions, but he couldn't stand looking into her sad eyes.

Grace's eyes began to pool with tears. Steve tried again to convince her, "Grace, I don't know how this happens. I don't. But I was

18 *First Continental Congress* – This was a gathering of delegates from 12 of the 13 colonies that would later become the United States. They met in Philadelphia for over a month, in September of 1774. Representatives of the colonies met to discuss the Intolerable Acts that Britain had passed against Massachusetts in response to the Boston Tea Party in December of 1773. The delegates wrote a petition to the King asking that the Intolerable Acts be repealed. The King ignored the request and eventually the colonies would unite to fight the most powerful nation on the Earth.

with Joseph Warren again, and he and a bunch of other patriots signed these Suffolk Resolves. And Paul Revere was taking them to Philadelphia." Even as he said it, he knew how crazy it all sounded.

Steve looked at Grace. She was sadder than he had ever seen her.

Grace asked, "So, this is the reason for the name?" Steve wasn't sure what she meant, and his expression conveyed his confusion. She went on, "You said that they signed the 'Suffolk Resolves.' I'm assuming the name comes from Suffolk County."

Steve got excited. "Exactly!" His voice carried new hope. "Yeah, I thought the same thing. Boston is in Suffolk County."

But his hopes for a change in her attitude flattened. Grace reached across the table and picked up the manuscript. She took a minute or two to turn through the old pages. Squinting closer to a particular page, she pushed the manuscript in Steve's direction. "Look at this word." Grace pointed to the top of a page in the middle of the document. He read *Suffolk* and the next word looked like *Resolves.* The words on this page and the next page were cracked and faded, but the term Suffolk Resolves appeared more than a few times. Steve looked up while Grace moved the manuscript back in front of her.

Gently she turned through the pages and flipped to a different section and asked, "What do you think these pages are about?" She looked straight at him.

Steve reached over and brought the document in front of him. Looking at the pages, he could make out a few words, such as *tea* in a number of places, and the words *Griffin's Wharf* and *Mohawks* also popped out. Steve looked up at Grace. "It's talking about the Boston Tea Party."

"Why are you doing this, Steve? Why are you making up these stories?" With tears on the edges of her eyes, she looked directly at him. "Are you trying to distance yourself from me?" Grace stood up and headed to the door looking back at Steve. "Is it because of the essay? Are you trying to show you are somehow patriotic? Do you think making up stories from your great uncle's old manuscript and telling me about traveling to the 1770s will make me think you're more patriotic?"

Grace reached for the door handle. "Or is it more than the essay? Is this your way to stop hanging out together? Did you get tired of being teased for hanging out with me? Just like Nick said." She paused, "Nick said some guys told him you were going to get rid of me, that you were tired of hanging out with me."

She tried to steady her voice. "I guess that's the reason for these crazy stories. I mean, I just wish you had been direct. You could've just told me. You didn't have to lie." Steve could see a tear rolling down Grace's cheek as she closed the door behind her.

Steve stood frozen. He stared at the closed door. Never in a million years – never could Steve have imagined this! He knew his stories of time travel were crazy. He'd questioned them himself, but he never thought arguing about them being real would wreck his friendship with Grace. And Nick – what the heck did he know about anything? Steve hated that guy! He was always trying to show off around Grace. What did he have to do with any of this? Steve stood there shaking his head, watching through the bay window as Grace hurried past his driveway.

Desperate to make things right, he ran towards the door still holding the musket ball. He began to pull the door open with his other hand, but the instant it started to open, the musket ball sizzled, an intense light flashed and Steve once again left his century.

Chapter 31

Paul's Plea

The sun shone bright, but a steady, icy wind pierced through Steve. He found himself in a long coat shivering next to Dr. Warren and Paul Revere. They all stood behind a large, red brick building with a steeple. It took a minute, but Steve recognized the Old South Meeting House as the place he'd visited just before dumping the tea. This back side of the church had large paned windows with one row of windows at eye level and two other rows of windows three stories up. Dr. Warren stood next to Paul Revere, dressed in a thick robe that was draped over him like a roman toga. In one of his hands, he held onto a ladder that leaned against the back of the meeting house. Steve stared. Why was Dr. Warren wearing a Roman toga?

Paul Revere shook his head, "Joseph, I can't let you do this." He stuck his thick arm between Dr. Warren and the ladder. "This is beyond dangerous!" Revere spit out the words, "It's fool-hardy!" Dr. Warren looked up the ladder to a second-story window and then back to his friend. Revere moved to position his whole body between his friend and the ladder. "Sam should never have accepted your willingness to speak. There's a reason, Joseph, that no one else would speak at this massacre commemoration."

Dr. Warren nodded acknowledgment and placed his hand on his friend's shoulder, then reached past Revere to the ladder. It was clear he was preparing to climb.

Steve saw Paul Revere's jaw tighten. "Joseph, if I allow you to enter that building, I may as well be placing the noose around your neck myself. You'll not live to finish the speech. If you're not shot, you'll be taken to the public square to be hung for treason! We all want to maintain the tradition, but I'm telling you this anniversary, this March, it's different."

As the doctor tried to reach around him, Revere continued. "In Sam's zeal, he's allowed you to volunteer for a death sentence. More than one of the Sons of Liberty have heard rumors that the troops intend to assassinate you. The Sons of Liberty would do anything for you, Joseph; you know that. Believe me when I tell you, they know your life is in danger. I plead with you to forgo the speech! For the greater cause we will yet achieve, don't end your life today." Paul's hands shook, and a vein in his neck pulsed as he stared at Dr. Warren.

Joseph Warren looked at his best friend, and his voice dropped. "Paul, for five years, every March since 1770, the massacre has been remembered; right here at the South Meeting House." Dr. Warren turned and glanced at the wall behind him. "The citizens and patriots of Boston have recognized the danger of gathering each year. Now, on the fifth anniversary of the massacre, should we forgo the event because the King's troops have succeeded in intimidating us? Never." Dr. Warren calmly put his hand on Paul's shoulder. "I know your concern for my safety. But I feel your prayers and intend to heed the peace I feel from the Almighty more than our mortal concerns. In this moment, I feel the prayers of all the Boston patriots. I feel at peace, Paul. And I feel Elizabeth, as if she stands with me."

Paul Revere closed his eyes and Steve wondered about this reference to Elizabeth. Revere mumbled almost to himself, "I just regret we allowed you to persuade us that you should be the speaker."

Warren quickly interjected, "Paul, this is my calling to complete. There was no one else who should make this speech."

Revere shook his head. "But there is no one the troops have greater cause to arrest! It was your pen that wrote the Suffolk Resolves. The Governor knows it was you who organized the meeting of delegates. The King, and probably all of England, hold you responsible for the Resolves. Your call for military opposition within the Resolves has been deemed treason, Joseph. Treason!" Revere's voice rose higher as his friend moved into position to climb the ladder. He continued, with what seemed to be almost a panic in his voice, "The Governor considers you responsible for spreading treason not only in Boston but across the entire continent. Joseph, Governor Gage has a standing order for your arrest because of the Resolves and the destruction of the tea. Given all this, how can you be the right person to speak today?"

Dr. Warren stepped up onto the first rung of the wood ladder, and said, "Paul, I'm at peace." Pausing and looking directly into his friend's eyes, the doctor added, "I'm not afraid to die for this cause for which we labor." Paul Revere closed his eyes, as Joseph went on, "And if the worst were to occur, the Lord has said, 'Greater love hath no man than this, that a man lay down his life for his friends.'"

Turning to Steve, Dr. Warren added, "And my trusted apprentice will protect me. My good friend, William, will pray for me."

Steve froze. Pray for him?

Still looking at Steve, Dr. Warren said, "Be diligent in surveying the streets, William, and alert Paul or John if anything arouses suspicion." Dr. Warren looked at Steve with a slight smile. Standing there, not knowing what to do, Steve just nodded.

"Paul, I'm afraid it's time to conclude these discussions. We each have our job to do and mine is to address this gathering." Dr. Warren began climbing up the ladder with his white toga blowing in the breeze.

When Warren slipped through the second-story window, Steve turned to Paul Revere, "Why is Dr. Warren entering this way?"

Revere said, "So as to be harder to apprehend and to avoid having to push through the crowd." He nodded toward the front of the chapel. "Now, you had better go quickly. Let's have you circulate around the roadways and paths near the meeting house. Remember, William, if you encounter anything amiss, report it immediately to me or Mr. Hancock. I'll be sitting near the front to protect Joseph if necessary. John will sit near the back door to receive any news you might have."

Revere pulled off his tricorn hat and waved it. "Now, go William!"

Chapter 32

Steve Foils the Plan

People had gathered everywhere, both within the walls of the church and outside. As Steve made his way into the Boston streets, he thought about Dr. Warren's conversation and how he'd asked Steve to pray for him. Pray for him? Nobody had ever asked him to pray before. He sort of believed in God, but he'd never tried to talk to Him. While Steve was definitely unfamiliar with prayer, Dr. Warren seemed to believe it could really help.

He thought of Grace and how she talked about prayer, how it was like talking to a friend. He stopped and looked up. After a long pause, looking into the Boston sky, he mouthed four words, "God, help Dr. Warren." Then thinking of chocolate eyes brimming over with tears, he got real sad and added, "Help Grace know I still like her." It was not a lot of words – nothing fancy. Steve knew that a lot better prayers could be said, but few could be more heartfelt.

Having walked over a block away from the church, with his thoughts still on Grace, he blindly turned a corner and ran right into a fellow pedestrian. The collision sent them both to the ground, with an audible "pop." Both parties lay in a tangled mess.

Grimacing with pain, Steve looked at the man he had collided with. He was about twenty and wore a bright red uniform, a real Redcoat. This man lay on the ground writhing in pain. Next to him lay a smashed egg. Looking at the egg and the Redcoat who was holding his knee, Steve struggled to stand. His right thigh throbbed. Although straining with his own pain, Steve asked, "Are you all right?"

Gritting his teeth and desperately holding his left knee, the young British soldier spat out, "No! Do I look all right? Look at this bloody mess you've caused!" The young Redcoat shook his head and spoke through clenched teeth, his face contorted. "I don't know how

I can manage. My knee, I cannot move it. I was to be arriving at the Old South to put an end to the cursed speech. And that there egg was intended to be worn by that bloody doctor! It was to be the sign to the officers to take him. After tonight he was to speak no more evil of His Majesty's troops." With a disgusted look on his face, the soldier, in slurred speech, commanded, "Well, now, don't just stand there. Help me!"

Steve was no expert, but the soldier's breath stank with a smell that Steve figured must be from alcohol. The soldier hissed, "Even with no egg, I'll still need to get to Old South." He reached for Steve, "Help me now. I've gotta get there before the bloody rebel finishes. The officers are expecting me. Now help!"

Steve backed away from the vile soldier's outstretched arm. The last thing he intended to do was help this Redcoat attack Dr. Warren, even if the Redcoats' plans were already ruined thanks to the smashed egg. Steve turned and scrambled to run with his own injured thigh, but stopped suddenly. He thought of Grace. He had an idea. Maybe there was a way he could prove to her that he'd told the truth. He hobbled back to the still-struggling soldier. With surprise and satisfaction on his face, the soldier said, "Tis right! You best pull me up." He moved his arm toward Steve.

Steve reached out and wrapped his fingers not on the outstretched hand, but firmly around the three brass buttons on the soldier's sleeve. Yanking his hand back, he ripped off the buttons as fast as he could. His success surprised him. Two of the three buttons were nestled securely in his palm. The stunned Redcoat, impaired by both the twisted knee and too much rum, spit a stream of obscenities at Steve. Steve ran with a throbbing thigh back towards the meetinghouse.

The swearing faded as he got closer. With the back of the church in site, Steve wondered what he'd done. The soldier would surely report Steve's actions to the British officers. What would the Redcoats do if they caught him? Put him in jail? Kill him?

Catching his breath, he looked over all the bricks and mortar at the back of the church that he'd noticed earlier. He needed somewhere to hide one of the buttons. He found the gap he was looking for between the bricks and a windowpane. Taking one of the brass buttons in his fingers and turning it to lay flat, he tried fitting it in the crack. Pushing until the button made an indentation to the bone, he wedged it deep into the slim opening.

Perfect! It could be hidden and secure for the next 225 years.

Chapter 33

1775 Boston Massacre Speech

Steve tried to get inside the church. Finally pushing through, he saw Dr. Warren's white toga and the pulpit draped in a black cloth. Sam Adams and Paul Revere sat behind Dr. Warren's podium at the front. British officers sat in the first few rows.

Steve leaned to the man next to him, and said, "Excuse me sir, can you tell me where I can find John Hancock?"

Examining Steve, the gentleman pointed to his right and leaning to Steve's ear, he said, "Mr. Hancock is there, near the other door, wearing the sky blue jacket with the large gold buttons."

Thanking the gentleman, Steve nudged his way through the crowd to the man who would be the first signer of the Declaration of Independence. Standing in the back, surveying the scene in front of him, John Hancock noticed Steve bumping through the crowd. As Steve finally squeezed through the last group of patriots, he said, "Mr. Hancock, I'm . . ." he hesitated. "I'm William Eustis, Dr. Warren's apprentice."

Hancock nodded. "William, I certainly know who you are. Is there something amiss?"

Steve said, "Mr. Hancock, yes, there's something amiss." It sounded funny, but Steve continued speaking this fancy, old English. In a hushed whisper Steve told John Hancock what had happened with the Redcoat.

When Steve finished, Mr. Hancock looked around at the British soldiers in the crowd. He said in a low voice, "William, your collision and the cracked egg may be the best evidence yet that the hand of Divine Providence is protecting the good doctor. As for what we should do, I think we have to hope that without this egg being thrown at Joseph to signify to the officers the need to apprehend him, the intended evil will not occur." John Hancock placed a hand on Steve's shoulder. "We will watch the officers in front and pray for Joseph. For now – I believe that is all we can do."

Listening to the doctor's speech, Steve realized that Dr. Warren was doing nothing to appease the British officers and soldiers sitting in front of him. The speech blasted patriotic fire. The officers and soldiers hissed at Doctor Warren's words. Then, some of the officers started shaking their heads, stirring and looking around. Steve could guess that they were probably waiting for an egg to fly.[19]

Dr. Warren's speech vividly recreated the nightmare of March 5, 1770. Dr. Warren called upon the widows of those who had died in the massacre to remember holding their children as they beheld the murdered husbands and fathers lying dead in the street. *"Take heed, ye orphan babes, lest whilst your streaming eyes are fixed upon the ghastly corpse, your feet slide on the stones bespattered with your father's brains."* Steve made a face at the gruesome image created by Dr. Warren's words. Then, suddenly, he saw one of the younger British officers jump out of his seat.

The sneering captain stood directly in front of the podium. He held pistol balls in an opened hand. Steve watched Dr. Warren walk toward him. Dr. Warren continued his speech, completely calm, while he dropped a white handkerchief, like a flag of peace, into the young officer's hand.

Dr. Warren's speech concluded, and he found his seat. Next Sam Adams stood and addressed the group. Steve stood in the back with his hands in his pockets, his hand wrapped around the musket ball and the remaining brass button. Holding the musket ball, he wondered, Why am I going on these trips? At the same time, he heard Sam Adams emphasize that the town of Boston must continue to remember, and never forget, the Massacre, including in March of the coming year, 1776.

19 *Broken Egg* – After the 1775 Massacre Speech, official sources showed that there had been a plan to arrest Dr. Warren and other revolutionary leaders that were in attendance. The arrests never happened because the arranged signal of pelting Dr. Warren with an egg never occurred. The British soldier bringing the egg to throw at Dr. Warren tripped on his way to the ceremony and the egg broke.

The British officers could endure no more. The red-coated soldiers bolted up and began banging their walking sticks and swords on the floor. Cries of "Oh Fie![20] Oh Fie!" rang out. Looking up, Steve instantly saw townspeople turning, running, and pushing all at the same time, like herds of passengers on a sinking ship. Shouts from the Boston citizens rang above the chaos, "They're going to fire!" Steve saw some people on the second floor of the building actually jumping from the windows to get away from what they must have thought would be a second massacre from firing British soldiers.

In all the chaos, Steve's hand began to heat up. Then, the jostling mob of patriots around him began to fade away as an old wooden door swung open. The bright light engulfed him, and Steve found himself on his knees outside his own home in modern times. Looking around, he saw Grace turning the corner onto the next street. Her hair flowed behind her, and just before she turned out of sight, Steve saw her wiping away a tear on her cheek.

Steve tried to get up to chase after her, but the shooting pain in his right thigh quickly brought him back to his knees. Kneeling on the ground, he opened his hand. He looked at the musket ball and the shiny brass button that had traveled over 200 years. Now he wondered, could a Redcoat's button really save his friendship?

Steve was not the only one watching Grace walk down his street. A polished man in a shiny black suburban with dark tinted windows followed her every step. Behind dark glasses, the man's eyes soaked in the scene: the tears, the haste, and the frustration. He had tossed the book he'd been reading into the passenger seat the moment Grace burst through the door. He now watched as Steve knelt at the edge of the driveway, staring in the direction the girl had gone. He watched Steve open his hand and was confused when he thought he saw two round objects. From across the street, the man strained for a clearer

20 *Fie* is an old English word that was used to express disgust or disapproval.

view. He removed his sunglasses to get a better look. He recognized the first object. It was the musket ball, but the other item seemed to glimmer in the sun as if it was made of gold. He watched as Steve struggled to stand and then turned with his head down. He limped back to the house.

The man pulled a small tape recorder from his pocket. He spoke slowly, "It appears the T3 is shining and now affecting others in O'Dell's life." He paused, then added, "It also appears that the boy suffered a slight injury to his leg." He said no more, and put the dictaphone back in his pocket. Then he reached over and picked up the publication he'd been studying before the girl had marched out of the house. The senior agent stared at the cover of the book, *Time Traveling Talismans (T3s), by The Boston Historic and Genealogical Society*. He turned back to the chapter that he'd been reading – Bunker Hill Musket Ball.

Chapter 34

A Modern Day Patriot and Grace

Grace didn't show up to school the next day. At first, as Steve waited in the cafeteria before school, he thought she was just avoiding him. When she didn't turn up in M-Rod's English class, he knew she had skipped. He stared at her empty chair. Unlike the rest of the kids, Grace loved school. She never missed a day. Did she really want to stay away from him that badly? Steve would've never guessed in a million years that sharing his stories about Dr. Warren would cause her to think he wanted to end their friendship. He wondered if she would avoid him forever. Would they ever be friends again?

He couldn't understand how he'd caused such a mess just by being honest, but he intended to prove that his stories had really happened. He felt in his pocket for the musket ball and the brass button. As long as he could get her to speak to him again, he'd convince her that he hadn't been making things up to wreck their friendship.

Steve walked home from school alone. He sat in the kitchen by the bay window alone. He did his homework alone. He hated it!

Lying on his bed, he put his book to the side. He couldn't concentrate; he just kept thinking about Grace and how sad she looked when she accused him of making everything up. He was still lying on his side an hour later, when his mom looked into his room. He thought she was coming in to tell him dinner was ready. Instead, she asked, "Steve, are you all right?" She eyed the book lying on the floor by his bed.

Steve lied as he turned away from the door. "Yeah, I'm okay, just tired."

His mom sounded unconvinced, but she said, "Well, Lee Warren is downstairs. He came to see you."

Closing his eyes, Steve rolled off the bed. He wasn't in the mood for this. Barely moving his feet, he grabbed his Sox hat and pulled it down over his face as he shuffled toward the living room. What could Lee want?

They met.

They talked.

Lee explained.

Lee left.

It was Tuesday morning and school would be starting in a few minutes. Steve waited in the cafeteria, looking for Grace. Would she miss two days in a row? If she showed up, he would talk to her and fix things. He watched the doors to make sure he didn't miss her. He saw tons of kids pour through the main entrance to the cafeteria.

Then someone tapped him on the shoulder from behind, and he heard her voice, "Can I sit with you?" Steve spun around. Grace Levy looked at him with her head tilted, nervously biting her lip, but when Steve's face lit up, her amazing smile burst through.

Moving to the side to make room on the white cafeteria bench, he said, "Um . . . yeah, yeah!"

Grace sat down and started to talk, then halted and started again. "Steve, I want to talk to you about Sunday. I guess, I mean, I shouldn't have said the things I said." She looked at him nervously, opened her mouth then closed it again.

Seeing her struggle with what to say next, he jumped in, "Grace, I had a terrible day yesterday. Do you know why I had such a bad day?" Grace shrugged. "I hated it because I wanted to see you." Grace looked at him with a relieved smile.

Bursting to get it all out, Steve said, "School stunk and then Lee Warren came by my house. He wanted me to sign his copy of my essay. So weird." Steve shook his head. "He also talked to me more about my great uncle and World War II." Steve paused before adding, "Grace, this is the really cool part. I didn't feel like I was lying or something. I could talk to a real patriot about my essay and I didn't feel bad."

Without waiting for Grace to reply, he added, "I promise, Grace, I haven't been making up patriotic stories about Dr. Warren. I promise I haven't been telling you stuff to end our friendship. I promise. I can prove I've gone back in time." Steve pulled his hand from his pocket and held out the brass button.

"This is a British Redcoat's button. I ripped two off a soldier's sleeve and brought this one back with me. I did it to prove to you that I'm really having these experiences in the 1700s. Here, you can have it." Steve put the button in Grace's hand. Shaking his head, he said, "I don't know why we both can be touching the musket ball and you don't come back in time. I don't get it. But I promise, Grace, that is a real soldier's button. You can take it to some metal tester or antique person or something and they'll tell you it's old and real; or you can do some other kind of test. But I promise it's real, and I promise I'm not making this stuff up."

Holding the button in the middle of her hand, Grace asked, "You ripped a button from a British soldier's jacket for me?"

Steve nodded. "I actually ripped off two. I brought this one back for you to keep, and stuck the other one in a crack in the Old South church – you know, the real old church on the Freedom Trail in Boston. I did it on my last trip when I was back there. We can go look in the crack; I'll show you where. I promise, in the back of the building under a window there will be an old button like that one – the other one will have been stuck in there for like 225 years."

Grace lifted her eyebrows, "Really?"

"Really. I promise. We can go find the old button in the wall and it will be like this one but probably all rusty and old, and it'll prove I'm not lying."

Steve would have bet a hundred dollars that he'd seen every variation of Grace Levy's smile . . . but not this one. Like always, her eyes twinkled, and her cheeks glowed. But this time her smile had a mischievous twist. Before Steve knew what was going on, she had leaned over and kissed him on the cheek

Still smiling that impish, really cute smile, she said, "You don't need to prove it. I believe you." She added, "I've got something to show you. Can I come to your house after school today?" With the first bell for classes ringing, and his head still spinning from the kiss, Steve nodded.

As they walked down the hall and he finally caught his breath, he asked "What's the surprise?"

Grace just smiled this new grin of hers, "You'll see."

PART THREE
REVOLUTION

Sparks make fire. Some sparks light a welcomed campfire. Others burn down forests.

We've traveled with Steve and his Time Traveling Talisman and have witnessed sparks. Sparks of soldiers killing rebels who became revolutionaries, patriots sparking protests against unequal taxation and unfair treatment of the colonies' tea, and resolves and speeches sparking a Revolution. The final spark is a shot heard around the world. This spark burns into a blazing battle on a hill outside Boston. This fire and the dead who lay in its embers will shout across the Atlantic, "Now – We are Enemies!"

Scene from Battle of Bunker Hill

Jason Russell House – Center of Fighting in Battle of Menotomy

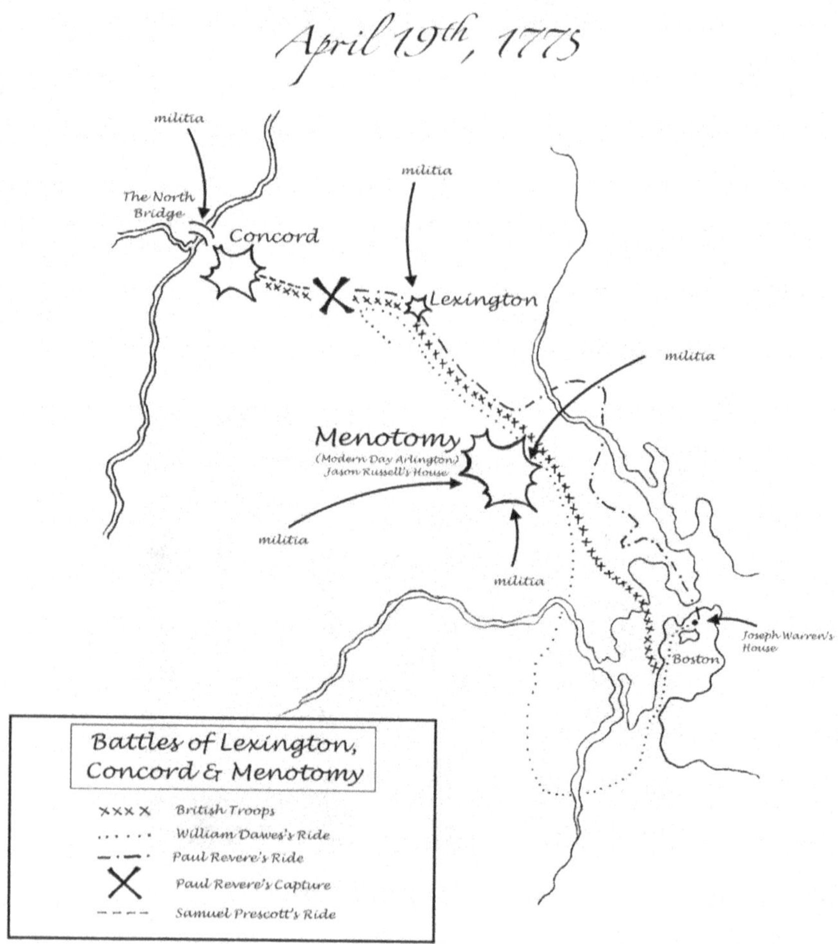

Battle of Menotomy

April 19, 1775 was arguably the first day of the Revolutionary War, and is recognized each year as Patriots Day. Although many Americans may remember the Battles of Lexington and Concord on this day, few remember the Battle of Menotomy. The confrontation at the Jason Russel House in Menotomy was an essential contribution to the events of April 19, 1775. It is believed that more Americans lost their lives in the Battle of Menotomy than in the Battles of Lexington and Concord combined.

Chapter 35

Grace's Surprise

After school, Grace came over to Steve's house with her surprise. As they sat together at Steve's kitchen table, Steve grabbed some chips from behind the pantry door while Grace pulled a huge ream of paper from her backpack. Steve stared at the mountain of paper and said in a disappointed voice, "This is the surprise?"

Smiling, Grace said, "Just wait and let me explain." She moved the printed pages in front of both of them. "After our argument on Sunday, I researched Joseph Warren on the internet and read and printed everything I could find about him. Like everything!" She pointed to the stack. "I stayed up all night trying to read it all. The next day I was so tired, but I wanted to keep reading, so I convinced my mom to let me miss school because I felt sick." Grace fidgeted a little, and looked at Steve, "It wasn't really a lie, after staying up all night reading and worrying about everything, I did have a headache." Grace gave a slight smile in Steve's direction.

Steve nodded. He was the last person Grace needed to convince. He just wanted to know what she found out. She kept talking, "Well, once my parents left for work, I kept reading and reading about Joseph Warren. I read all of it." She pointed to the two and a half inch stack. "And . . ." she made a conciliatory nod in Steve's direction. "Everything you talked about; the Boston Tea Party, the Suffolk Resolves – it was all right there on the internet."

Steve listened. He soaked in everything. Grace told him a bunch of things he already knew, and a bunch of things he'd never heard about the 1770s and Dr. Warren. They talked for almost an hour. After they'd looked through most of the information, Grace said, "Dr. Warren was like a great writer and all the leaders relied on him to write about what was happening. Apparently they would send his letters to these Committees of Correspondence[21] in the other 12 colonies." Excited, she added, "Here, see? When Dr. Warren wrote articles for the newspapers, he used a secret name. His secret penname was *A True Patriot.* Isn't that cool?"

She added, "He was the type of patriot I want to be like. He didn't just say the Pledge of Allegiance or just fly a flag or something – he really did things to help his country." As Steve listened to Grace, he felt a warmth fill his chest. For the first time, he felt at peace talking to Grace about these things. Now when Grace talked about being patriotic, he didn't feel like he was an imposter or a liar.

Grace added, "I want to show you this." She shuffled the pages, searching; then her eyes lit up. "Here, look." She pointed to a portion of an article talking about how Dr. Warren worked with Paul Revere at the start of the Revolution. Before he could read the piece, Grace bubbled over, saying, "He's the one who brought Paul Revere and a guy named William Dawes to his house on Hanover Street in Boston. And then he sent them on their rides. You know, the super famous one that everyone always talks about? His house is where it all started!"

As Steve started reading, Grace tried to wait but only lasted a minute. She started talking again, telling him the ending before he'd finished. "After the Battles of Lexington and Concord, Dr. Warren fought with the Minutemen at the Battle of Menotomy. It was the biggest battle of the day and there were huge groups of Americans that were waiting for the British. He got so into the battle that a British musket ball knocked a hairpin from the wig under his hat." He could picture his friend fighting with the militia, dodging bullets and taking care of wounded soldiers.

---

21 *Committees of Correspondence* – These were organizations set up by the Patriot leaders within all of the Thirteen Colonies during the 1770s just before the American Revolution. The purpose of the committees was to get information about what British leaders were doing, spread that information to all the major cities within the Thirteen Colonies, and just as importantly, to get the information spread to the rural farm communities where most of the American colonists lived. The Massachusetts committee formed by Sam Adams and Dr. Joseph Warren served as a model for other colonies, and was one of the most active and influential committees during the eve of the American Revolution.

Steve stopped reading. Looking up and seeing her excitement, he thought about all they'd talked about and all the pages that Grace had gathered – what a cool surprise. What a great friend.

Then Grace's smile faded, and Steve saw her hesitating. Noting the change in her expression, Steve asked, "What's up?"

Her face became more somber. She thumbed to the back of the pages. The sadness in her eyes deepened as she found the spot. "There is something – and it's real important."

After a long pause, Grace pulled a page from the pile, but then froze. Her eyes fixed on the window behind him. Steve turned and saw what caused Grace to freeze. Rob and his buddy, Curtis Christopher, were at the door about to come in. In a panic, Steve quickly started shuffling and gathering the pages as fast as he could, but it was too late.

Rob and Curtis entered together, and there he was sitting alone next to Grace. It could be worse. He could be buried up to his neck in sand, at the edge of the ocean, with the tide coming in.

Chapter 36

Rob and Curtis

They were trapped.

The two older boys poured through the door, howling and goofing off. Curtis slugged Rob, "You ain't got no hop. Man, you hop like a white boy," Rob was about to reply when he spotted Steve and Grace. He stopped his goofy gangster laugh. Curtis looked over too. Spotting Grace, he stuck out his chest and flashed his best lady-slayer smile in Grace's direction.

Curtis spoke first as he headed to the fridge. "Hello, Stevie and Miss Grace." With the fridge door wide open, Curtis called out, "I love coming to Stevie and Robby's house, cuz you white folk know how to fill a fridge."

Rob flipped a chair backwards and plopped down in front of Grace and Steve and all their papers. He turned to Curtis, "Well, you better get your black fingers off that Jell-O pudding pack, unless there are two." Curtis grinned and tossed one to Rob. "There's even one for Stevie and his little missus if they want to share it." Both Steve and Grace declined the offer.

Steve saw Grace's eyes bugged out as if at a crime scene when Curtis called Rob's family the "white folk," and when Rob told Curtis to get his "black fingers off the pudding." Later, Steve would make sure to explain that Rob and Curtis talked to each other like that all the time. Curtis and Rob were the best athletes in Needham, and had been best friends since fifth grade. They were the only 10th graders to play on the varsity football, basketball and baseball teams. Not only were they the only sophomores to play on these teams, but they also stood out as players. They were best friends on and off the field – always there for each other no matter what.

Looking at Rob and seeing that Curtis was now coming to the table too, Steve really wanted to get Grace and all their stuff out of the kitchen, and fast. Rob and Curtis closed in like hungry coyotes on a pair of rabbits. Curtis flipped his chair backwards before plopping down in it, and now scooted it closer to the table.

Curtis handed Rob a spoon for his pudding, and waving his own spoon around said, "So, Stevie, what's all this stuff? Are you trying to be some kind of professor or someth'en?" Steve didn't answer. He kept gathering papers. Curtis rested his spoon above his pudding pack and made a disgusted face. "So you just sit at the house with this pretty girl reading all this stuff for fun? Man, you must be crazy!" Looking around, Curtis noticed the tattered old manuscript. He reached for it. "What's all this yellow-lookin', old stack of papers here?" Curtis moved the manuscript towards him. Steve noted that at least Curtis treated the pages carefully.

Steve again said nothing, but Rob spoke, "It's some old stuff our World War II great uncle gave Steve."

Curtis lifted his eyebrows, nodded and turned back to the pages. Steve knew Curtis talked and acted like some tough gangster from the 'hood but Steve had sat next to Curtis' family during tons of basketball, football, and baseball games. Curtis' father worked in Boston as a lawyer, and his mom served as secretary for the Needham Historical Society. They lived just up the street in one of the nicest homes in the neighborhood. Why Curtis always talked like he'd grown up on the streets was weird and beyond Steve.

Curtis squinted at the pages. "Stevie, you can't really read this scribble, can you?" Steve watched Curtis focus on the old manuscript and could tell that he genuinely wanted to read it.

Reaching over and taking the document back, Steve said, "Nope. No one can, so give it back." Curtis made another one of his funny faces and threw up his hands like drawing a foul on the basketball court. He got a laugh out of Rob.

As Steve took the papers back, Curtis spotted the musket ball. "Well Stevie, now this is cool." Curtis snatched the ball before Steve could stop him. "Is this some kind of old bullet or what?"

Wanting the ball back but with no hope of getting it without Curtis' cooperation, Steve responded with a curt, "Yes."

"Yeah, Stevie, now this is something your Daddy Curtis wants to check out." Curtis held the ball and examined it.

Steve rolled his eyes. "Curtis, if you'll give me the musket ball, Grace and I'll leave." Grace had finished gathering the papers. She sat there with no smile, looking away from Curtis and Rob.

Curtis said, "Oh, now, you and your pretty lady friend don't have to leave. You can play professor and tell Rob and me all about this stuff."

Rob cut in. "No way Curt; not for me." Rob looked to the stack of papers Grace had gathered, raised his eyebrows and shook his head. He added, "I don't need some crappy history lesson, I get enough at school. But I do need to see that old bullet."

Rob reached for the musket ball, but Curtis yanked it away. "Not yet, Robbie boy, I'm not done lookin'."

Grace had everything gathered except the musket ball. She looked between Rob and Curtis, as anxious as Steve to get out of the kitchen.

Steve held out his hand to Curtis. "Curtis, if you'll give me the musket ball, we'll get out of here." Curtis ignored him.

Like everyone else who held the musket ball, Curtis looked at the ball as if trying to solve a hidden mystery. He looked up. "Not so fast, Stevie. Your big brother needs a turn." He tossed the ball to Rob, who easily caught it and smirked at Steve.

Again, Steve looked at Grace. He thought about all the pages she'd researched, printed and studied for him. He wanted to be alone with Grace. He wanted to read her research. He wanted to hear about this important thing she wanted to tell him about Joseph Warren. Rob had just started looking at the musket ball, but Steve was done. Grace had done so much for him; he'd get the musket ball and he'd get her out of here.

Balling up his hands into fists, Steve said, with as much power as he could, "Rob, give me that ball." Rob looked up. Steve could tell he took issue with the tone of his demand. Rob didn't say anything;

he just ignored Steve and went back to looking at the ball. Steve tried in a nicer way, and this time Rob at least acknowledged the request.

"Just a minute –" Rob paused. He looked to Steve and asked, "Do you think this ball killed anyone?"

The deep question coming from Rob surprised Steve but his reaction to the question surprised him even more. When Rob asked *if it killed anyone,* chills ran up Steve's spine, producing the same electricity as when Dr. Warren had said he hoped *to die for his country up to his knees in blood.*

"Rob, I'm sick of this. Give me the musket ball!" Steve's outburst made Rob turn to him in surprise. He wasn't flustered. He just glared at Steve. Curtis made a whistling noise, followed by another one of his funny faces, eyebrows raised.

Staring down his little brother, Rob was obviously up to something. Placing the ball on the table and turning to Steve, he said, "I wasn't done looking at it. But if you really want it, I dare you to take it." Rob lifted his hands, leaving the ball on the table for Steve to try to grab it.

Grace grabbed Steve by the arm. "Come on, Steve. Let's just go to the den. Get the ball from Rob later." Grace got up and started walking and Steve followed her lead. Steve noted the disappointment in Rob's face as he moved from the table. Then Steve turned back and lunged.

Even having let his guard down, Rob still moved too fast for Steve to pull off his plan. Rob's hand got to the ball at the same time Steve's hand came down on the table. Neither one secured the ball, and it flew into the air. Steve sprawled across the table, trying to grab it before it fell. His body and arms flew in four different directions. The ball fell to the kitchen floor, and the two of them dove in the direction it had landed. Both were now scrambling around on the ground.

During the fiasco, Curtis had jumped out of his chair to make room for the scramble. He stood watching the brothers crawling around on the floor, and pumped his fist while cheering for Rob. Grace stood nearby, yelling for both brothers to stop.

Chaos reigned in the kitchen, but neither Rob nor Steve heard the ranting or yelling. As their hands stretched for the ball, their fingers touched the simmering lead at the same time. In that instant, they both saw a wooden door appear. As if in slow motion, the O'Dell brothers rolled through the wooden portal.

The doorway sucked them through and a burst of light exploded from under their fingers.

Chapter 37

Rob Meets Warren and Revere

Dr. Warren stood in a room lit by candles, and Rob stood by the doctor's side. The candles produced enough light to illuminate his brother's face and the clothes he wore. Steve realized that he and Rob were both dressed like Dr. Warren, although Rob's long waist coat and black leather shoes were more faded and worn than Steve's, and far short of the quality of Dr. Warren's. Rob stared around the room, his mouth open. His eyes, twice their normal size, searched for something familiar.

Steve wanted to explain, but before he could get closer to his brother, there was a knock on the door. Dr. Warren opened it, and Steve immediately recognized the visitor. "Come in, Paul." Dr. Warren grabbed his friend's hand and got him inside quickly. "Thanks for coming."

Steve moved closer to Rob, who immediately grabbed his arm. "What's happening!?" His voice trembled with fear and anger. Rob acted like Steve was the one at fault for them being here. He ignored the accusatory tone and whispered to his older brother, "That's Paul Revere!" Now Rob looked even more bewildered.

Paul Revere held his three-cornered hat in his right hand as he nodded his head towards Steve and Rob. "Good evening, Mr. Eustis and Mr. Forbes." Steve nodded back, but Rob stood with his mouth open. They both watched Dr. Warren walk with Revere to the fireplace.

Steve noted that Revere had called Rob *Mr. Forbes,* but who was Mr. Forbes?

Paul Revere stood by the fire as Dr. Warren handed him a paper and spoke in quick sentences. "Paul, I've set it in motion. I sent Billy Dawes across the neck and through Cambridge." Paul Revere nodded as Warren continued, "I need you to cross tonight. Cross the bay to Charleston and ride to Lexington and Concord. Gage's troops will cross by boat as well. The Regulars leave by sea and will march north of Charlestown this evening."

Paul Revere stared directly into the eyes of his friend. "Joseph, you know this for sure?" The light from the fire glinted in Joseph Warren's eyes as he stared back at his friend and nodded.

Steve turned to Rob, who looked like he'd just seen ghosts talking. He wondered if his older brother understood the importance of what was happening. It was the night of Paul Revere's ride. This would be the spark that would start the Revolutionary War, and here they were, watching it all! Paul Revere asked, "Are Sam and John still in Lexington?"

Steve leaned over to his brother and whispered, "He's talking about Sam Adams and John Hancock." Rob's face looked pale. The overconfident jock attitude he had in their kitchen just minutes before had completely vanished.

Dr. Warren nodded, "General Gage[22] is sending the Regulars across the Charles River to march on Lexington. He's found out about the ammunition and he knows where Sam and John are hiding. We shall only protect them, and our supplies, by acting now. The element of surprise is Gage's main weapon. You or Dawes must get through their pickets and warn them and all the townsfolk. Awake all the militias." Warren placed his hand onto his friend's shoulder, "It's time – you must call all the patriots, all the Minutemen[23], all the farmers and fathers from here to Concord to arms tonight."

Paul Revere spoke, "Joseph, if all of this comes to fruition, we may be at war, even by sunrise." Dr. Warren looked from his friend to the fire's flames. He nodded. Paul Revere watched but said nothing. He placed his three-sided hat low on his head. He knew his role. His job would be to ride and warn. He turned towards the door, but stopped.

---

22 *General Thomas Gage* was a British Army General who also served as the Governor of the Massachusetts colony. He was sent by King George in 1774 after the Boston Tea Party. He was given the very difficult task of avoiding a war but enforcing the Intolerable Acts passed by Parliament to punish the citizens of Boston for destroying the tea.

23 *Minutemen* were civilian colonists in America who were expected to keep their arms and equipment with them at all times and in the event of an alarm or emergency, be ready at a minute's warning.

"Joseph, how'd you get word? How do you know for sure the Regulars march this night?"

Dr. Warren didn't respond. Finally, Paul spoke. "Did she tell you?" Steve wondered who *she* was, but he saw Revere duck his head as if he'd pried into an area that he ought to have left alone.

Joseph stepped toward Paul and patted his best friend on the back. It was clear he intended not to reveal his source. Steve wondered again who she[24] might be and promised himself that he'd look it up in all the stuff Grace had given him. Instinctively, he felt for and found the lead ball in his pocket. He felt some relief. At least he had the musket ball, and it hadn't ended up with Rob.

Despite the dangers of his own mission, Revere turned to Dr. Warren. "Joseph, take great caution. I'll warn Sam and John. But I worry about your decision to not leave with them."

Dr. Warren listened as they both stood in the moonlight. He nodded slowly. "My good friend, don't worry about me." Steve saw the doctor's gaze turn to the star-spangled sky. He figured Revere had a lot of reasons to worry about his best friend. Dr. Warren said, "All men who love this land and believe in liberty must make sacrifices to preserve our freedom. Many will face greater perils than mine in the days to come. Now, you must be off!" In the light of the moon, Dr. Warren forced a smile.

Paul wrapped his thick arms around Dr. Warren. Without saying more, Paul Revere quickly left down the narrow streets of old Boston. He would return to his home for his riding boots.

Steve remembered Mrs. Truman, his history teacher, telling the class about how the church was used to display two lanterns that would signal the colonists about the way British soldiers were planning their attack, "One if by land, two if by sea." He could see the Old North Church from the doorway, and he knew that soon two lanterns would be glowing from the white steeple in the sky.

---

24 *Dr. Warren's Source* is a mystery. He definitely knew the British were leaving Boston the evening of April 18, 1775. However, he never disclosed how he knew. Some historians speculate that his source of information came from General Gage's wife, Margaret Gage. She was born in New Jersey and considered herself an American. She once said that she hoped, "her husband would never be the instrument of sacrificing the lives of her countrymen."

Chapter 38

Words of Explanation from a Younger Brother

Dr. Warren spoke quickly, "Mr. Eustis, you and Mr. Forbes please ready my horse. We must depart." He motioned to an outbuilding that stood down a path a few hundred feet away. Gently, he pushed Rob forward, as if to shove him closer to the door and the readying of his horse.

Steve motioned to Rob to join him in getting the horse. Rob looked lost. He followed Steve, who had already started in the direction of the outbuilding. Remembering all the Redcoats at the Massacre speech with their guns, swords and steel bayonets, Steve shared Dr. Warren's desire to be on their way as quickly as possible.

"Hey, wait," Steve heard his brother call from behind him, but he didn't stop. Rob easily caught up, "Steve, what are you doing?"

Still walking, Steve said, "I'm getting a horse. And, I'm going to figure out how to get it ready like Dr. Warren asked."

Just as they got to the door of the carriage house, Rob grabbed his arm, "No! You're not doing anything until you tell me what is going on! Look at this," Rob waved his hands in front of his clothes. "This is messed up! I don't know what you did or how you did it, but this is over, dude. It's done! Get us back." As he said the last words, Rob thumped his finger into Steve's chest.

Steve was close enough now that, from inside the carriage house, he could see a cream-colored mare staring at them with large brown eyes. He realized he wouldn't be getting the horse to Dr. Warren until he satisfied Rob, so he started talking. "First, I didn't do this." He reached into his pocket and pulled out the musket ball. "It's this – this thing, this musket ball. Somehow, it can take me, and I guess now you, too, back to these Revolutionary times. Like back in time to the 1770s."

Rob shook his head and snorted, "Yeah, right! How can that work? You're such a stupid liar!"

Steve pointed to the blanket, saddle, bit and reins hanging on the wall. "Let me get the horse ready and I'll tell you all I know. I promise. I'll tell you everything." Steve knew his brother could be pretty terrifying when he was angry, but right now Steve was more concerned about Redcoats than he was about his brother. Dr. Warren had headed back to the house in a big hurry. Given Steve's experience with the Redcoats, he understood the urgency. In a voice that sounded more confident than he felt, he said, "I'll explain this crazy stuff as best I can. I promise." Rob just shook his head in disgust, but didn't stop Steve from entering the stall.

The cream-colored mare nudged Steve as Steve tried to remember what he'd read about readying horses in his books. In the book, *Johnny Tremain*, he remembered a scene where Dove, the stable boy, watched Johnny Tremain get the Colonel's horse ready. He was pretty sure the blanket came first, so he laid that on the gentle mare's back as he explained, "I promise it's the musket ball doing this. Somehow it shoots out light, like explodes with light, and then it transports me, I mean *us*, back. There's kind of this door, like a portal opening, and then light. When the light fades, the next thing I know I'm dressed like we are now, and people talk to me like I'm this William guy."

Rob stood quiet. He nodded and Steve could see by his brother's surprised expression that he'd seen the light explosion too.

Steve laid the saddle, with its hanging stirrups, on top of the blanket and reached under the horse to tighten the straps. Thankfully, the mare stood unruffled.

He tried to keep his mind working down the two paths: readying a horse for the first time in his life and explaining their time-travel experience. Looking at the bit and reins remaining on the wall, Steve paused and turned directly to his older brother. He'd do his best to explain what he was still trying to figure out for himself. He thought about the conversation he had the other day with Mrs. Okenspire, his honors science teacher. Before these crazy trips in time, he thought Mrs. Okenspire was the weirdest grownup he knew. But, the day before, when Grace missed school, he stayed late after class and talked with Okenspire about time travel. She showed him some different websites, and he had to admit that the stuff she showed him was pretty cool.

Remembering some of the things they'd talked about, Steve asked Rob, "Have you ever heard of Einstein's Theory of Relativity?"

Rob's eyes narrowed. "What are you talking about? What does that have to do with us being trapped in some crazy history thing?"

"It all connects. I promise." Steve tried to speak in his most convincing tone.

Then Rob at least made an effort, "Wasn't Einstein like a real smart guy or something?"

Steve reached for the bit and reins and said, "Yeah, way smart. Anyway, his *Theory of Relativity* says that time can bend, depending on speed. And if you get to the speed of light, then time contracts and kind of just goes away."

Rob moaned, closed his eyes, and slowly started shaking his head. He spit out in frustration and disgust. "That doesn't even make any sense! I don't get it."

Steve examined the horse's bit. It was a small metal rod with leather reins attached. He wondered how to get it into the mare's mouth without losing a finger in the process. He said, "I don't get it either," and he tried to muster the courage to stick the metal bar in between the two rows of horse teeth.

Steve paused, "Ok. Do you remember Mrs. Okenspire at the middle school?"

"The crazy science teacher?"

Steve nodded, "Yep. Anyway, she knows all about Einstein's theory and time travel, and has totally read about this stuff. Yesterday, she showed me a bunch of stuff on the internet and I read it too." He stopped; Steve wondered if Rob would think less of him after admitting that he read the stuff that Okenspire liked.

Rob just lifted his hands and said, "So?"

Steve continued, "And . . . there are some crazy websites on the internet about how, if you could travel at the speed of light, you could go back in time. There are scientists that call these time-traveling tunnels wormholes or an Einstein-Rosen Bridge. It's crazy stuff, but since all these time-traveling things have been happening to me, I've been wondering if the musket ball creates some kind of wormhole or time-traveling bridge. You know, like when the portal door opens and it explodes with light." Steve looked at Rob, wondering how stupid he thought this all sounded.

Rob just shook his head and muttered, "Wormhole?" He closed his eyes, squatted down like a catcher behind home plate, and put his hands on each side of his head.

Steve looked from his brother to the bit, to the horse, and then behind him out the large stable doors to where Dr. Warren was waiting for his horse. The doctor would be appearing there any second. He looked at the bit again. With a big breath, Steve lifted the metal piece and stuck it into the horse's mouth. Thankfully, the mare wiggled her head back and forth only slightly, as she opened and adjusted her teeth to the bit.

Steve flopped the reins, connected to each side of the bit, up and over the mare's head and looked at his work. Not bad! Hanging on the post next to the stall was a rope with a loop. Steve grabbed it, placed the loop over the horse's head, opened the stall, and began leading the horse out. Rob grabbed his arm again. "What do you think you're doing?"

Steve raised his eyebrows and shrugged. "I need to take the horse to Dr. Warren."

Rob shook his head, gripping Steve's arm even tighter. Rob asked, "How many times have you like passed through these wormholes, or whatever they are, with that musket ball?"

Steve looked at the house and saw Dr. Warren walk out. He nodded in the doctor's direction, and motioned for Rob to walk with him. "This is my fifth time." Steve was relieved when Rob dropped the grip on his arm, and walked out with him. Dr. Warren stepped off the porch and took long, hurried steps towards them.

Rob whispered with surprise, "Five times?" Steve nodded and stopped to wait for Dr. Warren. He realized he was at the point on the path closest to the road that Paul Revere had travelled down moments earlier.

Just then, Rob stepped in front of Steve and grabbed the front of his coat. "You need to tell him! You need to tell him everything so that this crazy stuff will end!"

Steve stared at his brother. "Tell him what? What are you talking about?" Dr. Warren's long strides were eating up the distance between them in a hurry.

Rob glared. "Tell him the truth! Tell him we aren't from here. Tell him we're leaving. Tell him . . ."

Dr. Warren reached them and Rob became silent. Warren took the rope off his mare, grabbed the reins, and inspected the saddle strap. "William," he bent over and cinched the strap up under the mare tighter, "you know it must be more snug." The doctor threw a sharp glance in Steve's direction, then mounted the readied horse. "You ginger Goblin so much, no wonder she likes you so."

Steve looked at the soft brown eyes of the horse and thought, Goblin – that's a weird name for such a nice horse. He patted the mare on the snout, glad that she liked him, or William Eustis, or whoever.

Adjusted in his saddle, the doctor turned to his apprentices standing in the cool Boston evening, "Mr. Forbes and William, I'm sure you know this home and office may soon see troops coming down Hanover Street." The doctor looked up the road. "It's time we all leave. For me, I cross tonight from the point in the bay at the Charlestown Ferry and then on to Menotomy. The Committee of Safety at Black Horse Tavern awaits my arrival. Before dawn, you must leave to join the patriots in Menotomy as well. Your association with me and my house compromises your safety here in Boston. I'll send a few of the Sons of Liberty across to escort you to Menotomy. You should plan to meet them at the south side of Mill Pond just before dawn. But, before then, my good friends, I hope to enlist your services."

Dr. Warren reached into his coat pocket and pulled out a small stack of envelopes. "These are for the children. Please see they get delivered to Miss Mercy." Steve's eyes lit up as he took the envelopes. He recognized that name from Grace's stack of internet research. Miss Mercy Scollay and Joseph Warren were engaged.

Dr. Warren continued, "If I'm captured by General Gage or worse," he paused, "Mercy and the children must have these letters and know my love for them." Steve reached for the letters and saw the names on each envelope: Mercy, Betsy, Josey, Dickey and Polly. "Also, I hope to enlist you to communicate the news of this night to Mercy's father. Mr. John Scollay is a true patriot. His services will be needed tonight. He must help Mercy and the little ones out of Boston. Please tell them to make their way to Worcester, then to Doctor Dix's. He is prepared to receive them."

Steve nodded, hoping he could remember it all. Dr. Warren turned Goblin with the reins as he prepared to gallop down Hanover Street.

Before Dr. Warren could spur the horse forward, Rob shoved Steve and spat into his ear. "Tell him!" Steve didn't say anything, so Rob continued to push him forward. Once Rob had something on his mind, Steve knew he wouldn't give in.

The moment before Dr. Warren was about to ride away, Steve blurted, "Wait!" The doctor reared back and looked to Steve. Rob's face relaxed.

"Yes William, what?"

Steve couldn't do it. He couldn't say things that could hurt the relationship he had with this awesome patriot. As much as he knew Rob wanted him to do it, and as much as he would like Dr. Warren to know who he really was, as much as he'd like Dr. Warren to count Steve O'Dell as a friend and not just this William Eustis guy, he couldn't do it. He tried to tell Dr. Warren the whole truth, but it wouldn't come out. He said instead, "Where should we go to find Mr. Scollay and deliver these?" Steve held up the letters while Rob closed his eyes and gritted his teeth.

"At his house, Mr. Eustis, where else at this hour?" Dr. Warren edged Goblin toward the road.

Steve said, "Yeah, well, where is the Scollay's house?"

Dr. Warren tilted his head in confusion. "Mr. Scollay lives next to Old South. Do you not recall that he is a deacon at church?"

Steve nodded. He actually figured he could find the Old South Meeting House. He'd been there twice in the last week – or in the last two hundred and twenty five years, depending on how he calculated it. Steve knew he'd face Rob's wrath, but he stepped aside to let Dr. Warren leave.

The doctor spurred his mare and in moments had disappeared into the streets of Boston.

"What's wrong with you?" Rob shouted as he pushed Steve in the chest. "How are we going to get home now?"

"Have you been listening to a word I said?" Steve shot back. "Telling Dr. Warren that we're from the future does nothing. The only way we get home is with the musket ball."

Steve had never stood up to his brother like this before. But here in the 1700s, things were different. Here in the 1700s, Rob didn't know what to do to survive. Steve did.

As Steve followed Rob back into the house, he turned back to look at old Boston. Just then, he saw them, two bright lights from the top of the Old North Church. He was about to tell Rob when the lights disappeared. He waited. It was done. The famous signal had been planned and now given – "One if by land. Two if by Sea."

Chapter 39

A Warm Fire and a Cold Musket Ball

The interior of the house felt much warmer than the April evening. Logs crackled in the fireplace, and Rob turned to warm his backside. Looking at Steve, he said in a simple matter-of-fact tone, "Okay. Let's get back to our house." He stuck out his hand. "Give it to me and let's go."

Without saying anything, Steve squeezed the ball in his hand. He felt no spark, no buzz, no warmth, nothing. They weren't going home any time soon. But he knew Rob wouldn't take his word for it, so he walked to the fireplace and handed it to Rob.

Rob held the ball and rubbed it with his fingers, then said to Steve, "So what do we do next?" Steve shrugged. Then in a booming voice that bounced and echoed off the dark walls and high ceilings, Rob shouted, "Do it! Make it work!"

Steve shrugged again, and said, "I don't make it work. It just works on its own; I don't know how to make it take us back."

Rob shouted, "What about the worm tunnel stuff you talked about, and that exploding light speed? How do we get through that door you talked about?" Cursing, he spit out the last words, "Do something!"

Rubbing the left side of his face, trying to think, Steve said, "Maybe we both have to touch it at the same time, like when we got sucked through the portal the first time."

"Well, then get over here and touch it." Rob held the ball out to Steve and shook it impatiently, until Steve reached out and touched it. Nothing.

"What the . . . !" Rob's cursing bounced off every wall in the room. "Can't you make it work?"

Steve shrugged and said, "Rob, like – I don't know. It – it gets weird, like kind of warm, and you just know when it's going to work. It's all cold now." Steve nodded toward the musket ball and said, "Usually it just sends me back when the trip is over. Maybe we have to finish what Dr. Warren asked? Maybe we need to leave here and go find Mercy Scollay." Steve patted the letters in the pocket of his coat. "We did say we'd get these to her. Maybe that's what we have to do before the ball will work."

Rob cut him off, "I didn't say I'd do anything, and I'm not leavin' this house. I'm going to wait here until the ball works again." Rob stood, shaking his head. He balled up his hand, squeezing the old bullet. "What do you mean by warm?" Rob glanced to the fire.

Steve watched him eye the flames and said, "It's like a weird warm. Every time I've gone back and forth in time, the ball's gotten this kind of warm feeling just before. But it's not like that," he added as he watched Rob bend down and put the ball in front of the fire on the stone hearth.

His older brother put his hand over the ball to make sure the fire was providing plenty of heat. Satisfied, Rob stood. "There, let's try that. Maybe when it's warmed up it will work."

Steve was pretty sure it wouldn't. The ball seemed to heat up from the inside, not the outside, and only when it someh*ow decided* the adventure was supposed to end. He didn't like his brother's plan to stay and keep waiting. Rob had to know that the British soldiers meant real danger. Steve said, "I think we need to get out of here. Dr. Warren kept looking for Redcoats and I'm worried they're coming."

Rob snorted, "Like real Redcoats?"

"Yeah, real Redcoats. I've seen 'em. I've seen 'em a bunch. I've seen them shoot people. I even crashed into one last time I came back in time and really hurt my leg."

"Whoa, wait, wait, wait . . . you're saying we can really get hurt here?" Rob ran his fingers through his hair. "Like really shooting people? Like this stuff isn't some dream or something?"

Steve nodded, "Yeah, I kind of thought at first these trips were a dream and it was all just happening in my head, but last time I hurt my leg really bad and it still hurt when I got home. I'll show you." Steve pulled down the side of his pants to show his brother. Rob looked at the black and blue bruise as Steve explained, "This hurt when it happened and even more the next morning when I got back – you know, to our time."

Rob didn't say anything. Steve added, "I've seen lots of Redcoats, Rob. Guys with guns and big, long knives on the ends of 'em." He spread his hands apart over sixteen inches to describe the blades. "I'm telling you Rob, we need to get out of he. . . "

Three hard thumps on the door interrupted.

In an instant, Steve hurled himself at the door and pushed the thick board down between the metal brackets on the doorframe. As the thud of the door brace secured the entrance, he heard voices shouting outside. More banging followed. "In the name of the King, open this door immediately!"

Steve turned to his brother and gulped, "I knew we should've left."

Rob stood frozen. He stared as Steve darted toward the kitchen, and waved frantically for him to follow. Rob looked to the front door just as a huge thump jolted both the door and doorframe. Without wasting another second, he raced to the kitchen to join Steve.

Steve lowered his voice and pointed, "There's another door." They scrambled towards it and both ran out into the Boston darkness.

Chapter 40

Rob and the Revolution

Rob followed Steve through the streets of Boston with his head aching and spinning. He was running from real Redcoats! All he wanted to do was look at Steve's musket ball and bug him. He didn't plan to end up in some crazy time trap with real guns and soldiers.

Steve had a head start but Rob knew he could catch up to him. He always did. The cold air pushed through his lungs as he sprinted closer to Steve. Just as he pumped his arms to go even faster, he glanced to his right and saw them. Two red-coated soldiers were coming around from the front. "Halt! By authority of the Crown! Stop this instant!" Rob's heart pounded but he had no plans to stop.

Rob raced harder to get around the corner that Steve had just turned. The second before he rounded the corner, Rob heard it – *Boom*! The zip of the discharged ball zipped past him. "Holy Shiz!" *That was a real bullet*, Rob thought as he put his legs into turbo. He caught up to his brother and together they continued to sprint through the old streets of Boston. After turning the last corner, Rob saw the church his brother seemed to be heading towards.

Rob couldn't believe any of this – Paul Revere, Redcoats, real guns with real bullets, and Steve a seasoned veteran traveling back to the 1700s. After a lot of hard running, Steve finally stopped at the end of a short alley hidden from the light of the moon by the building he was leaning up against.

Gulping down breaths of the cold, Boston air, Rob stood with his hands on the brick wall. Steve gasped, "That shot! I've seen Redcoats shoot at others, but I've never actually been shot at before." Still gulping for air, he said, "I'm worried about this trip. It's different."

He stared at Rob, "We've got to get off these streets." He nodded to the open road. "Okay. We just keep walking toward the Old

South chapel. We've got to act normal." He pointed to the steeple just a few blocks away. Still gulping chestfulls of cold oxygen, Rob followed Steve out of the alley to the new road. He couldn't remember ever following Steve's lead before.

His younger brother turned, walked, looked around corners and continued to the white steeple that served as a beacon above the rooftops. Together they went down the last street. Rob could see the church and the only house near it. Steve pointed to the house and nodded in that direction.

Rob hated following Steve. Ridiculous!

He wanted to get things normal again. He wanted to try again to get home. Just then, he froze. He looked back in the direction of Dr. Warren's house and the warm fire. His stomach sank. Rob closed his eyes and shook his head. His feet stood rooted in place.

Noticing Rob wasn't behind him, Steve stopped. The younger brother looked over his shoulder, and then hurried back to Rob. Steve said in a sharp whisper, "Come on! Let's go. It's the house next to the church."

A heavy dread settled like lead in Rob's stomach. Not wanting to lift his eyes and see his brother's reaction, Rob mumbled, "I left it."

"What are you talking about?"

"I left it. You know, the musket ball. I left it on the fireplace."

Steve's eyes widened. Then he closed his eyes and said, "We can't go back." Rob noted the double meaning in the statement. They couldn't go back to a house filled with Redcoats and they couldn't get back to their world.

Rob straightened, "I wasn't thinking. I just started running." He waited for Steve to make some know-it-all comment, like, "I told you not to put it by the fire," or "You still should've grabbed it." As soon as he did, Rob knew what he'd do. He'd punch Steve so hard in the ribcage that it would knock him off his high pedestal. He'd had enough of this craziness! They might be back in the 1700s, but he'd make Steve remember who was in charge.

But Steve didn't say any of those things. He just shook his head, and turned in the direction of the house that might be the Scollay's home. "Let's get out off the streets."

Rob nodded, a bit surprised. He let his right fingers come out of their tight fist. Both brothers headed to the home next to the old church.

Rob walked next to his younger brother, trying to figure out what bothered him more, the fact that they were stuck back in some crazy other dimension, or that in this other dimension Steve was the one in charge. Rob should lead. He should know what to do. Now, he followed behind his little brother as Steve's eyes darted across dark streets trying to protect them from Redcoats.

Rob had never been scared of riding a white-knuckle roller coaster or tackling a charging fullback. Steve couldn't do either. But now, Rob was the one who kept screwing things up. All he wanted to do was curl up in a tight ball and hide in the next dark corner.

As he stood behind Steve, his brother knocked on the door, waited and knocked again. Rob wondered if anyone would open the door this late, but then the latch clicked. A man, wearing what looked to Rob like a white bed sheet, opened the door just a crack. Then, seeing who was outside, he flung it open for Steve and Rob to enter. The man hurried them both through, saying, "Mr. Eustis, what are you doing at this hour?" The man, in his fifties or early sixties, with sharp gray eyes, square shoulders, and an energetic tone to his voice, put his candle holder on a small mantel attached to the wall near the front door.

Steve asked, "Mr. Scollay?" Rob watched Steve pause for a confirmation, but the older man didn't say anything, he just looked at Steve and waited. After two or three seconds, Steve continued, "Dr. Warren asked us to come and give you these, to give to Mercy and the children."

Rob watched Mr. Scollay take the letters, just as a woman with a thin, petite figure, and long, dark hair tied back in a side ponytail, entered the room. The lady approached Mr. Scollay and he put his arm around her, then placed the letters in her hand.

Rob stared at the woman. She looked at each letter, pressed them to her chest and, turning to Steve, said, "William, thank you. Thank you so much for bringing these." Her voice flowed with an Old Boston-English accent, and Rob tried to think if he'd ever heard words pronounced in a prettier tone. The sweet voice continued, "By chance, William, did Joseph say anything else to you?" Rob looked from Mercy to his brother and wondered why everyone knew Steve. How'd he get so popular?

Steve floundered. Rob had seen many a guy melt under a pretty girl's spell. The tongue gets thick, eyes get big, and words come out in a higher pitch. Steve squeaked out, "Yeah, uhmm, Dr. Warren wanted you to have these." Steve pointed at the letters. "He's worried about things happening tonight. He wants you to leave Boston and take the children to Worchester. I guess somebody named Dr. Dix lives there and he'll help you." Once Steve started, his words gushed out.

Steve looked to Mr. Scollay, then to Mercy. As the candlelight flickered on the faces of those in the entryway, he added the big news, "The war is starting tonight."

Mr. Scollay stared at Steve, and then turned to Mercy, "I'm to make some visits tonight. I think it best if you prepare to travel. I'll talk to Mr. Edes and find how to get you and the children out of Boston. We must get you to safety, to Worchester, and to Dr. Dix. If war is coming, there's no telling what the Regulars might do to Dr. Warren's children."

Mr. Scollay turned and walked to the back of the room, when a little girl stepped forward from the shadows of the hall. Rob guessed this could be Dr. Warren's daughter, and he was pretty sure she'd heard the warning about Dr. Warren's children. Mr. Scollay noticed the young lady too. He placed a hand on her shoulder. "Betsy, Miss Mercy will need help tonight. Will you be a strong girl and help her ready beds for Mr. Eustis and his companion?" Betsy nodded. Her young eyes, like a kitten's, looked for comfort, and wandered through the dark as the old man disappeared deeper into the house to fetch his clothes.

Miss Mercy motioned for Betsy to come to her. The girl, skinny legs sticking out from her white nightgown, made her way to Mercy, who bent down to wrap her arms around her. But before Mercy could share words of comfort, the little girl, looking in her adopted mother's eyes, asked, "Is Papa in danger?"

Mercy held Betsy, shut her eyes and said, "Oh, Betsy, we're always in danger every day of our lives. Sometimes more danger than others. But God grants us His grace and protection. He's mindful of your papa." Mercy stroked Betsy's hair, and her voice rippled with her soft Old Boston accent, "God's watching over your papa while he secures liberty for all of us and for all the colonies."

The little girl snuggled deeper into Mercy's arms. After a long silence, she looked up at the woman and asked, "Can we pray for Papa?" Rob didn't see that one coming. The girl looked about ten.

Miss Mercy dropped to both knees, and leaned back a bit to look into the little girl's eyes. "Certainly." She motioned for Rob and Steve to join. Rob paused, looking to his younger brother, who awkwardly knelt beside the two girls in nightgowns, ready to pray. Rob stumbled into a kneeling position, not quite sure of the procedure. Mercy asked Betsy, "Do you want to say it?" Rob looked curiously at the little kid, but Betsy quickly nodded.

Mercy squeezed her hand and Betsy closed her eyes as both girls folded their arms. Betsy spoke and Rob looked over to his brother, who had closed his eyes just as Mercy and the little girl had. Rob heard the little girl's voice, meek as a sparrow, say, "Dear God, thank you for Papa, and thank you for his friends. Please make them safe tonight. Please bless Papa and Mr. Scollay, and Mr. Revere and Mr. Edes and Mr. Eustis, and his friend with him . . ."

Rob kept his eyes open, watching the young girl pray. When she included him and Steve in her prayers, a wave of warmth filled him. He listened as the girl ended, ". . . Thank you, God, for Miss Mercy, and bless us that we can leave Boston safe. In Jesus' name, amen." Mercy Scollay said nothing. She hugged the little girl, stroking her hair as Betsy squeezed her eyes shut.

Rob noticed her little body tremble. He watched her lay her head on Mercy's shoulder. Steve and Rob looked at each other but said nothing.

After almost a minute of comforting the child, Mercy spoke. "Well, Betsy, I think we had better tend to our guests; what do you think?" Mercy pulled back to look at the little girl. With her small hand smudging across her wet eyes, Betsy Warren nodded, and both girls stood.

Mr. Scollay paced into the room. He'd changed from his nightgown into street clothes, and boots that were as dark as the night on the other side of the door. Quickly, he explained, "Mercy, I'm heading to Mr. Ede's. Be ready to leave Boston with the children upon my return. Until then, tend to Mr. Eustis and his companion."

As his daughter, Mercy, watched, Mr. Scollay put on his dark overcoat. He opened the door, blending into the night just beyond the entrance. Just before he stepped into the dark streets, Mercy burst forward. "Papa, must you leave tonight? The Regulars, will they not be everywhere, patrolling the streets?"

Rob, too, wondered about the old guy going out and confronting Redcoats. He wouldn't want to do it.

"Mercy, many are doing more dangerous things than me tonight, and many more will be in greater danger in the conflict to come." Putting his hand to his three-cornered hat, he said, "I've lived in Boston my whole life and know every alley better than the tomcats. I'll be back before dawn." Then looking to Steve and Rob, he added, "Try to rest, but be ready to journey when I return." Then he added, "I'll be back, God willing."

With these last words, Mr. Scollay disappeared into the night.

Chapter 41

A Night at the Scollay Home

Rob watched Mercy close the door behind Mr. Scollay. He stared at the flickering candle on the wall and at the eerie shadows in the room. He'd been shot at, prayed for, his brother was leading him all around 1775 Boston, and now he was supposed to sleep in some random house until some old Bostonian guy came back and sent him and Steve out of Boston with messages that would help start the Revolutionary War. His head throbbed.

Mercy moved her hands slowly over each of the letters Dr. Warren had sent. She gazed at them with such reverence, as if they were flowers on a funeral casket. Turning to Steve she said, "Mr. Eustis," she paused. "You've been Joseph's friend for a long time." She paused again as she stumbled, trying to find the right words. Placing the letters on a nearby table, she asked, "Did he . . . does he, say things to you about me?" Her eyes darted to the letters in order to avoid making eye contact with Steve.

Steve shrugged. Rob could see him trying to figure out what to say. "Yeah, Dr. Warren said to tell you and the kids that he wanted you to have those letters." Rob cringed. This wasn't what Mercy Scollay was hinting for.

Rob knew what Mercy wanted. She hoped to get information about what Joseph Warren thought about her. Steve, or this Mr. Eustis guy, was one of Dr. Warren's best buddies. Mercy hoped for some inside information about his feelings for her. When it came to girl and guy crushes, things in the 1770s weren't that different from 2001. Rob had seen this happen dozens of times at his lunch table in school.

Mercy bent down and started spreading blankets on the wood floor. She looked at Steve, and said, "I've talked to Rachel, Mr. Revere's new wife, more than once." As little Betsy handed her extra blankets that she then folded up as pillows, Mercy continued, "Rachel told me all about her and Paul, and what it was like marrying a widower with children. She listened to me go on about how much I wished to join her as a wife of a man dedicated to our cause of liberty. But, in the end she had no advice regarding Joseph." Again, Rob noted that look; that, "come on, tell me something he says about me" look. But Steve seemed clueless. Mercy turned to Steve and then patted the top of the folded blanket that served as the pillow.

Mercy paused and lifted the back of her hand to her lip. "Why can Paul remarry and have Rachel to worry for him as his wife and yet Joseph feels the need to delay our marriage?" Sadly she shook her head.

Rob looked to Steve. He could tell Steve had no answer. Rob jumped in. He might not be this Joseph Warren's best buddy, like his brother, but he wasn't going to let this pretty lady's night get any gloomier because his brother didn't know anything about romance and women. "Mercy," Rob knelt down by her as Mercy readied the beds on the floor. "Joseph made us promise we'd deliver those letters to you." Rob nodded to the letters Mercy had set on the table. "When he got on his horse tonight, he wouldn't leave until we promised to tell you how much he loved you." Mercy's face brightened and a small grin started.

Steve spoke again, "Yeah. Like, I know he loves you." Mercy looked at Steve. "Sure, he trusts Paul Revere and I guess, he, like relies on me as his apprentice or something, but he loves you." Steve looked at little Betsy, "If anything happened to Dr. Warren, who'd raise his children?" Mercy closed her eyes and nodded.

Mercy's cheeks were still a little flushed from asking such a bold question, but she said in a resolute tone, "When the conflict ends, God willing, I pray Joseph and I will be together." She looked to the letters again and her faint smile cheered up the dim room. Mercy grinned at both Steve and Rob as she stood and picked up the letters. She tidied the room with Betsy's help, and then left the apprentices to get a little sleep before her father's return.

Chapter 42

The Night Before

Rob lay on his back. The wooden floor pushed through the thin blankets and rubbed on Rob's shoulder blades. But the hard floor wasn't the reason he was still awake. He was worried about what was going on and what would happen to them. Rob stared at the ceiling. "Steve, what's happening? Are we really these William and Johnny guys?"

Steve turned on his side facing his brother. He waited and said, "No. We aren't really these guys." Then he paused, "I think it's the light. Somehow when we go back through the time portal, we come out appearing to everyone who existed back then like these other people. It's not like we're possessing their bodies or something weird like that. I think it's just the light that we come through must make different images for people to see. I'm not sure where the real William Eustis goes, but all the people see the images of William Eustis and Johnny Forbes when they look at us, even though we're still us." Steve rested his elbow on the ground and propped up his head to rest on his hand so he could look at Rob. He asked, "Does that make sense?"

He waited for a response but when none came, he changed the subject. "It starts in the morning." Steve waited. "Do you get it, Rob?"

Rob sighed. He'd wanted to know about the time-traveling stuff, not what was happening in history. He had no clue what his brother was talking about.

"The British," Steve explained. "They're marching right now. In the morning, there'll be a bunch of Americans waiting for them. Paul Revere is telling everyone right now, you know, all the Minutemen, he's telling them to get ready because the British are coming."

Rob just looked up at the grey spots on the ceiling from years of candle smoke. He remembered when he was 13, the family had gone to Lexington for the April 19th reenactment, but he didn't pay much attention. As Rob rolled over to face his brother, he figured this might be the first time he'd ever really wanted to know history stuff. He asked, "Do we, like, do the Americans, win the war tomorrow?"

His little brother shrugged. "Nobody wins the war tomorrow – it goes on for eight years. But tomorrow the British will claim we fired first, and we'll say the British did. We'll win the fighting tomorrow. We won't win at Lexington, but when the British leave Lexington and they march to Concord, we'll fight them at the Old North Bridge. They don't catch us by surprise, like they hoped. We are ready, with guns and lots of men. It's Dr. Warren sending Paul Revere out to warn the Minutemen, and the other guy, the William Dawes guy, and a third guy named Samuel Prescott that joins them along the way and makes it farther than anyone, that wreck the surprise. The British will get stuck fighting tons of Minutemen tomorrow because they'll all be ready and waiting. When the British retreat to Boston, we'll shoot at them, picking them off all the way back." Steve looked at Rob, "You know the town Menotomy that Dr. Warren talked about? Menotomy is like the old name. It's really Arlington. I read about it in the stuff Grace brought to the house. I just couldn't remember how to pronounce the weird old name, but the new name, the one on the map today, is Arlington."

Rob knew about the city of Arlington, Massachusetts. It was just a few towns north of Needham. He'd played in a baseball tournament there last summer.

Thinking about Dr. Warren in Arlington or Menotomy made Rob think about Dr. Warren's house and the musket ball he'd left by the fire. Rob looked at Steve. "I'm sorry I left the musket ball and I'm sorry I blamed you for everything that's happened." Apologizing to Steve came easier than he'd thought. He'd never done it before.

Steve smiled and nodded but then lay back flat on the floor and looked up. "Don't worry, we'll get it back."

Steve's voice had lost the positive excitement he had had when telling Rob about their nation's history. Rob reassured his little brother, "Yeah, we'll get the musket ball and then go to Menotomy and find Dr. Warren. We can tell him whatever news Mr. Scollay brings back, and then our mission will be done. And we can finally get back home." Rob waited for a reaction from Steve, but Steve just looked at the ceiling. Rob asked, "Right?"

Steve closed his eyes, nodded, and then turned on his side.

Hours later, Rob woke up to see two men standing over his brother. Rob recognized one as Mr. Scollay, the other was much younger. "Mr. Eustis?" Mr. Scollay bent down and shook Steve's shoulder. Steve sat up and looked at the two men. Scollay continued, "Mr. Eustis, I must send you and Mr. Forbes along quickly. I visited Mr. Edes tonight. The Regulars left his print shop in ruins."

Steve was barely awake but listened carefully as Mr. Scollay said, "Mr. Edes barely escaped with his family, as well with their apprentice, Mr. Lyte." He nodded towards the young man standing beside him, whom Rob assumed was Mr. Lyte. "I believe both you and Mr. Forbes met James Lyte when he was with the other Sons of Liberty from the north end." The other man nodded to the brothers. He had a look as stern as Mr. Scollay, but he was less than half Scollay's age.

Mr. Scollay went on, "The Regulars have ransacked every patriots' home and place of business like never before. Dr. Warren must know the damage and know it's deliberate. Tell him the Edes and Gill shop has been destroyed. The printing press was broken to pieces. His own home has been torn apart. General Gage's men are intent on starting a war. The men outside the city must know there is no freedom or liberty to be had inside Boston. It must be taken from outside."

Mercy entered the room holding a candle, with little Betsy by her side. Mercy approached her father and he put his arm around her. He said to her directly, "Mr. Edes told me the city is to be sealed. You and the children must leave tonight if we are to get you to Dr. Dix. You must leave for Worchester by way of the Roxbury Neck.[25] Mr. Edes said the Regulars stationed there are allowing women and children to leave, but he and I both question for how long. When you pass through the neck, you mustn't identify the children as Dr. Warren's. They will be known as Dix children and you are Mrs. Dix returning to Worcester."

The next ten minutes exploded into activity. Mercy woke and readied the children while Mr. Scollay helped prepare Steve and Rob for their next assignment. James Lyte stood by the door, pacing and peeking into the darkness beyond the safety of the Scollay home.

Dr. Warren's children stood huddled together in the drawing room. Betsy knelt down and talked to a smaller boy who stood with wide eyes, bewildered by the rush of activity. Rob was worried for them. He wanted to ask Steve, "Do they get out? Do they make it to Worcester?" But the questions would have to wait.

James Lyte stood ready to lead Steve and Rob, Dr. Warren's apprentices, to the rendezvous site where two Sons of Liberty would be waiting on the south side of Mill Pond. After getting them to their point of departure, James would retrieve Dr. Warren's horse and ride Goblin back to Mr. Scollay's house for safekeeping. Before leaving, Rob looked at Mercy and the children. He was glad the children had received their father's letters and happy he'd helped deliver them.

James Lyte opened the door. The black, cool air entered. Rob eyed the dark streets, then he turned to look back at Mercy and the children. He nodded to them in a way meant to say goodbye and good luck. Before he stepped into the darkness, Rob heard Mr. Scollay whisper in a somber tone, "May God bless and watch over us all tonight."

James herded the group from the house at a quick pace, keeping them close to the buildings. He looked constantly in every direction, watching for Redcoats. Before crossing the second street, Rob came right next to James and said, "Hum. Hey, excuse me, James, before leaving Boston, we need to stop by Dr. Warren's house."

---

25 *Roxbury Neck* was a narrow strip of land that connected the city of Boston to the mainland in the 1770s. Until the city of Boston filled in this back bay, the Roxbury Neck (also called the Boston Neck) was the only land route connecting the city of Boston to the mainland. On the night before the Battles of Lexington, Concord and Menotomy, William Dawes went by way of the Roxbury Neck while Paul Revere and the British crossed Boston Harbor in a boat.

James didn't slow his pace. He just glanced at Rob and said, "We can't." Rob waited for more explanation, but none followed.

Rob said again, "Like, I know you really want to help get us out of Boston, but we have to get something from Dr. Warren's house first."

Again, James didn't break stride. "The Regulars ransacked the doctor's house tonight, and may still be there. I don't particularly wish to confront Regulars on Hanover Street, with only two unarmed physician's apprentices."

Rob's stomach tightened. He knew Regulars meant Redcoats, the same group of soldiers that had shot at him earlier.

Steve abruptly stopped walking, pointing to a different road. "Isn't Dr. Warren's house in that direction?"

James turned around, shooting quick looks to the east and west, but didn't answer. Steve said again, "Isn't it?" and then added, "James, we're going there with or without you. We've got to get something and can't leave Boston without it."

James took his hat off and ran his hands through his hair. He looked in the direction of Hanover Street, towards Dr. Warren's house, but remained silent. Steve added, "Dr. Warren would want us to return and retrieve the item. We're going back."

James shook his head, "I would think Dr. Warren would most prefer his apprentices make it out of Boston alive." He stood his ground. Steve stared at the Son of Liberty and said, "What we are getting at Dr. Warren's house is a matter of life and death, and we are getting it with or without your help and protection." Steve emphasized the last word while eyeing the pistol James had tucked in his belt.

With a tightened jaw, James turned abruptly and quickened his already brisk pace towards the doctor's home.

Mr. Edes' report to Mr. Scollay proved true. Broken glass, cracked furniture and scattered papers filled the room and hallway, but luckily no Regulars remained. James and Steve stayed at the front door watching the street as Rob entered the house alone. He pushed his way past busted and knocked-over furniture. Upon reaching the fireplace, his heart stopped. Nothing remained of the fire. The logs had burned to ash and the hearth sat cold, but by some miracle the musket ball lay in the same place he'd left it. Rob bent down and picked it up.

He felt so relieved. He felt like he could cry. Then he thought, No way! Quickly he turned his head and blinked hard a few times. With Steve standing in the doorway, there was no way he was going to let that happen. He might apologize to his little brother, but there was no world or time period where he would ever let him see him cry.

Chapter 43

At Dawn with Sons of Liberty

James looked up and down the shoreline. Next to him, Rob and Steve stood by, quiet. James took quick strides in one direction and then the other. Although it was still dark, a glow from the East had just begun to light the edge of the sky. After several moments of looking for the Sons of Liberty, Rob began to worry a bit. Then two men, a little older than Rob, stepped out from behind the sea bushes and moved towards them. Neither group said a word until they were close enough to whisper.

James reached out his hand, speaking first, "These are Dr. Warren's apprentices." The two men nodded and extended a hand to Steve and then Rob. Rob listened as they said their names at a volume that was barely above the ripple of the tide.

The one with a square jaw and blond hair identified himself as Noah. The other had darker hair and brown skin. "I'm Nathan," he said in a hushed voice.

Before his companion had finished introducing himself, Noah had already stepped silently to the enclosure behind the bush. He uncovered a boat they had hidden in the brush and slid it into the water. The wooden craft looked no larger than an oversized bathtub and the distant shore, muted in the rays of the moon and an early morning glow, looked a mile away. Rob thought of the lifeguard training he'd completed in eighth grade and worried he might need it today.

Nathan whispered, "Come quick. We've already seen Regulars patrolling the shores."

James turned to Steve. Then putting a hand on Nathan's shoulder, he pulled him closer. As Nathan bent down toward Steve, Rob saw the medal hanging from a leather chain around his neck. Nathan, sensing James' purpose, put his hand to the medal and pulled it up for Rob and Steve to see. On the medal was engraved a tree and the word *LIBERTY*. Taking his hand from Nathan's shoulder, James said, "These are Sons of Liberty." Steve and Rob both nodded. James went on, "Tell the doctor that the Sons of Liberty who remain in Boston will gather information for him. Tell him what we discovered tonight, and that we are willing to fight from the inside." Steve nodded again. Noah and Nathan were both now waiting, casting anxious looks up and down the shore.

In less than two minutes, James retrieved Goblin, Dr. Warren's mare, and Steve and Rob sat with their knees to their chest in the boat, watching Noah row with strokes that fell as soft as snowflakes.

When Steve started to speak, Nathan placed his finger to his lips and shook his head. Rob watched Noah continue to lift, drop, pull, lift, drop, pull. Each stroke becoming quieter than the last. They continued in nerve-racking silence until a cry from shore caused all four of them to whip their heads around to the coast.

"Halt! In the name of the King, return to shore!"

Like an explosion, Noah plunged the oars deep into the bay and each stroke now thrashed and heaved at the water. The small boat jolted, and Rob gripped the wooden edge to keep from plunging face first into the black water. That's when he heard the crack of the first musket. Turning toward the explosion, he saw a fire burst from the second soldier's musket with another loud bang. The musket ball skipped across the water, right in front of the boat. The first soldier had straightened his musket and began pouring powder and loading a ball to try to get a second shot in while they were still in range. Rob's hands shook. Nothing on a football field could scare him. But now, being shot at by Redcoats, taught him that being brave on a football field was nothing compared to bravery in battle.

"Get down!" Nathan's voice cut between the shots. Instantly, they all ducked and Noah dodged as best he could while still pulling oars through the misty bay. By the time the two soldiers fired again, the noise echoed half as loud, and the threat from Boston's shoreline faded like the shoreline itself. As the second discharges landed somewhere far from them, the sun cracked the horizon.

With the threat of taking a bullet to the chest now gone, Nathan straightened and asked Noah if he wanted a break from rowing. Noah shook his head, and said, "We'll be 'cross shortly. I'm fine." Big drops of sweat pooled on his forehead.

Nathan turned to Rob and Steve. "Well, men, we've escaped Boston." He afforded himself a brief smile. "I feel we lacked time for a proper introduction on shore. I'm Nathan Chamberlain from Needham." Upon hearing the name of their town, Steve looked to Rob. Rob acknowledged the coincidence with raised eyebrows.

Noah paused rowing for a minute in order to shake their hands, "I'm Noah Russell from Menotomy." Turning to Steve, he said, "I think we met a couple of weeks ago when Dr. Warren was traveling through the town." The sun's morning rays were just beginning to bounce across the bay. Rob could see their destination lay less than a hundred yards away.

Noah positioned the tiny boat to approach a patch of sand on the Charleston shore. With three strong pulls of the oar, he brought the boat up onto the sand and then retired the oars inside the craft. "I've marched these trails from Menotomy to Boston over a hundred times. Today, we take the Old Indian Trail. It's longer and rougher, but free of Regulars." Noah pointed to their left. He then led them in, pulling the boat further ashore. They hid it in the bushes far above the tide lines.

Noah led them on an overgrown trail not much wider than a 12-inch ruler. As they marched on, the four of them rarely stopped and hardly talked. They did catch their breath a few times by streams, where they stopped to drink and fill water containers. During one of these breaks, Noah and Nathan shared biscuits they called hardtack. Rob decided the name fit. It felt like he was eating a white hockey puck. He figured if the Americans ran out of musket balls, they could shoot pieces of this stuff. But he was starving, and he found if you cracked a piece off in your mouth and drank some water, it softened enough to swallow.

After walking miles they reached the crest of a large hill. At the top, Noah pointed and said, "Just over there is Menotomy. When we get there, we'll visit my house so I can gather my musket and ammunition." Rob had noted that Nathan carried a rifle with him while Noah traveled unarmed.

Rob thought about Noah going to get his musket and ammunition. Having been shot at more than once, he liked the idea of being with someone who could shoot back. But he figured the best option would be to avoid the shooting all together.

Chapter 44

Menotomy

The sun had passed the midpoint in the sky and inched west by the time Noah lead them out of the woods. They'd walked for miles and had not seen a single house. Now, Rob saw a village far off to their right, popping out from the trees. The group headed parallel to the village, until they reached a wooden sign that said, Concord Road. Noah pointed up the road to the village and said, "Here's Menotomy. My house is next to the curve in the main road."

Rob looked ahead, dreaming of the golden arches of McDonalds or a red and white KFC bucket. Instead he saw a steeple and a few dozen buildings forming the center of the village, and a lot of homes dotting the surrounding countryside.

More than a few people now marched on the same road they were on. Six men marched 30 or 40 yards ahead, and behind them Rob could see two or three other groups making their way towards Menotomy. Nathan turned to Steve, "Mr. Eustis, this is a good sign." He nodded to the men ahead, "The militiamen are coming." Each man ahead and those behind their small group had a musket strapped across their back. Approaching the town limits, more and more men appeared. All carried muskets.

After entering the village and winding through a few roads, Noah stopped and looked in the direction of a group gathered in front of a building. He turned to the rest of them and said, "That's the Black Horse Tavern. Maybe Dr. Warren is here."

Rob and the others headed to the building that acted as the hive of activity. When they got closer, Rob saw the sign for the tavern, a black stallion standing with his front hoofs raised. They'd accomplished another task in this crazy world of Dr. Warren's – they made it to the tavern. Men spilled in and out of the building. The gathering sparked an energy that Rob could feel. Although he knew that getting ready for a battle and getting ready for a football season were very different, the energy at the tavern felt like the first gathering of players at the first practice of a football season. Rob walked with his group into the tavern. The men inside spotted Rob's companions and some nodded in their direction. One taller, younger man nudged his shorter friend and took his hat off, nodding toward Steve. Rob continued to be amazed at the reputation his little brother had everywhere they went.

The two men approached them. The shorter, stockier man said to Steve, "Mr. Eustis, I presume?" Steve looked at the young man and nodded. The man's eyes stayed focused on Steve, "I'm Perley Putnam of Danvers. I recall that you came with Dr. Warren last month. At that time, you and the good doctor counseled us to be ready, and the Danvers men heeded the doctor's words. Yes sir, we're ready in full force. We've come with over 150 men from Danvers. Heard the alarm, yes sir, and marched almost sixteen miles in four hours."

Steve turned to Nathan and Noah. He was confused about why the man would be telling him this. Perley went on, "About an hour ago, Dr. Warren asked Captain Foster to employ strategies here in Menotomy, rather than chasing towards the retreating Regulars, seeing as how's we'd already marched so much this morning."

Steve said, "Did you say Dr. Warren talked to your, um, captain today? Is Dr. Warren here?"

The other man with Perley stepped forward, "You just missed the doctor." He extended a hand to Steve. "I'm Dennis Wallis. You and Dr. Warren gave a mighty fine speech last month in Danvers. But I tell you, Dr. Warren's speech today has all the men ready to fight the entire King's army! The good doctor told us about all that's been happening today. Have you heard how the war's begun?" Steve shook his head.

With the same excitement and energy that rippled through the militiamen, Dennis shared the news, "Dr. Warren told us all about the Lexington standoff. Yes, sir, the Redcoats fired and fired, killing Lexington men, and then our militias met the Regulars. Things weren't like

Lexington at the Old North Bridge. No sir, we was firing back, and we chased the King's Regulars, all of them, right out of Concord." The tall young man nodded and said, "Yes, sir, if not for General Percy's reinforcements and cannons coming' up from Boston, General Smith and his men would've all been done in. The doctor left with buckets and buckets of men, over a hundred. Doctor Warren and Colonel Heath are marching now to meet retreating Regulars. They'll pick 'em off. Yep, pick 'em all off from along the roadsides and snipe 'em in the rear. The red snake winding down the road will be 'bout dead when it gets here, and we'll kill it! Yes, sir, we'll kill it! Kill it here, in Menotomy. It's not slithering past here, no sir!" There was a chorus of cheering and thumping on the tavern's tables. The man spit out the last words and Rob watched and listened in amazement at the passion and bravery this group had.

Just then, a man with a black beard and sturdy leather apron nudged past him towards his younger brother and said, "Mr. Eustis, I'm Ethan Wetherby, keeper of the Black Horse Tavern. Dr. Warren asked about you and Mr. Forbes before he left. He said you'd be bringing news from Boston. That you were to pass it to me, and I'd place it with other messages and letters he left." The man nodded in the direction of the counter. "You can scribe the notices and, God willing, Dr. Warren will read the information tonight after he and General Heath fix the King's Regulars."

Perfect! Rob liked the idea. His brother could write the information about Mr. Edes' print shop, Dr. Warren's house, and the big mess in Boston just like Mr. Scollay had told them. Steve would write the note and seal it up for Dr. Warren. Finally, they'd be done! They could get out of this crazy time trap before the King's Regulars or red snake or whatever you wanted to call it, got back to Menotomy.

The tavern keeper, Mr. Wetherby, had already stepped to the counter and pulled a piece of paper, feather, and inkwell from the back shelf. He placed the paper and ink on the counter, and handed Steve the feather. Steve looked at the light brown and white-lined plumage and said, more to himself than the tavern keeper, "I'm supposed to write with this?"

Hearing Steve's comment, Mr. Wetherby nodded as he reached for the knife in his pocket. "Sorry, Mr. Eustis, that pen's point is as worn as a dull rock." Rob watched the tavern keeper make two precise slices with his knife through the end of the feather to create a tight point. The innkeeper eyed his handiwork and said, handing the feather to Steve, "That'll do. Now you can pen the notices."

Steve took the sharpened goose feather, looked at the inkwell, and then back to the feather. He eyed the feather from top to bottom before dipping it in the glass ink jar. Ink dribbled across the paper as he started to write. Each time he reloaded the feather with ink, he dripped black across the page. His pen strokes only added to the mess, and pushing too hard, he broke the tip of the feather. Rob watched.

Steve turned to the innkeeper shaking his head and said, "I'm done. This feather doesn't work." Mr. Wetherby picked up the scribbly, ink-coated paper and raised his eyebrows. After examining the sloppy mess for a moment, the tavern keeper reached over to the shelf behind the counter and pulled out another sheet of paper. He took the broken feather from Steve and with a few strokes of his knife, he again sharpened the point. "Mr. Eustis, you may dictate the message you wish to share with Dr. Warren, and I will act as scribe. I'll make sure the doctor receives the news in a manner that he can decipher." In less than five minutes, the note got transcribed and was sealed with a wax seal. Mr. Wetherby placed it with other envelopes and said, "I'll keep safe the note, join it with these other messages of importance."

Rob gazed around the old wooden tavern. Men filled every space in the building. Many of the men were scraping food from wooden bowls. Rob's empty stomach rumbled.

Either the tavern keeper noticed Rob eying the wood bowls or he heard his stomach, because moments later he asked, "Mr. Eustis, would you and your men like some beef stew? We made extra today but after feeding half of the colony, I'm not sure how much remains."

Rob looked at Steve and nodded vigorously. In less than a minute, Steve, Rob, Nathan and Noah stood at the corner of the counter, the only open space in the tavern, with four bowls of Black Horse Tavern stew.

At this time, the Danvers men excused themselves. They'd already eaten and their company was readying to join the Danvers Militia and to prepare to face the Regulars. The taller Danvers fellow, the one named Dennis, asked them to join the militia in making sure no Regulars made it back to Boston. Noah and Nathan both stated that they planned on doing just that after gathering Noah's musket.

Steve looked to Rob. Rob shook his head. He didn't look up; he just lifted a bite of the stew and blew on it. Chased by Redcoats more than once. Shot at three times. He wouldn't be adding to that count by joining the Danvers Militia. He was going to finish his stew and then make the dang musket ball work. If it didn't work in the tavern, they'd go with Noah to his house and stay at the Russell house until they figured out how to make the crazy thing heat up. No fighting. No shooting. And no more Redcoats.

Chapter 45

Jason Russell's Home

Less than ten minutes after eating their Black Horse Tavern stew, they were walking up the Concord Road towards Noah's house. No one talked much. Steve got closer to Rob and started walking slower, creating distance behind Noah and Nathan. He looked ahead at the two Sons of Liberty. After a minute, he turned to Rob and said, "Are you sure you don't want to join them?" Steve nodded towards the other two. "Maybe we need to go with them. Like, maybe we need to somehow help Dr. Warren with this fighting before the ball will work again."

Rob shook his head, without making eye contact with his little brother. He wanted to swat Steve for saying something so dumb! Rob looked at the farmhouse they were approaching to their right. The house stood tall. But around it, everything was eerily quiet.

Turning to his brother, Rob groaned, "We're doing what we said. We're going to Noah's house and we'll wait there until all the fighting is done. That's it." Snarling, he added, "Come on, Steve. Don't be stupid! We don't belong here. I'm seriously not getting shot at again."

Rob got it. He knew that Steve couldn't just *make the ball work.* In his heart, he worried that Steve might be right, that the ball might never work unless they fought with the militia. But that wasn't going to happen.

As they turned a bend, Noah pointed a little further down the path. A house placed at an angle towards the old colonial road stood in front of them, and a swarm of men buzzed around it. They pushed shovels and swung picks, expanding an already lengthy trench. Long muskets rested in the corner of the deep earth seam that stretched the length of thirty yards. Rob looked at the house, and then stared at the men digging, building up banks and readying themselves for battle.

At the sight of it all, Rob squatted down and with bended knees like a baseball catcher behind home plate, he put his head between his hands. He'd tried so hard to avoid the war. Now, they were right in the middle of it.

Rob watched Steve come back toward him and saw two men from the earth fort hop up out of the trench and walk to greet Noah and Nathan. Dennis and Perley, the two men from the tavern, came up to the Sons of Liberty while Rob stayed in place. Steve bent down next to him, "Are you okay, Rob?"

Rob was disgusted at having his little brother feel sorry for him. He shook his head. "Oh, sure, I'm fine!" Rob spit out each word. "I-just-want-to-get-out-of-here." Almost pleading, he said, "Let's try the stupid ball again." Rob dropped his hand to brace himself on the ground.

Steve pulled the musket ball from his pocket. He showed no reaction to his brother's rudeness. Steve reached out to Rob to help him up, but Rob shook his head and stood on his own, ignoring Steve's help. Rob stretched his hand to Steve's right palm where the musket ball sat. They both touched the round lead ball.

Nothing.

Rob burst out, "Really? Seriously! What is wrong with this dumb thing?" He tried to shove the ball out of Steve's hand, but Steve had already wrapped his fingers back around it. Rob kicked a clump of dirt and then fell down on his knees.

Just then, Noah called over to them, "Mr. Eustis and Mr. Forbes, the Danvers leader, Captain Foster, intends to confront the Regulars at this bend in the road, here across the street from my house." Noah nodded to the nearby family home. "Nathan and I intend to join the Danvers Company here."

Dennis stepped forward, "Mr. Eustis, you and your apprentice are welcome in the trench. To be truthful, we will likely need a good doctor with us." The four men's eyes drilled into Steve, who turned to Rob.

Rob didn't hesitate. Staring back at the four men he replied, "No."

"Your presence in the fort will be sorely needed, and even if not needed, it would certainly boost the morale of the men."

Rob didn't wait for him to continue, "No. We'll both be in the house, or . . ." Rob looked down the road, "We may go to a different house."

Now, Noah spoke, "The other houses will all be locked and empty. The women and children have gone into the hills." Noah spat the words "women and children" at Rob, glaring at him, challenging him to stand up and fight like a man. "Only the men are left here to fight."

Rob shook his head. There was no chance he was going to risk his life fighting in some battle he didn't even understand.

Steve said, "We'll be in Noah's house and we'll be happy to help from there."

Steve, Rob and their group moved toward the Russell house. But before they walked past the trenches, a man rushed by towards the center of the company. One of the men in the trenches exclaimed, "That's Israel Hutchinson." Everyone in the group stopped digging and turned to listen.

Winded, Israel stood in front of an older gentleman and spoke between large gasps of air, "They're flanking! They're coming around the sides. The Regulars . . . the Regulars aren't marching straight. They're flanking their positions." Just as the words poured out of the gasping militiaman, the sounds of muted shooting and a cannon up the road highlighted his report.

The sweating and spent militiaman glanced up the road and then back at their older leader. Israel tried to catch his breath and speak slower, "Captain Foster, the Regulars aren't going to approach from the road, they are going around, sending parties of men to the flanks. We need to spread our forces to the sides." Israel swept his arm towards the Russell house and towards the other side of the road, emphasizing his point.

The Danvers captain stood thinking, then shook his head. He looked to the trench. "We can't. The front is the direction we face and the direction we protect. We stay together and use the redoubt[26] we've worked to build." The shots up the road continued, echoing a bit louder with each round.

Israel Hutchinson started to plead his case again, and Rob strained to hear. Noah looked up the road to where the battle sounded, and hurriedly motioned for them to follow him. Rob followed Noah in the direction of the house. But he could hear Israel's final plea, that the fort would do them no good when the Regulars attacked them from the sides. Rob looked off to each side of the road and then at the trenches that only protected the soldiers from the front. He worried. What would happen to those men if Israel Hutchinson's predictions were right?

Rob, Steve and Noah entered the house. Inside, Rob and Steve saw six or seven minutemen listening intently to an older gentleman speak. Upon seeing Noah, the older man stopped talking, brightened and embraced Noah in a hug. Rob immediately noted their resemblance.

Noah turned to Steve and said, "Father, this is Mr. William Eustis, Dr. Warren's associate, and this is Mr. Johnny Forbes, their apprentice." Noah continued, "These are the men that the committee of safety requested we retrieve from Boston. Mr. Eustis and Mr. Forbes, this is my father, Jason Russell."

Rob and Steve both nodded, while Noah placed his hand on Steve's shoulder. Noah added, "Father, I intend to grab the Brown Bess[27] and join the Danvers Company. With your blessing, Mr. Eustis and Mr. Forbes will stay here."

Unfortunately, no blessing would be given.

---

26 *Redoubt* is an older term used in former battles and wars referring to a temporary fortification, usually involving earth trenches and mounds.

27 "*Brown Bess*" was a nickname used for the British Army smoothbore musket, used from 1722 to 1838. Many Americans owned a Brown Bess from their time serving in the French and Indian Wars from 1754-63. Many Americans fought with the British against the French and certain Indian tribes. Or, they had a Brown Bess from having purchased one from an American veteran of the French and Indian War or from a British soldier.

Rob saw them first. From the side window, over two dozen red-coated soldiers appeared, stretching out through the trees. Rob lifted his arm to point. He tried to warn the others, but his tongue was frozen. Before the men in the room could follow Rob's pointed finger to the window, gunfire cut through the spring air.

The British soldiers had worked their way around the flank of the road, attacking the small party from the sides, just as Israel Hutchinson had warned. From Lexington and Concord, the Redcoats had been mercilessly fired upon by American Minutemen hiding along the road behind trees and rocks. The men in red were haggard, beaten soldiers, ready to do anything to get back to Boston alive.

Rob watched as other Redcoats set fire to a house across the road. Mr. Russell also stared through the window as flames begin to engulf his neighbor's porch. Immediately, Noah scrambled to organize the men in his father's house, while his father continued to stare in shock at the flames. Then Mr. Russell made a terrible mistake. He burst outside to plead with the approaching soldiers. Rob watched in horror at what happened next.

At the edge of his yard, Mr. Russell lifted his arms with his hands held high, demonstrating to the three approaching soldiers that he meant no harm. "Please, please!" he pleaded. "An Englishman's house is his castle. Please, spare this house." Rob watched the haggard and beaten soldiers approach within an arm's reach. Then, without the slightest hesitation and without saying a word, one of the soldiers leveled his musket with the bayonet pointed at Mr. Russell's chest. Rob's knees buckled as he saw the soldier thrust the blade forward and the bloody point of the bayonet protrude out of the old man's back.

Jason Russell crumbled to the ground. The other two Redcoats lifted their own muskets and thrust their bayonets into the crumbled old man lying in front of his own home.

Rob held on to the windowsill, his legs giving way underneath him. He'd seen people killed in movies or video games, but not like this . . . not real people, not in real life!

He saw Steve watching but no one else had seen the tragedy. Although Noah had been spared from seeing his own father killed, Rob realized that if Noah lived through the day, he'd find his father in his own yard with gaping holes through his chest.

Steve's face was as pale as an eggshell. Silently, he turned to Rob and pointed to the stairs. Distant sounds now grew closer as the men in the house began firing upon the Redcoats. The first floor filled with smoke, and musket balls from outside exploded into the Russell home.[28] Steve and Rob scrambled up the stairs, while wood cracked and splintered all around them. The British musket balls peppered the stairs and walls.

On the second floor, Rob and Steve found an unoccupied room with an open window facing the main road. Steve headed to the window to assess their situation. Rob leaned against a wall and slid down. He closed his eyes, trying to purge the picture of Mr. Russell's body and the bloodied bayonet from his mind. He sat on the floor and thought, *How did I get in this nightmare?*

Steve had been standing and looking at the battle from the window when suddenly he yelled, "Rob, it's Dr. Warren!" Rob struggled to pick himself up and stumbled over.

A man by Dr. Warren's side barked commands to the Minutemen around them as both he and Dr. Warren took cover behind an outbuilding near the Russell home. Rob stood near Steve and watched Dr. Warren sprint behind the shed. A militiaman following Dr. Warren was stopped short by a three-quarter-inch-wide ball of British lead. Watching the soldier struggle, Rob's stomach tightened. Then, to his amazement, the doctor left the protection of the shed to assist the fallen patriot. After providing aid, Dr. Warren dragged the injured militiaman back behind the cover of the outbuilding.

From their view on the second floor, Rob and Steve saw something Dr. Warren did not see. A British soldier had maneuvered behind

---

28 *Jason Russell House* still stands. It still has the holes in the stairs and walls from the April 19, 1775, battle in and around the home. The house is now a museum in the town of Arlington (formerly Menotomy), Massachusetts. Additionally, Jason Russell did make the fatal mistake of approaching British soldiers on April 19, 1775, and pleading that they save his home. The soldiers bayoneted and killed him on the spot, in his own front yard.

a tree near the shed and now had his musket leveled at the doctor. Steve shouted through the open window, louder than Rob had ever heard Steve yell, "Look out!" The doctor turned to look in Steve's direction just as the British musket discharged. The ball whizzed past the doctor's head so close that it knocked a hairpin[29] from his white wig. Having missed its mark by mere inches, the musket ball exploded into the wall of the shed. Dr. Warren's injured companion turned and fired his pistol in the direction of the British soldier, forcing the Redcoat to retreat.

Dr. Warren placed his hand to his wig and turned to see who had given him the signal that had saved his life. Looking up, he saw Steve, and mouthed, "Thank you, William." Steve acknowledged the gesture with a nod.

Watching Dr. Warren and the other colonists confront the British regiment,[30] Steve said, "I want to be with him." Rob's mouth gaped open. A bullet had just missed Dr. Warren's head by less than an inch and Steve wanted to be with him? Rob stared at his brother and wondered how the smartest person he knew could be saying the dumbest thing.

Rob was ready to tell Steve the millions of reasons why two teenagers from 2001 shouldn't be fighting in a Revolutionary War battle when his brother said in a thoughtful voice, "I think he needs us. He wouldn't be alive right now if it wasn't for us being here."

Rob kept silent. Pointing to the doctor, now a hundred yards up the road, Steve said, "Do you see him leading the attack?" With a slight nod, Rob acknowledged he did.

What Rob and Steve didn't see were the two British soldiers who had made their way into the upstairs bedroom.

---

29 *Dr. Warren's Hairpin* was shot out of his wig by a British soldier in the Battle of Menotomy, on April 19, 1775. The fighting in Menotomy was more intense than in any of the other battles fought on the first day of the Revolutionary War.

30 *Regiment* is a military unit of about 700 to 1,000 men, usually under the command of a colonel. Each infantry regiment was divided into 10 companies with each company having 8 to 10 officers, 38 to 70 private soldiers, and 1 to 2 drummers.

Chapter 46

The Way Back from Menotomy

Rob heard a floorboard creak behind them. He reeled around and saw the first red-coated soldier lunge forward with his musket. The second followed, both bayonets leveled in their direction.

Rob's only word "No!" could have been his last, but for his quick reflexes. The closest Redcoat made a quick, deep thrust that would have fileted Rob's chest down the middle but for his experience as a quarterback side-stepping attacking linebackers. His quick feet saved his life, but not his arm. Rob experienced firsthand the sting of British steel as it sliced through the flesh of his right arm.

Rob instinctively slapped his left hand over the wound. Blood began to ooze between his fingers and the stinging pain confirmed that this was no dream. Rob could see in the Redcoat's eyes that he wanted more than just a flesh wound.

The attacking soldier prepared for another lunge with the bayonet, but his comrade yelled, "Michael! They're unarmed." The less aggressive soldier placed his arm across Michael's chest. Rob and Steve stood at their mercy. After a moment of hesitation, the Redcoat named Michael tilted his bayonet upward, and reluctantly abandoned his plan to kill what he believed were two rebels.

The soldier vented his frustration by hocking back and ejecting forward enough spit to cover the left side of Rob's face. Then he snarled, turned to his comrade and nodded toward the doorway. With British spit oozing down Rob's left eye, and blood dripping to the floor, he watched the Redcoats leave.

With the soldiers gone, Rob could breathe again. He tried wiping the ooze from his eye with his left hand and accidentally smeared blood across his face. Steve swallowed, trying not to look at Rob's spit-covered face with blood mixed into the slime.

Rob had never felt so beaten in his life. He could take a fastball to the ribs or a blindsided tackle, but right now he stood bleeding, beaten, and scared.

Steve put a hand on Rob's shoulder. Rob looked at the hand. He'd never needed comfort from Steve before. Never. He didn't feel like the undefeated quarterback or the starting pitcher in the state playoff series that he was. Using a tone he'd never used before with his brother, Rob asked, "Steve, do you think we could try the musket ball again?" Steve nodded.

Rob hoped they'd experienced enough of the 1770s. Besides, Steve looked at his bleeding arm and both of them knew he needed a doctor. Even though Rob liked Steve's friend, Dr. Warren, he wanted his arm fixed by a 21st century doctor.

Pulling the ball from his pocket, Steve opened his hand and turned to Rob. Silently Rob reached out with his good arm and touched his fingers to the ball.

Nothing happened. After waiting a second, Rob shook his head and simply said. "We're never going to get back." Rob sounded defeated, broken. Steve eyed the blood flowing from Rob's cut. The red drops slowly dripped from his fingers. Steve glanced at the long gash. "I'm real worried. You've got to get that mess sewed up."

Still staring at Rob's right hand and the dripping blood, Steve suddenly had an idea. "Rob –" But just as Steve started to explain, a voice roared from below their room. "There's two more up there!"

"Dang! We've got to barricade the door. Quick!" Steve jumped toward the dresser.

The only thing big enough to block the door was this eight drawer dresser standing up against the wall. Steve grabbed it first and pushed with two hands; Rob joined him, pushing only with his good arm. Somehow, they managed to slide it against the door before the soldiers burst in.

Turning to the window, Rob eyed the distance to the ground. "Can we jump?" He stuck his head out the window to calculate the distance, but as soon as he did, a musket discharged from below, causing splinters from the windowpane to spray his neck and head.

Outside, the British soldier pointed in their direction and shouted orders to another group of Redcoats.

Rob looked back to the dresser; his brother was braced against it. The banging on the bedroom door had begun. They were stuck.

The soldiers pushed against the dresser barricade while Rob rushed to help hold it against the door. "Aargh!" He moaned in pain as the soldiers thrust against the door and the dresser smashed into his injured arm. The jolt pushed a surge of blood from the gash. The makeshift barricade wouldn't hold for much longer. Rob's arm ached while blood bubbled out.

Steve braced his back against the dresser and turned to Rob, his eyes glancing at the gash in his brother's right arm. Then he pulled the musket ball from his pocket.

"Let's try again! Quick, touch, with that hand." Steve nodded to the bloodied arm. Fighting the push of the soldiers, they were sliding backwards with the dresser. Rob lifted his injured arm, and placed his blood-soaked fingers on the lead ball. When the bloody fingers touched the ball, it exploded with energy.

The soldiers burst through the door, just as a blast of light raced past the Redcoats and engulfed the two brothers.

Chapter 47

A Revolutionary Wound in the 21st Century

Grace and Curtis stood beside the kitchen table as if no time had passed. But when the two boys suddenly stopped wrestling, Grace's eyes widened. She pointed to Rob's right hand, "There's blood!"

Rob and Steve pushed themselves up. Then, Rob reached over and hugged Steve with his uninjured arm. Awkwardly, Steve returned the side hug with a bear hug of his own. Curtis made a face. Grace just stared.

Curtis blurted out, "What's going on? You were rolling and fighting and now you're all huggin!" Usually real smooth, Curtis stood looking like he'd just shot two airballs from the free throw line.

Steve helped Rob to the table. Blood dripped from Rob's forearm and puddled on the wood surface. The wound was too high up on his arm to see with the long-sleeved shirt.

Rob grimaced, and said, "I need to take my arm out of my shirt." Steve helped him undo the buttons on the front of the shirt and together they gently moved his right arm out of the sleeve.

Grace gasped and turned her head. The deep slash spanned from Rob's elbow to his shoulder.

Curtis gaped at the wound, then gasped, "Whaattt haapppenned?" The words came out like a kid watching his first magic trick. He couldn't take his eyes off the red mess coming from the gash. Rob's 21st century shirt had blood stains all over but no rip or tear.

Rob winced and squeezed his eyes shut. Through clenched teeth, he begged, "I need a towel. Something. I've got to put …."

Grace grabbed her hoodie from off her chair, "Here . . ."

Rob bit his lower lip, "Thanks."

Taking deep breaths, Rob looked toward Curtis. "Steve can tell you all about it."

Ignoring Curtis, Steve looked at Grace and explained that Rob and he had traveled back to April 19, 1775. "We saw Joseph Warren send Paul Revere on his ride. We fought with the Minutemen at Menotomy. We saw the British soldiers retreating from Lexington and Concord back to Boston." While Steve talked, Grace looked at him and nodded. Curtis, on the other hand, wrinkled his forehead. His expression became tighter and tighter with each statement as he physically shifted his chair farther and farther away from Steve and his crazy story.

"Steve! Really. What are you talking about?" Curtis stood, shaking his head.

Steve looked directly at Curtis. "Curtis, you can believe me or not, but what I just told you is the truth. Rob's arm got slashed by a British Redcoat's bayonet while we were hiding in a house along the main street of a town called Menotomy."

"Steve! Seriously . . . where's your sense?" Curtis turned to his best friend. "Tell me what happened to your arm! Like, what really happened. Something on the floor cut it?" Curtis turned, looking for something sharp on the floor.

As he held the hoodie against the wound, Rob looked at his buddy. "Curt, it's all true, just like Steve said. When we were fighting, we both grabbed the musket ball on the floor, and it transported us back to this doctor's house. We saw him send Paul Revere to start the Revolutionary War. After all that, I got cut real bad by a bayonet, and we grabbed the ball together and found ourselves trying to get up off this floor." Rob waited.

Steve watched. Curtis looked hurt, as if he'd become the butt of a joke. Good at dishing out teasing, Curtis didn't like being on the receiving side.

Rob tried again, "Curtis, really dude, I promise that's how I cut my arm. I swear, bud."

Curtis looked at his best friend for a while. He glanced at Steve, and then back to Rob. "I don't know how you did it. I don't know how you got that nasty thing" pointing to the cut, "without ripping your shirt. But, I know you didn't get it from no British soldier's bayonet! Now you tell me the truth or I'm leavin'."

Rob looked up at him. "It's the truth, Curt. I swear."

Curtis eyed his friend. He waited as if hoping the story would change. Then he pushed his chair to the side and marched across the kitchen. When he got to the door, he looked back. "When you go to the hospital to get that thing stitched up, do me a favor and tell the doctor to look at your brains!" He slammed the door on his way out.

The three remaining teens sat quietly, staring at the door. Then Grace said, "Walking out of the O'Dell's kitchen because you think you're being teased about time travel stories . . ." looking at Steve, Grace raised her hand, "I can relate."

Steve smiled and so did Grace.

Their smiles quickly faded as the reality of their messy situation set in. Grace turned from Steve to Rob, "Guys, we've got to find a way to get Rob to the hospital to fix that up. And, speaking from experience, as someone who hasn't traveled back to 1770s Boston, I think it's best not to tell anyone else," her eyebrows raised, "about the British bayonet."

Rob nodded and, turning to Steve, said, "I think I've got a plan that will work." He opened a drawer and found some scissors. Dropping the bloodied hoodie, he took his shirt off and handed the scissors to Steve. "Okay, cut my sleeve above where the bayonet sliced me."

Steve hesitated. "You want me to cut your shirt?"

Without waiting for Steve to figure out the plan, Rob opened another drawer and grabbed a metal ice cream scooper. Wincing a little, Rob walked to the clear pane in the kitchen pantry door. He paused less than a second and then swung the scooper into the glass. Shards shattered everywhere. Rob jumped away and put the scooper back in the drawer.

Steve's face exploded with shock! "Rob, what the heck are you doing?" Grace just stood with her mouth open.

Rob pointed again to his shirt sleeve. "You need to hurry and cut my sleeve up." With clenched teeth, he nodded to his sliced arm, and added, "This really hurts."

Steve started cutting. Shaking his head at the glass on the kitchen floor, Steve said, "What were you thinking? What're you gonna tell Mom?"

Rob answered, "We're going to tell her that you were tossing me a pudding pack and that I ran into the pantry door. It broke and one of the pieces cut me." Rob put extra emphasis on the plural, *We're.*

Steve spent three precious seconds thinking it through. He turned to Grace, "Will you call my mom and tell her Rob's hurt?"

Grace ran her fingers through her hair, closed her eyes, and said, "Really?"

Steve looked at the glass on the floor, the broken pane in the door and Rob's sliced shirt. "Okay. I'll call her, but Rob's plan is what we need to stick to. Okay?" Steve eyed Grace and waited.

She was nervously bouncing while shaking her head. "I don't like this. I hate lying. I'm terrible at it."

Steve hunched his shoulders. "Will you just go along?"

Grace closed her eyes and turned her head. Steve waited. He turned to the shards of glass sparkling on the wood floor. Rob looked at Steve and nodded to Grace. Steve again looked to Grace. Reluctantly, she said, "I guess."

Ten minutes later, Steve sat with Rob in the car. With the corroborating story from Grace, Mom hurried to get Rob to the hospital. She was so worried about Rob's cut, she only scolded them for not being more careful.

As they sat in the back seat on the way to the hospital, Steve helped Rob apply pressure to the wound, correcting his grip twice so that he applied it the right way. Rob asked, "How do you know about this stuff?"

Thinking about the cold March 5th night in Boston, Steve said, "A doctor in the very old part of Boston showed me." Rob nodded and winked confirmation that he got the reference to Dr. Warren.

Mom went with Rob into the treatment part of the emergency room, while Steve sat alone in the lobby. As he sat there alone, he thought about the musket ball. He pulled it out.

Why did it work sometimes and not other times?

Why did the ball do nothing now but other times surged with enough energy to transport him back to Dr. Warren's life and times?

Why Dr. Warren?

Why did it take Rob but not Grace?

Why did his great uncle have it?

"Why? Why? Why?"

Not really meaning to, Steve actually spoke the last three words out loud.

Nobody in the waiting room was paying any attention to Steve, except one man. When he heard Steve mumble the words "Why?" the man with the black fitted sweater and tinted glasses put down his magazine. He stared at the boy. He knew all the answers to the "Whys?" The man's eyes focused on Steve's right hand. He wanted to make contact with Steve. He had asked the Society for permission, almost begged. The Society received his request and asked him to be patient. He needed to wait a little longer. So the man stretched out his long legs in his nice tailored pants, and waited in a hospital waiting room.

He studied the young man on the other side of the room. Soon he'd walk up to Steve O'Dell. Soon he'd explain. Soon the boy would learn all about the T3 he held in his right hand. But not today.

Chapter 48

Stitches, Bayonets and Kisses

Steve sat there for almost an hour, thinking. He never noticed the man in the corner. Finally, Mom's voice interrupted his thoughts. "He's done." Her words split the quiet of the room. "Seventy one stitches." Steve's eyes widened. Mom said it again, "Yeah, seventy one." Rob stood next to Mom with his sleeve cut off and a long line of black thread crisscrossing a slice of his arm.

Steve looked at the line of black thread down Rob's bicep and repeated, "Seventy one?"

He let the musket ball fall in his jacket pocket and pulled his hand out. Mom scolded again, "Now do you see why you can't horse-play like that? The doctor told us he was a medic in the army and said he hadn't seen injuries like this since he'd tended to GIs[31] cut from bayonets." Steve's eyes shot open. Rob stood behind Mom and raised his eyebrows and nodded.

Steve said, "Sorry. It won't happen again."

He didn't talk the whole ride home. Even when Rob asked him what he was thinking about – an acknowledgment that Rob rarely, if ever, had extended before – Steve just said, "Nothing."

But he was thinking about something. This old bullet from the Revolution had so much power and had come to him in such a weird way. *Why?* Steve thought about his great uncle. He thought about all the strange letters and stuff that come with the ball. It must have some purpose. He must be having these crazy trips for some reason. He thought about his experiences with Dr. Warren. Why did he go

---

31 *G.I.* is a term that stands for "Government Issue." During World War II, when soldiers were drafted and required to serve in the military, it became common to refer to new soldiers as G.I.s, "government issued." This became a common term for all soldiers. In the 1960s, a toy army action figure was named "G.I. Joe."

back this last time? Rob had almost been killed. Was the musket ball good or bad?

When they got back home, Steve moved his dirty clothes off the chair in his bedroom so he could sit at his desk. He pushed the reading light on and started thumbing through the stack of papers Grace had given him. He was trying to concentrate on the papers, but he kept thinking about Grace's smile, the hug and that kiss.

Steve looked through the stack of papers talking about all his adventures back to the 1770s with Dr. Warren. Grace had gathered it all and read it all. She was an amazing friend, or did she want to be more than just a friend?

Steve's head started to hurt. He wanted to read all the stuff Grace had given him, but his mind kept wandering back to that really cute, mischievous smile, just before the kiss.

Just then Rob burst in. Usually he only came into Steve's bedroom if he wanted to take something, but Steve could tell that something was different tonight. "Hey, what are you doing?" Rob never asked questions like that to Steve.

Steve pushed the papers to the side, "Oh, just looking at stuff."

Rob sat on his bed. Steve asked, "What's up?"

Rob talked to Steve like he talked to his basketball buddies, "Mom said I can stay home tomorrow. No school. One good thing about this." Rob smiled and pointed to his bandaged arm.

"What about basketball? Will you miss any games?" Steve knew that would be much more important than school.

"Only a few practices, but I should be able to play by our next game." Rob looked at the papers next to Steve. "Is all that stuff about Dr. Warren?" Steve nodded. Rob asked, "Is it like stuff about what we saw and the other things you've done with him?" He seemed genuinely interested.

Steve nodded, "Yeah. It's a bunch of information about Dr. Warren that Grace gave to me."

Steve stopped. He looked at Rob. Of course! Rob knew all about this kind of stuff. Why hadn't he thought to talk to him about Grace before?

Steve shot up from his chair, and closed the door. This needed to be private. As he sat back down, Steve said, "Rob . . ."

After a long silence, Rob finally said, "Yeah. What's up?" Rob's words had a caring tone, no mean bite. This gave Steve just enough courage.

"Rob, I've never kissed a girl." Steve paused.

Rob tilted his head. "Well, that's a bit random." He smiled. He looked amused but not mean. Steve didn't know how to keep going. Rob waited. When Steve didn't say anything, Rob asked, "Does kissing a girl have anything to do with this stuff Grace gave you?" He added, "It doesn't seem too connected, all this 1700s stuff and kissing a girl." He acted as if he really cared.

Steve said, "Okay. It's related." He paused again. He couldn't make the right words come out.

With eyebrows raised, Rob looked at the papers from Grace, then at Steve. Putting two and two together, he smiled, "You want to kiss Grace, but don't know how."

Steve paused, then half nodded.

Rob laughed, but not in a mean way. "Oh, Steve. I can help you." He sat up straight on the bed. "I've been there a hundred times." Steve questioned the hundred times, but he wasn't going to say anything. This whole conversation was a lot easier with Rob taking charge.

Rob kept going, "There's two things about kissing, Steve. It's like sports. First, you need to know when to make the play and second you have to do it right. Does that make sense?"

Seeing the confusion on Steve's face, Rob said, "Okay. Let me explain. First, the right time. If you try to kiss a girl and it's the wrong time, it's a disaster. Like throwing an air ball from the free-throw line." Rob had his hands in front of him, moving them to emphasize his point. "It can be really hard to know if a girl wants you to kiss her. There's, like, a certain mood – like a pumpkin pie moment."

Steve wrinkled his nose and tilted his head, "A 'pumpkin pie moment'?" This was getting more complex than he'd anticipated. He thought about the morning with Grace and wondered, "But what if a girl just kisses you?"

Rob shook a finger at his little brother. "Okay, I'll explain the pumpkin pie moment. But first, I've done this a bunch and I've never had a girl kiss me first. Sure, if a girl kissed you, that could tell you something, but don't wait for that to happen. It'd be like making a half-court shot just before the buzzer, it happens, but don't count on it. Trust me on that."

Steve was wondering about his brother's expertise. But he didn't say anything about his own experience earlier that day with Grace. He just kept listening.

"Okay, I'm going to explain the pumpkin pie moment. But first, you have to remember there is timing and then technique. You have to pick the right time. But, even more important, you have to know how to kiss." Rob nodded with confidence, "I'm telling you this as your brother. Kissing is like shooting free throws, you only get better with practice. And when it's game time, you've better put in the practice if you want to score points. Does that make sense? Curtis and I figured this out."

Oh, boy. Now Steve was getting some of Curtis' expertise too.

Rob waited. "Do you get it? You can't only practice when you're really kissing a girl. That's like a game- time free throw. You have to practice before it's game time or you'll mess up in the game." Rob leaned forward. "We're going to get you a pumpkin."

Steve stared in silence. He tilted his chin down, looked at his brother and said, "Pumpkin?"

Rod nodded, "Yep. You can still get them at the store even after Halloween and Thanksgiving."

"Rob, why do I need a pumpkin?"

Rob acted a bit surprised that Steve wasn't catching on. "To practice, of course."

Steve sat in his chair, just blinking. He couldn't tell if Rob was serious. He said nothing.

Rob nodded, "It works, Steve. Curtis and I figured this out in sixth grade. Curtis' big sister Cassie told him he should practice kissing his arm. Kissing your own arm? That seemed weird, you know kissing yourself. So, we tried pumpkins." Steve's mind was racing.

He was trying to figure out how kissing a pumpkin was less weird. "Kissing a pumpkin is the best way to practice kissing a girl. You can kiss it straight on, or from the side, and the curves and creases in the pumpkin are just like lips, but not as soft." Rob slapped Steve's leg, and pointed at him again, "Don't tell anyone. But, yeah, you need a pumpkin about the size of Grace's head and then you can practice. Kissing a pumpkin and shooting free throws, it's the way to practice before the real thing."

When he'd started this conversation with Rob, Steve never thought in a million years that he'd be thinking about kissing a pumpkin.

"I'm telling you, Steve, it works. I've had a lot of practice."

Steve stopped him, "With pumpkins?"

"No, bro. Pumpkins are just how I learned to kiss. Now it's with real girls. Do you know Mimi Braziel?"

Relieved that his older brother wasn't still kissing pumpkins, Steve said, "Yeah. I know who she is." Everyone knew Mimi Braziel. She was the prettiest girl in Needham, and a year or two older than Rob.

Rob smiled, "Mimi Braziel said I was a great kisser."

Steve had no idea his brother had kissed Mimi Braziel, or that she thought he was a great kisser. Or, most importantly, that Rob believed kissing greatness started with pumpkins. Steve was shaking his head. He wasn't a believer.

But Rob wasn't done; he had more to share. "Now do you get what I meant by the pumpkin pie moment?" Steve shrugged. Rob clarified, "There is just that moment when the air around you and the girl smells as sweet as pumpkin pie, hot out of the oven. You can feel it. Then when you kiss her, it's sweeter than any pumpkin pie you've ever tasted. It's awesome." Rob stood up. He'd imparted a lot of Rob and Curtis wisdom. Steve appreciated the effort, but really? Kissing pumpkins?

Smiling, Rob said, "We'll get you a pumpkin."

The whole experience with Rob in his room, talking to him like a friend, was nice, but very strange--in more ways than one. Then Rob did something that was even more strange. He pointed to the papers from Grace, and with a serious look said, "Good luck with all that. Maybe I could look at it, too, when you're done."

Steve nodded and said, "Yeah. Sure."

Rob smiled back and left.

Steve sat at his desk. It had been hard to focus on the stack of papers before Rob came in, but now, after his conversation with Rob, it was almost impossible to get his mind clear of pumpkins, kissing and Grace. But he was determined to do it. He was going to read every page.

As Steve read through the night, a man sat in his vehicle watching. He watched all through the midnight hours. The man's eyes were focused on the light in Steve's window that never went out.

The next day at school, Steve had deep grey bags under his eyes. A little before the first bell rang, he met up with Grace and told her about Rob and the hospital. He left out any mention of pumpkins.

"Wow! Seventy one stitches," Grace grimaced.

"Yeah, the doctor said the cut needed stitches on the inside and on the outside." Steve grimaced too as he thought about the long line of black lacings going up Rob's right arm.

"How's he doing?"

"Well, he says it hurts but he was glad because he got to miss school."

The bell rang for class, and Steve and Grace began walking. Steve took a deep breath, "Grace, I stayed up real late last night reading about Joseph Warren. Thanks for researching all that stuff. It's real cool." Steve was saying thanks, but he knew that Grace could tell that there was something else.

After a long pause, Grace spoke, "You read about how Joseph Warren dies at Bunker Hill when he's just thirty-four, didn't you?"

Steve's eyes drooped. "While reading the stuff you gave me, I kept asking, why are these crazy things happening to me? What's the reason?" Steve's words came slowly as he gripped his history book tight in his right hand.

They reached Grace's first period room. Steve looked down the hall to his U.S. History class. He knew the second bell would sound any second, but he had to tell her the answer to his *Why* questions. Without looking at Grace, he just blurted out the words, "I'm going to save him from Bunker Hill."

Grace turned from her class doorway to look at him. She stared at her best friend. "What did you just say?"

Chapter 49

He Should be Remembered

The second bell rang. Both Steve and Grace ignored it. Grace stood a few feet from her class waiting for an answer.

"I have the stuff to do it right here," Steve pulled a bag out of his pocket. It held the musket ball and a few white pills.

Grace shook her head. "Are you crazy?" Standing between her class and her friend, she said, "No. Really. What are you thinking? No way--we need to talk. Don't do anything before we talk about this, okay?"

Steve glanced around and nodded over to her homeroom, "I'll talk to you more after class." Then he turned and walked down the hall.

Entering his U.S. History class late, he was relieved to see a substitute teacher at the front of the room. The young woman stood by a television and VHS machine. Steve's mood brightened just a bit. A substitute and a movie – perfect. He was exhausted from planning all night how he was going to save Dr. Warren. He was in desperate need of a nap.

The substitute talked while Steve positioned his chin between his folded arms on his desk, eyes ready to close as soon as the lights went out. The substitute said she was a graduate student studying history at Wellesley College just up the highway. Steve didn't really care. Then she said, "This video we're going to watch today is called, *'The Conflict Ignites.'* It's the first tape in a series documenting the American Revolution. This video discusses how the Revolutionary War started."

Steve lifted his head. What had she said? "The American Revolution and how it started." He grinned. Joseph Warren was for sure going to be in this video. He wondered how similar the actor would look to the real Joseph Warren.

Even after the lights were out, Steve sat up straight, eyes glued to the screen. He watched the guys he knew, the men he'd met with Dr. Warren – Sam Adams, Paul Revere, and John Hancock. The video showed reenactments of stuff he'd lived through – The Boston Massacre, the Tea Party, Lexington and Concord. The video began wrapping up just before the bell, and Steve realized that there would be no mention of Joseph Warren. None. Tons of early patriots and a bunch of events were mentioned, but not one mention of Joseph Warren. Not one.[32]

The bell rang, and the class emptied. Steve got up slowly and walked over to the young lady bent over the VHS machine, rewinding the video for the next class. Looking up, the young teacher smiled. She looked pleasant, much more normal than other substitute teachers. Straightening up, she asked, "Do you have a question?"

Steve said, "Did you notice they didn't say anything about Dr. Joseph Warren in the video?" He looked back at the U.S. History graduate student. She seemed smart.

Her eyebrows knitted together, and her answer confirmed Steve's suspicion, "Doctor who?" She shook her head, "I don't think I recognize that name. Who did you say again?"

Without much hope, Steve said, "Dr. Joseph Warren, the patriot guy that sent Paul Revere on his midnight ride and like helped organize the Boston Tea Party."

The substitute shook her head again, "I'm sorry. I don't think I've ever heard of him."

The sudden feeling in his chest surprised Steve. Her words replayed in his mind, "I don't think I've ever heard of him." He didn't just hear the words. He felt them.

His thoughts now raced way past the classroom and the substitute. He nodded and said a dull "Okay, thanks." He looked out the classroom and into the busy hall, his hand hidden in his coat pocket,

---

32 *1994 Greystone Communication A&E Presentation – The Conflict Ignites* – The author watched this video. Just like Steve, he hoped to see Dr. Warren depicted in the early events leading up to the revolution. Many patriots from Boston were mentioned. Many important events were described. The author felt the disappointment that Steve felt when Dr. Joseph Warren was not mentioned. He had been forgotten.

fingers wrapped around the ball in the bag. How could a documentary about the beginning of the American Revolution not mention Dr. Warren?

Stepping out of his history class, Steve saw Grace bouncing and weaving through crowds of students to get to him. Out of breath, she said, "Steve, I've been thinking about what you said, you know about saving Dr. Warren?" Grace looked at him. "Steve, are you listening to me?"

When he glanced at her, she continued, "You're just a teenager. You can't somehow change history. You can't just save Dr. Warren from dying at Bunker Hill. Tons of people died in that battle – like more than any battle of the Revolutionary War."

Grace paused, "Steve, if you go back to Bunker Hill, you could die." Steve just stared silently down the hall. "Are you even listening?"

"Grace, I just know you're wrong." Finding the musket ball in his pocket, he squeezed harder. "It doesn't make sense that this time-traveling stuff is happening for no reason. Really, I can save Dr. Warren. He's not going to die in that battle." Turning from Grace he added, "I'm supposed to save Dr. Warren. I . . . "

Without allowing Steve to continue, Grace waved her hand, "Stop! Stop! This is stupid! How do you know this is what you're supposed to do? How can you say this? And how can you even save him? It's a major battle in a huge war!"

"Grace, there's a reason why these things are happening to me, and I think I finally know why. After I help Dr. Warren live past Bunker Hill . . ." Steve stopped. Grace waited for him to continue. "After I save him, he'll be famous. He won't be forgotten. He'll be like his friends, the other Founding Fathers we talk about, you know, like the ones who are in movies and textbooks and stuff." Steve's voice choked up. Quickly he stopped. What the heck, why was he getting emotional?

Embarrassed, he whispered, "I know he'll do great things after Bunker Hill. Everybody will remember him. It's not fair that he's lost from history."

Grace closed her eyes and gripped her books so hard her knuckles turned white.

Steve continued, "Grace, in the stuff you gave me off the internet, President Reagan quoted Joseph Warren in one of his speeches. I don't remember exactly what he said, but something about most Americans don't know Joseph Warren because he died so early during the Revolution. Do you remember that?"

Grace shrugged, but her silence didn't stop Steve, "What about the stuff from the *Daughters of the American Revolution* that you gave me. Do you remember that article?" [33]

Grace looked clueless regarding this article too. She said, "No. I have no idea what the article said, but it doesn't matter. Your idea about changing history is crazy! You can't stop him from dying."

"You're wrong. The article you gave me does matter. It said that out of all the Founding Fathers, the men who started our country, only George Washington has more stuff, like cities and counties named after him than Joseph Warren."

Steve emphasized his point, "Grace, everybody used to know Dr. Warren and named a bunch of things after him to honor him. But, now, nobody has a clue who he is, or what he did. Grace, not even a history teacher knew who he was."

Grace listened. She bit her lower lip, then said, "Steve, I know Dr. Warren is important to you, but changing history is impossible. Seriously, how would you even do this?"

Steve pulled his hand from his pocket and showed her the musket ball next to two full-sized white pills. "Sleeping pills. Dr. Warren is going to sleep through the battle." Grace made a face. Steve continued, "The white pills are from my dad's dentist office at work. They

---

33 *Daughters of the American Revolution* is a patriotic organization deeply committed to the memory of the American Revolution. While researching about Dr. Warren, many internet articles from the Daughters of the American Revolution, including those from the Joseph Warren Chapter, were very helpful. I learned that numerous geographical landmarks were named after Joseph Warren. Since then, the information from the Daughters of the American Revolution is no longer found on the internet, but this quote from the Warren Township Historical Society; Warren History, Volume One, No. 1, Spring 1989, is helpful. "Young America remembered the heroes of her revolution by bestowing their names on towns and villages still only wilderness when independence was won. Washington gave his name to innumerable counties, cities, towns, lakes, rivers and mountains. A close second in popularity was Dr. Joseph Warren."

are, like, way powerful. My sister Elizabeth took these when she got her wisdom teeth pulled last summer and not even the blast of a cannon could've woken her up."

Grace's eyes filled with worry. She opened her mouth to speak, but Steve didn't wait to hear her arguments. "No matter what you say, I'm going to do this." He wrapped his fist around the ball and pills, plunged them back into his coat pocket, and started walking away. Grace caught up, and they both walked to their next class in silence. Grace arrived. Steve took a few more steps before turning to look at her. "I just don't think my experiences with Dr. Warren are just for me. Or, I guess now for Rob, too." He looked at Grace. "It doesn't make sense that these crazy trips to the past are happening for just two teenagers. I think it's happening so I can help our country."

Grace shut her eyes and rubbed her hand across her face.

The second bell rang and they both ignored it for the second time that day. "Steve," Grace said, her voice softer now, "There's something eerie about that musket ball. You know it. You even said so yourself."

Steve knew what she was talking about. He slid his hand into his pocket and rubbed the rough lead. A familiar warmth caused his fingers to tingle and immediately spread up Steve's arm.

Looking to his hand and then back to Grace, he watched the image of Miss Grace Levy blur. Then in a second, she'd vanished in light.

Chapter 50

A Toast

When the flash from the light dimmed, Steve found himself sitting at a large wooden table in a room lit by a dozen or so candles on the walls. The light flickered across the faces of those present. Joseph Warren sat at the head of the table, while eight other men sat listening. Steve looked around but recognized no one.

"This is the report." The man speaking sat down. Dr. Warren nodded and Steve watched as he pushed his chair back and stood. His gaze fixed momentarily on each man around the table.

Finally, Dr. Warren spoke, "Well then, the wheels are in motion. In the morning the British will wake and see the redoubt. As we speak, men are swinging picks and heaving shovels in order to build their earthen fort. And, tomorrow, these same men will defend it with their lives against King George's Regulars."

Dr. Warren straightened himself and glanced at the men around the table. "More than anyone in this room, I am responsible for sending the men to the hill." He paused as if anticipating backlash, and then said, "When the British cannons fire tomorrow, I intend to be with the men I have sent."

A wave of disapproving murmuring began to circulate around the table. "Absurd!" An older, heavier gentleman pushed himself from the table to better direct his statements at the young doctor. "You are the President of the Provincial Congress[34] as well as the Chairman of this Committee of Safety.[35] The idea of you being on the Hill tomorrow is ridiculous!" The man lifted his arms. "Surely you recognize this."

34 *The Provincial Congress* was a law-making body that Massachusetts and other colonies formed in opposition to the ruling British government. Dr. Warren was the head of this governing assembly.
35 *The Committee of Safety* was a group in Massachusetts and other colonies that worked to root out those who were not loyal to American independence and they worked to prepare the Colony for war if necessary.

All the men in the room nodded in agreement. Some even pounded their fists on the table to show their agreement.

Dr. Warren tried to appease the group, saying, "These statements are true. However, I am also to be a commissioned General. As a General, the men I command must know I am willing to accompany them into battle and that I'm willing to pay the same price for this nation that they are being asked to pay." Dr. Warren motioned to the wall behind Steve, "Gentleman, the men we are sending to the Hill tomorrow must confront the King's army behind a wall of earth they construct in one night. They are farmers and fathers. Not a one is a paid soldier, nor are they learned army engineers. Tomorrow, behind this mound of dirt, they are to exchange blows with the world's greatest military might." Placing his hands on the table and leaning in closer to the men so that the light of the candles flickered in his eyes, the doctor said in a voice filled with conviction, "My men need me, and I swear before God, I will not let them down."

The older man also leaned forward, looking eye to eye with Dr. Warren. In a deeper voice he said, "The men have Colonel Prescott and Colonel Putnam. You are to be a Major General. Generals do not fight in battles. Generals orchestrate them! Captains and colonels fight battles." Pounding his fist, the larger man added, "More than a general, you are the chairman of this Committee of Safety and the selected President of the Provincial Congress. If you leave in the morning for the redoubt you will be the most rash, reckless, and ridiculed leader we could have chosen! You, Sir Joseph Warren, will not be worthy of the titles you bear or the trust that has been placed on you."

The man's words hung over the table. The older man sat back down, still fuming.

Dr. Warren straightened and walked around the table to where the older gentleman sat. Everyone's attention was riveted on the two men. Recognizing his opportunity, Steve sprang into action. Everything had fallen into place. No one was looking in his direction. He reached into his left pocket and felt around. His fingers found the musket ball, but where were the pills? Stretching his fingers to the far corners of his pocket, he finally found them.

Pulling the pills out, he placed them on the table, and quickly crushed them with the backside of his spoon.

Dr. Warren was addressing the group again, but Steve was too consumed with his task to pay much attention. Steve kept smashing the pills, but soon realized he'd made a mistake. He should have ground the pills on a plate and not on the old wooden table. Much of the powder from the pills had fallen into the grain of the wood. He scraped as much as he could off the table and sprinkled what was left into the glass of red wine at Dr. Warren's seat. Dr. Warren just needed to return to his seat and take a drink before the meeting adjourned.

The older man now stood. He reached for Dr. Warren's hand and said in a soft voice, "I don't mean to be critical, my friend. May God grant to you the wisdom to see that your talents are needed for the duration of the conflict. We need you beyond tomorrow's battle."

Joseph nodded, acknowledging his colleague's concerns. "Fair enough, my good friend. We will leave it to the graces of our good Lord. We will let Him that rules all influence these events that affect so many. Only He knows how this will end or the best course to follow."

All the men nodded and began to rise from their seats. Steve could tell they were wrapping up the meeting. He panicked.

Ignoring his nerves, Steve grabbed the goblet in front of him and stood. Raising the glass in the air, he screeched in a higher-pitched voice than anticipated, "A toast! A toast to tomorrow's success and God's blessings."

All eyes turned to Steve. The men around the table hesitated, looking a bit bewildered. Steve now realized it might have been inappropriate for the apprentice to be making the toast. He stood in front of the crowd with a glass held high and everyone staring at him. The back of his collar was wet with nervous sweat.

Thankfully, Dr. Warren came to his aid. He put one hand on Steve's shoulder and with the other, picked up his glass of wine. "A finer, more loyal friend and apprentice a man could not ask for. Surely, we can all drink to success and God's blessing." The doctor held up his glass and drank his wine.

The men all raised their glasses and "Here! Here!" echoed throughout the room.

Chapter 51

June Morning

After the meeting the previous evening, Steve had walked with Dr. Warren from the parlor of the West Cambridge home to a nearby guest house. As they started walking, Dr. Warren began complaining about how tired he felt. Steve helped him to his bed and within minutes Dr. Warren was sound asleep.

Morning came, but Dr. Warren did not wake up.

The sun shone and its rays warmed Steve's face. He sat in a wicker rocking chair in front of the house and tried to enjoy the day. He knew that today, June 17, 1775, meant the Battle of Bunker Hill. He knew that many men would die today, more than in any other battle of the Revolution. But he also knew that thanks to him, Dr. Joseph Warren would not be one of them.

Steve looked over the gardens with their summer flowers. The bees meandered from flower to flower in the warm summer sun. He thought about how history would change because of what he had done.

First, Dr. Warren and Mercy Scollay would get married. This would mean that Betsy and the other children he saw at the Scollay house would grow up with a mom and dad.

Next, Dr. Warren might become as important as George Washington. If Dr. Warren lived to help fight as a general in the other battles of the Revolution, there was a good chance he would become one of the nation's early presidents, maybe even the first president. Or, he might help write the Declaration of Independence. Steve had read that Dr. Warren's ideas in the Suffolk Resolves had inspired Thomas

Jefferson when he and John Adams wrote the Declaration of Independence. And if not a writer, Dr. Warren could at least be a signer of the Declaration of Independence.

There were so many other things Dr. Warren could do with a longer life – things that Steve couldn't even think up. But no matter what he ended up doing, he would live and he would be *remembered.* To Steve, that seemed the important thing.

Still, as he sat back and rocked on the porch, something bothered Steve. Since waking up and coming outside, he'd thought more and more about what would happen in the battle today if Dr. Warren didn't show up. He knew that Bunker Hill was going be the biggest battle of the Revolutionary War. Hundreds of Americans would die. But, in the end, many more British officers and British soldiers would die today because the Americans did not retreat. Steve kept thinking about how the Americans were going to stand their ground through three charges. The article Grace gave him had said that the Americans ran out of bullets, but even then, they didn't run. They fired rocks. They defended their fort; they defended their country.

Steve had read about how George Washington would have just been made General of the Continental Army[36] and would be marching from Philadelphia to take command of the army outside Boston. When the news of Bunker Hill reached him, the first question Washington asked was *Did they run?* Steve wondered what the answer would be without Dr. Warren at the battle.

Steve sat in his chair looking at the hills and thinking about just how much one person's life could change the course of history. The sun crept higher in the morning sky.

More than an hour passed as Steve sat on the porch. The June sun felt good on his skin. His eyelids began to close. The next thing he heard was the rattling of the door handle. His head popped up, and he saw Dr. Warren standing in the door frame.

---

36 *The Continental Army* was created by the Second Continental Congress in 1775. It was formed to coordinate the military efforts of the Thirteen Colonies that had gathered around Boston after the Battles of Lexington, Concord, and Menotomy. George Washington commanded the Continental Army until 1783 when the Treaty of Paris was signed, officially ending the Revolutionary War.

The doctor wore a pale blue waistcoat with silk fringes laced with silver. His breeches were white satin, with silver loops, and under his coat was an immaculate white ruffled shirt. Dr. Warren was dressed to impress. He may not have had a major general's uniform, but he looked the part. Steve's heart sank. He watched his friend step out and adjust the sword on his side, and Steve saw the musket strapped across his back. He stood up to block Dr. Warren's path.

"Good morning, William." The doctor scanned the horizon, then stared at Steve. "Well, if we can hold the hill through the day, we'll control the high ground around Boston. If we control the high ground, we will control the fate of the King's Regulars. But . . ." The doctor's voice trailed off, "Whatever happens on that hill today, the men need encouragement to stand their ground." His voice was confident, though his face was somber.

Dr. Warren spoke with certainty, "Those men waiting on the hill will stay their ground if they have leaders that stand with them." He pointed in the direction of the hills and continued, "Now, as to those hills, I must and will go. I made the decision to place the men on the hill and I will be there with them when we defend it."

Dr. Warren nodded to his apprentice and stepped around Steve. In a desperate voice, Steve said, "Dr. Warren, if you go, you will be killed."

Dr. Warren stopped. He turned back and looked at his young friend. Then with a nod, he said seven words that Steve did not understan – "*Dulce et decorum est pro patria mori.*"

The words lingered. Their meaning remained unknown. But, a shiver sprang up and around Steve's spine.

Chapter 52

William Accompanies Dr. Warren

Still staring at Steve, Dr. Warren said, "William, I'm certain your skills as a surgeon will be needed at the field hospital. Will you accompany me to the edge of the hills?"

Steve's mind raced. His first plan had failed, Dr. Warren was awake, and he had no back-up plan. But, staying close to Dr. Warren until he thought of Plan B made sense. So, with nothing to protect him but a three-cornered hat to provide some shade, he decided to join Dr. Warren.

As they walked, neither said anything. Steve tried to devise Plan B, but he kept thinking about the seven weird words that Dr. Warren had said. He didn't understand what the words meant, but the feeling they created when he spoke them was still bubbling inside Steve.

Walking next to a field with a rock wall, Steve turned to Dr. Warren and asked, "What were those words you said earlier?"

Without breaking stride, and with his focus on the approaching hills, Dr. Warren said, "My former apprentice, has your Latin become so misplaced that you can't interpret a simple phrase?" Now Steve knew why he didn't understand the weird words – Latin. Not knowing how to answer, Steve remained silent.

Finally, while maintaining his brisk pace and with a feeble grin, Dr. Warren said very slowly, "*Dulce et decorum est pro patria mori* means, my friend, 'It is sweet and fitting to die for your country.'" This time the phrase produced an even eerier feeling inside Steve. Still maintaining pace with the doctor, he repeated the words under his breath, *Dulce et decorum est pro patria mori*. Steve's whispering of the phrase and the sound of dirt and gravel under their feet were the only sounds the doctor and apprentice made as they walked to the hill.

After a long stretch of silence, Dr. Warren said, "You know, William, I said my goodbyes to the children." As if offering a confession, Dr. Warren continued, "Oh, how hard it was to hold little Richard in my arms and hug him and not know if I shall see him again in this life. My little Richard is only three. Betsy is not yet ten." The patriot stepped over a fallen tree across their path. "Four children without a mother and their father marching into battle." Dr. Warren's voice trailed off. "William, I pray my friends and my Elizabeth will forgive me. But I feel the Lord approves."

Steve thought about the little kids he'd seen with Mercy at the Scollay's house. He thought about Betsy's prayer for her dad. Her tears. He really had to figure something out. How the heck was he going to save this man who seemed so intent on fighting?

Moving steadily up the path, the doctor continued, "If I die, I do so for a cause far greater than one man. William, I feel I must do my part to sustain this land. For over a hundred years, it has been a land for those that no one else wanted. It has been a land where they could come and find refuge and freedom." As they crested the back side of a large hill, Steve could see the battlefront. As he walked, Dr. Warren said, "America must prevail. If I die, all on this continent may know my conviction to country was beyond all that life has to offer. I pray to God that if I die, my death will stir the hearts of every American to the cause of liberty." Steve lifted his head. Dr. Warren's last words caused the same strange feeling as had the Latin words.

When they arrived at the west shoulder of Breed's Hill, Dr. Warren turned to Steve, "Mr. Eustis, I believe this is where we must part. I will continue to the top of that hill and join the men. My brother John will welcome your assistance in the field hospital to the north." Dr. Warren pointed to a path some distance up the road.

Steve recognized that his entire purpose in altering Dr. Warren's fate would be lost if he let the doctor leave and allowed the course of history to unfold. He quickly said, "Dr. Warren, I won't leave your side."

Dr. Warren looked puzzled. "William, I intend to be in the heart of the battle. Your services will be needed in the hospital, not on the battlefield. We shall part here."

But Steve jumped in quickly. "If I follow you to the heart of the battle, I'll be able to help those needing care immediately."

Dr. Warren's eyes warmed as he looked at Steve. "William, you are a true friend and patriot, but I must insist . . ."

Steve didn't let him finish. "Dr. Warren, I know what you're going to say. But I know how dangerous it will be. Believe me, I know." Steve thought of the internet articles and all the American deaths he'd read about. The doctor started to speak, but Steve spoke first, "Remember you were the one who said," Steve paused, hoping it would come out right, "'*Dulce et decorum est pro patria mori.*'" Saying these words caused a deep warmth in his chest and his eyes stung and brimmed with tears.

Standing quiet for a moment, Dr. Warren placed his hand on Steve's arm. The true patriot surrendered. Nodding he said, "We go together." Then pausing and looking toward the battlegrounds, he added, "May God guide us at the battle front."

Chapter 53

Colonels Putnam and Prescott

Climbing the backside of Breed's Hill (which Steve knew from Grace's material would eventually be called Bunker Hill), Steve and Dr. Warren heard the rumbles of battle. Looking across the face of the hill to the other side, they saw smoke coming from Charlestown. Buildings were now aflame; smoke engulfed the hill. The British cannons firing from their warships tore through the small village. From the harbor, a constant stream of booms echoed across the landscape.

Steve's mind flashed to the stories his great uncle Harold had told him. He thought about the battles Walter and Harold had fought in for this country. Despite how crazy scary it all looked, as Steve stood on the hill, he felt his heart swell for everyone who had ever fought for his country's freedom, from this Revolutionary War battle to the battles in Afghanistan after 9-11. He wished he could somehow thank them all.

Dr. Warren approached the first American soldier they came to and asked where he could find Colonel Israel Putnam. The soldier pointed in the direction of a rail fence some distance to the side of the hill. Steve walked with Dr. Warren toward the fence, and noted a short, heavy-set man with a square jaw and gray hair shouting orders.

Pointing at the hordes of men in red and nodding toward the fence, Colonel Putnam shouted, "This fence is our ground and we will stay our ground!" The men along the fence wore dirty shirts of different colors, while the British soldiers at the water's edge wore their shining red uniforms. If the battle would be decided by who looked the best, the Americans had no chance!

As Steve and Dr. Warren made their way toward the colonel, one of Colonel Putnam's men headed away from the fence. Colonel

Putnam saw the man and hurried in his direction. He grabbed him by the arm and the younger man mumbled, "Sir, I don't feel well. I request permission to leave. I'm sick." The man's voice trembled as he looked at his commanding officer, and then toward the hordes of British soldiers pouring out of their ships.

"I'm sorry, son, but I need you here." Putnam stood directly in front of the soldier and his voice was firm. Still complaining about being too sick, the soldier tried to edge by his colonel, despite the lack of permission.

Maneuvering a few feet in front of the soldier, the colonel drew his sword and pointed it at the younger man. In a steady, stern voice, he said, "Get back in that line or I'll run you through on the spot." The man did not move. The other men at the fence all stared as the colonel prodded him in the shoulder with the sword. The man still did not move. Putnam suddenly jabbed his sword until the tip sank into the man's arm. The man groaned and grabbed at his bleeding shoulder as blood colored his shirt. Putnam barked, "Do you believe me now?" The man stumbled back to the fence, while Putnam looked at his men. "If anyone else is thinking of leaving, he'll get more than the tip of this sword!" Steve watched the man holding his shoulder and looked at the other men staring at their colonel with his sword still drawn. No one else would be leaving, no matter how sick they got.

With the men at their posts, and order in the ranks once again established, Israel Putnam noticed Dr. Warren and Steve for the first time. With a quizzical look and a slight smile, the old colonel welcomed them, "Joseph, I didn't anticipate this honor." Putnam stared at the doctor and then straightened and said, "General Warren, command is yours." Standing straight and saluting, the colonel added, "Sir, what would you have me do?"

Dr. Warren shook his head. "Israel, I haven't come to relieve you of your command. I have not yet received my commission from Philadelphia. I've only come as a volunteer. Besides, I know nothing of your dispositions, nor will I interfere with them. I only request your direction in telling me where I can be of most use in the great cause today." Dr. Warren stood straight and spoke in a strong voice.

Looking into the eyes of the doctor, Colonel Putnam nodded. Steve could see the respect the colonel had for the young doctor.

Pointing to the redoubt on the top of the hill, Putnam said, "There you will be covered."

With an edge to his voice, Warren responded, "Colonel, don't think I came to seek a place of safety. Tell me where the battle will be most furious."

Again, the seasoned veteran pointed his friend to the recently constructed fort on top of the hill. "That is the object of the British soldiers. If we can keep them from it, the day will be ours. Your presence up there may make all the difference to the men waiting to face the British assaults. I'm sure Colonel Prescott will welcome the help."

Understanding now that the old colonel and friend wasn't trying to protect him by sending him to the redoubt, Joseph nodded a thanks, and set out towards the top of the hill. Steve followed as together they marched higher towards the earthen fort. Behind them, Steve noticed the hordes of red-coated soldiers gathering outside Charlestown at the base of the hill. He could feel the battle's gloomy presence. The feeling today was different from the fighting on the road between Concord and Boston. On April 19, 1775, Steve and Rob saw the bloody skirmishes at Menotomy, but today, June 17, 1775, on this hill, they were prepared for a lot more. This wasn't just a skirmish, this was war.

Steve and Dr. Warren entered the fort at the top of the hill. Behind the earthen wall, Steve saw the dirt-laden faces of men watching intently as the enemy poured out of ship after ship. The cargo of crimson warriors seemed endless. British soldiers dressed in red who had been seasoned in battles across the world waited on shore for the command to charge the homemade dirt fort of the rebels. Like the summer sun itself, confidence radiated from their red coats and reflected off their shining bayonets, making the tattered clothes of the Americans seem even sadder. As the Americans watched their enemy's numbers increase and the Regulars' preparations intensify, it was clear to Steve that those in the redoubt had grave questions regarding the wisdom of their position on the hill.

Many of these Americans had helped oppose the Regulars at Concord, Lexington, and Menotomy. This was different. On the road from Concord, the American soldiers had melted into the woods every time the Regulars charged them. Now, the Minutemen were trapped behind a wall they had built in one night, with nowhere to go. Steve wondered about how these untrained men could stand up to the King's Regulars who approached with their bayonets leveled and cannons roaring. What would the men behind the earth walls do when a cannon ball struck and plunged through a fellow soldier? Steve now wondered what he himself would do when blood was spilt.

The leader, Colonel Prescott, walked between the men and froze upon spotting Dr. Warren. He looked confused, but regaining his composure, he saluted the soon-to-be-commissioned General. All the men watched as Prescott approached Dr. Warren and said, "General, do you have any orders? I didn't expect you, but I am certainly at your command."

Greeting the colonel with a hearty salute, Warren announced in a voice loud enough for all of Boston to hear, "Colonel Prescott, I have no commands for you or your men. As you and the men are aware, I have not yet received my commission." Dr. Warren looked at all the men in the redoubt, and spoke so loud that everyone could hear. "I come as a volunteer with my musket and powder horn to serve under your most able command, and I shall be happy to learn from a soldier of your experience. I only wish to join you and fight with the finest men on the continent!"

The arrival of Dr. Warren and his speech created no small stir. The men quickly spread the word that Joseph Warren himself was in the redoubt. Men pointed, smiled, slapped backs, and actually laughed. The concern that had been on their faces melted away. Like a shadow disappearing when the light of the sun is directly overhead. Dr. Warren's presence removed doubts regarding their mission.

A man came up to Steve and said, "Mighty proud I am, to be fighting with Dr. Warren. Yes, sir." The young man had skin as dark as the black barrel of the musket he gripped with both hands. "My name is Salem Poor."[37] He extended a hand to Steve, "I'm a free man. Yes, sir, I bought my freedom." He shook Steve's hand with vigor. "I've been enlisted with Captain Ames since the Regulars started things in Lexington. We came down from Andover." The man looked around him. "Yes, sir, I figured what's the good of being a freeman if my wife and my son is going to have Redcoats telling us what we can and cant's do?" Staring at the British soldiers below them, he continued, "I intends to fight. Yes, sir. I ain't scared to fight, not one bit." Salem Poor gripped his musket. Steve nodded, hoping all on their front line were as committed as Salem.

After talking to other soldiers, Dr. Warren made his way back over to Steve. He greeted Salem and the three turned to Colonel Prescott as he began to speak loud enough for all in the fort to hear. Steve noted that the red-coated army below had now begun their march up the hill.

Prescott bellowed, "You are all marksmen. There's not a one of you that can't kill a squirrel at fifty paces." Colonel Prescott's group of untrained soldiers stared down the barrels of their muskets, as all the Americans now watched the greatest army in the world marching closer and closer. "But today you reserve your fire! You conserve our ammunition." The soldiers continued climbing the hill, coming nearer and nearer. "And if you do, we will destroy every one of them! Aim at the handsome coats. Pick off the commanders!"

With the enemy now getting so close you could hear their boots pounding the ground, the colonel raised his voice to a thunder echoing under the June skies, "But remember, my men, above all things . . .

Don't fire until you see the whites of their eyes!"

---

37 *Salem Poor* was a real person who fought at Bunker Hill. He had been a former slave who purchased his freedom. He is credited with shooting and killing the British Colonel James Abercrombie, and was praised by Colonel William Prescott as one of the bravest men to fight at Bunker Hill.

Chapter 54

The Stand on the Hill

Watching red soldiers push up the hill from every direction, Steve realized that any chance of saving his friend was fleeting. He and Dr. Warren were trapped. Thousands of British bayonets flashed in the sun. Each twisted the sun's rays off razor edges. Steve thought back to Rob in the upstairs room of Jason Russell's house. He remembered the blade being pulled back through his brother's arm. He remembered Rob's look when the steel knife did its slicing, and the bubbling blood fell onto the floor. Steve's stomach tightened. He stood with Dr. Warren on one side and Salem Poor on the other, as all three watched thousands of soldiers march closer and closer. The rumble of the advancing soldiers steadily increased.

Despite his efforts to be strong, Steve's face drained of color and his shoulders shuddered. Dr. Warren touched his arm. "William, I should've never let you come. You belong at the field hospital. You should be with my brother, not at the battle front." Dr. Warren looked behind them and nodded in that direction, "Make haste. John will need you on the adjoining hill. Quick! You were supposed to be there anyway." Dr. Warren's eyes flooded with concern.

Steve asked, "Is John your brother?"

"William, I fear you're falling into a state of shock. You are not fit to fight. Find John, who is most certainly my brother. You have worked with him on many occasions. Now go! Rest! And get ready for the onslaught of casualties that must surely follow." Dr. Warren turned to the red wave, which was now closing in on the redoubt.

Steve grasped for courage. He'd come to help Dr. Warren. How could he leave now and go to a field hospital? Besides, what could he do to *help* at the hospital? He'd pass out the first time he saw a leg amputated. If future Americans, ordinary Americans, like the substitute teacher, were to remember Dr. Warren, he had to make him live through this! Steve had to change history. He certainly couldn't do that at a field hospital.

Hurriedly he said, "Come with me! Please come. We can both help your brother at the field hospital."

Dr. Warren started to speak, "William . . ."

Steve would never know what his friend intended to say. At that moment an American soldier seven or eight men to their right discharged his musket. The second the charge exploded, Colonel Prescott jumped on top of the wall. The colonel raised his sword towards his own men. Ignoring the host of Redcoats approaching, the colonel roared, as he stood above the man that fired, "If you believe in me enough to follow me here, you best believe me now when I tell you I will run through with my sword the next man that fires before ordered!" The colonel looked around, challenging his men. Steve stood close enough to see Colonel Prescott's eyes and knew he would follow through with his threat.

Warren never answered Steve's request. It was impossible to leave safely at this point anyway. Both Dr. Warren and Steve were stuck in the battle. They watched the Regulars lower their bayonets into the charge position. Every American held their fire.

With a roar from the British officers, 350 of the finest of the King's Regulars surged forward. The battle of Bunker Hill had commenced.

The fastest Redcoats came within a few feet of the wall. A British soldier in front of Steve got so close he could see that the lapel on his Redcoat had torn and was flapping below black stubble on his chin. Then, the word finally came. Prescott's voice boomed–"FIRE!"

The closest Regulars stood at point blank range when the patriot colonists shot into the British ranks. The lead balls smashed through the company and left over half the Redcoats on the ground. The survivors continued the attack, but a second round of fire cut the remaining number to less than a dozen. This rag-tag group of patriots had perfectly executed Prescott's orders.

Smoke filled the redoubt. Through the chaos, Steve spied another regiment of the King's Regulars. The second wave marched up the hill, stepping over the bodies of their fallen comrades. As they came closer, the second wave plunged forward. The marksmanship and accuracy of the American rebels demolished them. Behind the haze of musket fumes, the farmers reloaded. Even with approaching British bayonets thirsty for their throats, they filled their muskets with new balls and powder. Salem Poor was as quick as any. Pulling his powder horn and ramming his ball through the musket's barrel, he was one of the fastest of the men.

The sound of the British cannons and the American muskets shook the earth and throttled the sky like thunder. Steve thought about Grace. She'd been so right. He shouldn't be here. He stood, barely peeking over the earthen wall. He watched Dr. Warren work his musket, firing and reloading. He saw sweat drench Salem Poor's shirt so that the muscles in his chest and dark arms rippled through the thin fabric. Then, like the worst point in a horrible nightmare, two paces past Dr. Warren, a man's neck snapped back. The man's hands flew to his head as he crashed flat onto his back. His body bounced once, quivered for only a brief second, and then lay still. His hands going limp, Steve looked at the fallen man's head and immediately wished he hadn't. He would never forget the mutilated face and cracked skull. The seven Latin words Dr. Warren had said earlier and that he had repeated flashed through Steve's mind. As he watched the carnage of fallen men pile up around him, he began to think that dying for one's country was not as noble and glamorous as the fancy Latin phrase made it seem.

The battle raged on. All around him, he watched men dying on both sides of the dirt fort. The cries of the wounded echoed in Steve's head, and the smoke and dust all around him stung his eyes. After a third wave of Redcoats fell, the King's Regulars had no choice but to retreat down the hill and regroup.

Looking at the bodies of the British Regulars scattered across the ground, a soldier behind Steve said, "I never saw sheep lie as thick in the fold as the mass of Redcoats on this hill." Although pleased at the

Americans' success, Steve figured the man and others in the redoubt knew this was no time to celebrate. Everyone could see the troops reorganizing below.

Once again, the Redcoats held a steady march up the hill and the Americans waited. These fathers and farmers were holding their ground against the finest army in the world. Just as Steve began to think that the Americans would win, he heard Colonel Prescott discuss with Dr. Warren the issue of ammunition. There would not be enough to repulse another attack.

This was it. History had not changed. Unless by some miracle Steve could think of a new plan, Dr. Warren was going to die, and Steve would probably be right next to him!

As the third assault assembled, Steve thought back to Menotomy. He remembered how Dr. Warren narrowly missed being shot in the head because Steve called his name. Although a risky way to try to save someone, he had no options left. He would watch for the redcoat that would shoot Dr. Warren and then warn him just in time.

As the Redcoats neared the wall of their fort, Salem Poor stood his ground. The former slave had just one last charge in his musket. He leveled his weapon at the soldier with the fanciest red jacket and pulled the trigger. The officer's hands flew to his chest and his body yanked back as if caught by a trip wire. Two soldiers near the officer fell to his side. "Help!" cried one soldier, "Colonel Abercrombie has been shot!" Steve turned back to Salem, who had flipped his musket around in his hands, ready to use it now as a club. Even without ammunition, this man had no intention of backing down.

As the third assault continued, all the Americans ran out of ammunition. With no firepower to repulse the Regulars' march, the battle became British bayonets versus the swinging butts of Patriot muskets. A forest of bayonets poured over the side of the redoubt and the Americans prepared for hand-to-hand combat.

Dust poured upwards in a thick, brown cloud. Steve could barely see Dr. Warren with his sword drawn, trying to coordinate a retreat. Steve scrambled to stay by Dr. Warren's side and watch him as best he could.

The Americans had lost the redoubt. With so much dust from the loose soil, it was almost impossible to see the fort's back opening for escape. Dr. Warren helped the defeated men out of their self-created barricade. The doctor stood guard with his sword drawn, allowing the others to pass through the fort's exit. Steve got to the back wall, but didn't leave. He watched dozens of men make their way out and move down the back of the hill, including Salem Poor.

Dr. Warren shouted encouragement as the remaining soldiers fled. Suddenly a British officer spotted him. While the doctor focused on helping the last of the patriots retreat, the officer reached inside his red waistcoat, never taking his eyes off Dr. Warren, and pulled out a small-sized musket, somewhat bigger than a pistol. The officer leveled his arm and closed one eye as he drilled his sites into the doctor.

Seeing this final event unfold, Steve froze. He tried to cry out, but his throat tightened. The words that could've saved his friend couldn't escape his mouth. Steve looked on in horror as the British officer began squeezing the trigger of the mini-musket.

Finally, one word burst through – "*Drop*!"

Dr. Warren never processed the command. Hearing the sound of his friend's voice, Dr. Warren turned in Steve's direction just as the shot was fired.

Steve and Joseph's eyes met for less than a second before Steve watched his friend's head violently snap forward. At the same instant, a searing pain burned through Steve's upper leg. The pain dropped him to his knees. It felt like a white hot poker had been stuck into his thigh at the bottom of his right pants pocket. Screaming and grabbing his own leg, Steve watched Joseph Warren plummet to the ground.

"No!" burst from the recesses of Steve's heart. His scream was louder than any before it, but the noise merely melted into the chaos of battle.

The searing pain passed as quickly as it had come. Steve scrambled to pick himself up off his knees and tried to get to Dr. Warren's body. He took a few steps in Warren's direction. Just as he started to kneel by his fallen friend, a British soldier swung the butt end of his musket full force, crashing into the side of Steve's skull.

PART FOUR
LIFE IN THE 1770s

Dr. Warren's death cements a pivotal point in American history. I was present then and throughout every one of America's pivotal moments. From the Pilgrims stepping off the Mayflower in 1620, to a future President winning her election, I'm present. Stepping back and stepping forward – for me, both are as easy as turning a page.

Light has no boundaries in time. Within the light of the time-traveling talisman, I step in and out of decades and centuries – back a lifetime to World War II or back centuries to the dawn of this great nation.

I'm the one who helps Steve remember. Do you know me?

When you finish Steve's story, you will.

Abigail Adams

John and Abigail Adams House, Quincy, Massachusetts

Chapter 55

Failed Mission

"Look over there at that Rebel Dandy!" The voice echoed like a Chinese gong in Steve's swollen head. He listened, but lay still as a stone. "Oh, yes'm, that there silk fringe waistcoat alone ought to fetch a fancy nickel in them Boston markets!"

Steve was barely able to open his eyes. He could scarcely make out the scene in front of him. As he forced his eyes to process his surroundings, he saw Dr. Warren's body being rolled from where it had fallen. British soldiers were rudely removing the silk waistcoat that had been the recent topic of their conversation.

Steve continued to watch as they flung his friend's arms around. The doctor's arms flapped in the warm summer breeze like a rag doll. The filthy, crude soldiers pushed and dragged his friend through the dirt while wrestling the waistcoat from his dead body. Dr. Warren, the person who proved to be the one constant in all these crazy trips to the past, lay lifeless.

Steve looked around, taking in more of his surroundings. Bodies were stacked up like rows of firewood. As Dr. Warren's body was dragged towards the other fallen soldiers, Steve closed his eyes. He recalled the few other deaths he'd experienced. His grandmother's death in her sleep when she was almost eighty fell short of a tragedy. He'd been only four when his grandfather died. Similar to his grandma's passing, the death of his grandpa did not seem to tear at his insides the way that Dr. Warren's death did. Steve's stomach tightened when he thought of Betsy and the four little children he'd met at the Scollay house. The skinny legs, the big eyes, the soft prayer – Betsy and the other children would never hug their father again. Steve closed his eyes.

Everything about his being ached. His head pounded from the soldier's fierce blow. But there was an even stronger pain in his chest, the kind that only comes from experiencing a deep loss. Dr. Warren was dead.

Chapter 56

View from Penn's Hill

Twelve miles from Bunker Hill, a mother and her ten-year-old son climbed a different hill. They'd been hearing the sounds of war for hours. Now, they chose to see it.

The orange flames of Charleston, a city burning, were bright enough to be seen from the other side of the bay. All the citizens on Penn's Hill stared in shock. There was no doubt this was the source of the billowing, black clouds. The cannon fire that had rumbled for almost an hour continued to echo across the ocean. Johnny did not know what he had expected, but to see the fire spreading all over the hill and the whole community across the bay in flames made his stomach sicken. He looked to his mom and neighbors; all of them stared in disbelief. Johnny knew many standing on the hill had sons or husbands who had left Braintree weeks earlier to help fight with the patriots. An eerie and reverent silence covered the hill.

His mom reached over, touching his shoulder. Seeing the full scene of war, she merely whispered, "Oh Johnny." Johnny now noticed the hordes of red-coated soldiers marching up the distant hill, while hundreds more streamed off the massive ships stationed in the harbor.

With no other noise, the distant thud of cannons made Johnny's bones tremble. Mother and son edged next to the Turner family. The Turners had lived across from the Adams' farm for decades. Abigail reached for Mrs. Turner's hand. Neither woman said a word, but Johnny saw the fear in Mrs. Turner's eyes. Johnny knew her son was somewhere on that burning hill.

With no other sound but the echoing of distant cannons and a woman softly weeping, they all watched war.

Chapter 57

Failure

Steve lay among the dead soldiers, trying to figure out a way to escape. The handful of living soldiers in his line of vision were all turned away from the area where he lay. If he was to escape, this was his chance. Using all the strength he could muster, and fighting a powerful nausea stemming from the intense pain in his head, Steve managed to get on his hands and knees. Barely crawling, he proceeded down the northwest side of the incline.

He made it unnoticed down the hill and quickly crawled into a grove of trees, where he managed to stand up. Once on his feet, though, a new wave of nausea hit. Overcome by the pain in his head and the stench of warm blood and gunpowder that seemed to cling to his clothes, Steve doubled over and his stomach emptied itself. He stayed that way for a minute or two, concentrating on taking deep breaths. Once his head stopped spinning, he wiped the mess from his face and began to slowly move deeper into the cover of the woods, avoiding the more-traveled path leading to the redoubt some twenty yards to his left.

Wobbly and halting with each step, he gradually put distance between himself and the battle scene. The memory of Joseph Warren's tangled and twisted body being dragged and piled with the dead continually replayed in his mind. When he could go no further, he crumbled to the ground with his back to a tree. He looked to the hill. He saw the redoubt and the path leading up to Bunker Hill. Thinking out loud, he muttered, "Why am I here?"

He'd been so certain the reason for his time travels was to save Dr. Warren. Now Dr. Warren lay dead. Steve felt broken and utterly exhausted. His head throbbed. He had a pit in his stomach and absolutely nowhere to go in this crazy time trap. Why was he still here?

Suddenly his eyes jerked fully open. He jolted upright, causing a flash of white hot pain to surge through his head. Instantly and instinctively, he reached first into his left pant pocket and then his right. Ignoring the increased pain caused by his quick movements, he began feeling for a pocket in his shirt, then in the back of his knee-length pants. No other pockets existed. With his head aching more than ever, he scrambled again to feel for the musket ball in his front pockets. Again, he found no ball.

Steve crumbled beneath the tree. He lay there like a piece of driftwood on the beach after being pounded by the waves. No musket ball. No Dr. Warren. He was completely alone.

Under the umbrella of the tree's branches, Steve covered his face and let the tears come as he buried himself beneath the dark blanket of despair.

Chapter 58

THE FIELD HOSPITAL

Near the burning hill, but far enough away to provide safety for the wounded, Dr. John Warren heard, smelled, and saw the results of war. The moaning of dying men encircled him. How could just two doctors confront this avalanche of casualties? Although there were certainly more doctors in and around Boston, there were only two willing to help the patriots. The makeshift hospital sat on a neighboring hill from where he and his fellow doctor had watched the battle unfold.

The wounded flooded the hospital. The two doctors worked and toiled to save and help the mountain of wounded patriots. Dr. John Warren knew he should not leave. Yet, he had to know the fate of his older brother. He began examining the next wounded patriot. He saw a musket ball lodged into the upper thigh. Thankfully, there was no damage to the bone. Before John Warren began to extract the bullet, he asked the question he'd repeated over a dozen times to other soldiers. "By chance do you know the fate of Dr. Joseph Warren?"

Moving himself onto the table with help from the doctor, the injured patriot gritted his teeth. With his eyes crunched together in pain, he said, "Aye. I saw him. Yes, I saw him get shot. At about the same time as me, he took a ball. I can't say where. As the men pulled me out, I shouted to him within the redoubt. He lifted his head towards my voice. I'd hoped they would pull the new general out, but he remained to the last. I don't believe there was anyone else left in the fort to help the good doctor."

Upon hearing yet again that a soldier believed his brother had been injured but not killed, John Warren cracked. The younger Warren extracted the ball from the leg of this most recent patient. He tied the wound shut and then turned his back to the dozens of others waiting. The thought of his brother lying wounded on the battlefield with no one to help him pushed all rational thought from his mind. He just couldn't help other soldiers while the thought of his brother dying alone from his wounds danced in his head.

He would inform his colleague. If anyone could support this crazy decision to leave the overflowing field hospital it would be the one remaining doctor on the hill. As Joseph Warren's former apprentice, the other doctor had been the last one to see his brother before he walked to the battlefront.

Upon reaching the other doctor, he saw him staring down upon a young soldier. Tears flowed, staining a most distressed face. The terrified patient cried out, "Mr. Eustis, Dr. Eustis! Spare the leg. I beg you!"

Yet, despite the soldier's efforts, the younger doctor gripped the saw and the amputation continued.

When Dr. Eustis had finished, John walked up to him and tried to explain himself as best he could. With immediate and complete support from Joseph Warren's former apprentice, Dr. John Warren set off on a fast jog to get to the conquered redoubt before complete darkness.

Chapter 59

Meeting John Warren

Steve could not say how long he'd been under the tree. He stayed there because he had no place to go. Stirring from his semiconscious state, he had no idea what to do. His head felt like there was a crack right through it. At some point, he must have fallen asleep, and now all he knew was that there were voices in the distance.

Looking from his vantage point under the tree, he saw what was causing the stir. Along the path, and not too far down the road, the commotion was a result of a confrontation. Two men were in a heated debate. One was a British soldier with two other Redcoats by his side, and the other was a man carrying a bag, trying to get past them. Steve could see that the soldier was prohibiting the man from continuing down the path to Breed's Hill. The man confronting the soldier presumably wanted to follow the trail that Steve had just come down.

Straining to listen, Steve heard the exchange. One of the soldiers hissed, "I don't care what your intent is. You're not taking another step beyond this point. In the name of the King, I've my orders."

"I'm a doctor! There are wounded men who need my attention."

"That may be the case but I'm certain I know your loyalties. I'll not allow assistance to be given to rebels of the crown. Not on my watch."

Despite the British soldier's firm stance on the issue, Steve could see that the so-called doctor wasn't willing to accept the soldier's terms. "My brother is among the wounded. I'm going!" the young American shouted, and made a sudden attempt to dart around the sentry.

The King's Regular swung his musket in the direction toward where the young man had lunged. As the soldier thrust his musket forward, the bayonet sliced into the doctor's left shoulder. He staggered backwards, dropping the bag.

"Aye! I tell you my bayonet can do more damage than that! Now, turn around and head back the way you came."

Unarmed and now wounded from the sharp edge of the British bayonet, the patriot acknowledged defeat. Dejected and clutching his injured shoulder, the young man turned, grabbed his bag and began to walk away. He started down the road in Steve's direction. As he drew closer, Steve could not help but note the resemblance between this man and Dr. Warren.

Standing up carefully, so as not to cause more pain in his throbbing head, Steve stumbled toward the man. As he climbed out of the brush and onto the road, the young physician noticed Steve for the first time. Steve wondered who the man was, but sensed that the man this doctor was looking for might be Dr. Warren. Steve stopped him on the path. "Eh, excuse me. I heard you talking down there – with the soldier." Steve motioned in the direction of the British sentry.

Stopping, the man acknowledged Steve, "I only wanted to see if my brother survived. No one from the redoubt has been able to confirm whether he's alive or dead."

"I was in the redoubt. Who is your brother?"

"Joseph Warren."

Steve held his gaze for a moment. The man's eyes reminded him so much of the kind and friendly eyes of his fallen friend. Steve's own eyes dropped. He spoke almost in a whisper, "Dr. Warren and I were close. I was with him from the beginning of the battle . . . to the end."

Ignoring his injured arm, Joseph's brother dropped his bag and grabbed Steve's shoulders, "How do you know him? What happened? Please tell me everything!"

Thinking about the tragic afternoon and the last seconds with his friend in the fort before he was shot, Steve spoke slowly. "I'm Dr. Warren's apprentice." Steve paused, "I'm William Eustis."

Chapter 60

THE MORNING AFTER

The day before, Abigail had heard the rumors. First one and then another messenger stated that Joseph Warren had died. Hearing the news, little Johnny buried his face in her apron and wept. Dr. Warren had healed his hand and saved him from having crippled fingers. He remembered when he was a small boy and he and Dr. Warren had cared for his sister, Susanna, before she died. Dr. Warren was like an uncle.

Now, the morning after, Abigail and her son Johnny had set out to confirm whether the rumors of Joseph's death were true. They were accompanied by several others from their small town of Braintree. They all had questions about friends or family members who fought in the devastating battle.

Upon arriving at the battle site, Abigail and Johnny headed for the field hospital. Abigail was sure that Dr. John Warren or William Eustis would certainly be there, and she hoped that one or the other would know the truth regarding Joseph.

A colonial soldier directed Abigail and Johnny to the doctors' camp. With her son by her side, it took her little time to spot John Warren. Just before the young doctor began serving his next injured patriot, Abigail called, "John . . . John, over here."

Turning towards the voice, the tired doctor made his way to her. John hadn't spent as much time with Abigail Adams and her family as his brother had, but he certainly knew who was calling him.

Abigail watched the doctor walk toward her. Dark lines circled red, drained eyes. She saw the blood on his hands and arms. She now looked about and questioned her decision to bring Johnny into the military hospital. Men moaned as they waited. Blood stained the ground around the men. She gasped at the sight of a soldier's amputated limb in a basket. While trying to regain her composure, she stepped in front of Johnny to block his view of the basket.

"Hello, Mrs. Adams," John said with a bewildered look. In a tired voice, he added, "What brings you here?"

Pulling Johnny closer to her, Abigail turned to the younger Dr. Warren. "John, I apologize for disturbing you. However, Johnny and I must know if the news we heard yesterday is true."

As Abigail continued, the brother's expression confirmed what she had been dreading. In a voice filled with restrained emotion, John replied, "The rumors are true. Joseph is dead."

Abigail felt the muffled sobs of Johnny, as he hid his face in the folds of her dress. Dr. John Warren watched the boy, his own eyes admitting that he too longed to weep.

Turning back to Abigail, he motioned for her to follow him. He directed the two of them a short distance from the military hospital. They walked until they came to an area where a young man sat alone. His back was up against a tree, and a forlorn expression was etched on his face.

Still some distance from the young man, John turned to Abigail and said, "Abigail, the young man behind me states he was with my brother and witnessed his death." The younger Dr. Warren continued, "His description of the three charges of the British before the fall of the redoubt is impeccable and he even talked about serving next to Salem Poor, a former slave, in the redoubt. I know Salem was there because I've heard the reports of how valiantly he fought. The boy told me in great detail the story of Joseph's death and it corresponds with what others have stated, except that the boy was knocked unconscious. He says that when he woke, he saw Joseph dead, not injured."

John paused, "He saw him dead. No one claims to have been as near Joseph as this young man. In fact, he claims that when Joseph was shot in the back of the head, he tried to run to my brother's aid and that's when a British soldier used the butt of his musket to strike him. Surely, he does have a terrible bump on his head to attest to this part of his story." Abigail noticed the emphasis on the last few words and the strange look now on John Warren's face.

John added, "But I'm not sure he can be trusted."

Wrinkling her brow, Abigail responded, "I don't understand. You are stating that everything about the boy's story seems consistent with what you've heard from others, but yet you act like I should be careful in accepting what he may tell me as the truth?"

John cautiously nodded and then confided, "Abigail, it's true, he knows a lot about what happened at the battle yesterday. But when he told me his name –" John stopped.

Abigail prompted him, "And, what did he say?"

Speaking in a lower tone, he leaned towards her, clearly trying to keep the conversation from the young man in question. John whispered, "The boy claimed to be William Eustis."

Abigail tilted her head back, "Why? How odd. Why would he claim to be Dr. Eustis?"

John nodded, "This is the exact question I asked as well. When I questioned him further, he acted surprised that I wouldn't think he was William, but readily acknowledged that he wasn't him." Shrugging slightly, John went on, "On my return here to the hospital, I talked to William. He was not aware of anyone trying to impersonate him."

Abigail now looked at the boy with a puzzled expression. She could not imagine a child who could look more forlorn and rejected. A surge of motherly compassion overtook her. The longer she looked at the young man, the greater her desire to help him. She turned to John. "Surely this boy must have a mother or family?"

John Warren shrugged. "I'll be honest. I've been so preoccupied with Joseph's death, and the wounded, I have not asked additional questions." Looking into his bloodshot eyes and remembering the carnage at the field hospital, Abigail didn't question the truth of his statement. The doctor continued, "I do know that he spent the night here and has not left that spot at all today, not even for food or water. I believe he has nowhere to go."

Abigail had heard enough. Despite John's protests, she brushed past him and headed towards the boy, stating in a firm but gentle tone, "Anyone who was your brother's friend is a friend of mine."

Abigail approached the solitary figure. "Hello, young man. My name is Abigail Adams." Looking up into her face, the boy acted like he recognized her. Lighting up he said, "Abigail Adams!"

A bit startled at his expression and recognition, Abigail straightened her dress. Hearing him speak, she got a strange feeling, as if they had actually met. Trying to shake the odd sensation, she continued, "My friend, Dr. John Warren, tells me that you were with his brother in the redoubt yesterday. Is that true?" Abigail watched the boy's countenance cloud over. He nodded but volunteered nothing regarding their mutual friend's death.

"Dr. Joseph Warren was a very close friend of our family." Abigail placed her hand on her son Johnny's arm, and went on. "I want you to know, young man, that a friend of Dr. Warren's is a friend of our family in every way." She smiled, holding her smile until she noticed the faintest flicker of light in the boy's eyes. "Do you have anywhere to stay?" she asked. The boy shook his head and looked away. "All right then, it's decided. You will stay with us for the time being." She smiled down at him, and the poor boy actually smiled back.

Abigail Adams looked almost exactly as Steve remembered her. He'd met her that first night, during his first experience with Dr. Warren. He recalled sitting at the bedside of a little boy named Johnny, recounting bedtime stories. The memories brought a ray of light into his soul. They were the first good feelings Steve had felt in over twenty-four hours. His hopeless expression brightened, and a smile even escaped the gloom when he recognized the young boy standing next to Abigail. It was Johnny!

Abigail said, "Tell me your name."

Steve looked at the friendly face. She patiently waited for what should have been an easy answer to a simple question. Realizing his 1770s world was different without the ball and with Dr. Warren dead, Steve did the only thing he could think to do. He told the truth. "My name is Steve O'Dell."

Chapter 61

Days, Weeks, Months

Twelve miles from the field hospital, Steve found a new home. Braintree[38], Massachusetts was settled in 1625. The Adams' family farm anchored a corner of the pleasant community for almost that long. If not for the constant concern about his future, Steve would have enjoyed the experience of spending a vacation on a real colonial farm. However, he thought about his own family and friends constantly, and had no idea how he was ever going to get back to them; he had no choice but to live each day in the 1770s.

Thankfully, Mrs. Adams took Steve, or Stephen, as she called him, into her quaint home and treated him like one of her children. Abigail called him Stephen because it was the name of the Lord's disciple in the Book of Acts in the Bible. Steve quickly learned that Abigail Adams loved the Bible. The children all treated Steve warmly; Steve especially liked Johnny, the oldest child. Like his mother, Johnny had showed kindness to Steve from their first meeting on Bunker Hill. Now, months later, they were like brothers.

Although a few years younger than Steve, Johnny was mature for his age and very bright. Most importantly, Johnny loved to read and write. In this regard, he and Steve were kindred spirits. On more than one occasion, Steve thought about his first visit to Colonial America and the evening he'd spent at the Adams' home when the family lived in Boston. Steve remembered the bedtime stories he shared with the young boy who was now somehow much older.

---

38 *Braintree* was the name of the town where the Adams family lived for many years. In 1792, part of Braintree, which included the Adams family farm, became the town of Quincy. For this reason, when referring to the community before 1792 it is called Braintree and after that date it is called Quincy.

With the days turning to weeks and the weeks turning to months, Steve became more and more a part of Colonial America. During this time, he adopted a routine. He had specific chores, getting water from the well, chopping wood daily for the cooking and for fueling the fires, and feeding the farm animals. On Sundays, he went to church with the family for most of the day, and when not in church, he read the Bible with the family. In fact, he learned that reading the Bible was a fundamental part of daily life for the Adams family. It was the first book the younger children learned to read from, and was used as part of the regular lessons Abigail gave to the children. Before the end of Steve's first week in Braintree, he was certain he'd read more Bible verses and stories than he had in his entire life. Occasionally, Steve accompanied the children to the town's schoolhouse to learn lessons, but for the most part the family's education stemmed from their mother.

Once, while discussing how much they enjoyed reading, Johnny told Steve that he hoped to read the entire Bible once a year throughout his life.[39] Steve marveled at the goal. He figured he'd feel good if he could manage to read it once in his life.

Usually, when Steve wanted to be with someone or talk to someone, Johnny was around. They enjoyed many mornings or afternoons discussing books or other writings. The Adams family had a respectable library, and to Abigail's delight, both Steve and Johnny made good use of it.

Steve adjusted to his new home in Colonial America while the American Revolution raged on. Johnny's father, John Adams, was a delegate in Philadelphia and part of the recently formed Continental

---

39 *John Quincy Adams* lived over 80 years. He did read the Bible cover to cover each year of his life and recited the Lord's Prayer each night before going to bed. When he died in 1848, he was one of the last surviving Americans who could remember personally watching the Battle of Bunker Hill. He never forgot the day as a young boy when he and his mother watched the hill burn. He cried when he learned his friend and doctor had died in battle. In the decades leading up to the Civil War, John Quincy Adams became one of our nation's fiercest opponents of slavery.

Congress.[40] Steve would sit with Johnny and listen to Abigail read the letters explaining what was occurring in Philadelphia. Within the Continental Congress, Johnny's father had been instrumental in getting an army formed and appointing George Washington as General.

Abigail often wrote letters to her husband. Steve was fascinated by how she could use the goose quill pen to write. Noting Steve's interest, one day Abigail turned to him. "Stephen, I would like to read to you a portion of my letter to my dear husband. As a friend of Dr. Warren, you are certainly a friend of Mr. Adams." Turning to her letter, she read, "Not all the havoc and devastation they have made has wounded me like the death of Warren. We want him in the Senate; we want him in his profession; we want him in the field. We mourn for the citizen, the senator, the physician and the warrior. When he fell, liberty wept." When she looked up, Steve noted her sadness. "I will miss him, Stephen."

As Abigail read the letter, thoughts of Grace kept popping into Steve's mind. Grace had often read to Steve things she'd written. When Steve imagined an adult version of Grace, he pictured Abigail Adams. Like Grace, Abigail had a natural beauty that was more beautiful because of her goodness from inside.

Thinking about Grace made him ache for home. It had been months since he'd seen his mother and father. He really missed them and even longed to see Rob and Lizzie. The Adams family had been wonderful to him, but they couldn't replace his family.

As he walked out of the room, his world in the 1770s now felt a bit gloomier. Once again, he tried to push away the nagging question that always hung around in the back of his mind, "Will I ever see them again?"

---

40 *Continental Congress* – This was an assembly of representatives from the thirteen colonies that would soon become the first thirteen states in the United States. The Congress met just prior to and during the Revolutionary War. It was the highest governing organization during the Revolutionary War. Each colony selected representatives to meet in Philadelphia and make decisions for the new country, including the approval of the Declaration of Independence.

Chapter 62

A Goose Quill Pen and 1770s Manuscript

Although Steve had adjusted to his new life in Colonial America during the past several months, there were certain conveniences of the 21st century that he sorely missed. As the days became colder, a trip from the farmhouse to the privy when nature called was definitely no fun. And if he used the chamber pot in the middle of the night it always had to be emptied in the morning. However, as strange as it seemed, one of the items Steve missed most about the 21st century was a good ink pen.

With an ink pen, he could write about Dr. Warren. He could preserve the memories and experiences. Because he let Dr. Warren die, this was all he could do to save him and holding the feather in his hand, he felt he'd lost his ability to communicate.

Johnny watched Steve struggle to contain his frustration as he tried to write with the quill pen.

"You better be careful, or you're going to break another pen," the young boy said, smiling. "Momma says we're going to have to stop farming and do nothing but raise geese to keep you supplied."

Steve was not in the mood for humor. "I know what your mom said and don't worry, I won't." As Steve was writing and talking to Johnny at the same time, he failed to concentrate on what he was doing. He pushed too hard on the quill in his hand and the tip broke.

Johnny shook his head and Steve could see him trying not to laugh. "Steve, I think you're a great writer, even if you've broken a pen a day since you've been here."

Without looking at his friend, Steve barked, "Johnny, this is a goose feather! It's not a pen!"

Johnny looked confused about his outburst. Steve quickly attempted to remedy the situation, "Johnny, what I mean is that I can't pen what I want when I keep breaking the feathers. My lack of penmanship creates an inability to write well." Johnny raised his eyebrows but asked no questions.

Some weeks later, Johnny looked at the thick document in Steve's hands. Johnny had watched Steve start all this writing last summer, the very first week at his house. His friend from Bunker Hill had continued writing through the winter and now into the spring. No matter how cold, under the light of a candle, Steve labored to pen his memories.

As Steve looked over the document, Johnny could see frustration in his friend's eye. "Steve, don't worry about the first part. Your penmanship is much better now." Johnny was trying a stab at humor. He emphasized the word *much* in a way that clearly conveyed what he and Steve both knew. Steve might be writing better now, but his writing was still nearly impossible to read.

Johnny stood up, "Well, for now let's leave the writing and go to dinner. I think guests are coming tonight, so there should be something good." Nodding to the stairs that led down to the parlor, Johnny added, "Besides Steve, you can always rewrite your story when your lettering is better. Or, if you like, I'd be happy to act as scribe for you."

Johnny had made this offer before. He thought it would be perfect. He had excellent penmanship for his age, and if he could help pen it, then he could read it. He was curious about the document his friend spent so much time working on. Steve shared parts of the stories about Dr. Warren, but Johnny wanted to read and know it all. He'd never seen someone work so hard at writing something as Steve did, while writing about Dr. Warren.

Steve put the quill down and stood up. He shook his head. "Sorry, Johnny. I may rewrite the first part but for now it will be without a scribe." Slumping his shoulders, Johnny stood by the door.

Steve announced, "Let's forget about the manuscript for now. Dinner smells great. Let's go eat!"

Chapter 63

Familiar Dinner Guests

Their suspicions were confirmed by the two extra place settings. Abigail Adams was planning for two dinner guests.

Just as Steve came down the stairs, there was a knock on the door. Turning towards the door, Steve saw one of the younger children invite two men into the parlor. Abigail wiped her hands on her apron and moved towards the door. Steve suddenly recognized both men. It was Paul Revere and Dr. John Warren.

While Mrs. Adams greeted the guests and the men thanked her for having them to dinner, Steve's mind began to race with memories. As everyone was making their way to the table, Steve became excited about the prospects for the dinner conversation. These were men who loved and respected his old friend as much as anyone. Just last month, Abigail had shared the news that Paul Revere had christened his newly born son Joseph Warren Revere. Steve was certain they would both share memories and stories of their mutual friend.

"Stephen, it is nice to meet you." Paul Revere nodded to the man next to him. "Dr. Warren, here, mentioned that you were staying with Abigail." Revere shook Steve's hand as he pointedly stared at him.

John Warren extended his hand to Steve as well. "It's good to see you again, young man. I must say, you look much better now under the care of Mrs. Adams than when we last met under the shadow of Bunker Hill." John looked first at Steve and then at Abigail.

After a prayer of thanks for the food that Abigail asked Steve to say, one of many prayers that Steve had offered in the Adams' home, the guests wasted little time in getting to the point of their visit. John Warren began. Addressing both Abigail and Steve, he said, "I presume you've heard, General Washington's troops have forced the Regulars out of Boston." Both Steve and Abigail nodded. For approximately a year, the British troops had occupied Boston. Once they were removed, the news had been a cause for celebration all over Braintree and the surrounding areas.

John continued, "Well, with the Regulars now out of Boston and headed to New York City, I ventured up the path where we first met." John paused. "This time, however, there were no British bayonets to prevent me from going to the top of the hill. I walked all around the hill, and every step I took felt like I was walking on hallowed ground. With each step, I wondered if I was walking on my brother's grave." At this last statement, John Warren's expression grew solemn.

Still looking at Steve, the younger Dr. Warren continued, "I plan to find my brother's body and give him a proper burial. I think I know where to start and I would like to begin tomorrow. Paul and my younger brother, Samuel, are going to join me. Since you saw where the Redcoats dragged him, we would like you to join us as well." John Warren paused, "Will you?"

Steve was shocked. At first, he didn't know what to say. After a moment he said, "If Mrs. Adams doesn't mind me missing my chores," looking at Abigail, "then yes, I'd like to come." Abigail nodded with approval.

Chapter 64

Finding Joseph

The April morning started cold. Light rain blurred their view of the hills. Steve had left Braintree the previous night with Warren and Revere. They'd all slept at Revere's home in the north end of Boston, just across the bay from Bunker Hill.

They woke at dawn to get an early start, and the two men and Steve met John's younger brother, Samuel Warren, at the base of the hill. As they hiked up the hill that had been the site of so much death, they stopped at the top, examining the remains of the redoubt.

John looked first towards the American fort and then to Steve as he spoke. "Well, I assume it was in this area that Joseph was shot?"

Steve nodded. "I stood here, and Dr. Warren was there." Steve pointed to a spot less than ten yards away. "I remember seeing the British soldier's pistol pointed directly at Dr Warren and I tried to warn him." Steve walked to the spot where Dr. Warren had fallen. "Just as I yelled, the British soldier fired, and the next thing I knew he was falling." Steve pointed down to the ground. "He would've landed here."

He paused, remembering that tragic moment. All three men watched and listened. "I wanted to run to him, and I tried. I started toward him, but as I did another British soldier standing somewhere around here," Steve made a circle with his hand, "swung the butt of his musket into my head. It knocked me out and I don't remember anything after that." Steve's voice trailed off and a heavy silence fell over the small group.

Revere asked in a reverent tone, "Did you see where they placed the body?"

Steve nodded, "I did. When I came to, the battle was over." Steve reflected on the distasteful memory. "I saw two Redcoats take

Dr. Warren's waistcoat and drag his body over that way." Steve pointed towards a group of trees. "Follow me," he said, as he began walking in the direction of the trees.

"It seems like they dragged him over here." Steve pointed to the area just in front of the trees. "That's all I can remember. After I watched them take Dr. Warren, I decided I needed to escape. That's when I crawled towards those." He pointed to a large grove of trees some distance behind the redoubt. "From there, I somehow made my way down the road," Steve looked towards John Warren, "and then you found me . . . or I found you." Steve shrugged. "That's all I remember."

Nodding, John stepped forward. "Well, I think I know where we need to start digging." He looked at the other men and turned towards the small grove of trees. He was silent for a long moment. A shadow of grief had fallen on his face. Sticking the point of his shovel into the dirt, John cleared his throat, "I say we start here."

The group began digging, and it didn't take long before they uncovered the remains of a soldier. Samuel Warren, Joseph's youngest brother, made the discovery. He thrust his shovel down past a few feet of New England dirt and announced, "Fellows, I've found a bone." When the others gathered around, they began shoveling more carefully around the location of what turned out to be an American soldier's arm. No one spoke as the remains of one soldier appeared to be the remains of two, then three and then many more.

Steve thought it would be hard to think of a more repulsive undertaking. The bodies had been buried for over nine months, and little remained but the bones. Steve looked at the skeletons under the severely deteriorated clothes, and he knew it would be really difficult to identify which of the skeletons was Dr. Warren. Nothing was said as they all tried to endure the awfulness of their task. After some time, John stopped and stepped back, and the others likewise stopped. They knew they had clearly uncovered a number of soldiers. The question everyone was thinking was, "Which one, if any, was their friend and brother?"

Remembering something he'd read from Grace's material, Steve asked, "Is there anything that could identify Dr. Warren?" The three men looked at the skeletons. There seemed nothing that could help identify the remains. Steve asked again, "Did Dr. Warren have any missing fingers or toes or maybe any false teeth that would still be intact in his mouth?"

Revere's face lit up. "Aye! A couple of years past I helped make and fit two false teeth for Joseph. If we find the skull containing the ivory teeth and silver band holding them, we've found Joseph."

A new sense of hope sprung up among the wet and tired diggers. Although none of the skeletons currently exposed had two ivory teeth[41], the group took heart in the fact that their friend and brother could now be identified. They just needed to unearth his remains.

After another hour or so, Revere announced, "I've found Joseph." Although it should have been good news, Steve noted that Revere's voice was low and somber.

As they stopped the search, all came to where Revere stood. With the remains half uncovered, Steve examined the facial part of the skull facing upward, and saw the two ivory teeth and a silver clasp connecting them.

All felt joy in finding Dr. Warren, but were deeply sad to see him like this. Joseph Warren would now receive a proper funeral and burial. The morning rain had stopped. Rays of sunlight were beginning to shine through the clouds.

The day had been a success.

How successful – Steve had no idea.

---

41 *Dr. Warren's ivory teeth* were truly crafted and wired together by his best friend Paul Revere. Additionally, it was by this means that Dr. Warren's body was identified among the many dead Americans in the mass grave on the top of Bunker Hill. Paul Revere may have been the first to use forensic dentistry in the United States.

Chapter 65

YES!

They all reburied Dr. Warren's fallen comrades. Skeleton after skeleton was placed back in their dirt graves. Steve watched as John and Samuel carefully arranged Dr. Warren's skeleton and prepared it to be moved. Revere had brought a large wool blanket for this purpose. The blanket was placed next to Dr. Warren's grave. Gently, the brothers and closest friend of the fallen hero moved the fragile remains from the dirt coffin onto the waiting blanket.

The three men moved the bones as best they could, struggling to keep the remains together. Steve watched, trying to imagine how these bones being placed on a blanket had, just ten months earlier, been his friend. These men were moving the skeleton of someone who had really impacted his life and the lives of millions of other Americans. After walking side by side with Dr. Warren, Steve was no longer the same. His feelings towards his country and those who fought to protect it weren't the same. He owed this change to Dr. Warren, and was unsure how to repay him. He really loved the hero of Bunker Hill.

Dr. Warren's body had been moved to the blanket where it was securely wrapped. The men placed a second blanket around the body, and then ropes were tied around both blankets to hold the bones of the skeleton in place. The remains of the great patriot were now ready to be transported down Bunker Hill.

As the group finished and gathered their equipment, Steve went back to refill the hole. He shoveled his first scoop of dirt into the opening. Leaning over the top of the hole and preparing to scrape a second pile of dirt, Steve stopped. Looking in to where Dr. Warren's head would have laid, there appeared to be a round, grey stone. But could a stone be so round? Throwing the shovel aside, Steve bent down and picked up the object.

It wasn't a stone. It was a musket ball. No, it was *the* musket ball!

A surge ran up his spine.

Remembering that Dr. Warren had been shot in the back of his head, Steve realized that the musket ball must have fallen from the doctor's skull as its contents had deteriorated. The thought was not pleasant, but it did explain why the ball was laying in the dirt.

As Steve examined the ball, his hand shook. Could the musket ball responsible for Joseph Warren's death be the same one that generated his time travels?

Steve knew that there were likely thousands of musket balls that could be found on this hill. But the feeling that burned through his fingertips, up his arm and into his chest when he first touched the ball removed any doubt. Placing the ball in his pocket, Steve was sure he held the missing link between his current life in Colonial America and his life in the 21st century.

While walking to join the other men, the question bubbled inside him as his fingers wrapped around the ball in his pocket, "Would the musket ball still work, and if it did, when?"

Chapter 66

The Funeral

Four days after having retrieved Dr. Warren's remains, a grand funeral and burial ceremony was planned for the hero of Bunker Hill. Those around Boston said the event would surpass any ever produced in the thirteen colonies.

April 8, 1776 arrived and Mother Nature delivered a beautiful day. The Adams family arrived in Boston, along with many others from the surrounding communities, in order to give Dr. Warren a fitting burial. Steve and Johnny joined the others lining the streets to see the elegant coffin housing the remains of the fallen hero. The procession began at the State House and stopped at King's Chapel, where a large audience paid their last respects.

As they walked to King's Chapel, Steve and Johnny both noticed that the local businesses, or what was left of them after being under the control of the British regiments for over a year, had closed in order to honor Dr. Warren. Everyone wanted to pay their respects to the beloved doctor and the hero of the revolution against Britain.

The whole town tried to fit into the chapel to hear those speaking about Dr. Warren. Steve and Johnny had managed to squeeze in. Steve quickly realized as he listened that those honoring Dr. Warren believed his name would never be forgotten. He and Johnny listened to speaker after speaker who stated that his honor and fame would last forever.

At the conclusion of the speeches, the boys watched as Dr. Warren's casket was removed from the church and placed in the Granary Burying Ground. Steve went to the Granary Burying Ground. He watched the burial and left the old cemetery a bit confused. He knew that, in modern times, Dr. Warren's remains were no longer at this cemetery. In his 21st century Boston, the Granary cemetery was at the beginning of the Freedom Trail. He'd seen a photo in Grace's internet stuff about Dr. Warren's gravesite being in a cemetery called Forest Hills, not the cemetery they had just buried him in.

The Granary Burying Ground would become famous. Paul Revere, Sam Adams and John Hancock would all be buried here. Steve had seen their headstones. Everybody walking the Freedom Trail in Boston could see their graves. Steve wondered how the remains that he helped find and bring from Bunker Hill could be buried here in 1776 but somehow end up in Forest Hills in 2002.[42]

He thought, "If Dr. Warren had remained here, he'd be with all his other famous friends. If he'd been with them, he wouldn't be so forgotten."

42 *Burial Locations of Dr. Joseph Warren* – Dr. Warren may have been buried more times than any other person in history. He was buried four times. First, on June 18, 1775, he was buried on the battlefield by the British, after the Battle of Bunker Hill. Second, on April 8, 1776, he was reburied with great honors at the Old Granary cemetery in Boston. Third, in 1825, the year of the fiftieth anniversary of the Battle of Bunker Hill, he was reburied in a family tomb at St. Paul's Church in Boston. Fourth, on August 8, 1856, he was reburied in what was, at that time, a very prestigious location with his other family members, at Forest Hills Cemetery in Roxbury, Massachusetts, just outside Boston. On October 22, 2016, the author attended the installation and dedication ceremony of a life-sized bronze statue of Dr. Joseph Warren at Forest Hills Cemetery, honoring and better marking what had become an almost abandoned location.

Chapter 67

Debate on Penn's Hill

The day following Dr. Warren's funeral began bright and pleasant. With his morning chores completed, Steve sat with his back against the oak tree near the house, examining the musket ball in his hand. Since finding it, he'd kept it with him at all times. Yesterday during the funeral, he held it the entire time. He hoped that during the funeral some event might activate the link to his century. But nothing had happened. The ball sat cold then and now.

Squeezing the ball in frustration, Steve saw Johnny approach. Looking at Steve's hand, Johnny said, "Don't you ever give it a rest? It's a fine souvenir, but are you ever going to stop holding it?"

Steve didn't answer, but instead asked a question of his own, "Johnny, would you like to go up to Penn's Hill and show me where you watched the fighting? I've never been up there." Steve had been wondering if maybe that special place could trigger the musket ball. Johnny nodded and pointed, and they both began walking through the open fields and pasture to the hill.

Sitting on top of Penn's Hill, Steve could see everything. He could even make out the vague shape of the redoubt. From there, he could follow a line to the grove of trees where Dr. Warren had been buried by the British. Seeing Bunker Hill and Boston, Steve thought about the funeral the day before. Still staring across the bay, he said, "There sure were a lot of people at Dr. Warren's funeral."

Johnny turned to his friend, "I've never seen anything so big. Could anyone besides the King of England be more famous?" Johnny looked back towards Boston. "Everyone in Boston and even in the faraway colonies knew Dr. Warren. I doubt there will ever be someone so grand or someone that everyone will remember more."

Steve puffed out a sigh of disgust, "Yeah, well, guess what? He'll be totally forgotten. " He, too, stared across the bay to Boston.

"No." Turning from Boston and the bay, Johnny traced something in the rich dirt with his finger. "No, he won't. Like Jesus, when you die for others and live for others, you're remembered." Johnny looked up, "You saw all the people yesterday, thousands."

Steve sighed again, shaking his head. "I promise, there will come a time when nobody will even remember Dr. Warren's name. They'll have no idea about all the things he did."

Johnny sat up straight. He looked hard at Steve. "I guess you're more right than those that spoke at the funeral yesterday? Didn't you listen?"

"I heard the speeches," Steve said, "but I promise people won't remember him."

This time Johnny made a face like he was sucking a lime. He lifted his hands, rubbing the dirt from them. Johnny said, "I heard Mom talking after the ceremony to someone from outside Boston about a new town being named Warrenton, after Dr. Warren. But you think he won't be remembered? How can he not be remembered like you say when people are naming towns after him?"

"The people that spoke at the funeral are wrong. Dr. Warren will be forgotten." Steve spoke with certainty and sadness.

Johnny shook his head. "You aren't making sense. You act like you are so sure."

Steve stood up, still holding the cold musket ball. "Let's go back to the house. I need to show you something." They went up the narrow stairs to their room and, once inside, Steve closed the door. He knew sharing his story was a risk, but Johnny deserved to know the truth.

Chapter 68

Believe

Johnny sat down on the edge of their straw bed. Steve reached behind him and pulled the stool from the table where he had recently penned the final chapter of his manuscript. He only briefly thought about what he was going to do, and then he did it. He told Johnny all about his home, his school, his family – his time. His story of modern America rushed out like a torrent of water through a broken dam.

Johnny sat stunned, shaking his head, "What do you mean you were born in 1987 – in a country called the United States of America? That's over 200 years from now." The boy's face twisted with concern.

Steve didn't like how this was turning out, but he continued. "I told you. The United States of America is this country. The Americans will win their independence. They will form a new country. The colonies will be the first 13 states, and then more will come. I promise. You have to believe me; I'm not from this century. I've traveled through time."

Reaching for the manuscript on the table, Steve continued. "Remember when you asked how I knew so much about the events in here?" Steve held the pages toward Johnny. Johnny sort of nodded. "When I read to you the account of the Boston Massacre and the Tea Party, you asked me how I knew so much about them. Do you remember?" Reluctantly, Johnny nodded. "Now do you see why?"

Johnny didn't respond. He just looked distressed. "Johnny, I knew so much about each event because I was with Dr. Warren. Somehow, I was brought from my century to your century. I thought I was, like, having these special experiences for a reason. I thought I was supposed to save Dr. Warren at Bunker Hill." He wasn't sure

Johnny believed anything, but he continued. "If saving Dr. Warren was the reason I was having these trips, I messed up."

After a moment of silence, he added, "I'm telling you this because I wanted to save Dr. Warren from dying at Bunker Hill so he would be remembered. That's the point of what I've been trying to explain – Dr. Warren is not remembered by Americans 200 years from now. I promise. He's not."

Johnny didn't say anything. In a softer tone, Steve said, "Johnny, I wish I was wrong. I wish Dr. Warren was remembered in my day. But, he's not. He'll be forgotten. That's why I've been writing with these feathers," Steve nodded to the desk and inkwell, "because it's the only way I can change that."

He stopped and looked to his shell-shocked friend. Johnny looked more petrified than believing. Eyes full of alarm, he asked, "Are you a witch?"

Steve hung his head. "No. I'm not a witch." He didn't know what else to say.

Johnny watched Steve, and then he asked, "Well, if this really happens, how do you do it? How do you travel through time?"

Snapping his head up, Steve saw for the first time the slimmest ray of hope in Johnny's eyes. Reaching into his pocket he pulled out the musket ball. He opened his palm in the direction of his friend. "This is the link. It somehow connects my century and yours." Steve added, "I got it from a great uncle. He was a war hero, a guy who was a future relative of Dr. Warren. I mean, I'm, like, related to Dr. Warren, too. I'm a distant relative, way in the future."

Johnny reached over and took the ball out of Steve's hand. As the ball left his hand, Steve felt something flow from him. His first reaction was to snatch it back, but he restrained himself as Johnny inspected the ball.

Johnny made a face, "This is the ball you found at the redoubt. How can this make you travel through time? How could you have received this from a great uncle related to Dr. Warren?" Johnny shook his head, "You just found it."

"I know. I just got it back. I didn't tell you the whole story." Steve scooted to the edge of his seat, "I always had the musket ball when I was in your century, except when I lost it during the Battle of Bunker Hill. I didn't have it all the time I was here with you." Steve nodded in Johnny's direction. "I didn't have it until we found Dr. Warren's body."

Johnny looked spooked. "What are you talking about?"

"Johnny, I didn't find it at the redoubt by a wall. The ball was in Dr. Warren's grave."

Johnny popped up from the bed. Steve had pushed things too far. To a young boy in colonial New England, this was pure and simple witch talk.

Hurrying to his feet and putting his hand on Johnny's shoulder, Steve nodded back to the edge of the bed. Johnny looked to the exit and then to Steve. He sat back down, and Steve said, "Your dad is going to sign the Declaration of Independence this summer." Although still "witch talk," this caught Johnny's attention. He loved to hear anything about his dad. "Your dad will be very important in creating the United States of America. He'll be the second president of the country that they'll form this year, on July 4th."

Steve could see Johnny was listening. He may not believe what Steve was saying, but he listened. "Your father will be remembered."

Johnny raised his eyebrows, "You mean my father will be remembered 200 years from now, but not Dr. Warren?" Johnny shook his head. Few colonists outside of Boston would've known who his dad was at that moment, while everyone in the colonies knew about the hero who died at Bunker Hill.

Steve nodded. "Johnny, you'll be remembered 200 years from now, too."

"What? How will I be remembered, and not Dr. Warren?"

Looking directly into his friend's eyes, Steve explained, "Your father will be the second president and you will be the sixth president. I know this because in my time, President Bush is president and he became president a few years after his dad. My history teacher, Mrs.

Truman, said the only other time that happened was with you and your dad."

Johnny looked so confused. He mumbled, "President? Do you mean Governor of Massachusetts Colony?"

Steve shook his head. "No. You'll be President of the United States, like governor of all the colonies, all united together." Steve watched Johnny trying to process these new ideas.

Steve knew everything sounded bizarre.

In a voice warmer than Johnny had used since coming up to the room, he asked, "How do you know this?" Then, as if answering his own question, he shook his head. "How can I know all this is true?"

Steve felt a surge of hope. "You just need to believe me."

Johnny stared at Steve but said nothing.

Steve could tell that Johnny wanted to believe. Finally, the younger boy nodded in the direction of the manuscript on Steve's lap and asked, "Now that you've told me your secrets, are you going to let me read the document?"

Lifting the pages from his lap, Steve asked, "If you will believe it, you can read it." Johnny almost smiled.

Handing the musket ball back to Steve so he could take the large stack of pages, Johnny's eyes twinkled. "I don't know what will be harder, reading your penmanship or believing your stories?"

Steve would never know.

While Johnny was handing the ball back to Steve, they both touched it together at the same time. At that second, the ball was caught between Johnny's life in the 1700s and Steve's life in the 21st century. Steve realized that Johnny was on the other side of a door that was closing. As it closed, there was a blast of light.

When Steve opened his eyes, M-Rod stood motioning him to class.

PART FIVE
REMEMBER

There are over 100,000 words in the English language, but which is the most powerful?

Do you remember that seventy men stood their ground on a Lexington field, in the first battle of the American Revolution? Eight never returned home. Their blood nurtured the soil of the national tree described in Steve's essay.

Do we remember that 2,977 people died on September 11, 2001? A total of 412 were firefighters, police officers and other first responders who rushed into the burning towers and never saw their friends and family again. At the 9/11 Memorial & Museum, the most hallowed location in New York City, all those who died are remembered, as their names are etched in bronze and read aloud.

More than 1,350,000 American military men and women have fought and died while defending our country. On Memorial Day and Veterans Day, do we remember them? Or, like Steve in November 2001, are these just days off from school?

If we fail to remember our history, if we fail to remember our veterans, and if we fail to remember those who have sacrificed for our freedom as Americans, America will lose the roots that make it strong. A tree without roots cannot survive.

There are over 100,000 words, and the word REMEMBER may be the most powerful.

Bunker Hill Monument

Statue of Dr. Joseph Warren at Bunker Hill

Dr. Warren's Footprints on the Freedom Trail

The Freedom Trail is a red brick path in Old Boston that is used to mark the location of important events, places and homes of patriots that contributed to the Revolution. While there is no spot on the trail specifically dedicated to Dr. Warren, it's hard to think of a person whose life is more intimately connected to the Freedom Trail.

Chapter 69

Mr. Frothingham

APRIL 2002

Steve had been back from living at the Adams Farm in the 1770s for about four months. Since returning, he wanted to visit what was now the Adams National Historical Park. He'd learned that the Adams Farm had been turned into something like a museum.

He told Grace about his plan. Together they selected a special date, April 19, 2002[43], the anniversary of the Battles of Lexington, Concord and Menotomy. Steve hoped that a visit to the Adams Farm, on this special day, could reactivate the musket ball for one more trip to see Dr. Warren.

Steve thought that when they left on that April morning to go to the old home of John and Abigail Adams, that it was just him, Grace, and his mom who were traveling from Needham to the Adams Farm.

He was wrong.

Continuation of Chapter One . . .

In the Adams' farmhouse, Steve stood in front of Dr. Warren's portrait. The man in the black suit watched Steve stare at the painting. He watched him pull his hand with the ball out of his pocket.

The man flattened his coat with his hands and the lines of his tailored suit jacket fell in perfect sync with his professionally-pressed pants. He stood to the side of the hall, hidden from Steve's view. He'd removed his designer sunglasses and raised his eyebrows. Pressing forward, he tilted his body toward Steve's right hand. Steve opened his hand and looked at the round piece of lead. In a murmur that the representative of the ancient organization strained to hear, Steve said, "Can't I have one more adventure – just one more?"

---

43 *April 19th is Patriots' Day* – A few states celebrate this date as a holiday. In Massachusetts, it is a school holiday. I'm sure a lot of readers wished they lived in Massachusetts in April.

It was time.

The agent who had followed Steve O'Dell from Needham stepped forward.

"Fine day on the Adams Family Farm, isn't it?" The man saw Steve startle. "My name is Richard Frothingham and I'm from the Boston Historic Genealogical Society." He handed Steve a business card.

Steve mumbled, "Who . . . what group?"

Mr. Frothingham spoke quickly. "I'm here representing the Society. I've come because of it." He directed his coal black eyes to Steve's extended, but now closed right hand. "You have a Time-Traveling Talisman. They call these antiquities T3s in the Society." Steve just stared, his mouth open. "What?"

"We must meet again. I'll be at Forest Hills Cemetery on June 17th." The information was already printed, not written, but printed on the back of the card. "Meet me at 4:34 in the afternoon – at his gravesite. This is the precise time it occurred. Lastly, today is April 19th. You and Grace have until June 17th to complete the book. Finish it before his death day. We will discuss the book and Dr. Warren." Mr. Frothingham began moving away. He ended with three final words, "Bring the ball." He nodded towards Steve's hand. With a final nod, Frothingham walked back the way he and his group had come, disappearing into the next crowd of visitors.

Steve stood rooted to the spot for several seconds. When he came to, he tried to follow the man. Questions bounced around in his head. But the mysterious man had vanished into the crowds. Turning around, Steve walked back through the doorway into the Adams Family Farm and pushed forward to catch up to Grace and his mom.

Steve's mom was engaged in reading a plaque about life on the Adams Farm in the 1770s. As he caught up to them, Grace said, "Where were you?" Steve slipped the card into Grace's hand and gave her a look that said, "We need to talk."

About an hour later, they sat at Steve's kitchen table.

Grace stared at Steve. "This Mr. Frothingham knew *my* name? Me?" Grace's voice rose enough that Steve looked to the kitchen door to make sure his mom hadn't heard. He made a face and put his finger to his lips.

In a softer voice, Steve said, "Yeah, and he knew we were writing the book about Dr. Warren. He said we needed to get it done before meeting him on June 17th." Steve shrugged, "I'm not gonna lie, Grace. It was freaky how much he knew. He knew everything."

"Steve, you're not really planning to meet this guy at this Forest Hills Cemetery in June, are you?" Nervously running her fingers through her hair, she added, "This is crazy. He knew our names. How'd he know our names? How'd he know we were working on the book? How'd he know you had the musket ball? He even knew we were going to be at the Adams Farm or why would he just show up!" Grace shook her head. "This creeps me out."

Steve nodded, and added, "Yeah, he knew Dr. Warren died June 17th and even said 4:34 was the precise time it occurred. How would he know the exact time he died? I was there when Dr. Warren died, and I didn't know that. And, all this information is printed on the back of the card, like this card was just made for me." Grace flipped over the card with the printed information on the back – *Meet at Forest Hills Cemetery June 17th 4:34pm.*

Still looking at the card in Grace's hand, Steve said, "Even though everything about meeting this Mr. Frothingham guy is crazy, I really want to know more. I need answers. Grace, I think this guy will have them. Yeah, meeting with him at the Adams house was psycho, but he wasn't like evil or anything. He seemed normal; he just knew things that I didn't think anyone knew." They both looked at the information printed on the back of the card. Then Steve said, "We're going on June 17th."

Grace looked at Steve and asked, "We?"

Steve nodded. "Grace, how are we supposed to write a legit book about Dr. Warren if we don't talk to this guy who seems to know more about Dr. Warren than the two of us combined?"

Grace quickly responded, "Steve, how could anyone know more about Dr. Warren than you? You were right there with him. You walked side by side with him!"

Grace's words made Steve think about his adventures in 1770s Boston. Everything now meant so much more to him, compared to when he'd originally learned about all the places on his school field trip to the Freedom Trail.[44] Just then, an idea popped into his head. He turned to Grace, "Okay, so I know you don't like the idea of talking to this Mr. Frothingham and getting information from him for our book. But what if we just go on the Freedom Trail together. We can visit all the sites I visited in the 1770s, and then I'll meet with this Frothingham guy alone."

Steve waited. Grace was silent. Finally, he said, "Will you come with me? We can take the Boston subway line from here. It stops right at the beginning of the trail."

After a few seconds, she agreed. "Yeah, I'll go with you. We'll see these sites in Boston. But," her eyes widened. "I'm not going with you when you go to Forest Hills Cemetery and meet with this Frothingham guy." Grace shook her head, "That whole thing weirds me out. I'm sorry."

Steve grinned, "Deal."

44 *Freedom Trail* – Since 1951, millions of people have enjoyed following a line of red bricks placed into Boston's sidewalks, streets and plazas. The 2.5 mile brick trail weaves through downtown Boston, connecting 16 historical sites. From the Boston Common on one end to Bunker Hill on the other, those following the trail can learn much about the events leading up to the American Revolution. Over 4 million people from all over the world walk the Freedom Trail each year.

Chapter 70

Freedom Trail and Famous Cemetery

Steve and Grace hopped out of the downtown subway station and onto the Boston Common, the oldest public park in the country. With permission from their parents, they'd taken the subway, with the requirement that they return before dark. So now, they had a full day of adventure ahead of them.

The June morning burst with energy. Grace looked around.

Crowds filled the sidewalks. Women in long dresses, thick aprons, and hair pulled up in buns that were covered with bonnets from the 1770s, gathered groups of people in Bermuda shorts and t-shirts that said *I Love Boston.* Men in long jackets with tails and knee-length pants with white stockings waved their three-cornered hats to get the attention of the crowds.

Sunday, June 16, 2002, was abuzz with tourists and Boston guides. All were converging at the beginning of the red bricks that marked the world famous Freedom Trail.

Grace followed Steve as they dodged through groups, following the carefully placed red bricks. Not far from the Boston Common, Grace saw one of the main stops, the Granary Cemetery. Hundreds of grey headstones, most slanted and some cracked, all sprang up from the open plot of ground in the busiest part of downtown Boston. Hundreds of years of history lay beneath those markers. Hundreds of tourists walked through the rows of headstones, all experiencing one of Americas most visited cemeteries.

The black gates around the cemetery were made from cast iron that would've been forged before electricity ever lit the dark corners of the graveyard. Steve passed through the iron bars and walked on. Grace examined a map showing the location of the important people who had been buried in the cemetery. Paul Revere, Sam Adams, John

Hancock, the five victims of the Boston Massacre, including Crispus Attucks, and Benjamin Franklin's mother and father were all buried at this site.

After reading about the cemetery, Grace spotted Steve in the middle of the grounds. He stood looking around him. He scanned the groups of tourists as if counting each individual. Grace could see gatherings at all the famous graves. Steve started walking in the direction of one of those groups and Grace quietly followed.

A guide who was dressed like a maiden from the 1770s stood near an old headstone. The large stone had a brass plaque stating that the man buried there, Sam Adams, had been a signer of The Declaration of Independence. Grace could see from the old plaque that the Sons of the Revolution had placed the special monument on Sam Adams' gravesite in 1898.

Steve listened to everything the guide said. He followed the group as they made their way to the huge John Hancock gravestone and then to the one for Paul Revere. The guide in the old-fashioned clothes talked a lot about all these different men in America's history. Grace knew what Steve was thinking. Each time the guide would tell a story about the 1770s, there was never any mention of Dr. Warren.

Grace and Steve stayed on the edge of the group as they walked to the memorial honoring the five people who died on the night of the Boston Massacre. Grace saw the name Crispus Attucks on the Boston Massacre memorial. Seeing that strange name, Crispus, made her think back to the first time Steve told her about his time-traveling experiences and how she hadn't believed him.

Steve stood there, looking at the marker. The names of the five men killed during the Boston Massacre were etched in stone. A small flag had been placed in the ground next to this marker and next to the other distinguished gravesites. Patriots lay there.

Grace noticed another name below the five. The marker read, Christopher Snider – Aged 12 years, Killed February 22, 1770. The innocent, first victim of the struggles between the Colonists and the Crown, which resulted in INDEPENDENCE.

Turning to Steve, she asked, "Do you know anything about this Christopher?"

Steve nodded. Again, he looked around at all the people. Pointing to the name, he said, "I heard Dr. Warren talking to John Adams about him the night of the Boston Massacre. Dr. Warren said this kid's death made everybody in Boston really mad."

Turning towards Grace, Steve spoke slowly, "I guess he was just standing outside some guy's house. The man in the house was super loyal to the British and got in a big argument with the patriots who wanted the British troops gone. The man in the house got scared and randomly shot a gun-full of buckshot out into the street. He killed the boy. Dr. Warren found eleven pellets in his body."

Grace repeated, "Eleven?"

"The guy had really packed the gun." He added, "In some ways, it was this kid's death that began the events that lead to the Revolution."

Steve walked away from the group. He started slowly back to the middle of the old, famous cemetery. He stopped. Grace stood next to him. She waited for him to talk. She didn't know what to say.

Steve pointed to a side wall in the direction of John Hancock's monument, "He was buried there." Grace looked towards the wall. Steve went on, "Grace it would be so cool to see him here. Look at all these people that come here." He nodded towards the crowds. "I wish Dr. Warren's family had just left him here instead of moving his body to Forest Hills Cemetery. Sure, it was the best cemetery back then, but now it's like in nowhereville. If they hadn't moved him, he wouldn't be forgotten, he'd be remembered – like his friends."

Steve sucked in a bunch of air. "It's so dumb."

Chapter 71

OLD SOUTH

Grace didn't know what to say. Steve seemed so frustrated. As they left the cemetery, they both walked in silence along the trail. After a few blocks, they came to the church called King's Chapel.

"This is where Johnny and I came to listen to the funeral speakers." Steve looked at Grace. "He was here at King's Chapel after we took his body from the battle site. From here, we all walked to the Granary Burying Ground. Everyone from Boston was there."

Steve stood for a minute with his right hand in a fist. He looked toward the Granary Burying Ground, then turned back to King's Chapel. After a minute, he said, "Let's keep walking."

They walked in silence. Finally, Grace asked, "Steve, are you sad because you're seeing these places that remind you of Dr. Warren's death or because you haven't had another trip in time?" She reached over and briefly touched his right hand.

Steve nodded, lifting his hand. "You saw me holding the musket ball?" Grace nodded in response. "Yeah, I still hope, you know, that it's not over." He turned his gaze to the upcoming building. "Every spot along this trail is super-connected to him. Dr. Warren walked and lived and died along this trail." He turned to Grace. "I guess I just keep hoping something will trigger this ball to work again." He nodded towards his hand. "It might be one of these spots."

Grace understood. She nodded and really wished Steve would put the musket ball in his pocket so she could reach down and hold his hand.

At the end of the block, they came to a church. Grace read the sign, The Old South Meeting House. The sign explained that this was where everyone gathered just before the Boston Tea Party.

Steve walked past the sign and said, "Let's go in. But," he pointed to the side of the church, "when we're done inside, I have to show you something back there. I think you're really gonna like it." This time Steve's smile spread across his whole face.

Grace followed Steve as he walked to where a group was standing. The group's guide was dressed like Paul Revere and had a deep voice. Grace looked at the guide and imagined the famous rider himself having the same voice as he rode through the towns announcing the coming of the King's soldiers.

"Look above you and around you." The guide's words echoed from the front of the church. "This was the largest building in colonial Boston. Every March 5, on the anniversary of the Boston Massacre, from 1772 to the signing of the Declaration of Independence in 1776, Boston patriots met here to commemorate the deaths of the citizens in their streets and to protest their unequal treatment by their King. On the eve of the Boston Tea Party, over 5,000 patriots met here to again protest the fact that tea in the colonies was being taxed and treated differently than tea in England.

"All the leading patriots of Boston spoke from that podium." The guide pointed to the pulpit in the front. The wooden pulpit had a velvet drape hanging down the front. As the group walked closer to the platform, Steve remained where he was. Grace knew that Steve hated calling attention to himself. But she was sure he would have liked to mention that one of those "leading patriots" had been his friend. She saw the knuckles on his right hand turn white as he gripped harder.

She walked over to him. "Do you want to go join them in the front? Maybe it will work there." Grace glanced at his hand.

Steve waited a bit and then shook his head. "I have a better idea." He looked out one of the back windows. "I want to show you something." With a bounce in his step that she hadn't seen since before they'd entered the cemetery, Steve walked out and around the old church to a back alley, away from the crowds. They were the only ones in the alley. Steve looked, walked, and looked some more at the back wall of the church. Grace could tell he was trying to find something.

"I think it's here under this window." He put the musket ball away and pulled a small, flathead screwdriver from his other pocket. "I brought this," holding up the tool, "just for this reason."

Grace watched as Steve bent down, looking up under the window ledge. He scooted over a bit to his left. Then he pushed, twisted, and with his second hand helped maneuver the screwdriver like a wedge.

Moments later, Steve was holding a brass button. Despite having spent over 225 years in a crack, it looked pretty good. The one Steve had given to her six months ago was certainly shinier, but they were definitely the same buttons.

Steve looked at Grace, "Maybe if I hold both of these?" Grace nodded. It seemed like a possibility. Putting the screwdriver back in his pocket and holding the musket ball with the button, Steve squeezed his hand into a fist. After a few seconds, he shook his head.

Grace watched as Steve jammed his clenched hand deep into his pocket. Trying to help, she said, "There are still a lot of other places it might work. You said it always works in random ways."

Grace smiled. Steve just started down the red brick trail.

Chapter 72

Massacre Memories and Hanover House

As they traveled across the path, Grace saw the fancy gold lion and unicorn statutes. Each stood on the top edges of the building's roof. A huge ornate clock had been built into the building between the gold statutes. It was easy to note this building as a site on the Freedom Trail. Surrounded by the many modern buildings, the beautiful three-story brick building floated in a sea of gray skyscrapers. White framed windows with ornate panes and wavy glass created a mirage in modern Boston that made those dressed in colonial costumes look perfectly in place near the Old State House.

Steve walked towards a cobblestone circle in front of the building. The five foot circle marked the site of the Boston Massacre. "I was standing there," Steve whispered.

Grace knew exactly what Steve meant. "Over here," he pointed back near the marker, "this is where Crispus Attucks was shot. There was blood everywhere," Steve paused, "and there," he pointed to the other side of the street, "is where I sat after all the shootings, until Dr. Warren came."

He breathed out a really long breath. "This is where I first went back." Grace looked at him. He closed his eyes and shook his head. He stuck his fist in his pocket, "Let's keep going."

Looking up at the clock, he added, "It's almost lunch time. I want to eat at the Green Dragon Tavern, but first I really want to try standing where Dr. Warren's house used to be."

Grace knew Steve was anxious to stand on the spot where Dr. Warren's house had been. He'd researched all he could on the internet. He'd even talked on the phone to the historian at the Paul Revere House.

With help from the historian, Steve figured out generally where Dr. Warren's home would've been. He decided he could find it in modern Boston because he'd been to the actual house in 1775. Grace looked around at the huge buildings and modern skyscrapers. Nothing much of the 1770s remained. She didn't say it, but she wondered how Steve would ever recognize anything from Dr. Warren's day.

She just smiled, "Let's go to where the house was and then we can eat."

They continued following the Freedom Trail, passing by Faneuil Hall and a statue of Sam Adams. Steve said, "Dr. Warren lived on Hanover Street, just up that direction." He pointed in between two huge buildings.

"How can you and the historian guy be so sure?" Grace asked.

As they crossed the busy streets and walked towards a barren, cement plaza bigger than four football fields, Steve explained, "The historian I talked to said he worked with other historians and they studied old maps. Putting a new map over an old map, they could tell the house would've been between the Boston City building and this federal building."

Grace could see the huge building to her left was the Boston City Offices and the one on the right was named the John F. Kennedy Federal Building. Steve pointed to the stairs in the middle of the plaza, "The historian at the Paul Revere House said it would be above those stairs. He said up the stairs and towards the federal building." Steve turned to their right. "I think if I can stand around the area, I can figure out where Dr. Warren's house would've been."

Grace tilted her head. She wondered how he'd figure that out, but Steve seemed happier than he had all day. Before they even got to the plaza stairs, he'd already reached into his pocket and balled his hand into a fist.

At the top of the stairs, Steve stared to his right. He walked about half-way to the John F. Kennedy building and stopped. He then turned and looked across the city toward the Boston Harbor. He glanced at the skyline. He kept staring, looking for something.

Grace asked, "What are you doing?"

"I'm looking for the steeple. I remember seeing the two lights from the Old North Church Steeple. Back when I saw the lights, the steeple was the highest thing in the sky. It was a lot easier to see."

Suddenly he froze, then pointed. "There! See the white steeple?" Grace nodded.

Steve hopped back and slid over to his left. He shuffled a few feet farther back down the plaza. "Here. Here is where I would've been standing when I saw the steeple. I remember that angle. That night the two lantern lights went out from the steeple that way." Steve pointed towards what was now a bridge across a bay. "This would be," he looked to a spot just behind them, "where Joseph Warren's house would've been.

"It all started here, Grace. I mean, it really did. You know the Revolutionary War started when Joseph Warren sent Paul Revere and the other rider, William Dawes, to warn all the militias that the British soldiers were marching to Lexington and Concord."

Steve looked at Grace. "We're standing at the Starting Place of the American Revolution." [45]

Grace looked around. There was not one person over here. Unlike all the other places on the Freedom Trail that were crowded with tourists and regular people making their way through downtown Boston, no one was over here on this plaza between the two government buildings.

Steve smiled at Grace. He stared back at the steeple. He looked so hopeful. "This may be the best place." Gently he moved his hand and right arm. Grace waited. After ten, then twenty seconds, Steve's arm stopped swinging. He looked at the steeple and then at Grace. All the light in his eyes faded.

---

45 *Starting Place of the American Revolution* – Although other places can claim to be where the American Revolution started, Dr. Warren's house is the author's first choice for the designation. Yes, the first shot was fired in Lexington. The first real battle was at the Old North Bridge outside of Concord. However, there would have been no Lexington or Concord if Dr. Warren had not begun the warnings to the militias the evening before the battles. Someday, the author hopes there will be a memorial marking the location of Dr. Warren's home, and designating the location as the Starting Place of the American Revolution.

"I really thought that of all the places, it would happen here." He spoke in a low voice. "I stood right here with Rob. We both watched Dr. Warren and Paul Revere leave from his house. I thought this might be the place to make it work again." He went to put the ball back in his pocket. His hope seemed gone.

Then Steve's head popped up.

He looked at Grace. "I have an idea. Grace, can you come and stand by me." Steve held in his hand the ball and the brass button. "Here, you hold these, and I'll touch them with you." He was smiling again. "See, when I came back here, to Joseph Warren's house, I came with Rob. Maybe this needs two people to work."

Grace tilted her head. She wasn't so sure she wanted to go if they'd end up in the middle of the Revolutionary War. But also, she wasn't so sure this would actually make it happen. Without voicing her doubts, she thought about her friend. She knew how badly Steve wanted to go back. Squashing her own fears and doubts, she stood next to him.

Steve placed the button and ball in Grace's palm. Then, he placed his hand over hers. He held her hand. She felt the ball; she felt the button; she felt his hand holding hers. Grace looked into his eyes, and smiled. His hand felt warm, and she felt butterflies in her belly even though the musket ball remained cold. She hoped he'd smile back. She hoped he'd keep his hand on hers.

"Dang!" Steve spat out the word and looked away.

He turned and picked up the ball and button from her hand. He shoved them back into his pocket. Then he said, "Tomorrow this guy is going to want the ball. I just know it. I'm not giving it to him. I'm not giving it up until I have another trip. I want to see Dr. Warren again."

The butterflies and the special moment now gone, Grace questioned, "What did you say?"

"Tomorrow, this Richard Frothingham guy is going to want the musket ball. He told me specifically to bring it to Forest Hills Cemetery." Steve looked back at Grace, "I want to go back; I just want one more visit when Dr. Warren is not dead. I don't want to give the ball back until I have another visit."

Turning to Steve, Grace said in a soft tone, "Steve, it might still work at Bunker Hill."

Chapter 73

Tavern, Steeple and Paul Revere

For a while, they walked in silence. Finally, Steve said, "I could imagine myself traveling back in time at any of the sites we've visited." He paused, "But I could never think about it happening at Bunker Hill." He paused again. "I wanted to see him alive. Bunker Hill is where I let him die."

Grace remained silent because she didn't know what to say. After a minute, Steve pointed to a sign above the place where they'd stopped, *Green Dragon Tavern.* Steve opened the door, "Let's eat."

As Grace walked in, the wood planks creaked, and the old, musty smell of the restaurant greeted her. The tables and chairs were made of dark, heavy wood that would've been popular when King George ruled. The place sat on the Freedom Trail between where Dr. Warren had lived and the Paul Revere House. They sat at a table near a window with white panes and wavy glass, just like the Old State House by the Massacre site. Grace asked, "Is this like the real Green Dragon Tavern?"

Steve shook his head, "No. This is just a restaurant they made to look old. It's not the real one."

Steve saw the old bulletins and maps on the walls from the 1770s. "Yeah, the real one was a lot bigger and had a big long room on the second floor. I met Sam Adams and John Hancock there."

Hearing Steve talk about his trips, Grace understood why he wanted to take another. How cool to have been in the real Green Dragon Tavern with Sam Adams and John Hancock.

Steve opened the menu, "Did you see the stuff to order?" He nodded at the pages, "You can order a Sam Adams burger or a Paul Revere one with bacon, or the one I'm getting, the Joseph Warren burger." For a brief second, a smile poked through his sadness. Grace loved seeing Steve's smile.

They ate, talked and planned the rest of their afternoon.

As they left the tavern, they turned right and followed the red bricks of the Freedom Trail for a few blocks until they came to Paul Revere's house. They waited in line to tour one of the oldest and most famous homes in Boston.

As they left Revere's house, Steve had the same disappointed look on his face that he had at all the other sites.

From Paul Revere's house, they crossed a few streets and turned two corners before they entered a lush courtyard with trees and flowers. From the courtyard, Grace could see the back of a church. From the height and white glow of the old steeple, she was sure they were next to the Old North Church.

Groups of people and their colonial-dressed guides stood all around the courtyard. Near the church, a huge bronze statue memorialized Paul Revere. His right arm was flung behind and outstretched, his body leaned back with riding boots firmly astride a gleaming stallion. The tourists snapped photos from every angle. Grace overheard a tall, skinny guide telling his group, "This is the most photographed site on the Freedom Trial." A young father handed him a camera and requested that the guide take a photo of him with his kids. The guide directed them. "Okay, move over to this spot. From this angle," he said, pointing towards the steeple, "you can get the statue and the steeple in the photo. Smile!" The dad, mom and their two daughters, who looked a little younger than Steve and Grace, now had a lifetime memory from their trip to Boston.

"Steve," Grace said, "let's ask someone to take a picture of us. My new flip phone has a camera."

They stood in the same spot where the young family had stood. Grace turned to the family and asked the mom if she would take the photo. Grace explained to her how the camera in her phone worked. The mom nodded, while the dad stood behind with the girls and watched.

The dad smiled, "Now come on, put your arms around each other." His daughters giggled. Grace certainly didn't mind, but didn't want to act first. The dad's smile grew as he lifted his arms and pushed his hands together in the air, "Come on, closer now, go ahead."

Grace felt Steve's arm wrap around her waist and she did the same for him. The dad had a big grin. His wife did her best to catch Grace and Steve's moment in the flip-phone photo.

"There you go!" The dad thought he was pretty clever and smiled at the young couple. His two daughters still had a few giggles left as they looked admiringly at Grace. Grace thanked the young mother.

Having recovered from the embarrassment of this getting-close moment, Steve looked at the photo. "Wow, that's so cool that your phone can take photos." Steve loved anything to do with new technology. Grace looked at the photo too, but she only focused on how cute Steve's smile looked when he was embarrassed.

She followed him as they walked towards a nearby bridge.

Chapter 74

The Last Spot

Grace stopped and turned around. They were halfway across the long bridge stretching from Boston to Charlestown. She looked at the Old North Church's steeple. Grace pointed back towards the church. "So from here, Paul Revere's friends climbed up into the steeple and hung two lanterns, right?" Then she pointed to the end of the bridge, "So that people over there would know the troops were coming out of Boston by boats. Is that right?"

Steve looked in both directions, and nodded. "Yep. It's weird to think Boston used to have just one little land strip to get into the city. And, at the highest tide, the old city would become an island." Steve pointed in the other direction, "I guess it would've been harder for the soldiers to go out by land because they were sending so many that night."

Grace repeated what they'd just heard at the Old North Church, "So, 'One if by land, two if by sea.'" She smiled, "It makes a lot more sense now. I never really understood that saying, and I've lived just outside Boston my whole life."

Steve saw the sun getting lower. He thought about the day. Grace had been so great. Every time the stupid ball didn't work, Grace's smile always helped him feel better. Steve raised his eyebrows. To be honest, what boy wouldn't feel better when Grace Levy smiled at him? It was by far the best part of this disappointing trip.

They'd now followed the red brick trail across the Charlestown Bridge and through a couple of blocks in Charlestown. They could see the red bricks of the Freedom Trail ending at the entrance to the Bunker Hill Monument.

Every step up the street, Steve thought about June 17, 1775. He thought about what was under the roads and cement sidewalks. He'd watched the red-coated soldiers coming up this hill. He could remember the bullets from the Americans tearing and ripping through the approaching Redcoats. Over 1,000 British soldiers were killed or injured. And as much as Steve tried, he would never forget the expressions on the soldiers' faces as their bodies were riddled with bullets.

Steve looked from the ground to the top of the hill. Walking closer to the top, closer to where the fort had been, made his stomach tighten.

The white monument pointed upward, soaring above everything else on the hill. The Bunker Hill Monument, the last stop on the Freedom Trail, loomed just ahead. The ground was dedicated as a special site and construction on the huge monument was started June 17, 1825, the fiftieth anniversary of the battle. The fiftieth anniversary of Dr. Warren's death.

"Wow! That is way tall." Grace was looking up at the 20-story granite tower. "How long did you say it took to build?" Steve said, "Almost twenty years, it was started in 1825 but wasn't finished until 1843."

Grace asked, "Can we walk up inside the monument?"

Steve nodded, "Yeah. There are stairs that go all the way to the top." He figured that he should sound excited, but coming to Bunker Hill just hurt. He kept thinking of the dirt fort, the men, and the death. He thought of Salem Poor standing next to him with his smooth black skin shining with sweat as he loaded and fired, and Colonel Prescott as he jumped on top of the wall, kicking guns and shouting not to fire early. He'd already calculated where Israel Putnam would've been with his men on a lower part of the hill. But the recurring vision that felt like a scalding burn was seeing his friend shot.

Without saying anything, Steve walked through the main gate. He and Grace passed the huge statue of Colonel Prescott with his sword in hand and his long cape behind him. They walked away from the tall, white monument and the crowds waiting to climb to the top. They walked past it all, and Grace said nothing. She followed Steve to the other side of the National Historical Park where no one stood.

Apart from everything else, on the far edge of the hill, placed flat in the ground, was an old marker, weathered and abandoned. With Grace standing next to him, they both read, *The Monument Erected in 1794 Intended to Stand Where Warren Fell was Opposite on Concord Street.* Grace spoke first, "So there was a different monument on Bunker Hill before this one?"

Steve looked at her. He'd been holding the ball since they had walked through the front gate. He knew they were now at the right spot. When nothing happened and the ball sat cold, he said slowly, "The first monument was built by the Masons in honor of Dr. Warren. They wanted it on the spot where he had died. It was like two stories high, but nothing like this one." Steve looked back to the towering monument and the visitors surrounding it, "There's a replica of the 1794 monument in the big one." Steve had researched every site on the Freedom Trail, including this place.

He opened his hand and looked down at the round lead ball. When he looked up, he could see his own sadness reflected in Grace's eyes. He didn't want her to be sad. Grace had done so much. She'd spent hours and hours with him. For weeks they'd worked on the book and reviewed what he now knew to be his manuscript, the one he wrote with a feathered pen over 200 years ago. Grace knew more about Joseph Warren and the crazy time-traveling adventures than anyone else he knew. No one cared more than Grace.

She said, "I'm really sorry, Steve." She didn't say anything else. There was nothing else to say.

Chapter 75

HIS NAME IS LAFAYETTE

As they both walked silently, Steve held the ball in his fist, and put it back in his pocket. As he did, he felt the British soldier's button under his knuckles reminding him of his plan. He'd almost forgotten about it! Since he had first hidden the button, he'd wanted it to go to Grace. No one deserved it more. He just wondered when would be the best time to give it to her. He thought about the cool view from the top of the monument. Perfect! He looked up at the monument's top peak, but was blinded by the sun. Steve looked away. He shook his head. But this brightness didn't go away.

When the glare in his eyes finally disappeared, he saw a man next to the monument. The man stood like a king, straight and tall. He held a cane and a black top hat in one hand. He dressed in a suit, with the jacket coming down past his knees and his collar turned up just under his seasoned chin and distinguished cheekbones. The gray streaks in his hair told Steve that the cane was not just for decoration. His strange clothes looked like they were from a different time period. The warmth Steve began to feel in his right hand confirmed it.

As quickly as the man appeared and the warmth had come it all started to fade. The man looked directly at Steve and said in a flowing French accent, "Follow theez path." He pointed his cane to the other side of the monument. The ball went cold, and the man disappeared.

Steve yanked his hand with the ball out of his pocket. Forgetting about the button and how he might give it to Grace, he looked in the direction where the strange man had pointed his cane. Grace watched the weird reaction and asked, "Did something happen?"

Without responding, Steve abruptly changed their course. Instead of heading to the visitor's center entrance to the monument,

Steve started walking in the direction the strange man had pointed. Grace followed, but asked again, "Steve, what happened back there?"

Steve said, "Yeah, something happened," as he lead them forward. On the opposite side of the monument from the visitor's center, there were a number of displays. These displays were waist-high and depicted Bunker Hill at different phases. One depicted the hill before the 1775 battle, another told about the battle scenes, and then there was the last.

Steve stopped. He pointed to the Fiftieth Year Anniversary display. The display depicted the enormous June 17, 1825, celebration. Tens of thousands of Americans had gathered for the laying of the cornerstone to begin construction of the current Bunker Hill Monument on the fiftieth anniversary. He turned to Grace, "I just saw him."

Pointing, he said again, "I just saw that man. He was over there." Steve now looked back to where the tall, distinguished man with the cane had stood.

Grace looked to the place he pointed and then back to the June 17, 1825 display. She bent closer and then looked up. "You saw General Lafayette?"

Chapter 76

Bunker Hill Soil

Steve shrugged and bent down to look at the name to answer Grace, but when he tried to read the display, the ball burst with electrical energy in his hand and the display and everything around it exploded in light. When the burst faded, he was sitting in a chair, on top of Bunker Hill. The hill had no houses, no buildings, no huge monument, just tons of people. Everything around him looked like the June 17, 1825 display.

A man stood on a podium and in a very loud voice projected his words all the way down the hill to the huge crowds. Steve ignored the words as he soaked in the scene. He sat in a chair. He looked down and put his hands to his neck. He wore long black pants, a white shirt with a collar that went up to his chin and cheeks, and a silver silk band tied across his neck. He sat in a group of about forty really old men, all dressed like him. They all sat in the front, at the top of the hill on a decorated platform with flags and banners made from red, white and blue cloth. This group overlooked everything, and Steve could see thousands and thousands of people all around the hill below them.

On his lap, Steve saw what looked like an invitation. The paper had a rich quality and the print was super fancy. Everything talked about this June 17, 1825 Commemoration and Dedication. There was a line in the middle of it that said in large, bold letters, *Distinguished Guest of Honor – Veteran of the June 17, 1775, Battle of Bunker Hill* and then had a line. Above the line, in fancy cursive with flowing curves and handsome swirls, was written the name Dr. William Eustis.[46]

---

46 *William Eustis* was a real person. He was a doctor and did serve as Dr. Warren's apprentice. They were close friends and Dr. Eustis helped alongside Dr. Warren in the first battles of the Revolutionary War. He tended to the wounded during the Battle of Bunker Hill. Later, he would become the Governor of Massachusetts. Unfortunately, he would not have attended the fiftieth anniversary of the Battle of Bunker Hill. He died February 6, 1825, four months prior to the huge anniversary celebration.

Steve looked around at the elderly men sitting near him. He figured these forty or so old veterans were all that remained of those who had fought on the Hill fifty years earlier. He looked at his comrades on either side and wondered if he looked as old as they did. Steve suddenly noted that the man with the strong voice had turned to look at the distinguished guests.

His voice boomed, "Venerable men! You have come down to us from a former generation. Heaven has lengthened your lives that you might behold this joyous day. You are now where you stood fifty years ago, this very hour, with your brothers and your neighbors, shoulder to shoulder, in the strife for your country."

The voice continued, "God has allowed you to behold and to partake of the reward of your patriotic toils; and he has allowed us, your sons and countrymen, to meet you here. In the name of the present generation, in the name of your country, in the name of liberty, thank you!"

At this point, the speaker started clapping. He turned to the thousands of observers and they started clapping. Steve heard the entire hill thundering. Then the speaker motioned for the veterans to stand. Old knees and worn feet raised these men, some standing straight but many bent over with age. Steve stood with them. The roar of the crowds became deafening. The men and Steve bowed to another wave of roaring appreciation.

Sitting down, Steve looked again at his special invitation. The main speaker was Senator Daniel Webster.

This Webster guy went on, speaking to the multitudes. As he took in the scene, Steve remembered the Veteran's Day Celebration where he had met his great uncle for the first time. He felt a pang of guilt as he recalled that he'd only wanted to go to see what his great uncle would give him. Rob had complained for over an hour about having to go honor our country's veterans. Yet here, thousands stood outside in the sun to honor those who fought for their liberties.

The Senator raised his voice to a booming volume and drew Steve away from his thoughts. "But, ah! What of Him! What of the first great martyr in this great cause! Him! The premature victim of his own self-devoting heart! Him! The head of our civil councils, and the destined leader of our military bands, whom nothing brought hither but the unquenchable fire of his own spirit! Him! Cut off by Providence and falling before he saw the star of his country rise; pouring out his generous blood like water, before he knew whether it would fertilize a land of freedom or of bondage! How shall I struggle with the emotions that stifle the utterance of thy name? Our poor work may perish, but that of General Joseph Warren shall endure!

"This monument that is to be built may molder away; the solid ground it rests upon may sink down to a level with the sea; but thy memory shall not fail!"

The speaker kept talking, but Steve's thoughts stayed on that point. Wow! In 1825, in this super huge event, this Senator said the crazy big monument that they were going to build might molder away, but Dr. Warren's memory would not fail. How cool! Steve just wished it was true.

Steve thought about the book he and Grace had written about Dr. Warren. He thought about how he hoped Senator Webster's speech[47] could come true. He wished Grace could've come back with him to see and hear all this. And he wished Dr. Warren stood here with him.

He sat holding the ball. Senator Webster announced that it was now time to lay a ceremonial cornerstone for the Bunker Hill Monument.

That was when Steve saw the man, the one he'd seen earlier with the cane. The man Grace called General Lafayette stepped forward to lay the cornerstone. He looked exactly like he had when he'd directed Steve with his cane to the Bunker Hill displays. Steve now watched him walk. Though he limped, the man walked straight and deliberate.

---

47 *Senator Daniel Webster's Speech* – Senator Webster did speak at both this groundbreaking event and when the monument was completed almost twenty years later. The words that are repeated above for the dedication speech are almost exactly the words he spoke. Senator Webster was noted for his great ability to speak to large gatherings. It is believed his speech on June 17, 1825, on Bunker Hill, was given to the largest crowd ever to listen to a speaker unaided by a microphone in the United States. Estimates of attendees at the event range from 100,000 to 200,000. And, General Lafayette did lay the cornerstone.

He performed the ceremonial laying of the first stone for the monument with great respect.

After General Lafayette finished, Steve watched as hundreds of people came to congratulate the general. They shook his hand. They thanked him for his service to George Washington and their country. His celebrity status clearly eclipsed that of Senator Webster and Steve decided he would look him up and learn more about General Lafayette when he got back.

Steve watched while Lafayette seemed to be moving as best he could toward Steve. Steve remained on the red, white and blue platform. As he held the musket ball in his left hand, he waited to shake the hand of the man who had directed him to this event – 175 years in the future.

Finally, after almost an hour, General Lafayette reached Steve. The tall, notable man said, "Mister William Eustis, I presume." He extended his hand and bowed. Steve shook his hand and looked at all the people who were still standing behind this man with the French accent. Steve said, "Yeah. I'm Mr. Eustis."

The Frenchman smiled, "I've been told that you knew Doctor Joseph Warren better than any man now alive. You were hiz apprentice and you fought here, on this hill, with him during the battle, no?"

Steve nodded and said again, "Yeah."

Lafayette's eyes lit up, "I need your help then." The French general slowly started walking away from the group and Steve got up and followed. "You see, when I was nineteen and living in France, I was told of the Revolution in America. I heard of the first battles at Lexington, Concord, and of course Bunker Hill. I could not think of anything else. I was consumed with a passion to fight for liberty, to fight for the freedom of mankind. At only nineteen, I was a Mazon as well." Lafayette said the last words slowly. He looked at Steve. Steve raised his eyebrows. Lafayette noted the interest, "I am still a Freemazon. I've been true to the order all through my service to your country and my people as well." Steve enjoyed listening to the man's breezy French accent.

They walked in the direction of the two-story grey statue to their right where Dr. Warren had died. Lafayette pointed, "He, Doctor Warren, was a Mazon as well. I knew of him. As a young man, I knew of hisz death on this hill. I knew he served as the Grand Master of Mazons in North America. I knew he'd given hisz life for the most noble and great cause – libertyé!"

He was silent for a moment, then said, "I am an old man whose heart beats still in France as well as America. And now, I ask your help." Lafayette looked directly at Steve. "Where on thiz hill did he die?"

Steve pointed to the marker. "He died by that marker." Lafayette nodded and said, "As hisz friend who stood by hisz side in death, come help me." Looking to the spot ahead, Lafayette said, "The principle of free government lives in American soil. I wish to have the soil of thisz hill placed over me when I die. I am a man who has lived two lives. God willing, I will be buried in France, but it will be under the best of American soil."[48]

They'd arrived at the spot. Steve looked around and Lafayette asked, "Is thisz where he died? Is thisz the place?" Steve nodded.

With a few slow steps and the help of the cane, Lafayette knelt to the ground. He turned to Steve, "As hiz friend, pleez will you help me?" Steve watched as Lafayette pulled a cloth bag from his jacket. He reached his hand deep into the Bunker Hill soil and scooped dirt into the bag. Steve knelt beside this former aide and friend to George Washington. He watched Lafayette, who continued scooping the dirt with his hands. Steve dug his hand into the warm June earth. Together they filled the bag with Bunker Hill soil.

They both stood. Lafayette placed his soiled hand on Steve's shoulder. Looking at him, he smiled and whispered, "Merci." The

---

48 *Marquis de Lafayette* – Was born in France to one of the wealthiest families in all of Europe. At age 19, he sailed to America and played a vital part in helping George Washington and the American army defeat Great Britain. President James Monroe invited Lafayette to return to the United States in 1824 to be part of the nation's upcoming 50th anniversary. He laid the cornerstone for the Bunker Hill Memorial and when Lafayette left America, he took soil from Bunker Hill with him so that the dirt could be sprinkled on his grave. He died at age 76, on May 20, 1834, in France, and was buried under the soil from Bunker Hill.

general extended a dirt-covered hand. Steve lifted his right hand and stuck his left hand in his pocket.

The second Steve's fingers reached the ball, a bright burst exploded from their joint grip. Lafayette lifted their hands. He smiled. Then, he disappeared in a blanket of light.

Chapter 77

The Moment and the Visitor's Center

"Steve!" Grace grabbed his drooping shoulder, and called again, "Steve!"

Steve's head snapped up and he popped out of the trance. Grace stared at him. "Wow!" she said. That was really weird. You just totally zoned out!"

Steve straightened and looked at her. Grace waited a few seconds and Steve finally said, "It happened."

Grace's eyes widened, "Did you see him? Where were you?"

Steve shook his head, but with a smile brighter than he'd had all day, he said, "No, I didn't see Dr. Warren. I hardly moved. I mean, I was right here, but in 1825." Steve turned to the waist-high display, "It was just like that." He pointed, "I got to be part of the June 17, 1825 celebration. I was a special guest with a bunch of other Bunker Hill veterans."

Grace listened. His eyes brightened as he looked at her. The moment made Grace's chest warm and her heart beat faster. No one was around them.

Steve seemed to be thinking. Grace held her breath. Then he asked, "Do you like pumpkin pie?"

"What?" Grace just looked at him. Then she said, "Yeah. I mean, I guess. Pumpkin pie is good. But, what does that have to do with anything?"

Shaking his head, Steve mumbled, "Just wondering."

Ignoring how Steve's strange question had destroyed the previous moment, Grace thought about the amazing day that they'd spent together. She thought about the weeks they'd spent working on writing the book. It all made Grace want to hug him.

She started to blush, but she didn't care. She wanted to show Steve how much everything meant to her. She took a deep breath and reached for his hand. Just as her fingertips brushed his hand, he turned and started walking to the visitor's center. His cheeks seemed to have a red tint to them. Grace was pretty sure that Steve was blushing.

They both entered the visitor's center.

The room was full of people. Visitors walked through the rooms full of displays as they made their way to the stairs that led to the top of the monument.

Steve walked to a center display. He stood reading it as one of the park rangers began talking to him. Grace watched and then turned and left the main room. She began to explore the other places in the visitor's center.

Grace entered a room with high ceilings and large, bright windows all around. In the middle of this room stood a towering seven-foot marble statue. The statue was of a man with high leather boots cuffed at the top, a long coat and cape draped over a shoulder, and the face of a gentleman of the 1770s. His right hand rested on a long sword pointed to the ground. A four foot, dark marble pedestal lifted the figure into the air high above everyone and everything in the room. Grace looked at the one word etched with gold lettering into the black and grey marbled pedestal. She read, *WARREN*.

Grace stopped. She looked up again at the man holding the sword. She noted all the flags around him and the people passing. Some people stopped. Some read the name. Most just continued their path to the Bunker Hill Monument.

Her heart raced. Her eyes darted back looking for Steve. She spotted him walking towards her with the park ranger from the first room. Steve was talking to the ranger, but stopped when he saw Grace. "Hey, Grace, this is Ranger Taylor."

Grace wanted to burst out with her discovery, but she waited. Steve turned to the ranger. "He knows a ton about Dr. Warren."

The ranger smiled, "So Grace, Steve said that you two are working on a book about Dr. Warren." The ranger looked up and pointed to the statue. "I think that's awesome. I'm a huge fan of Doctor Warren."

Grace turned to Steve, "Look! I was coming to show you."

Steve now saw Dr. Warren's statue. The Ranger walked with them towards the statue, saying, "I've worked here for almost ten years." He looked up at the statue, "Hardly anyone that comes here knows anything about Joseph Warren. I love telling his story, but a book or movie or something about him is what Americans need after 9-11. I hope your book sells a million copies. I really do. America would be a better place if more people remembered the patriots who sacrificed so much for it." Mr. Taylor looked back at Grace. "I told Steve he needs to send me a copy before I deploy to Afghanistan." Grace made a mental note of the man's name tag, "Major Brent Taylor."

Grace knew that since September 11th, a whole bunch of soldiers had been sent to Afghanistan to hunt for the terrorist groups that caused the attacks on the Pentagon and the Twin Towers. She asked, "Are you like a major in the army?"

He nodded. "I'm a park ranger full time and major in the National Guard part time. My reserve unit has been called up." The major added, "Since being called up, I've thought about Dr. Warren having to leave his four children and his fiancé, Mercy Scollay. And he did it before he even knew if we'd be a country." Grace studied the park ranger as he stood staring at the statue, "I like to think that I'm just one of many who have followed Dr. Warren's example. It's the price Americans pay for freedom."

Grace nodded and Steve turned to the ranger. He started asking Major Taylor a bunch of questions about the statue and about Dr. Warren. Major Taylor could answer them all.

Grace listened but her mind had wandered back to what Major Taylor had said. Leaving a family to go to war. It's a really high price. She wondered about the price paid by Dr. Warren; he didn't come back. Grace looked at the tall, lean man talking to Steve. She liked this Major Taylor with handsome silver streaks in his wavy grey hair. In her heart, Grace said a silent prayer for Major Taylor.[49]

After about fifteen minutes, Major Taylor patted Steve on the back. "Wow. So great talking to someone who knows so much about one of my heroes." Then they all shook hands and started saying their goodbyes. As they left, Major Taylor added, "Please don't forget to send me a copy of your book." Grace nodded and smiled back.

49 *Major Brent Taylor* is a real person. You can look him up on the internet. He was not a park ranger, but he was a major in the Army National Guard. He served fifteen years in the Army National Guard. During that time he was called upon to leave his family four times, to serve two tours of duty in Iraq, and two in Afghanistan. On his fourth tour, he did not come back. Major Taylor was killed in Afghanistan. He left behind a wife and seven children. This is a very high price for our Freedom.

Chapter 78

Top of the Monument

Step 100. Grace looked at the number "100" painted on the next step.

Step 175. She kept walking, step after step after step, up the spiral staircase, over halfway.

Step 275. They were almost there. Steve looked over his shoulder, "I can see the end."

Step 294. Finally. They stood at the top.

Grace looked around. Each of the five or six windows on top of the twenty-story monument had people peering out at views all around Boston.

Grace turned to the window closest to them that faced west. The sun was lowering over the bridges and waterways that connected Boston. Climbing and descending tourists came and went. An opening at a different window brought Steve and Grace together to gaze out over the Charles River and into the old part of Boston. They both looked through the thick glass to the places along the Freedom Trail. They could see the white steeple of the Old North Church and the area of Paul Revere's house. Up the road was where Dr. Warren had lived. In the small space, their cheeks were just inches apart as they stared out the window.

On this side of the room, there was no one but Steve and Grace.

Turning to face Grace, Steve opened his hand. He held in his palm the ball and the brass button. He smiled at her. "Grace, I want you to have this button. It's the one I hid for you, kind of like over 200 years ago." Steve acted a bit awkward, like he didn't know what else to say. He looked so cute when embarrassed! Grace felt butterflies begin whizzing in her stomach again. They both stood facing each other, their lips just inches apart.

Grace reached for the button, but as she did so, her fingers brushed against the musket ball. A warmth sprang up her arm. Steve's eyes widened and he began to say, "Do you feel . . . " when a sudden flash of light burst through the window. As it faded, all the modern buildings in the city disappeared. Grace squeezed Steve's hand in the excitement, with the ball and button between them.

The next thing she knew, she was looking at Dr. Warren. Grace saw the image in the sky, and it looked exactly like a full-colored version of the seven-foot statue she had just seen in the visitor's center. Next to Joseph Warren on the left appeared General Lafayette. Grace recognized him from the display twenty stories below. Finally, there was a man with a three-cornered hat and riding gear who came stomping up next to Dr. Warren and placed his arm around him. This man, who was surely Paul Revere, smiled a large broad grin.

Grace next saw an older man who looked a lot like the statue of Sam Adams they'd passed along the Freedom Trail and a man next to him in a very fancy coat and frilled shirt. These two patriots stood to the side of the first group. A shorter man, with a balding hairline stood by a woman with a beautiful smile and rich brown eyes. Another beautiful woman appeared with four small children, the little kids waving in their direction. Then, Grace noticed that there was a young boy standing next to the balding man and the pretty lady with the lovely smile.

The boy stepped toward Grace and Steve. Grace could see that he was holding something in each hand. He walked towards them and Grace realized that as he did, he got older with each step. While she watched in amazement, he grew from Johnny the boy, who had been standing next to his parents, John and Abigail Adams, to a full-grown man, John Quincy Adams, right before her eyes.

The sixth President of the United States now stood in front of Dr. Warren and the others. John Quincy Adams and Doctor Warren and all the other patriots from 1775 turned to their left. Grace now saw a handsome man appear. He wore the blue dress uniform of a United States Marine with crisp white gloves. Around his neck, just below a shaved and chiseled chin, hung a medal with a light blue ribbon.

The young Marine lifted his hands and John Quincy Adams placed the items that he had been holding into the hands of the Marine. The Marine turned on a dime, and walked towards Grace and Steve. Grace could now see the objects. Stopping in front of them, the Marine nodded but said nothing. He simply held out a manuscript and a musket ball. The Marine's grey-blue eyes lit up as he looked at Steve.

Grace watched Steve smile, then whisper, "I can't thank you enough, Harold."

Then, just as quickly as it had happened, it all disappeared.

Chapter 79

Forest Hills Cemetery

The next day, June 17, 2002, came with clouds and some drizzling rain. Steve stood by a large grey rock with a patchy, light-green coating. The large rock stuck out from the ground and the greenish coloring of the moss added to the antiquity of the spot. Steve was glad he'd taken an early subway train from his house, and given himself enough time to find the spot. Forest Hills Cemetery was like a small town. It had roads, hills, bridges and groves of trees.

He looked around and waited. He glanced at his watch, 4:31. Mr. Frothingham had said to meet at 4:34. He looked all around. There was nobody.

While he was waiting, Steve had walked around the rock and noted that many Warren family members were buried at this location. Small flags and an aged marker noted that Major General Joseph Warren lay here. This was definitely the spot.

Steve stepped away from the large rock with the markers and flags behind it. He walked ten or twenty yards to the street within the cemetery to look up and around. No one.

He looked to his watch, 4:34.

Just as he turned back around . . . "Good afternoon, Steve."

Holy surprise! Frothingham stood right behind him. He wore a smooth, perfectly-pressed black suit with sunglasses and black leather lace-up shoes. His hair was dark, and his cheeks were tight over his high cheekbones.

Catching the breath he'd lost from Frothingham's crazy appearance, Steve said, "Uhh, I just didn't know you were there."

Steve thought he saw a slight grin. Frothingham said, "I'm glad you could make it. At the Society, we've been anticipating this day for a long time." Mr. Frothingham stood with his hands neatly folded in front of him. He nodded to Steve's right hand. "I believe you are holding something that is older than our nation."

Steve just stood there. Frothingham waited. After almost a minute, Steve opened his hand. The musket ball lay in his palm like a regular lead marble. Steve knew Frothingham understood that it was so much more. After another long pause, Steve asked, "Why did you call this a T3, or something like that?"

"Yes, it is a T3 – A Time-Traveling Talisman. It has been held by my society since the 1840s. As you know, it is directly linked to the great patriot, Dr. Joseph Warren." The man pulled a small container from a pocket inside his suit coat. "The T3 goes here." Mr. Frothingham flipped the lid up and Steve could see a perfect place within the container for the ball. Steve had thought about this moment for weeks, even months, and now it was here.

He reached out and placed the ball into the spot within the container. Although Steve wanted to keep the T3, as this Mr. Frothingham called it, it just felt right to give it back. It was much easier than he'd imagined. Definitely, the experience yesterday with Grace had helped.

Frothingham closed the lid over the Joseph Warren musket ball. Gently he placed a hand on Steve's shoulder, "You are now part of the Society."

Steve looked at Frothingham, and said, "I really don't understand how that musket ball could've been held by your Society since the 1840s. John Quincy Adams gave it to a member of my family, and it got passed down to me."

Frothingham said nothing. He removed his hand from Steve's shoulder and placed the container back in his suit pocket. From the other side of his suit coat, he pulled a set of four or five neatly folded papers. He handed the papers to Steve. The pages were copies of newspaper articles from the mid-1800s. The articles covered the Revolutionary War musket ball, held by the Boston Historic and Genealogical Society. They discussed how the ball had been given to the Society from one of the founders and that it had been the ball that killed Joseph Warren at Bunker Hill.[50]

Steve was confused. The agent from the Society could see it. He said, "Steve, in this line of work, time continuums are not always easily understood. I can only assure you that you are correct – the musket ball was passed down through your family members. Also, I am also correct that the Society has had continual possession of the T3 since the 1840s." This didn't clear anything up for Steve. Frothingham added, "I know that didn't help much. You will learn more through attendance at the Society meetings. For now, I'll just say that if you hiked in a forest you might find two paths. Although they go in different directions, the paths can both reach the same destination. You and I can only travel one path. But what if you could travel both at the same time? A T3 can. It travels different paths through history with different contacts and different effects, but eventually ends up in one place." Mr. Frothingham patted the suit where he had placed the T3 container. Then, looking at Steve, he just nodded. "Trust me, you'll learn more at the meetings."

This got Steve's attention, "What meetings?"

"Steve, you have experienced firsthand a T3. Others around you have also experienced the effects of the T3." Frothingham stopped, "There are three others. Your brother, Rob. Your friend, Grace. And Curtis Christopher."

At this point, Steve wasn't surprised that Mr. Frothingham knew the names of everyone around him, but he was surprised that he'd listed Curtis. Steve replied, "Curtis has nothing to do with this."

Mr. Frothingham shook his head. "I believe he was present when a time continuum experience occurred with you and Rob – the afternoon before you both went to the hospital."

Steve said, "Yeah, like he was there, but does that mean he's part of this society stuff and supposed to come to these society meetings?"

"It means you invite him. All four of you are invited. It is important that all four of you know that additional experiences with

50 *Joseph Warren Musket Ball* does exist at the historic and genealogical society in the old part of downtown Boston. With the musket ball, there are many newspaper articles from the 1800s, arguing whether this musket ball is the actual musket ball that killed Dr. Warren.

other T3s may happen to you again in the future. You don't have to run home and tell the others right away, but you should share this with them in the near future. You'll know when the time is right." Frothingham paused, "All of them could have similar experiences."

Richard Frothingham added, "Please know that your invitations are of the most exclusive category. You will be asked and must remember your personal passwords. The four of you will be granted entry into the long room of the Society upon repeating the words, 'T3s Help Humanity.'" Frothingham nodded, "This password cannot be shared and is only for you four that have been exposed to the effects of the T3."

Now Mr. Frothingham started walking in the direction of a vehicle that Steve hadn't noticed before, "Steve, you will learn much more about the Society. You will learn the role it plays in safeguarding and caring for the T3s. They're rare in the world, but not within the Society and its members."

They were getting closer to Frothingham's shiny, black Suburban. "Please know, Steve, that not everyone who works at the Boston Historic and Genealogical Society or the many patrons who come to study their family lines, are part of the Society that I'm referencing. The Society that guards the T3s is exclusive. Only a select few understand the true nature and power of the T3s housed within the collections." He stopped across from the vehicle. "Those select Society members who know about and guard the T3s meet when the need arises. You'll be notified when needed and you should inform Grace, Rob and Curtis that they'll be notified as well."

Mr. Frothingham pulled a set of keys from his pocket and asked, "Would you like a ride?" Steve hesitated and Mr. Frothingham smiled, adding, "Steve, I know exactly where you live. I've been following you every day since you won the essay contest in October. If I was going to kidnap you, I would've done it a long time ago."

Steve didn't say anything. Frothingham waited. Then, Steve said, "Okay. But I just want to know if there's anything you don't know about me?"

Frothingham opened the door, "I'll drive and we can talk more. We can talk about your book."

Well, Steve thought, as he opened his door, it looks like he doesn't know that Grace and I have already finished it. We just need the right title.

As Steve got in, Frothingham said with a grin, "Now that you've finished it, we can talk about how the Society can help you publish it – after you decide on the title, of course."

Chapter 80

Saving Dr. Warren

"Steve, I just want to know what you mean." Grace sat at the kitchen table in her light blue soccer shorts and team practice jersey. Her legs crossed in front of her. Her right leg swinging back and forth impatiently on top of her left knee. She waited for an answer.

"I don't know. I told you. It's nothing. She just kind of reminded me of you. That's all." While working together on the book, before their trip to the Freedom Trail, Steve had told Grace that Abigail Adams reminded him of her. Now, since they'd both seen her, when they were up in the Bunker Hill Monument, he faced Grace's grilling.

"So, I saw her on Sunday. I guess I'm just trying to figure out what you mean." Grace looked right at him. She followed up with another question, "You said you liked her a lot, but why?"

Steve contemplated telling her how he felt, but didn't break. "I don't know."

Grace shook her head, "You have to know! What did you like about her?"

Steve just shrugged, "I'm not sure."

Grace rolled her eyes and dropped her head to the table with hands and arms on each side. While her face was planted down on the table, Steve smiled.

After a few seconds, Grace looked up at the clock and then toward the door. "Alright, I've got soccer practice. But you'd better promise that you'll tell me later." Turning to leave, she glanced at him from the side and, grinning one of her irresistible grins, asked again, "Promise?"

He smiled back, liking the game, "I promise – someday."

She slanted her eyes and shook her head. "At least make sure to tell me how it goes today when you drop off our book. That's way cool that Mr. Frothingham's Society is going to publish it for us." Grace hurried toward the door. Watching her leave, Steve thought about what they'd done together over the last few months. Day after day, they'd labored to type the experiences Steve had painstakingly written with a feather pen over two hundred years ago. Last week they'd finished the book, and yesterday Mr. Frothingham said the organization he represented intended to publish it for free, with Steve and Grace receiving one hundred percent of the royalties. Although Steve told Grace a lot about what happened with Mr. Frothingham, he hadn't told her yet about her invitation to the Society meetings. He figured he'd wait until they had success with the book. After publishing it, Grace would like the Society and would be less suspicious. Then it would be easier to tell her that she was actually a member of the group.

Steve watched her walk down the driveway. He turned from the window and looked at the papers forming one neat stack.

Nine months earlier, when he originally wrote his essay, he cared a lot more about the $500 than he did about the men and women who had sacrificed for his freedom. Now, looking at everything he had written with Grace, he laughed at the situation. Steve's only purpose now was to help others remember the men and women who sacrificed for their country.

Steve turned from the freshly printed pages and looked at his tattered manuscript on the other end of the table, that he'd struggled to write over two hundred years ago. He thought about the boy he knew as Johnny. He now understood that John Quincy Adams, as an older man, had started the chain of passing the manuscript and musket ball to Dr. Warren's descendants. Johnny had remembered the conversation in their room. He wanted Steve to get the ball and manuscript. Being a good writer and a boy descendent of Dr. Warren were the only clues John Quincy Adams had. With these clues, he had started a chain that lasted over one hundred and fifty years.

Despite Johnny's doubts, he kept and passed on the stack of ink-blotted pages. He gave it to a grandson or great-grandson of Joseph Warren. Based on the letters and histories that accompanied the old manuscript, John Quincy Adams had instructed that the ball and manuscript be passed on to a good writer. Steve now understood why, when Harold learned of Steve's essay, he wanted so badly to give these items to Steve.

Looking at the tattered manuscript, Steve thought about the words penned on the last page, "March 4, 1825, I now believe. Johnny." Steve had looked up the date on the internet. He learned that John Quincy Adams was sworn in as the sixth President of the United States on March 4, 1825. Just as Steve had told him, Johnny had seen the 13 colonies win the Revolutionary War, he saw his father become the second president of the new nation. And finally, on March 4, 1825, he must have remembered his crazy friend from the future telling him that, like his father, he would become president. [51] Now, as Steve read these few words, *"March 4, 1825, I now believe. Johnny,"* written by his friend, when he was actually President Adams, it made complete sense. Johnny, who had become President, was sending a message to his friend Steve into the future.

Steve turned back to the 2002 version of Dr. Warren's story. Typed and printed, it was a lot more legible than the original. Tomorrow, the Society would receive these pages and begin turning them into a book.

He thought about the past few months. Steve was certainly more patriotic. He no longer felt ashamed of his essay. He didn't feel awkward about being around guys who loved the flag. He visited Lee Warren to look at his World War II antiques and his collection of patriotic papers. He liked hanging out with the "Flagman." Steve worried about Lee's health. He was over 80. Lee acted like Dr. Warren more than anyone Steve knew. Lee Warren was surely part of the old

---

51 *John Quincy Adams' Election* – The election of 1824 was the most unusual election ever. Four candidates all from the same party, all won certain states. Not one of the four won a majority of the 24 states' electoral votes. Because no one won a majority of the states' electoral votes, the election was decided by the vote of the congressmen in the House of Representatives. After this very unusual process, Johnny became the sixth President.

oak tree that represented patriotism in Steve's essay. Steve felt part of that same old tree.

He placed the title page on top of the stack of papers. From the ashes of September 11, to honoring World War II veterans, to walking the streets of 1770s Boston with Dr. Warren by his side, his journey was all in one book.

He had once believed his time travel adventures were meant to save Dr. Warren from Bunker Hill. Saving Dr. Warren's life made sense. Now, he knew the purpose. Steve could save Dr. Warren by retelling his story. He could save the memory of the great American Patriot. Every American could know Joseph Warren. Every American could remember him. And, every American could honor those who have given and are giving so much for our liberty. *"Saving Dr. Warren . . ."* it was a perfect beginning to the title.

Over the past few days, as Steve and Grace tried to decide on a title, Steve remembered the pen name that Dr. Warren used when writing rebellious articles about the British. At the end of each article, Joseph Warren would sign, *"A True Patriot."*

Dr. Warren died on Bunker Hill, but within these pages this patriot lives on. Steve and Grace had combined the two ideas.

Saving Dr. Warren . . . "A True Patriot."

Steve stared at each word.

It was perfect.

You finished Steve's story.

Can you see how it became my story as you read through the pages? Thank you for allowing me to be your guide. Are you still wondering who I am?

Although I can be found in large and great things like aircraft carriers, tanks, federal banks, or acres of national parks, I am also found in small and simple things like a musket ball, a boy, or even an essay. It is through these small and simple things that the grand things are possible.

Who am I? I'm America's Spirit.

I'm what you feel when you look up the hills of Arlington Cemetery and see the changing of the guard at the Tomb of the Unknown Soldier, or the chills down your back you feel when you visit Gettysburg, walk the Freedom Trail or spot the USS Arizona at the bottom of Pearl Harbor, where over a thousand Americans lay entombed forever in their ship. I'm the hope the world felt when three firefighters placed the Stars and Stripes on top of Ground Zero on September 11, 2001.

It's books like this that tell my stories, it's people like you who read these stories, and it's Americans of all ages and colors who remember these stories, that make me stronger.

Remembering those who have given so much, and those like Dr. Warren who have given all, is a duty of every American. Whether your family recently crossed borders to come to America, your family line goes back to the Mayflower, or your family roots are intimately tangled with the great and ongoing repentance of slavery, all who live in America must remember this nation's history and heroes. If we fail to remember our heroes, they will disappear. They will vanish from history. By remembering our nation's heroes and America's Spirit, we can together live on.

THE END OF BOOK ONE

Thanks for reading. If you enjoyed this book, please consider leaving an honest review on your favorite store's website. If you would like to learn more about Dr. Joseph Warren, I highly recommend the biography *Dr. Joseph Warren: The Boston Tea Party, Bunker Hill, and the Birth of American Liberty* by Dr. Sam Forman, a historian and Harvard faculty member. Additionally, *Founding Martyr: The Life and Death of Joseph Warren, the American Revolution's Lost Hero*, by Christian DiSpigna, is a great resource. Lastly, I would love to hear from you. Please contact me through my website **jefferyjmckenna.com**. I am happy to be a guest speaker in classrooms and love to partner with patriotic organizations in their fund-raising endeavors.

Patriots' Page

"I'm thinking patriotism means – other things. I think it's like doing something for others, you know for the people in your country. Someone isn't patriotic just because they say they are. They need to be doing something." —Grace Levy p. 18

Mercy Scollay – 1770s Boston Patriot

Mercy Scollay was a strong, beautiful woman and an amazing patriot. She was willing to give everything for the American cause, while supporting her fiancé who did give his life for American liberty.

Lee Warren – "Flag Man"

Lee Warren is a legend in Southern Utah. As one of the last Pearl Harbor survivors, he gave away over 100,000 flags and organized a day of remembrance every Dec. 7th for city officials, veterans, and families.

Robert Eugene Bush – Medal of Honor

Robert Eugene Bush was the real Navy Corpsman behind Walter's WWII story, who risked his life to save his Captain. He received the Medal of Honor and Purple Heart for his acts of valor on Okinawa.

James L. Day – Medal of Honor

James L. Day was the real Marine behind Harold's story, who led his men in holding enemy ground on Okinawa for four days by firing rifles, a machine gun and hurling hand grenades. He received the Medal of Honor and Purple Heart.

**Todd Beamer –
Leader on Flight 93**

On 9-11, Todd Beamer with other passengers formed a plan to take back their hijacked plane. With his final words "Let's Roll," they stormed the cockpit. Because of them, the plane crashed in a Pennsylvania field instead of the White House.

**Brent Taylor –
Major Army National Guard**

Like Dr. Warren, Brent Taylor left a young family to fight for liberty on four deployments – twice to Iraq and twice to Afghanistan. On his fourth tour, he was killed, leaving a wife and seven young children.

AUTHOR'S NOTE

I've enjoyed American history all my life. In 1978, as a sixth-grade student in Las Vegas, Nevada, the book, *My Brother Sam is Dead,* written by James Lincoln and Christopher Collier, transported me from desert lights to colonial taverns filled with adventures and tragedies of the American Revolution. But, after many years of reading and studying American history, I only learned of Dr. Joseph Warren in the spring of 2000. The more I learned, the more I wondered why I'd never heard of him. By the end of 2000, I dreamed of telling his story to young Americans.

On the morning of September 11, 2001, as I was driving to work, the world changed. The year before I had wondered, *How could I tell Dr. Warren's story?* After September 11, the story materialized. I just needed to write it.

As I learned to paint with sentences, to tell the stories of World War II heroes and our country's Revolutionary War icons, my dream came together. I mixed and combined true events throughout the book. I will point out a few of the many aspects of the story based on true accounts.

First, the most famous musket ball from the Revolutionary War really is safeguarded at The New England Historic Genealogical Society.[52] I've held it.

Second, one Navy Corpsman, Robert Eugene Bush (Walter's Story), and one Marine Corporal, James L. Day (Harold's Story), truly fought through the onslaught of Okinawa during World War II. You can read their stories on the internet. Both lived. Both received our nation's highest award for military service, The Medal of Honor. They weren't brothers and weren't foxhole companions. But, by linking these stories together, we can relive the sacrifices made by families and war buddies during World War II and all wars.

52 In the novel, I referred to this organization as the Boston Historic and Genealogical Society.

Third, I've tried to be true to the events surrounding Joseph Warren during the 1770s. America's sixth President, John Quincy Adams, lived in Braintree just outside Boston, when his family's beloved doctor became a soldier in America's fight for liberty. Paul Revere demonstrated his love and admiration for his best friend by naming his son, who was born after the battle of Bunker Hill, Joseph Warren Revere.

I've marveled at Dr. Warren's ability to gather, organize and lead America's first army of fathers and farmers during the earliest light of the American Revolution. Up to fifteen thousand Minutemen came to his call and launched a siege around Boston after the first battles at Lexington, Concord and Menotomy. I'm amazed at his immense fame for 100 years and his subsequent disappearance from American history. My purpose in writing this book was to re-tell his story and infuse his love for America into the hearts of those who read it.

Lastly, Lee Warren, known as the Flagman within my community, is real. He served in the Navy. While stationed at Pearl Harbor, December 7, 1941, he helped operate a gun on his navy destroyer, the MacDonough DD351. Lee watched the bombing and sinking of ship after ship in that now-hallowed harbor. He was a friend from 1997 until his death in 2014. I never tired of hearing his accounts. He and his shipmates were credited with shooting down a Japanese Zero and helping to shoot down a second during the onslaught. Lee never forgot that Sunday in 1941, when he watched the Harbor burn. He spent a lifetime helping others remember Pearl Harbor. Throughout his life, he honored the men who died that day and all veterans by giving away over one hundred thousand flags.

Lee Warren remains the most patriotic man I've ever known. He and Dr. Warren are my heroes. I love them. I love the country they loved. I love the young men and young women who make up the future of this land. I dedicate this book to them.

I hope you enjoy their stories.

I hope you nurture a love of country through reading about their sacrifices.

I hope you remember those who gave all, for us to enjoy so much.

AUTHOR'S FINAL WORD – APRIL 2020

When I started this book twenty years ago, I never imagined it would be published in the middle of a world-wide pandemic. The coronavirus has impacted every person in the United States.

As I reflect upon the story of *Saving Dr. Warren . . . A True Patriot*, I think it is a fitting time for this book to reach young Americans. The stories of 9-11, World War II, and the beginning days of the American Revolution were extraordinarily trying times – similar to what we're experiencing today.

At this time, we as Americans are all wondering about the future. What will our lives be like beyond these times of quarantine? After 9-11, we worried about future terrorist attacks. During World War II, Americans worried we might be speaking German or Japanese at the end of the war. In the beginning days of the Revolution, patriots knew that if this small group of thirteen colonies did not succeed in defeating the immense British Empire, everyone involved in opposing the King would be killed for treason.

My final words are a quote from President Reagan, during another trying time. When President Reagan won his first election in 1980, the United States was experiencing a long-lasting recession, with millions of Americans unable to find jobs. Beyond our borders, there was a terrible hostage crisis. For 444 days, fifty-two American citizens and diplomats had been held hostage in Iran. As President Reagan took office, the future did not look bright.

In his inaugural speech to Americans, he quoted Dr. Warren. I share his words, as the final words for this book, because they applied to the 1770s, the 1980s and to our present day.

> "On the eve of our struggle for independence a man who might've been one of the greatest among the Founding Fathers, Dr. Joseph Warren, president of the Massachusetts Congress, said to his fellow Americans:

Our country is in danger, but not to be despaired of. On you depend the fortunes of America. You are to decide the important question upon which rest the happiness and the liberty of millions yet unborn. Act worthy of yourselves.

Well, I believe we, the Americans of today, are ready to act worthy of ourselves, ready to do what must be done to insure happiness and liberty for ourselves, our children, and our children's children. And as we renew ourselves here in our own land, we will be seen as having greater strength throughout the world. We will again be the exemplar of freedom and a beacon of hope for those who do not now have freedom."

Ronald Reagan – First Inaugural Address, January 20, 1981

May God bless America and the youth of this great land.
Jeffery J. McKenna

Book Two

Chapter One

He didn't care.

He didn't care if his parents weren't coming.

He didn't care if they were mad.

As he walked, Curtis tried to stop thinking about the huge fight he'd had with his mom and dad. His thoughts turned to his former best friend. He frowned as he pushed out the crisp New England air in a long sigh of disgust.

Rob had gotten weird. Since that afternoon in his kitchen when he'd cut his arm on the floor, Rob was different. He'd gotten nice – too nice. And, he'd started going to history meetings in the old, downtown part of Boston.

Really! History meetings! What was Rob thinking? What had happened to his friend? Curtis kicked a rock off the sidewalk as hard as he could.

He kept his quick pace. He'd be late for the awards assembly, but he didn't care. It was his parents' fault. Besides, he was the regional football MVP. He was getting the most important trophy. A late entrance might make it better, more dramatic.

He'd just started jogging towards the school's front entrance when he saw him, a lone figure standing out in the cold. Curtis knew the old man was waiting for him. "Hi, Grampa."

The man nodded in reply. He stood under the overhead lights of the school entrance. He was a tall, fit man who stood straight. Shifting under his gaze, Curtis asked, "Should we go in?" His grandfather continued to stare at him with pained eyes. Curtis added in a soft tone, "Uh, thanks for coming."

His grandfather stopped staring and closed his eyes. "I went to your house." His aged voice always had a soft, scratchy sound. "Your parents told me you'd left." He paused. Curtis didn't need to be Sherlock Holmes to know his grandfather wasn't happy about the fight. He thought his grandfather was going to tell him again about how education is what makes a man more than an animal. Grandpa had talked to him about the importance of education since before he'd even started elementary school.

"I saw the trophy. I've been inside looking for you. MVP of the entire region. That's something." Grandpa Elijah had been Curtis' personal Superman ever since he'd learned about the gravity-defying hero. The older man continued, "Curt, do you know what MVP stands for?" Curtis nodded. He thought this was pretty obvious. His grandfather went on, "What does the V stand for?" Curtis answered, "valuable."

His grandfather stared at him for a long time. "What's 'valuable' about you Curtis?"

Curtis shrugged. "I'm 'valuable' cuz I score a lot of touchdowns."

"Your parents told me what you said." His grandpa waited until Curtis met his gaze. His voice carried deep emotion. "Is it true you told your parents you didn't need school? That you don't need them, or your family? You're headed to the NFL?"

Curtis looked down in silence. He knew he'd said a lot more things, but his mom and dad deserved every word. They never stopped nagging about his grades, his homework, or his attitude.

Grandpa Elijah reached out and touched his arm, "If you have no education, how 'valuable' are you, Curt? When you step off the football field, what happens if you've abandoned your family? When you can't make touchdowns, who will care about you? If that's your only *value* now, scoring touchdowns and getting into the NFL, you're on the wrong path."

Curtis grit his teeth. He looked through the door's window at the lights inside. They were at least a half hour late. "Grandpa, I don't care." He'd never talked to his grandfather this way or with this tone. Curtis stepped towards the door, but the older man moved in front of him. His grandfather reached into his pocket. When he pulled his hand out, a large coin sat in the middle of his brown and calloused palm.

"What's that?" Curtis asked running his hand over his head.

Grandpa said slowly, "It's a 1793 chain penny." He turned the penny over.

Curtis could see the ring of chains around the words, "One Cent." The words United States of America were around the chains. "Cool, Grandpa. It's an old penny. Real cool." Curtis pointed to the doors. "I really need to go in."

His grandpa shook his head. "Not yet." He extended his hand closer to Curtis. "This is for you." He paused, then said, "Slaves used to keep them. Look at the word on the front."

Curtis flipped the penny over. Above a woman with long hair, was the word Liberty. Curtis again looked at the date – 1793. He reached out to hand the huge penny back to his grandfather. But Grandpa Elijah shook his head. "It was given to me, to give to you."

Curtis looked up, "What do you mean?" He thought about his grandmother, who had passed away just last year. "Is this from Nana?"

"No, it was a strange gift." Grandpa paused, gazing down at the coin, thinking. "It's from a friend of mine at the Boston Historic and Genealogical Society." He looked at Curtis. "His name is Richard Frothingham."

Made in USA - Kendallville, IN
82137_9780999901205
05.12.2022 1154